"It's been a while since…well, I've done this."

"How long is 'a while'?" Dean asked.

She closed her eyes, took a breath and then tipped her head back to look straight at him. "Six years."

Dean's heart stopped for a moment, before it went into overdrive. To be the first man she'd slept with after such a long time…

"Shelby, maybe we should think about this—"

Her fingers halted his moving lips. "I have been thinking about this, in ways I never allowed myself before I met you. Please tell me I'm not the only one."

He nodded, his throat too constricted to allow him to speak. How many times had he woken up, reaching across his empty bed, wanting and wishing she was there?

"No thinking about the past or the future, okay?" Her voice was soft. "Not tonight. Tonight is about right here, right now…you and me. That's enough."

"Is it? Is what's about to happen here enough for you?"

"It's everything."

THE MAVERICK'S SUMMER LOVE

BY
CHRISTYNE BUTLER

MILLS
BOON

First published in Great Britain 2013
by Mills & Boon, an imprint of Harlequin (UK) Limited,
Eton House, 18-24 Paradise Road, Richmond, Surrey TW9 1SR

Special thanks and acknowledgement to Christyne Butler for her contribution to the MONTANA MAVERICKS: RUST CREEK COWBOYS continuity.

© Harlequin Books S.A. 2013

ISBN: 978 0 263 90133 7
ebook ISBN: 978 1 472 00515 1

23-0813

Harlequin (UK) policy is to use papers that are natural, renewable and recyclable products and made from wood grown in sustainable forests. The logging and manufacturing processes conform to the legal environmental regulations of the country of origin.

Printed and bound in Spain
by Blackprint CPI, Barcelona

Christyne Butler fell in love with romance novels while serving in the United States Navy and started writing her own stories six years ago. She considers selling to Mills & Boon® Cherish™ a dream come true and enjoys writing contemporary romances full of life, love, a hint of laughter and perhaps a dash of danger, too. And there has to be a happily-ever-after or she's just not satisfied.

She lives with her family in central Massachusetts and loves to hear from her readers at chris@christynebutler.com. Or visit her website, www.christynebutler.com.

Chapter One

"Well, aren't you the picture of domestic bliss."

Dean Pritchett didn't look up from his e-reader. Even though his most recent download was an old favorite he'd already read numerous times, there was no need. He had a feeling his brother wasn't done yet.

"Hmm, you seem to be enjoying that spin cycle a bit too much," Nick continued, his voice laced with typical sarcastic humor. "I think you've been cooped up in this trailer too long, little brother."

Shifting his weight as the decades-old washing machine beneath him finally switched into high speed, Dean stayed put despite his brother's teasing. He'd learned the first weekend of staying in this government-sponsored mobile home that perching something heavy, like himself, on top was the only way to keep the appliance from dancing across the tiny laundry room's floor during the last cycle.

"You're just jealous because I got here first."

"I'd rather do my 'spinning' the old-fashioned way." Nick

propped one shoulder against the open doorway. "And it's about time you did, too."

He finally looked up. "I'll pass. Thanks."

"Wrong answer, bud. That might've worked when Dad and Cade were still here, but now I need a new wingman."

Dean stared at his brother. He was the shortest of all the Pritchett kids, but built like a football player. All muscle. He had the same blond hair and blue eyes as their oldest brother and baby sister, unlike Dean who had inherited their mother's deep green color.

Nick also had the charms that made sure he was rarely at a loss for company.

"You haven't needed a wingman since you were fourteen," Dean said, "and came home with the phone numbers of three cheerleaders in your pocket. All seniors."

Nick returned his smile. "Yeah, those were the days. But if you think I'm going to let you sit here and stare at that gadget all night—" he snatched the tablet from Dean's hand "—you're wrong."

"Hey!"

"At least tell me you're reading something hot like the latest issue of *Biker Babes Gone Wild*—" He peered at the screen, then guffawed. "Wait, *The Collected Works of Jane Austen?* That's chick stuff."

"Jane Austen is a literary giant," Dean shot back. "Her work is classic and timeless and she was Mom's favorite author. She gave me my first book."

"Okay, professor. At least it's not Shake-N-Stir."

The washing machine ended its run. Dean hopped down and reclaimed his e-reader, flipping the cover closed to put it to sleep. "That's Shakespeare, you doof."

"Whatever." Nick pushed away from the door. "Come on, it's time to put the books away and suck down a few cold ones. And change that shirt."

Dean looked down at his gray T-shirt with the big block

letters stating REAL MEN READ. "Abby gave this to me at Christmas. And it's the last clean shirt I have."

Nick eyed the pile of freshly folded laundry before yanking a snap-front Western-style shirt still warm from the dryer and tossed it at him. "Here, put this on. Girls in Rust Creek Falls love cowboys."

Dean snorted. The Pritchett family had a working ranch back home in Thunder Canyon, about three hundred miles south of here, so technically they could be called cowboys. Lord knew he and his siblings had all worked the land alongside their father from the moment they could walk. And yes, he often wore a battered Stetson while he'd worked here in town to keep the sun out of his eyes.

But it was the family business, Pritchett & Sons Fine Woodworking, known for producing beautiful handcrafted furniture, where both he and his brothers made their living.

And what had brought them to this small ranching community last month.

Rust Creek Falls had been hit hard over the Fourth of July holiday by what was now called the Great Montana Flood. Dean had been one of the first to answer the call for volunteers to help rebuild the town, and soon his entire family joined in, setting up shop in the cluster of trailers on the west end of town.

Thankfully, most of the businesses in Rust Creek Falls were up and running again, except for the elementary school that suffered a lot of damage. Many private homes and ranches were still in need of work, especially those located south of the creek, which had become a raging river breaking through its levees during the storm.

Dean and his family had worked long days those first couple of weeks, but now their father and oldest brother had gone home to take care of the ranch and family business while Dean and Nick had chosen to stick around for the duration.

And maybe, for Dean, even longer.

"Come on, time's a wastin'." Nick nudged him out of the way and opened the lid of the washer. "I'll take care of loading your dryer. You get pretty. We both know you're going to take longer."

Dean cuffed his brother on the back of the head before turning toward the tiny bathroom to wash up and change. It wasn't as if he'd never been to the one bar in town. He'd gone a couple of times, but he tended to prefer books to most people he met.

Catching sight of the faded scar that ran down the center of his chest in the mirror as he buttoned up his shirt, Dean blamed his preference on a childhood filled with mysterious health problems that had kept him on the sidelines most of the time. Everything had changed, though, when surgery his freshman year in high school had fixed a faulty heart valve. Soon he was as athletic as the rest of his family, but that didn't mean he'd morphed from a quiet kid to a charmer like Nick overnight.

Hell, most times he just kept his mouth shut and let the ladies do all the talking. He'd learned over the years that most of the female population found his silence a challenge they couldn't resist. So he'd let them try. Even if they got him to talk, they rarely stuck around for long after that—a lesson he'd learned years ago.

Pushing away the memories, he shut off the light and walked down the hallway to the front of the trailer.

"See? You did take longer. We ready to go?" His brother waited in the living room, already sporting his familiar black Stetson. He grabbed Dean's off a nearby hook and tossed it to him.

Deciding to go without the hat, Dean laid it on the coffee table, then checked his watch, surprised to find it already after nine. He figured he'd only have to stay for a beer or two before his brother found someone else for company. "Let's go."

They left their pickup trucks parked and took the short

walk in the still summerlike night air from the group of trailers to the Ace in the Hole. It was a rough-around-the-edges bar, popular with everyone, from cowboys to millworkers and now the volunteers helping the town get back on its feet.

The bar's parking lot on this Thursday night was filled mostly with trucks, a few cars and a handful of motorcycles. There was even an old-fashioned hitching post out front because local cowboys had been known to ride into town on horseback, even after dark. Lighted beer signs shone in the windows and an oversize playing card, an ace of hearts, blinked in red neon from its perch over the front door.

Once inside, Dean's eyes adjusted to the dim lighting as he followed his brother to the already-crowded bar that ran the length of one wall. Booths hugged the outer walls and round tables surrounded a small dance floor in the middle of the room.

There was a sorry excuse for a stage in the far back corner, but tonight's musical entertainment came from an antique Wurlitzer jukebox that still played three choices for a quarter. Pool tables filled the space in the far back and a couple of dartboards hung on the wall next to the exit door, all perpetually busy.

Dean and Nick grabbed two empty stools at the bar, but a lull in the music and the sound of a man's voice had them, along with the rest of the crowd, turning to face a booth in a far corner.

"Hey, everyone, could I have your attention for a moment?"

Dean recognized Collin Traub as the man rose to his feet. The pretty brunette next to him was his wife of less than one week, the former Willa Christensen. Both Dean and Nick had attended their wedding last Saturday. In fact, the entire town of Rust Creek Falls had been there to watch them exchange their vows.

"I have something I'd like to share with you," Collin said. "Something my wife and I just decided on."

"Are we hearing the pitter-patter of little feet soon?" someone called out.

Collin laughed along with the crowd, but waved off the suggestion. "Ah, I think it's a bit early for that, seeing how Willa and I have put off our official honeymoon to work with all of you, and the many volunteers who have joined us, on rebuilding our town."

Several people clapped and Collin waited until the noise died down again.

"We've pulled together since the flooding, and we've accomplished a lot in a short time, but there's still a long way to go. I know this town is going to come back stronger than ever." He looked down at his wife, who gave him a quick nod, then he addressed the crowd again. "Part of that strength is missing however with the tragic loss of Mayor McGee. His death during the flood has left a void in our town, so I've decided to join the election as a candidate to fill the mayoral seat."

A cheer rose from the crowd and soon Collin and his wife were surrounded by well-wishers.

"I guess folks around here think that's a pretty good idea," Nick said as a group of men greeted him with friendly hellos. He made a few quick introductions to Dean, including two waitresses who stopped by, one of whom wrapped an arm around Nick's shoulders for a quick hug before she continued on her way.

"Traub seems pretty popular. Just like you." Dean leaned closer to be heard over the jukebox. "Why am I here again?"

Nick shrugged and reached for the bowl of unshelled peanuts in front of them. "If you're talking about Faith, there's nothing there, man. She's old enough to be our...aunt. Besides, she's married."

"Never stopped you before."

His brother shot him a dark look. "You know, I was serious. You need to find yourself some company of the female persuasion. You're either working, cooped up in that trailer by yourself or hanging around with a bunch of kids."

Dean had to admit his brother had a point. When he wasn't relaxing in the trailer he could be found at the town park. He'd been taking a walk one night when a fight broke out during a pickup football game. He'd stepped in before two kids, barely in their teens, had gotten more than a few jabs thrown at each other and defused the situation. From then on, he'd been playing referee, spending more time at the park with the kids who hung out there.

Before he could reply to Nick's suggestion, a sweet voice called down to them from the center of the bar.

"Hey there, boys. Welcome to the Ace! I'll be right with ya."

Dean's gaze zoomed in on the petite blonde bartender. Now, there was someone he hadn't met yet in this small town.

Her shoulder-length hair whipped against her neck as she moved in a hurried but practiced pace, filling drink orders from both customers and staff. Dressed the same as the other waitresses in dark jeans and a black T-shirt that featured the bar's logo, she hadn't done any alterations to the shirt to show off the maximum skin possible like some of the others.

No, she just wore it pulled back in a knot at the base of her spine. A move that allowed a sliver of creamy skin to appear from time to time, and the deep V at the neckline offered a nice view of her curves. She stood in profile to him, so he could see only half a smile, but the cowboy she placed a tall, frothy beer in front of seemed to enjoy it.

"What can I get you, Nick?" she called down to them again, directing her words over one shoulder as she continued to work.

"A couple of longnecks." Nick added after tossing out their favorite brand, "Each."

She nodded her head and turned away, pulling two icy beers from a cooler beneath the bar.

"Damn, she hardly looks old enough to be in here." Dean felt a slow curl of heat ride low across his gut when she reached back and casually wiped her hands across her perfectly shaped backside. "Please tell me you haven't tried to go after someone who's almost jailbait."

"Shelby? Naw, she's not my type."

Good.

Happy he managed not to say the word aloud, Dean forced his gaze from the girl, surprised at the instant attraction coursing through his veins. An attraction that was all wrong considering how young she must be.

"Besides, she's twenty-two, so don't go all righteous on me, Grandpa." Nick grabbed a second handful of peanuts and started cracking the shells over a bowl filled with discarded casings.

Jeez, that was young. Not that at twenty-eight he was that much older, but still. "You're not interested, but you know her age?" Dean asked.

"Rosey told me."

Before he could find out who Rosey was, the angelic blonde headed their way. She placed the bottles on the bar in front of them, quickly popping off the caps. "Sorry, Nick. You know Rosey's rules. No double fisting allowed. Except on Sundays."

"And then you better be praying," Nick added, finishing what Dean guessed was a well-known proverb around the bar. "I thought I'd give it a shot anyway. Shelby, have you met my brother Dean?"

This time she looked right at him and that heat burned just a little bit hotter when he caught the full power of a pair of baby blue eyes, a perfectly straight nose and lips naked of any dressing but a sweet, if not aloof, smile. "No, I don't think I have."

For a reason he couldn't explain, Dean shot out a hand across the bar at her. "Dean Pritchett."

She stared at him for a moment before she placed her hand in his, the tips of her cool fingers gliding against the calluses on his. "Shelby Jenkins."

"Pleased to meet you." Thankful the words came out sounding normal, he tightened his grip just a bit. "Shelby."

"Likewise." An emotion he couldn't read flickered across her eyes as she pulled free from his touch. "You boys have fun. I'll check back with you in a few minutes."

Gripping his beer, Dean watched her walk away before drowning his suddenly dry throat in a rush of cool liquid. His next thought popped out of his mouth before he could stop the words. "What's a nice girl like her doing working in the Ace in the Hole?"

"Who are you talking about?" Nick pulled his attention from the flat-screen television showing a ball game.

Dean tipped his bottle in Shelby's direction. "Our bartender."

His brother's voice dropped to a low whisper. "Well, the word around town is she's too nice actually, if you know what I mean."

The meaning behind the words stung. Nothing got Dean's ire up more than stupid rumors.

He'd dealt with them as a kid when his weight gain and lack of stamina in gym classes had caused the other kids to talk about him behind his back. Even after the surgery, when long-distance running had brought him lean muscles and track awards, there were still comments about him being the guy in the class that girls loved to be friends with, but nothing else.

Dean looked down the bar at Shelby. With her big blue eyes and glossy blond hair, she looked like an angel. An innocent angel. "That's a crappy thing to say."

The hard edge in Dean's words brought forth a confused frown from his brother. "I guess you're right." Nick straightened and reached for his beer. "I'm just repeating what I've been told."

"You can't believe everything you hear."

Nick nodded in agreement, but then turned his attention back to the game.

By the time they were on their second beers, delivered by Shelby without a glance in his direction, even when Dean had paid for the drinks, he felt a tap on his shoulder.

Turning around, he found Jasmine "Jazzy" Cates and Cecelia Clifton, two more of Thunder Canyon's volunteers.

"Look who's here!" Cecelia offered a big smile. "Dean, I think this is the first time I've ever seen you in the Ace."

"Yeah, my brother thought he might need a babysitter tonight."

The girls laughed and Nick greeted them, suggesting the four of them grab an empty table. Dean added a couple of singles to the change Shelby had left on the bar, pushing the pile toward the inside edge so she'd see it.

He started to follow when his phone vibrated in his pocket. Pulling it out, he saw it was a call from Abby, their brother Cade's wife. "Save me a seat," he called out. "I'm going to take this."

Stepping into the corner near the door, Dean pressed the button. "Hey, Abby. Did Dad and Cade make it home okay?"

"A few hours ago. I'm calling from your dad's place. He and Cade are parked in front of the television watching the Rockies get their butts kicked."

"Yeah, we're doing the same at the local watering hole."

"Ah, Cade told me about that place. Not quite the same as the Hitching Post, huh?"

Dean pictured the Western-style restaurant and bar back home in Thunder Canyon that had gone through a complete renovation last fall. "Not even close."

"At least the town has a place where people can relax and

have some fun. Your dad and Cade told us about all the work you guys have done since you've been up there."

"There's still a long way to go," Dean said. His sister-in-law went quiet for a moment and Dean thought they might have lost their connection, something that still often happened as the town had gotten its cellular service back only a few days before the volunteers arrived.

"That's one of the reasons I'm calling, Dean." Abby's voice was low, but he could hear the concern in her words. "My sister, Jazzy, went up there with the first group and the family has heard from her only a couple of times since she's been gone."

"She's been a great help, Abby, working right alongside the guys when we cleaned out the flooded elementary school." Dean looked over at the subject of their conversation, sitting next to his brother with a beer in her hand. "In fact, she and Cecelia are here tonight with me and Nick."

"Oh, good." Relief colored Abby's tone. "Could I ask a favor? Keep an eye on her? She went through a pretty bad breakup last month, one that none of us in the family understand, because the guy she was dating seemed perfect for her."

As if babysitting Nick wasn't bad enough. "Ah, look, Abs, I don't think it's my place—"

"I'm not asking you to spy for me. Just make sure she doesn't do anything…stupid. Please?"

Dean blew out a breath. He couldn't say no to Abby. "Yeah, I can do that."

Seconds later, Dean had shoved his cell phone into his pocket when the sound of shattering glass caught everyone's attention.

He turned and found one of the waitresses standing toe to toe with Shelby over an upturned tray and broken beer bottles on the floor. He wondered for a moment if they were going to go from shooting evil glances to swapping right hooks, but then Shelby seemed to check herself and took a step back.

"Well, someone is getting lucky tonight." Shelby's voice rang out as she bent down to grab a couple of the broken bottles, holding them aloft in concession to the cheers and laughter from the crowd before tossing them into a nearby trash bin. "At least lucky enough to get a beer on the house."

Dean fought the urge to help her clean up the mess. Especially after the waitress only grabbed her tray and went back to a nearby booth.

Shelby spotted him and the foot he'd put forward shuffled back. The message in her gaze was loud and clear.

Back off.

He turned instead to join his friends, taking the empty chair next to Jazzy. Nick and Cecelia were on the crowded dance floor with separate partners. Dean angled the chair to face the bar. Yeah, so he could keep an eye on Shelby and no, he didn't know why, but something about her tugged at him.

Moments later, she emerged with a tray full of beers for the cowboys at a nearby table. Chatting with the group, she even allowed one of the men to trail his fingers along her forearm before stepping back with that same aloof smile for the interloper she'd given to him.

When she turned around, she caught him watching.

Her eyes narrowed for a moment and Dean wondered if he should be the one to look away. However, Shelby simply spun on the heels of her cowboy boots and made her way back to the bar.

Dean downed half of his beer before he noticed the growing pile of scraps on the table. "You determined to peel that off in as many pieces as possible?" he asked Jazzy, watching her pick apart the silver label with her fingernail. "I thought the object was to remove it in one—"

"Don't start, Dean. Not tonight." Her grip tightened on the bottle, but then she swiped a hand across one cheek.

Ah, damn. Tears. "You okay?"

"Just dandy."

He thought back to what Abby had just told him. "Want to talk about it?"

She flipped a long blond curl over one shoulder and then looked directly at him, her eyes now dry. "As a matter of fact, I don't, but thanks for asking."

Boy, he was doing worse than the Rockies, who were getting beat up by the Atlanta Braves to the tune of a dozen unanswered runs. "How about we dance instead?"

Jazzy placed her drink back on the table. "No, thanks. I just want to sit here, okay?"

Dean nodded. "Okay, but if you need someone to talk to—"

"You're a good friend, Dean." Jazzy leaned in close and placed a lingering kiss on his cheek. "But please shut up."

Doing as he was told, Dean leaned back in his chair, his gaze automatically going to the pretty bartender.

His brother's words about Shelby played again in his head. There was no way those rumors could be true. Not with the way she'd dismissed him. And why did he even care that she looked at him as if he wasn't much more than something she needed to scrape off the bottom of her boots?

Chapter Two

Typical man. Never satisfied with what's right in front of him.

Shelby Jenkins could be thinking about any of the male patrons at the Ace in the Hole tonight, but no, the man who continued to occupy her thoughts, even a day later, was Dean Pritchett.

All because she'd caught him looking her way more than once last night.

Despite the fact he'd had a pretty girl practically sitting on his lap, kissing him. The same pretty girl he'd left with a few hours later.

Okay, so Shelby would admit she'd been looking at him first when their gazes had met in the mirror behind the bar, but only because she had finally counted the money he'd left behind on the counter when he, his brother and their friends had moved to a table.

A 100 percent tip on a bar tab for four beers?

Her first thought had been to give the cash back to him.

She was well aware of the many barroom games and Shelby wasn't interested in being a player.

Or being played.

Then again, her bank account needed every dollar she managed to squirrel away and if the handsome blond cowboy thought a hefty tip was going to score points, she had no problem letting him think that way.

Or setting him straight if he tried to use his generosity to his advantage.

Shelby looked over the dwindling Friday night crowd as closing time approached, automatically double-checking the beer taps to make sure they were shut down. Last call had been twenty minutes ago and she was already deep into her nightly routine, knowing all the necessary steps by heart.

Being eighteen and needing a job that kept her days free, she'd started working at the Ace in the Hole as a waitress. Moving behind the bar a couple of years later had been a breeze as she'd easily picked up the necessary skills watching the other bartenders and practicing after hours.

Along the way, she'd also learned a few hard lessons about hooking up with a random cowboy or two. After two attempts at human companionship failed even before the first dates ended, Shelby decided casual sex just wasn't for her. She didn't enjoy being a means to an end.

Besides, once they found out she wasn't as wild and unattached as they first thought, their interest in her vanished quicker than morning dew. So, being lonely was something she'd learned to deal with.

She'd suspected the Pritchett boys had been talking about her long before the ladies joined them, especially after the way Dean had held tight to her hand when they were introduced, but she never let on. She was used to the gossip—it'd been tailing her since she was sixteen—but it made her sad that even newcomers seemed to judge her.

Then again, Dean had almost come to her rescue last night

when Courtney, one of the bar's newest waitresses and one of Shelby's oldest enemies, had walked right into her with a tray full of drinks. She'd held her tongue when Courtney hissed the accident was all her fault. Then made it clear to the cowboy she could handle things like she always did.

On her own.

She'd cleaned up the mess, played to the crowd as expected and even smiled sweetly at the cowboys when delivering a fresh set of drinks, courtesy of the house.

She flinched remembering the hot, sweaty touch from one guy who got a little too friendly. Something one too many of her customers felt they had a right to do from time to time.

Small towns. Born, raised and vilified as one of Rust Creek Falls' fallen angels, Shelby had just about all she could take of small towns.

Which was why her long-held goal of getting out of Rust Creek Falls had moved up from someday to as soon as possible.

"You keep rubbing the bar that way, you're going to put a hole clean through it." The raspy voice drifted over Shelby's shoulder. "Or make the last few cowboys in this joint jealous."

Realizing she'd been wiping down the same section of the scarred surface for the past few minutes, Shelby tossed the rag into the sink. "I thought you had headed home, Rosey." She turned and eyed her boss. "Don't you have company waiting back at your place?"

"Sam kept me waiting for the last three months. He can keep his pants zipped for a few more minutes." The owner of the Ace in the Hole walked around the end of the bar, pausing to easily flip over a couple of the stools so that they rested upside down on the bar's surface. "Besides, I can't head out without the proper send-off. Just wouldn't be right."

A nearby table of cowboys didn't bother to hide their obvious stares as Rosey, looking mighty fine in her tight jeans, blousy pirate-style top and cinched leather vest, walked by.

With her shaggy, jet-black hair brushing her shoulders, high cheekbones and slender build, Rosey looked years younger than someone who'd recently celebrated her sixty-fifth birthday.

Still, their low groans filled the air when Rosey stopped in front of the jukebox, digging into her jeans pocket. Anyone still in the bar knew what was coming.

The musical tastes of the Hole's clientele ran strictly country, from the old standards of Johnny Cash and George Strait to the latest hit from Nashville's newest queen, Taylor Swift, but not Rosey. A child of the sixties, Rosey loved her golden oldies, especially the doo-wop classics.

Shelby propped her elbows on the bar and grinned. By the time her boss deposited four quarters and started punching in her choices, a group of people in one booth headed out. When the first "shoo-doop, shoo-do-be-doop" filled the air, one of two tables packed with cowboys finished the last of their beers and departed, as well.

"Really, Rosey? Must you play those old songs every night?"

The sweetness of the feminine voice coming from the corner booth didn't hide the snarkiness that easily wiped the smile from Shelby's face.

High school antics reared their ugly heads again.

"Nobody likes that ancient music," the prissy blonde, sitting across from two of her friends, continued. "Except maybe for those born back in the dark ages."

Rosey stopped by a recently vacated table and cleaned up the mess left behind. Walking past the booth, she waved an empty beer bottle in the girl's direction. "Finish up your froufrou drinks, ladies. It's past your bedtimes."

The smiles disappeared from their faces and they went back to talking among themselves. Shelby took the bottles from her boss and deposited them in the nearby recycling bin, pleased that she'd somehow managed not to break a single one. "How do you do it?"

"Hey, I've been dealing with wiseass remarks from customers barely over the legal drinking age too long to let one that lame bother me." Rosey leaned in close and gave her a quick bump, hip to hip. "Don't let them get to you."

Easier said than done. Even with years of practice.

Shelby forced a smile back to her face as she turned to her boss. "I'm barely over the legal drinking age, remember? I went to school with those girls."

"Yes, but you've got an old soul. Not to mention a totally different perspective on what's important in life. More so than that cosmopolitan crew over there." Rosey jerked her head toward the booth. "Although they've been pounding the drinks pretty hard tonight. You okay closing up alone?"

This time Shelby's smile was genuine as she leaned in and gave Rosey a quick hug. She considered her boss one part Cher, one part Betty White and 100 percent best friend despite the years separating them.

"It's just the sorority girls and that last table of cowboys in the corner, new hires out at the McIntyre ranch." She took a step back. "I'm sure everyone will be gone before Elvis leaves the building." Rosey always ended her selections with a love song from the King. "I'll be fine."

"Ah, excuse me. Am I too late to get a beer?"

The deep male voice had Shelby spinning around.

Dean Pritchett.

He stood just inside the bar's front door dressed more casually tonight in faded jeans and a simple black T-shirt. A ball cap that had seen better days sat perched on his head.

"I thought you might be closed," he continued, tipping up the cap's frayed brim as he moved farther inside a few steps. "Then I heard the jukebox and decided to try my luck."

"Last call is done, gone and put to bed." Shelby's standard answer fell from her lips even as her mind registered that he was alone. No brother and no pretty blonde friend in sight. "Sorry. We're closing in less than fifteen—"

"We-e-ell, we might be able to find a spare cold brew," Rosey drawled, interrupting her. "That is, unless you have a problem with the music selection?"

Cocking his head to one side, he seemed to listen intently for a moment before he spoke. "How can anyone have a problem with The Tokens? 'In the Still of the Night' is a classic."

Rosey's face lit up with a bright smile as she pointed a perfectly manicured fingernail at him. "You can stay. Shelby, get this man a beer."

"Thank you, ma'am."

"Oh, please, don't 'ma'am' me. The name's Rosaline Marguerite Shaw with too many other former last names to get into." The older woman stepped forward and held out her hand. "Everyone calls me Rosey."

Shelby grabbed a cold beer from the cooler, watching as Dean shook hands with her boss and fell under her charming spell, just like every other man who met her. So why the sudden twist in her stomach?

"Dean Pritchett." He leaned forward after ending the handshake, his forearms braced against the bar. "This is a nice place you got here, Rosey."

"My last ex wanted his freedom more than he wanted the Hole. Sometimes I wonder who got the better end of the deal."

Shelby plopped the icy bottle, twist cap still in place, on the bar. "That will be three bucks."

Dean straightened and reached for his pocket.

Rosey waved off his efforts. "No need, sugar. This one is on the house."

"Thanks, Rosey." Dean spoke to her boss, but his deep green eyes were trained on Shelby.

His steady gaze bothered her more than she would admit. Why was he here? And coming by so late?

Not to mention he's alone.

Shelby tried to ignore the little voice inside her that had to point out that fact. Again. It'd been years since a guy had managed to occupy any space in her head. There just wasn't room with everything else she had going on in her life right now.

Rosey was right. For someone so young, she was an old soul and sometimes that old part seemed to reach out from deep inside her to take over every weary bone in her body.

"Shel, honey? Did you hear me?"

Blinking hard, Shelby realized she hadn't heard a word her boss had said. Knowing Rosey, that wasn't a good thing. "I'm sorry, what?"

Rosey's deep red-painted lips twitched, as if she was fighting a losing battle with a grin. Oh, boy, Shelby was in trouble. What exactly had she missed? Her gaze flew to Dean, but he seemed very interested in the bowl of unshelled peanuts sitting on the bar that hadn't been there a minute ago.

"I asked if the cash register is all set," Rosey said.

"Oh, right. Yes. It's ready to go." Turning away, Shelby walked to the other end of the bar, her boss on her heels. She quickly opened the register, handing over the locked money bag knowing Rosey planned to take it home with her tonight.

Shutting the drawer with a push, she remembered something. "Hey, did you see my letter? I thought I left it tucked beneath the cash drawer."

Rosey sighed. "I thought I told you to burn that thing after you showed it to me yesterday."

She had, using a few colorful adjectives that were typical for Rosey. "I know, but—"

"But nothing. What did your mama say when you showed it to her?"

Shelby remained silent.

"She didn't say anything because *you* never told her what you were doing in the first place." Rosey guessed correctly. "Oh, sweetie. Why not? Your mama would have supported you."

"I know that. She would have supported me so much that she couldn't have kept her mouth shut about it. Everyone in Bee's Beauty Parlor would have known and then…" Shelby's voice faded for a moment. "I just didn't want it to be public knowledge."

"Look, you earned that degree the hard way. While I don't even want to think about how it'd be harder than a whore's heart to run this place without you, they should have considered themselves lucky to get you. Their loss."

"They didn't want me." She kept her voice low. Damn, it still hurt more than it should to say those words aloud. "Even after all that volunteering I did last month with the summer school program…they didn't want me."

"Then they're morons and I'm worried for the younger generation of this town."

Shelby nodded, swallowing hard against the lump in her throat. "Thanks, Rosey."

"Honey, you need to get your mind off all that stuff." She tucked the money bag beneath one arm and cocked her head toward the end of the bar. "Something tells me that hunky cowboy could assist you in that endeavor."

Pushing the strands of blond hair away from her face, Shelby refused to look even though she could feel his gaze on her. After last night it felt…familiar. "Pass."

"You're alone too much."

"I'm never alone." Shelby reminded her. "Not for the last five years and that's exactly how I want it."

"That's not what I meant and you know it."

Yes, she did. It was a heated topic of discussion they'd shared in the past, but she just wasn't up to it tonight. "Weren't you on your way out?"

"Yes, I am, but you play nice. I have a feeling that young man came in here for a particular reason."

Shelby had no doubt that was true. Nipping that reason in the bud was next on her to-do list. "Have a good night, boss."

"Oh, honey, when my Sammy's in town, it's always a good night." Rosey shot her a quick wink and then disappeared into the back.

Focusing her attention on the register, Shelby pressed the sequence of buttons to run the end-of-day reports and sent them to Rosey's computer. She then logged off and shut down the machine.

No sense in putting off the inevitable, Shelby squared her shoulders and started back to the end of the bar.

"Oh, teacher, teacher…"

Shelby froze as Darlene Daughtry's voice rang out across the bar. She looked over at the booth, spotting both her high school nemesis's phony expression of innocence and the folded piece of white paper she fanned herself with.

Was that her letter? No, it couldn't be!

"Oh, my bad. I guess I should have just called for a waitress." Darlene's pageant-practiced smile disappeared. "And you would have come running."

Shock filled Shelby as she realized what Darlene held in her hand. Shock that gave way to a long-familiar, burning shame.

She hated that certain people in this town still had the ability to make her feel that way, after all these years, with just a few choice words.

For all her hard work, there were some things a person never stopped paying for no matter how much time had passed.

Refusing to give Darlene the satisfaction of rushing to the booth, but determined to get everyone out of this place, Shelby set her gaze straight ahead and kept walking, grabbing a nearby tray just so she'd have something to hang on to.

First things first.

Dean looked up as she approached. She expected to see a familiar flirty gleam in his eyes, the same look she'd seen so many times from so many others. His calm and steady gaze confused her, as did the still-unopened beer bottle in front of him despite the growing pile of peanut shells next to it. "Look, I know why you're here. Not interested."

"Excuse me?" He tapped the side of the bottle with one finger while cracking open another shell with a simple squeeze of his fist. "I just came in here for a beer."

"Then I suggest you drink it because the bar is shut off and so am I." Her mind flew back to the girl he'd been with last night. "Can I say it any plainer? I have zero interest in anyone who's obviously already taken."

He started to speak, but Shelby kept on walking. Rounding the end of the bar, she started for the booths, but a warm hand gripped her arm.

She spun around, jerking from his hold, an unnecessary move as he'd already let her go.

"You're wrong," Dean said.

The story of her life. "Am I?"

He moved in closer, his work-scarred boots snugging up against the tips of her sneakers. She automatically lifted the round tray to her chest, placing it between them, almost like a shield. Dean's gaze dropped to the tray for a moment before he took a step back.

"I'm not taken." He pressed a hand to the center of his chest as if to emphasize his words, his voice a low whisper. "Jazzy, the girl you saw me with last night, is an old friend from back home. She was having a rough time and just needed someone to talk to."

Shelby pulled in a deep breath through her nose, fighting for control. It didn't work. All she did was take in the clean, outdoorsy scent that seemed to radiate from this man, a scent that managed to make its way through the typical smoky and boozy odors of most who hung out in the bar.

Suddenly very tired, she was ready for everyone to leave. Including Dean Pritchett.

Grabbing the beer bottle off the bar, she pushed it against

the back of his hand, forcing him to grab it before it crashed to the ground. "Well, I *need* to close up. Take your beer and find somewhere else to drink it."

She spun away from him and stalked over to the booth where Darlene and her friends sat, ignoring how her heart hitched when she heard the Hole's front door gently bang shut behind her.

"I'm afraid it's closing time, ladies," Shelby said with her best phony–customer service voice. "Are you all finished?"

"Hmm, are we finished?" Darlene spoke to her friends, ignoring Shelby as she propped a bent elbow on the table, her fingers tightened around a piece of paper in her hand.

"Oh, did you see the news today?" she continued, batting her mascara-heavy false eyelashes. "Preseason football starts this weekend. Isn't that exciting?"

The other two smirked in unison. Shelby knew what was coming. The contents of the letter were just the tip of the sword that Darlene planned to jab right through her.

As much as Shelby tried to avoid any talk of the biggest news to hit Rust Creek Falls in decades, even with the flooding last month, it didn't work. The extensive damage to the town had stemmed the tide a bit, but now things were looking better with the reconstruction going on, and suddenly everybody was a fan of a certain East Coast professional football team thousands of miles from here.

All because of local boy Zach Shute.

The best high school football player to come out of western Montana in years, Zach had graduated from college with a stellar career and was drafted in the first round. At twenty-four, he was a little bit older than most rookies, but his college days had been delayed for almost a year.

Thanks to Shelby.

"You must be very excited about Zach's prospects." Darlene looked at her now. "I heard professional ballplayers make very good money."

All three girls turned to her and waited. "I wouldn't know," Shelby said, forcing the words out.

"Really? One would think you'd be the first in line to hit up that poor boy for a big fat check." Her fingers relaxed and the letter fell to the table, soaking up the moisture from their now-empty glasses. "Seeing how your career as an educator seems to be over before it even started. But is that really such a surprise? Did you really think the town would want *you* teaching their children?"

Shelby's fingers itched to snatch up the letter, but she wouldn't give her old rival the satisfaction.

Not that it mattered. The contents had been short and sweet. Just two paragraphs telling her she'd been turned down for a teaching position at Rust Creek Falls Elementary School.

Despite the loss of the building in last month's flood, the town was still planning to hold classes any way they could and now that she had her early-childhood education degree, she'd wanted to teach. Shelby had hoped a year in the local school system would add more cushion to her savings and give her some experience to help her find a job in a new city far away from Rust Creek Falls.

She'd done her student teaching in nearby Kalispell, but when she found out the elementary school had openings, she'd jumped at the chance to prove to everyone, to herself, that there was more to Shelby Jenkins than her dubious past.

None of that mattered now.

"I think it's time for you all to leave."

"Really?" The girl in the corner, Shelby couldn't even remember her name, smirked. "We're not the only ones still here, you know. What about that table of cowboys back in the corner? Why aren't you kicking them out?"

"Probably because she wants to keep them all to herself."

Darlene reached for her wallet and cell phone as the three of them scooted out from the booth. Shelby's fingers gripped the drink tray so hard that she feared her bones would crack.

She forced herself to take several steps back, putting as much space between her and this witch as possible without looking as if she was running away.

At one point, she'd tried to understand Darlene's stinging malice toward her. After all, Darlene and Zach had been a steady item for two years before Shelby joined the cheerleading squad her sophomore year in high school. By the following spring Zach had ended things with Darlene right after the junior prom and moved on to Shelby, who'd foolishly thought dating the star quarterback was the answer to her dreams.

But that had been five years ago. High school should be ancient history for everyone by now. Except one of them had a daily reminder—

"Oh, here's a tip for you." Darlene paused, her friends already waiting at the door for her. She unzipped her wallet, yanked out a square foil packet and tossed it onto the table. "Use one of these this time, okay? I think everyone will be happier in the long run."

All the air disappeared from Shelby's lungs. The strength in her legs went as well, causing her to sway as Darlene brushed past her. She jutted her foot out to keep from losing her balance and Darlene's platform sandals caught the edge of Shelby's sneaker. Arm twirling couldn't save her and seconds later, Darlene face planted on the floor.

Her friends gasped as she scrambled to her feet and spun around, her face contorted in an angry sneer. "You did that on purpose, Jenkins."

Had she? Shelby wasn't sure, but there was no way she could convince Darlene of that. Nor would she try. No, what she wanted to do was yell, to get into this evil girl's face and tell her she couldn't talk about the most important thing in her life....

She turned away, her gaze drawn back to the table. The slamming of the door told her Darlene and her friends had left, but she didn't move as everything in her line of sight faded to black except for that single item on the table.

She blinked hard, hoping it would disappear. When it didn't, she cleaned away everything, the empty glasses, used napkins—the trash—with one sweep of her arm. Dropping the tray on the now-empty table, she leaned forward, bracing her arms to keep herself upright as she struggled to catch her breath, familiar accusations rolling through her mind.

How could you be so stupid?

This is the last thing I need right now.

There goes my life!

The loud laughter behind her stopped Shelby from heading down a road that led only to heartache. She shook her head, pulled in a deep breath and quietly reminded herself that she was the lucky one.

Turning around, she walked across the room. "Okay, boys, it's closing time. You all need to head out."

The four cowboys did as she asked, two helping their one friend who was having trouble putting one foot in front of the other. She smiled her thanks as they walked away, and started to clear away their empties, but froze when she felt an arm snake around her waist.

"Hmm, why don't I stick around so we can have some fun?" Heavy, beer-ladened words slurred in her ear as male fingers tightened on her hip.

Shelby fought against the tears that threatened by blinking hard. Could this night get any worse? She never let her guard down and got this close to customers, especially those who stayed until closing time.

"No, thanks." She tried to angle her body away from him, but he practically had her pinned against the table. "I still need to clean up."

"I'll help ya." His breath stank of cigarettes and his rough beard scraped against her cheek. "My buddies are already gone—"

"And you should join them."

Suddenly, she was free from his mangled hold. Shelby hurried away, moving around to the other side of the table in time to watch Dean escort the sputtering cowboy toward the door.

"H-hey! I wasn't go-going to do nothing!"

"I'm sure the lady is pleased to hear that in case you ever want to come back again." Dean's voice carried back across the bar as he strong-armed the man outside. "But it's time for you to leave anyway."

This time she couldn't hold on. She'd reached her limit and when her legs gave way, Shelby sank into the closest chair.

"I need to get out of here." Dropping her head, she covered her face with her hands, rocking back and forth repeating the words again and again. "I need to get out of here. I need to get out of here."

"Any special place you want to go?"

She jerked upright. Dean had returned and knelt in front of her. He'd tossed his hat on the table, making it easy for her to see the sincerity in his gaze.

"Just name the spot, darling." His mouth hitched upward in one corner, making his smile tentative and sweet at the same time. "Name it and I'll take you there."

Chapter Three

Incredible blue eyes stared back at Dean. Eyes the color of the crystal clear falls located in the mountains outside of town. They were also wide and unblinking, which worried him as much as the way he'd found her huddled in one of the simple wooden chairs, after he'd come back inside from making sure that the drunken cowboy left with his buddies.

"What are you doing here?" she whispered, her hands clenched tightly in her lap.

Her voice was as shaky as the rest of her. He found himself wanting to pull her into his arms, hold her close and tell her everything was going to be all right.

Which was probably a lie.

He had no idea what the heck was going on other than a drunken cowboy manhandling her and a booth of female customers that took childhood bullying to a new level.

"Offering to play chauffeur?" That got him a small smile, so he continued, "I came for a beer, remember?"

She nodded, still holding his gaze. "But you left."

"No, I just stepped outside to get some fresh air. When I saw your last customers leave, minus one, I figured I should come back in and make sure you were okay."

This time she closed her eyes and turned away. Two deep breaths didn't seem to help. She was still shaking. When she captured her bottom lip with her teeth and bit down, he just about lost it. "Hey, can I get you anything? A glass of water maybe?"

She shook her head.

"Something stronger?" It felt wrong to ask her that. She looked so innocent, but his brother had assured him she was of age and they were in a bar after all. "I'm pretty sure you've got just about everything here."

That got her attention. Eyes open, she looked at him again and he was glad not to see any tears in those blue depths. She drew in another breath, this one a bit more steady, and nodded.

"Okay." Dean backed away, rising to his full height. "Pick your poison."

"Hot chocolate."

Hot— What? "Hot chocolate?" he repeated.

She nodded again. "And don't spare the marshmallows. I need lots and lots of marshmallows."

He looked around, spotting the swinging door that led to the kitchen. "I'm guessing I'll find what I need in there?"

"No, the cabinet beneath the register. There's one of those automated machines with the tiny cups. Just pop one in and press the button."

Dean knew what she was talking about. They'd bought one of those gadgets for their father a few years ago for Christmas. The old man loved it. "And the marshmallows?"

"There should be a fairly new bag and a couple of mugs, too."

Dean crossed the bar and found everything just where she said. An assortment of single cups featuring flavored coffees, teas and hot chocolate lined the top shelf and the mugs, both looking well-used, sat next to a bag of miniature marshmallows. One of the mugs was stamped with Property of SEAL Team One, Naval Amphibious Base Coronado while the other featured a group of cartoon princesses.

He grabbed the princess mug, made the hot chocolate and returned. By the time he got back to her, her fingers were relaxed when she reached for the mug.

"What made you choose this one?" she asked, still a bit shell-shocked. "Don't think I know any Navy SEALs?"

He shrugged, having gone purely on instinct and handed her the spoon he'd brought with him.

"Well, I do." She paused to blow on the contents of her mug and poked at the melting marshmallows on top. "Samuel Jackson Traven, retired SEAL. He's Rosey's special someone."

Dean leaned against the nearby table. "I guess a spitfire like Rosey would need someone with the stamina of a Special Forces kind of guy to keep up with her."

This time she smiled, still looking down at her mug before bringing it to her lips to take a sip. "You figured that out after only just meeting her?"

"I'm a pretty good judge of people."

Shelby choked, but waved him off when he reached for her. "I'm—I'm fine. It's just still too hot."

Dean watched as she stirred her drink, then scooped the gooeyness on top into her mouth. A small sigh escaped when her lips closed over the spoon, a sigh that went straight to a part of him that had no business responding.

He tightened his grip on the table's edge, remembering the anger that flared in his gut when he'd come back in and found that drunk manhandling her. A protective—no, almost possessive—instinct he'd never felt before reared its ugly head and he wanted to do more to the guy than just haul his ass outside.

Why? What was it about this girl that brought out that side of him?

"Boy, that's good." Shelby's words pulled him from his thoughts. She sat a little straighter in the chair, resting the now half-empty mug in her lap. "Ah, thanks." She lifted her gaze to his. "Thank you for coming to my rescue."

"You're welcome."

She held his stare for a long moment, then broke free and looked around the bar as if she was seeing it for the first time. A quick shake of her head and she was on her feet.

Turning her back to him, she started cleaning the table. "I've still got a lot of work to do."

He moved out of her way. "Let me help you."

"No." Her reply was sharp and biting. She glanced over her shoulder, bit down on her lower lip for a second time, then said softly, "I've got this, but thanks again."

"Okay." He took a step backward, hands held wide in mock surrender. He then jerked his thumb over his shoulder. "I'll just get the trash from the booth over there."

"No!" She whirled around, clutching the bottles and her mug to her chest. "I don't need any help. Really. Everything is fine... I'm fine. The Ace is closed now and you've done your good deed, so you can just head on home."

After witnessing that lost look in her eyes a few minutes ago, and knowing the cause of it was still out there some-where? Not gonna happen. "I'm guessing you upend all the chairs and stools to sweep the floor?"

She sighed and stared at him for a long moment. He could almost see the internal battle she had going on inside her head. Not that he blamed her. Working in a bar probably meant she was hit on a lot and sometimes not as directly as what had happened a few minutes ago.

Was he hitting on her? Yeah, okay, maybe he was.

Finally, she gave him a quick nod before brushing past him in the direction of the dirty booth. Dean started with the closest clean table and by the time Shelby had wiped down the booth and locked the front door from the inside, he was working on the barstools.

"Hey, where should I put this?"

She turned, surprise on her face when she saw him holding the still-unopened beer bottle in his hand. "The beer cooler is behind the bar on the far left. I guess you weren't really interested in a beer, huh?"

No, he'd come back here tonight for just one reason. To see her.

Yeah, he was definitely hitting on her.

Shelby hadn't waited for an answer before disappearing through the swinging door. She returned a minute later with a couple of brooms and a dustpan. She paused but relented and passed one over to him when he held out his hand. Their fingers brushed and that same flicker that had crackled between them when he touched her before was still there. The widening of those beautiful eyes told him she felt it, too.

She spun away and headed for the back corner of the bar. He went to the front and they worked silently as an Elvis ballad filled the air. When they met in the middle of the room, Shelby grabbed a nearby trash barrel and took command of the dustpan. They finished just as the last notes of the song faded away.

She never once looked directly at him.

"Is that it?" Dean asked. "Or are we breaking out a mop and a pail of soapy water?"

"No, we don't wash the floors until the weekend is over unless a customer gives us a reason to—" A faint buzzing filled the air, cutting off Shelby's words. "Oh, darn it!"

She handed him the broom while fishing a cell phone out of her rear pocket. Tossing the dustpan into the trash can, she grabbed it and headed around the end of the bar while the thumb of one hand flew over the phone's flat screen.

Replying to a text message? Was someone wondering why she hadn't come home yet?

Dean hadn't considered that. There was no ring on her finger, but that didn't mean anything.

He'd been surprised after walking Jazzy back to where she was staying at Strickland's Boarding House last night to find Shelby Jenkins still on his mind. He was intrigued by her, a feeling he hadn't experienced in a long time, and he found himself wanting to know her better.

Now he knew why she'd spent most of last night frowning in his direction.

She thought he was already involved with someone. A misconception he'd cleared up earlier before she kicked him out of the bar. Not that he'd planned on leaving, at least not until he was sure she believed him. Now he was glad he'd stuck around.

"Well, that's it. Thanks again for your help."

He noticed her cell phone was gone, back in her pocket he guessed or inside the leather purse that hung from her shoulder.

"You might want to put these away." He walked over to her, holding out the brooms.

"Yeah, that's probably a good idea." She took them from his grasp, not allowing their hands to touch this time. "You can—"

"Walk you to your car?" He cut her off, offering a wide smile for the offense. "Great idea. You parked out back?"

"What are you— Why are you doing all this?"

"I'm a nice guy?"

"Or maybe you think I'm an easy—"

"I think you've had a long night." Dean cut her off again. "That includes being manhandled by a drunk and I just want to make sure you get to your car safely. That's all."

She nodded, and moments later, they were outside in the warm summer air. The parking lot was empty except for a couple of pickups and a car. Dean was glad to see the area was well lit. He glanced quickly at his watch. Almost two-thirty in the morning. He guessed there were many nights when Shelby left the bar this late.

She headed for the used four-door that looked as if its best days were long behind it, her keys already in her hand.

"You know, I was planning to come by earlier than I did," Dean said, falling into step beside her. "I worked until sunset at the elementary school and then fell asleep reading."

"All of the volunteers have been working so hard to help the town get back on its feet." Shelby reached the driver's-side door and quickly unlocked it. "Everyone appreciates all you've done."

He realized his time with her was ending fast. "Well, you know what they say about all work and no play. I was wondering if you'd like to go out with me sometime."

She yanked the door open and hesitated for a moment before sliding in behind the wheel. "I don't think so."

The door closed before he could stop her. Defeated, Dean could do nothing but stand there as she jammed her keys into the ignition. A quick turn and the highlights came on, but nothing else did except for a rapid clicking noise.

He watched her mouth move in what he guessed were a few colorful word choices as she tried to start her car again with the same results. Twice.

Tapping on the window, he waited until she rolled it down to lean forward and peer in at her. "Pop the hood. I'll take a look."

"Dean, you've already done so much for me tonight." She stared straight ahead out the windshield. "I can't ask you—"

He liked the way his name sounded coming from her lips. "You didn't ask. I offered. Now, pop it."

She did as he asked and he walked around to the front of the car, lifting the hood. She'd parked beneath a light, which helped somewhat. He fiddled with the battery connections but they were tight.

"Here, this might help."

He turned to find Shelby standing next to him with a flashlight. "Thanks."

Ten minutes later, he shut off the light and closed the hood with a light bang. Shelby stood leaning against the driver's-side door. "Sorry. I don't see anything that's a simple fix. It might just be your battery. More likely it's the alternator or the starter."

"It's money I can't afford to spend right now, that's what it is." She took the flashlight from him and tossed it back inside her car, locking the door behind her. "A perfect ending to a perfect night."

Dean wasn't happy this happened, but at least he was going to get to spend more time with her. "Come on, I'll take you home. Can we walk from here?" Considering the size of Rust Creek Falls, a person was able to walk from one end of town to the other in a few hours.

Shelby was shaking her head before he finished talking. "I can't ask that of you."

"I'm not going to let you walk alone." He remembered her cell phone. Damn, he hated to ask, but he had to. "Unless there's someone you can call to come get you?"

Shelby tightened her grip on her purse, an array of emotions playing across her face before she turned away into the shadows. Silence filled the air and he wondered what she wasn't telling him.

"No," she finally said. "There's no one. And I don't live in town. I'm on the east side of the creek, over on the edge of the Traub ranch."

Dean had met most of the Traub family when they'd held a barbecue out at their place last month inviting the whole town, including the volunteers.

"Are you related to the Traubs?" he asked.

She shook her head. "My daddy used to work at the ranch."

"Well, my truck is parked at the trailer I'm staying in." He motioned with one hand. "Let's get you home, huh?"

They made the quick walk across the street and into the makeshift trailer park. Dean held open the passenger-side door for Shelby, ignoring her look of surprise. He got behind the wheel and headed down Sawmill Street, knowing it headed straight out of town.

"How long have you lived in Rust Creek Falls?" he asked to fill the silence as they left the center of town.

"All my life." Shelby kept her gaze toward the window. "Born, raised and never been farther than Kalispell."

Kalispell was the next closest town to Rust Creek Falls, about thirty minutes away and where Dean had hoped to take Shelby out for dinner and maybe a movie. She'd already turned him down once. Should he try again?

He followed her directions on the back roads once they left the town limits, noting they soon passed a house for sale, and the five acres it sat on, that had caught his eye last week. Uninhabited for a few years because of the elderly owner's death, it had survived the flood unscathed. Dean had checked out the place on a whim, his head already filled with ideas to fix it up.

If he went through with his idea of being more than just a temporary resident of Rust Creek Falls, he'd need a place to live.

Shelby pointed out the road that led to her driveway just a few miles away. Dean turned, noting how the gravel drive inclined as they drove. "Did you have much damage from the flooding last month?"

"No, my daddy built our place up on this rise. There was a lot of water around us, and the driveway was impassable for a day or two, but that was it."

Dean was happy to hear that. Lord knew there were a lot of homes that had suffered damage ranging from flooded basements to entire homes being condemned. The biggest loss to the town, in terms of buildings at least, had been the total destruction of the elementary school.

He had to admit it'd been hard on his heart to be part of the team that gutted the entire place from the ceiling downward, tossing out tons of debris that included everything from books to pencils before a structural inspection could take place.

"Your father's a smart man."

"Was. Was a smart man. He died three years ago."

Damn, that sucked. Shelby must have been a teenager when that happened. Dean, too, knew what it was like to lose a parent at that age. His mother had died suddenly the summer after he graduated from high school.

"You can turn in here."

He did as Shelby instructed. The headlights of his truck passed over a simple, one-story ranch-style house with a front porch.

And a pickup truck parked in front of a two-car garage.

He thought back to the text message she'd received, not liking how his gut twisted at the sight of the extra vehicle in the drive. Pulling into the empty space near a side entry door, he saw an outside light shone bright in the dark night. A soft glow also came from inside the house. The kitchen, he guessed, wondering again if Shelby had someone waiting up for her.

He put the truck into Park and shut off the twin beams of light from the headlights that bounced off the garage, putting the cab's interior into a shadowy darkness.

"Well, it's pretty late." She reached for the door handle. "Thanks for the lift."

"Shelby, wait." He rested his arm across the back of the truck seat, his fingers inches from her shoulder. "You must have figured out that I came back to the bar to see you."

That got her attention.

She turned to look at him, the soft cotton of her T-shirt

brushing against his fingertips. With her back to the outside light, it was hard to see her face, but he could see when her tongue darted out to swipe across her lips.

Yeah, there went his body's involuntary reactions again.

"Do you believe what I told you earlier about me and Jazzy just being friends?" he pressed.

She nodded but remained silent.

Having no idea if that was a good thing or not, Dean decided he was going to try this again. But first things first. "You know, I'd really like to take you out, but I guess I should find out if you're involved with someone."

"Dean, I…" Her voice trailed off as she looked out the windshield, her fingers tunneling through the shoulder-length strands of her hair. "I'm not involved. Most of my nights are spent working at the bar. I don't have time to date."

He was glad to hear she was single and she hadn't turned down his offer quite yet. "Look, I was planning to take a picnic lunch up around the falls Sunday afternoon. I found this great spot, an open area with marked paths, right next to an outcropping of rocks where there's the remains of—"

"—of a bridge." She turned back and finished his sentence with him. "Wait, did you say the *remains* of a bridge?"

Dean nodded. "As far as I can tell, yeah, there used to be a bridge of some kind over the creek. I guess the flooding took it out. Do you know the place?"

"Yes, I know it."

He waited, wondering if she was going to say more. When she didn't, he plowed ahead. "So, how about joining me? I make a pretty mean fried chicken."

She smiled at that. "You cook?"

"It's an old family recipe that earned my mother a blue ribbon at the Gallatin County Fair three years running." Dean grinned at the memory. "I'll even throw in macaroni salad and freshly sliced watermelon."

Shelby studied him for a long moment, and Dean held his

breath. He hadn't worked this hard for a date in a long time. A couple of the female volunteers on his construction crew had made it clear from the first day they were willing and able to spend time with him. He hadn't been interested and not just because mixing work and pleasure could be a formula for disaster either.

But this? This he wanted with every ounce of his being.

"Well, how can a girl say no to freshly sliced watermelon?"

Shelby stepped inside her house and closed the kitchen door with a soft click, pausing to lean up against the cool wood for a moment. She couldn't believe she'd done the exact opposite of what her head had told her to do.

She'd said yes.

For an evening that had gone from bad to worse in a matter of minutes just an hour ago, it had ended with Shelby agreeing to go on a picnic with a total stranger.

A stranger who'd already earned Rosey's stamp of approval, saved her from a drunken cowboy, helped her clean up the bar and insisted on seeing her safely home after her car died.

A regular knight in shining armor.

Too bad Shelby no longer believed in fairy tales or happily-ever-afters, despite the princess mug.

"Are you okay, honey?"

Shelby turned at the voice, wondering how many times she'd been asked that question in her lifetime. "I'm fine, Mama."

"When you replied to my text you said you'd be home any minute. What happened? And where's your car?" Vivian Jenkins shuffled into her kitchen, tying the sash of her cotton bathroom tightly around her waist. "And who brought you home?"

"My car died." She flipped the lock on the door, deciding to go with the short version of the night's events. "That was

Dean Pritchett. He was at the bar and nice enough to bring me home."

"Oh, don't tell me you are hooking up with another one of those cowboys." Her mother's tone switched from concerned to protective. "I don't want to see you get hurt again."

"Dean isn't a cowboy. I think. I'm not really sure what he does for a living, but he's part of the volunteer crew that came from Thunder Canyon to help with the repairs of the town."

Her mother's demeanor changed in an instant. For a woman who had fallen in love and married a cowboy within weeks of meeting him twenty-five years ago, she sure held a disdain for the species nowadays. "Oh. Well, that was very nice of him."

"Yes, Dean Pritchett is a nice guy." Shelby walked past her mother and out of the kitchen, waiting until she was in the hallway before dropping the next bomb. "Which is why I agreed to go out on a date with him."

"Shelby Marie!"

"Shh!" Turning around, Shelby put her finger to her lips despite the partially closed door to her left. "I don't want you to wake her."

Her mother dismissed the request with the wave of her hand. "Oh, please. That child sleeps through a Montana thunderstorm. You know her."

Yes, she did.

Shelby pushed open the door, the night-light bathing her daughter's bedroom in a warm light. The entire room was decorated in princesses, from the bedding to the toys, but the most important princess of all lay asleep, a stuffed yellow bear held tight in her grasp.

Crossing the room, Shelby automatically picked up the stuffed toys that hadn't been selected as bedtime companions and her daughter's clothing, tossing each in their respective baskets. She perched gently on the edge of the twin-size mattress, marveling at how small Caitlin looked curled up in a ball in the center of the bed.

Brushing back the blond strands that matched her own, Shelby gazed at the little girl who changed her life five years ago. Caitlin was born on Shelby's seventeenth birthday, a present ten days early.

And two weeks after the end of Shelby's junior year in high school.

Two weeks after Caitlin's father, football star Zach Shute, had graduated, still proclaiming the baby wasn't his.

Shaking off the memories, Shelby leaned in and placed a kiss on her daughter's forehead, taking a moment to breathe in that simple fragrance of bubblegum-scented shampoo and talcum powder.

"Did she give you any trouble with her bath tonight?" Shelby whispered, knowing her mother stood behind her.

"Are you kidding me?" Vivian laid a hand on Shelby's shoulder. "She loved it. As long as I sang 'Under the Sea' over and over again. And then we had to read the book connected with that movie at least four times before she would settle down."

Shelby smiled. Her daughter did love to read. A trait she'd picked up from both her grandparents. She didn't have any idea where she or Caitlin would be today if it wasn't for the love and support of her parents.

Telling them she was pregnant at the tender age of sixteen was the hardest thing she'd ever faced, but both her mom and her dad had been by her side from the very beginning.

Rising, Shelby motioned her mother from the room. She was suddenly very tired and she had to be up with Caitlin in the morning as her mother worked at the local beauty salon on Saturdays. Thank goodness her daughter tended to sleep in, but even an 8:00 a.m. wake-up was going to be tough to handle at this point.

"Good night, Mama." Shelby gave her mother a quick

kiss on the cheek after they left Caitlin's room. "I'm heading to bed."

"So when is this date of yours?"

Shelby sighed. She should have known. "We're going for a picnic Sunday afternoon. Is that okay? Are you and Caitlin still going to the movies in Kalispell?"

Her mother nodded. She'd insisted on special afternoons with her granddaughter even though she stepped in as baby-sitter while Shelby worked at the bar. "And we're going out for junk food afterward."

"Mama—"

"I know, but it's my right as a grandmother. Healthy stuff here in the house, junk food during nana-and-me dates."

She was too tired to argue about it now. "Okay."

"Does this man you're going out with know about Caitlin?"

No, he didn't.

She'd thought about telling him she was a single mom to a five-year-old. Just to see how quickly he would backpedal from his invite, much like the last two guys did after finding out about Caitlin.

But the idea of spending a few hours up by the falls with another adult of the opposite sex, especially one as good-looking and well, nice, as Dean Pritchett, was too tempting to pass up.

Besides, she wasn't looking for anything serious. Goodness knows she had enough seriousness in her life, especially now. Her plans to move away from Rust Creek Falls had implanted even more fully in her head after the school board's rejection of her job application.

"Well, does he?" her mother asked.

"No. At least not yet." Shelby had a feeling he would have mentioned Caitlin if someone else had already told him. "Don't worry, Mama, Sunday afternoon is nothing more than a one-time thing."

She closed her eyes to the seed of hope that was already rooting inside of her. The one that said maybe this was more than that.

Much more.

Chapter Four

Sunday was another glorious summer day.

Bright sunshine and an afternoon temperature that reached almost eighty degrees, even though it was a bit cooler up on the mountain. The day was a carbon copy of the weather they'd been blessed with for the past few weeks that allowed the steady rebuilding of the town.

Still, a chill raced through Shelby. Glad that she'd pulled on her jeans and boots while getting dressed for her date with Dean, she second-guessed the short sleeves of her T-shirt that left her arms bare and susceptible to a ridge of goose bumps that rose on her skin.

She stared at the spot where a simple wooden bridge used to cross this section of the creek.

The majestic upper falls were still two-thirds of the way to the summit of Falls Mountain, but here in these twin open fields, popular with so many of the townspeople for parties and picnics, the lower falls were a more gentle cascade of water over an outcropping of boulders and rocks.

A month ago the flowing water must have been anything but gentle.

"I can't believe it's gone." She rubbed her arms to chase away the tingling. "The bridge had been here a long time."

Dean dropped to one knee, closely examining the broken sections of timber embedded into the ground, the only parts of the structure still there. "From what I heard, the rising water was more than enough to wash it clean away. How sturdy was the bridge?"

"Very. My daddy and his friends built it back when he and my mom were dating." Unable to look at the empty space any longer, Shelby backed away. "He told me their crowd used to come here a lot when they were teenagers. Back when no one else used to. At the time there'd been just a big old log across the divide until the guys from the high school wood shop decided to make it easier to cross."

Dean rose, gathering the backpack that carried their lunch, a small cooler and a well-loved quilt in his hands. He joined her again on the trail they'd been following for the past twenty minutes or so. "I wonder if it's on the town's master list of structures that need to be rebuilt or replaced."

"Doubtful." Shelby shrugged, working to add indifference to her tone as they walked. "With all the destruction down in the valley, I bet no one has even thought about the bridge."

The truth was she didn't want to care about the bridge anymore. It'd be one more thing that would make leaving harder when the time came.

Right up there with her mother.

As much as she'd tried to convince her mama that moving away from Rust Creek Falls was the best thing for her and Caitlin, the older woman refused to even think about going with them.

Even after Shelby had finally shared how she'd been turned down for a teaching position early this morning while Caitlin slept.

"I'll check tomorrow at the weekly meeting."

She stopped, Dean's words cutting into her thoughts, and looked at him. "Why?"

"Because it's important." Dean stopped, too, his gaze serious. "Not as much compared to someone's home or business, but that bridge is part of the town's history. It'll probably take a while. Heck, the calendar is so jammed it might not be until next spring, but that bridge should be—will be—rebuilt."

The conviction in his voice warmed her deep inside, chasing away the chill from the sight of the splintered ruins.

Dean Pritchett continued to surprise her.

Like when she'd called Tyrone at the garage about her car yesterday morning only to find out Dean had already made arrangements to have the vehicle towed there. And again later that same night when she'd expected him to show up at the Ace, and she'd eyed the front door every time someone walked in.

Only he never did, even after she'd dawdled at closing time until Rosey hurried her along, agreeing to give Shelby a ride home.

Then today, he'd shown up looking impossibly gorgeous in jeans and a simple white T-shirt beneath an open plaid shirt in shades of green that matched his eyes.

He'd practically shoved a bouquet of daisies into her hand as if they were burning his fingers. He said he'd gotten them at Daisy's Donuts. The owner always had bunches of her namesake flowers for sale, and when he'd stopped by to get dessert he thought she might like them.

She did. She loved them.

No one, other than her parents, had ever given her flowers before. She'd been so touched by the gesture that she'd almost invited Dean inside while she put them in a vase full of water. Thankfully, he'd already stepped off the back stairs, saying he'd wait in his truck for her.

"Shelby? Did you hear me?"

Realizing she'd missed what Dean had asked, she focused her attention and found he'd moved off the path to a shady area a few feet away at the base of a group of birch trees. "I'm sorry. What did you say?"

"I asked if this was an okay place to lay out the blanket." He pointed to the grass. "Or did you want to keep walking?"

She had planned to move farther up the winding path after stopping to see what was left of the bridge. Just in case anyone else in town had the same idea to come to the park for a picnic.

Not that she was ashamed to be seen with him. Just the opposite. The last thing she wanted was to run into someone like Darlene. There were others in town who felt the same way the cheerleader did about her. They might not be as straight-forward nasty as her former teammate, but the insults and hurtful barbs did manage to hit their intended target every once in a while.

Then again, despite the beautiful day, there hadn't been any cars in the lower parking lot and no one else was in sight now. Maybe she should be worried, not about someone ru-ining their date, but about being out here in an isolated area with a man she barely knew.

"Shelby?"

Realizing she'd once again drifted off, she forced a quick laugh from her suddenly tight throat. "There I go, spacing out on you. I'm so sorry. Yes, this spot is perfect."

"Rough night at the bar?" Dean set the backpack and cooler at his feet and unfurled the quilt. "You do look a bit tired."

"Don't you know it's impolite to tell a woman she looks anything but perfect?" Shelby knelt at the edge of the patch-work quilt and smoothed the material with her hands.

Dean mirrored her action, then reached across the blanket to take her hand. Surprised, she looked up and found con-cern in his gaze.

"I just meant if you want to cut this afternoon short—" he gave her fingers a gentle squeeze "—I'd understand."

Refusing to allow anything, including her fears, to mess up this afternoon, Shelby knew at that moment there was no place else she'd rather be. She might not know much about Dean, but she was certain of one thing.

He was a good man.

And that scared her in every way possible.

She eased from his touch, using that same hand to tuck her hair behind one ear. "No, I don't want to go home. Everything was fine last night at work. Like most nights."

"I was planning to stop in, but I had to drive to Missoula to pick up supplies. I ended up running into a friend from high school, so I stayed overnight, crashing at his place."

"Well, you didn't miss much. What happened Friday night was…unusual."

"Meaning Rosey doesn't always play oldies music as a way to get customers to leave at closing time?" Dean sat, placing the backpack and the cooler between them.

Smiling, Shelby joined him but made sure to stay on her side of the blanket. "No, *that* she always does. Sometimes she even hurries their exit along by singing."

"Not much of a voice?"

"Tone-deaf, but what she lacks in talent, she more than makes up for in effort and volume."

Dean laughed as he removed a container from the bag that smelled heavenly, even with the sealed lid. Shelby opened the cooler and pulled out two icy-cold water bottles, wiping them down with one of the napkins. Next was the pasta salad in a separate bowl. He dished everything onto two plates and handed one to her along with a set of plastic flatware.

The silence between them as they ate was…well, nice.

It allowed the natural sounds of the forest to mix with the rushing waters of the creek. The deep greens and rustic browns of the trees stood out sharply against the famous blue Montana sky. It was amazing how quickly nature re-

covered from natural disasters, unlike the man-made structures in town.

Not wanting to think about the flood or the recovery efforts today, Shelby concentrated on the wonderful food. "Boy,
you weren't kidding. The chicken is wonderful." She couldn't
resist licking the crumbs from her fingers. "Your mom must
be proud to know you can cook her secret recipe so well."

"My mother died about ten years ago." Dean's voice was
soft. "I'd like to think she'd be happy to know we still use
her recipes. She loved to cook and seeing people enjoy her
creations made her very happy."

He spoke the words with ease, but Shelby could see the
sadness move across his face for a moment before it disappeared.

"I'm sorry."

"It's okay. It was a long time ago. Though it did make for
a tough freshman year at college." He took another bite of
salad, the only thing left on his plate except for chicken bones.
"At first I didn't want to go. California seemed so far away
from Thunder Canyon, but she'd been so excited when I got
accepted at Berkeley. My father insisted I stick to the plan."

Shelby wondered what it was like to attend such a respected university. She'd patched together her degree with a
lot of day, night and online classes, taking them year-round
in order to get it done in four years.

"Not that everything went according to plan," Dean continued. "I ended up leaving school after my junior year because of financial issues. It took a couple more years to fully
earn my degree."

Well, maybe they weren't so different after all. "So what
is your degree in?"

"History. With a minor in structural engineering."

Good-looking and smart. Somehow she'd known there
was more to him than just a cowboy who worked construc-

tion. "Wow, I don't think I would have ever put those two subjects together."

"I couldn't decide if I wanted to be a teacher or an engineer."

Oh, how crazy would it be if Dean was a teacher like her? Not that she was a teacher; one needed an actual job to have that title, but still. It would also explain why he was free to help this summer. "So, what is it you do when you're not volunteering your time for disaster victims? I guessing you must have a pretty understanding boss to let you have so much time off."

"I do." Dean set aside his plate and reached for the container of watermelon. Removing the lid, he gestured for her to take the first slice. "My old man. We have a working ranch back in Thunder Canyon, but the family business is fine woodworking and furniture-making."

She never expected that. "Really?"

"Yes, really. I always knew I shared the family talent for carving and shaping wood, so I joined my father's business when I returned from college. Still being there seven years later is a surprise to me sometimes when I think about it." Dean paused for a moment. "But life doesn't always go according to plan."

A fact Shelby knew all too well. "So, I guess you're using your engineering knowledge more at the moment than in your regular job."

"Yeah, after doing some brushup work on my education when it comes to rebuilding homes, but I like it. I like Rust Creek Falls, as well."

"You do?" She lifted the triangle-shaped piece of watermelon to her mouth. "Why?" she asked, before taking a bite.

Dean smiled at her, as if surprised by her question. Shelby was surprised she'd actually said the words aloud, but she found she really wanted to hear his answer.

"Your town reminds me of what Thunder Canyon used to

be like. Back when I was kid, long before the gold rush, the fancy resorts and shops," Dean said. "It's still a good place to live, don't get me wrong, but we get a lot of tourists now, so it's kind of lost that 'everyone knows everyone' feel."

Shelby chewed the bite she'd taken and swallowed, knowing the bitter taste in her mouth wasn't from the sweet fruit. "You mean everyone knows everyone's business."

"That, too, I guess." He shrugged. "I tend to stay away from the small-town gossip."

"Easier said than done most times." *Especially when you're continuously the subject of that gossip.* Shelby managed to keep those words from spilling out of her mouth.

"Maybe, but what I really like about Rust Creek Falls is how everyone is coming together, not only to survive the flooding, but also to rebuild, to make things the way they were or even better than they were." Dean leaned forward, his eyes bright with conviction. "Neighbors opening their homes to those who need a place to stay, opening their barns to take in homeless animals, doing what they can to keep things normal for the kids. Giving of their time, their money, hell, I've seen people give the clothes off their backs, literally, for each other."

Shelby nibbled on the watermelon, admitting that Dean was right about how the town had come together since the crisis. She'd done her part by volunteering with the summer school program last month held in the town hall.

Still, she hated that she'd wondered just how giving everyone would have been to her and her family if help had been needed out at their place.

"And the way they pause to celebrate the simple things, like Collin and Willa's wedding last weekend. I mean, everyone was invited. It didn't matter if you've lived here your entire life or had only come to town to help with the recovery."

Dean asked if she wanted more. Then, when she shook her head, he took her plate. Putting their trash in a separate bag he'd brought with him, he finally looked at her again, a chagrined smile on his face. "Boy, I can't believe I just said all that. I'm not usually the kind of person who talks a lot."

Shelby laid a hand on his arm. "Please, don't stop. I like listening to you."

"Yeah?"

She nodded, releasing him to toss the watermelon rind into the trash bag. Wiping her hands, she tried to erase the tingling sensation that danced from her palm to her elbow thanks to the warmth of his skin.

"My brothers and I have worked on projects together, but usually it's just me and whatever piece of furniture I'm working on." Dean moved the cooler and the trash bag and now sat closer, leaning on his hip with one arm braced behind him. "Now I'm enjoying the day-to-day construction work, being part of a crew, functioning with a group of people to accomplish a collective goal. Furniture-making can be a bit solitary at times."

"Solitary sounds good to me. My job is nothing but working with people. Sometimes that can be hard, too."

"Especially when those people aren't so nice?"

Shelby nodded, wrapping her arms around her bent knees as she stared out at the nearby creek. "There are times I feel like I'm two different people."

"How so?"

"Well, there's the one who's responsible, oh-so-polite and always offers a smile even while telling customers they've reached their alcohol limit or apologizing for a food order being messed up."

Biting on her bottom lip, she was surprised at how easily those words had slipped past her defenses. She never did that, never let anyone get close enough to see the real her. Since her life had taken such a dramatic turn five years ago, she wasn't sure who the "real" her was anymore.

At sixteen it'd been all about making the cheerleading

squad and dating a popular guy while studying her butt off to get the grades she needed to get out of this Podunk town. Now, she was Caitlin's mother, Rosey's right hand and her mother's support system since the sudden death of her husband three years ago. And a wannabe teacher who needed to start applying for a position. Away from Rust Creek Falls.

"And the other person?"

Tilting her head, she looked at him while adding lightness to her tone. "Oh, that girl can be a real witch at times. With a capital *B*."

Dean leaned closer, brushing back the hair that had fallen against her cheek, his thumb staying behind to move back and forth across her cheek. "I find that hard to believe."

Her breath caught, then vanished completely the moment he touched her. *Move away. Now.* The command filled her head, but she was frozen in place, her arms locked around her knees.

Held captive by the simple press of his thumb, he gently lifted her head while lowering his. The warmth of his breath floated across her skin, his green eyes darkening to a deep jade as he looked down at her.

Before their lips could meet, Shelby broke free.

Dropping her chin, she kept her gaze focused on the sliver of blanket between them as heat blazed across her cheeks.

Dean stilled for a moment, then eased away. "Okay. This is a bit awkward."

"I'm sorry." She closed her eyes, not wanting to see the disappointment, or worse, in his eyes as the apology rushed past her lips. "I haven't— It's been a long time since I've—"

"It's okay, Shelby. No worries. I'll wait."

She looked up and found nothing in his gaze but tenderness mixed with banked desire. "You will? Why?"

"Because when the time is right, kissing you is going to be so worth it."

* * *

"Hey, bro!" Nick's voice rang out across the empty space that used to be the reception area/waiting room of the Rust Creek Falls Clinic. "That hammer you're choking works a whole lot better if you had something—you know—to hammer with."

Dean ignored his brother's smart-ass remark, even though the man was right. Without a nail, the tool he held tight in his grip was pretty useless.

Much like him.

It was only three in the afternoon, still early as most workdays lasted until the sun went down, but Dean couldn't seem to get anything done right today. Yesterday hadn't been much better either.

All because Shelby wouldn't go on another date with him.

He'd asked on the way back to her place Sunday afternoon, but she claimed she was working all week. So he tried to set up a lunch date, figuring eating with her would be more pleasant that chowing on a sandwich with his brother and the crew, but she'd turned down that idea, too.

He did see her at the bar Monday night, purposely showing up at last call under the guise to see if she needed a ride home. Her car had already been repaired, thus killing that plan, even though she did seem glad to see him, especially when he told her about getting the lower falls bridge added to the town's repair list. They'd talked after everyone had gone, cleaned up the place together and he ended up walking her to her car before heading back to his trailer.

Alone.

The same thing happened Tuesday night, which went even better as he managed to talk her into a slow dance to one of Rosey's jukebox choices after the place emptied. Dean smiled as he remembered how nervous she seemed at first, tripping over his feet. Then he'd pulled her close, loving the press of her curves against his chest, the flowery scent of her hair as it brushed against his chin. But when he pushed about her plans for the coming weekend, suggesting dinner and movie in nearby Kalispell, she never gave him a straight answer.

He'd gone back again last night, earlier this time with his brother who'd stopped by the trailer, but Rosey said Shelby had called in sick.

Was he just too stupid to get the hint?

He thought they'd had a good time on the picnic. Yeah, he'd talked too much about himself, something new for him. And she'd backed away when he'd misread what he thought was an intimate moment and tried to kiss her.

Another new experience. Not that he'd been doing a lot of kissing—or much of anything else for that matter—over the past couple of years, but to be so wrong about something so simple?

To be so wrong about her?

He thought back to what his brother had alluded to the night he first met Shelby, about her having some kind of reputation, but quickly rejected the idea. He just couldn't reconcile that image with the sweet young woman who seemed so shy around him.

And who wouldn't even go out on a second date with him.

"Here, try one of these. I hear they work wonders."

Dean turned. Nick stood next to him, a box of Sheetrock nails resting in his palm. "Very funny."

"Hey, the crew is ready to mud and tape as soon as we give them the green light," Nick said. "Emmet is anxious to get this place up and running. Everyone is."

Emmet DePaul, the local nurse-practitioner, had managed to save a good deal of his supplies and equipment before the creek overflowed its banks during the storm. He'd set up a temporary shop in his home near Strickland's Boarding House for the duration. With the clinic at the top of the list of needed repairs and a quick reopen, Dean's crew was just about finished with getting the new drywall in place. By

Saturday morning they could be priming the walls and laying the new floor.

Thinking about the wood flooring reminded Dean of another project he wanted to get done. Something that he hoped would keep him busy enough this weekend so he wouldn't care that Shelby was doing her best to give the impression she didn't want him around.

He grabbed the box of nails and then flipped his hammer in the air. Catching it by its head, he slapped the tool handle into Nick's now-empty hand. "Here, take over. There's just a few more nails needed along this seam. I'm going to talk to the crew for a minute before I head out."

"Out? It's not beer-thirty yet."

"It's always beer-thirty in your world." Dean brushed the dust off his T-shirt as best he could and unhooked his tool belt from around his hips. "I'm off to talk to Maggie Roarke about funding."

"I thought you did that at the meeting on Monday."

"This is something new. A project that just came up."

Nick groaned. "Don't tell me this has to do with that daycare center?"

How in the hell— "Why would you say that?"

"Because you stopped by that place twice last week." His brother twisted his paint-splattered ball cap around until the brim rested against the back of his neck. "When's the last time you got some?"

Dean's grip tightened on his belt, his gaze quickly darting around the space. There was no one here except him and his brother, which was why Nick felt comfortable ragging on him. Still, any one of the crew could have walked in.

"That's quite a switch. Talking about a day-care center in one breath and asking me about my sex life in the next."

"You know how my mind works. Besides, I think if you just scratched that itch that makes you want to do nothing but work seven days a week, you might be a happier guy. What do ya think?"

"I think it's none of your damn business."

"Come on, bro." Nick walked over to him. "I'm not telling you to get married and have a bunch of kids of your own."

Nick was treading on thin ice now. "Don't go there."

"Look, all I'm saying is, there are plenty of ladies looking for someone to spend a little time with this summer. We're going to be here for only another few months. There's nothing wrong with temporary."

His brother's whole life was a study in temporary—a lifestyle Dean wasn't interested in.

In fact, he'd been doing some hard thinking about turning this short-term construction job into something more permanent.

He and Matt Cates, a friend since high school, had already talked a bit about Matt's father wanting to open a branch of Cates Construction here in the Rust Creek Falls area.

Matt had no interest in moving north, but Dean had already half fallen in love with this remote Western town.

Still, it was just an idea, nothing Dean wanted to talk about aloud yet. "Don't worry about me. I'm fine."

"What I'm worried about is your wrangling me into working on Sunday. That's a sacred day. It's God's day."

Dean didn't fall for his brother's attempt at his innocent, choir-boy face from their youth. "Sunday is sacred to you because of football."

"Darn right." Nick grinned, leveling the hammer in Dean's direction. "Did you know a kid from here is playing pro ball for the Jets? They're playing Sunday."

"It's only the preseason. The games don't count."

"You're only saying that because the 49ers played last Sunday. A game which you missed, by the way. Where were you anyway?"

"I'll be back in about an hour." Dean headed for the door. "I want to see plenty of mud slapping the walls when I get back."

"Slap this, little brother," Nick called out.

Knowing his brother's sense of humor like he did, Dean didn't bother to turn around. He checked in with the crew of five men, all experienced in the construction trade, and then grabbed a water bottle from the nearby cooler before climbing into his truck.

Minutes later, he pulled into an empty parking spot at the town hall, pausing to admire a Heritage Softail Classic motorcycle sitting nearby before heading inside.

Maggie Roarke, a lawyer by trade, had taken a leave of absence from her job in Los Angeles to set up free legal counsel for home and business owners needing assistance in dealing with their insurance companies. She was also spearheading the private fund-raising drive that was helping Rust Creek Falls get back on its feet.

He took the stairs to the second floor, pausing when he saw Rosey step out of Maggie's office. He smiled, taking in her dark jeans, leather jacket and boots, not to mention the shiny black skull helmet decorated with red roses she held in one hand.

"Hey, lady. Don't tell me that Softail outside is yours?"

"Hey, there, handsome. Of course it's mine. What brings you down this way?"

He gestured toward the door she'd just exited. "Money. I need to talk to Maggie."

Rosey looked back at the door for a moment, a mysterious smile on her face. "Yeah, I just did the same." She turned back to him. "Do you have a minute? I'd like to talk to you."

"Sure. Did you put in a request for work to be done?" Dean followed as she moved down the hall and stepped into a small alcove. "I know the bar didn't suffer any losses in the flooding. Is something damaged at your home?"

"My place is fine." Rosey poked gently at his chest with her helmet. "The damage I'm worried about is what you're doing to Shelby's heart."

Chapter Five

"**Y**ou've been in the Ace the last three nights in a row. That's five visits in less than a week." Rosey dropped the helmet to her side but kept on talking. "The businesswoman in me is quite happy about that. As Shelby's friend? That's a different story."

"Wait a minute." Dean was amazed at her precise listing of his activities in relation to the bar, considering she'd been gone both Monday and Tuesday before he'd shown up. "How do you know all that? Ah, Shelby told you."

"Shelby hasn't mentioned you once."

Hmm, that stung more that it should have. "She hasn't? Then, how did you—"

"I know everything that happens in this town, including the fact that my girl was spotted riding shotgun in your truck, heading down from Falls Mountain Sunday afternoon." Rosey leaned in close. "And I'm sure I'm not the only one who knows that."

"What exactly does that mean?"

"You grew up in a small town. Whether it's discussing the newest fool willing to run for public office or who is and isn't attending Sunday services, people love to talk about… people."

Dean squared his shoulders. "I'm a pretty boring guy. No one should be talking about me."

"Or talking to you?"

"About what?"

"Who you're knocking boots with?"

Did Rosey think he and Shelby were— Was that what his brother was trying to get at back at the job site?

No, if Nick knew what happened Sunday afternoon, or what he thought had happened, he would have claimed his brotherly right and grilled him on the subject. "I'm not knocking boots with anyone."

That got Rosey to arch one perfectly shaped eyebrow at him. "Did you know your left eye twitches when you lie?"

"I'm not lying." Dean rubbed his hand over his face. His brother might not know anything about him and Shelby, but Rosey sure did. "Yes, I took Shelby to the lower falls for a picnic on Sunday, but that's it."

"A picnic?" The disbelief in her voice was plain as day.

"Yeah, a picnic. We went up to see where the bridge her father built used to be and had something to eat. She was home before six o'clock." Jeez, this was like being back in high school all over again. "Without saying she'd go out with me a second time, if you want to know the whole truth."

Rosey's posture changed. She suddenly looked more relaxed, almost happy. "You want to date her again."

Her words came out as a statement, not a question, but Dean answered her anyway. "Yes. She's smart and pretty and easy to talk to and…"

"And?" she prompted when his voice faded.

"And I like her," Dean finally admitted, wondering again what it was about the females in this town that got him to speak so freely. "Not that it matters. She keeps turning me down. Says she's busy."

"Maybe she is."

That was what Dean was afraid of. "Maybe she's already got someone in her life keeping her busy."

Rosey didn't speak for a long moment, hesitancy playing across her features. His gut told him he wasn't going to like what she had to say.

"Well, I can tell you she is busy from now until the weekend is over," she finally said. "I'm taking a road trip with my honey, which means Shelby will practically live at the bar."

"Okay. That's good to know." But it didn't explain why he had a sneaking suspicion she was going to say something else.

Rosey leaned forward, her voice a low whisper. "Don't give up on her, Dean. For someone so young, Shelby's been through…a lot. Tread lightly."

Dean waited, but she just centered her helmet on her head and tightened the chin strap.

"That's it? That's all the advice you're going to give me?"

Rosey gave him a bright smile. "You're a smart guy. You'll do just fine."

She brushed past him and headed down the hall. Shaking his head, Dean went to Maggie's office, giving a light knock on the door before entering.

"Dean!" Maggie Roarke, looking very lawyerly in a dark blue suit with her long blond hair pulled back in low ponytail, greeted him from a desk overflowing with paperwork. "Twice in one week. Must be something important to get you off the job site."

Locking his thoughts about Shelby away for the moment, Dean concentrated on his reason for coming here. "Do you have a minute?"

Maggie waved at a nearby chair. "Sure. What's up?"

"There's a place in town called Country Kids. It's a daycare center run by the Johnston sisters." Dean mentally braced himself, knowing how Maggie loved to spew off facts about the local businesses.

"Yes, I know the place. The center is run by Suzie and Sara, twins who had seven kids under the age of five between them when they started the business. They decided an orderly setting was the best way to care for their kids and keep their sanity, especially after Sara's husband was killed in a car accident when her youngest was just a few months old." Maggie rattled off even more details than he'd known. "Thankfully, they're north of the creek, so they suffered only the loss of their back fencing and a wet basement, but nothing drastic as they were in the process of a remodel anyway."

Impressed, Dean decided to jump right in with what he was looking for. "That's all true, and new fencing is in place, thanks to the parents who volunteered to help. Thankfully, the sisters were in the process of upgrading the fence and had the supplies on hand. But while they've got a big yard for the kids, I noticed there wasn't a structure for them to play on."

Maggie nodded. "I remember the assessment stated there were two swing sets out back, but they were washed away during the storm."

"That's what Sara told me when I stopped by Tuesday afternoon. Replacing them was part of the upgrade. They even have a new play set on order, currently sitting in a warehouse in Kalispell."

"Dean, I know where this is going—"

"But they can't pay the final invoice because they decided to waive any fees for the rest of the summer to help those in need," Dean pushed on. "They know their kids' families have enough to worry about without being concerned about child care."

"Which is very commendable, but there's no way we can justify that kind of purchase." She rested one hand on the closest stack of folders. "There are just too many homes and businesses that need help first. Our biggest priority is the elementary school. You know how completely destroyed the building was by the flooding."

Dean nodded. He and his family had spent their first two weeks here helping a large crew gut the brick building down to its steel interior framing. They'd had to empty the place of everything from damaged walls to desks to floor tiles. At the moment they were waiting on a structural inspection before any reconstruction work could begin.

That meant funding because the school needed new everything.

"The people here have been amazing about donating their time, resources and money," Maggie continued, waving a piece of paper at him. "Rosey, the owner of the bar, just dropped off this personal check. No questions asked and no demands on how the money should be spent." She tucked the check into a bank security bag. "Unlike some others."

He knew exactly who she was talking about.

Nathan Crawford.

A member of the town council, he stepped in to lead the town after the mayor died of a heart attack during the storm. Dean hadn't been too impressed with the man's demeanor the few times they'd interacted. Nathan always seemed more interested in becoming the next mayor than helping. That and dictating how any private funds donated to the recovery were spent.

Not that Dean had a vote, but he figured Collin Traub was the better man for the job. Collin had been the only member of his large family around when the storm hit and had been instrumental in helping the town during the confusing days that followed.

It was only August, but the campaign was already causing a major power struggle in the town, because the Traubs and the Crawfords did not get along. Even more so now that Sutter Traub had decided to be his brother's campaign manager.

Maggie leaned forward, her voice low. "Just between us,

I've almost closed a deal with a national rescue organization called Bootstraps, where my cousin Lissa works. I'm going to have to head back to Los Angeles soon, but she is amazing and is trying very hard to get the town everything it needs, especially when it comes to getting the school back up and running."

Dean remembered the school's principal addressing the meeting on Monday with the news that the school year would start on schedule next month with the teachers agreeing to hold classes in their own homes because the high school, while not affected by the storm, was already overcrowded.

In light of all that, Dean guessed a simple play set was pretty insignificant. But not to those kids. Or the staff. "Okay, I get it. No additional funding is available."

"I really wish we could help." Maggie reached for her pen and made a note in the leather folder in front of her. "I'll add the request for the play set to the list. If I get any donations earmarked specifically for child care I'll let you know."

"Thanks, I appreciate it."

Dean left the office, a bit deflated. There had to be a way to get that play set out of that warehouse and to the day-care center where it belonged. And not just because he wanted a project to keep his hands and mind off a certain pretty bartender.

He liked kids.

He liked seeing them happy.

Maybe because as a kid he'd been pretty unhappy.

School recesses were spent off playground equipment and trailing after his brothers, unable to keep up with their active sports schedules. Even roughhousing with them around the ranch had been tough. He'd been the one to stay behind, taking care of the horses while Nick and Cade had gone riding for hours with their dad. He'd helped his mom around the house when he could until his body would give out and he'd curl up on his bed with his books.

Even after everything changed and he was one 100 percent healthy, he still kept an eye out for kids, volunteering at a sports center for kids while in college and mentoring the local teens back in Thunder Canyon at ROOTS, a community outreach program.

Seeing the kids in the backyard, kind of walking around with not much to do, at the day-care center made him determined to not give up on this idea.

Climbing into his truck, he thought back to what Rosey had said about— Rosey! Of course! If she could write a check, whipping out his credit card to take care of the problem would be easy.

Dean grabbed his phone and called Nick, thankful when it went to voice mail. "Hey, bro, I'm going to be out longer than I thought. Need to run a few errands, including heading down to Kalispell. I'll stop by the clinic when I get back into town."

Four days later and his savings account a bit lighter, Dean inspected Nick's precision mortise-and-tenon joint construction. A staple at Pritchett & Sons Fine Woodworking by all the men, he had to admit his brother had a way with a chisel and a mallet.

Not to mention the rest of the tools needed to put together the play set that sat amid a sea of rubberized wood chips in the backyard of the Country Kids Day Care.

A play set that would allow hours of climbing, swinging and sliding fun for the kids. Many of whom had their faces pressed against the windows on this early Monday morning.

After stopping by the center and convincing the sisters that he had a way to pay for the set, they'd handed over the invoice. He'd called the warehouse during the drive to Kalispell, explaining the situation. When he arrived, he found the manager had waived the storage fees that had accumulated for the last month and agreed to a Saturday afternoon delivery.

Because so many components came preassembled, Dean

and Nick had built the set themselves in one day. Nick, who grumbled when Dean first told him he needed his help, caved when Dean played the "uncle" card, reminding his brother of the set they'd put together a couple of months ago for Sabrina, their three-year-old niece.

And Nick still made it to the bar in time to watch the Jets lose. All in all, a good day.

"You know, my sister and I still can't believe you did this for us. For the kids."

Dean turned and found one of the Johnston sisters standing behind him. Which one was anyone's guess. "We were happy to do it…Sara?"

"Suzie." She smiled and pointed to the top of her head. "You can tell by my hair. I always wear it pulled back while working—former bunhead, that I am."

"I'm sorry?"

"I used to dance ballet and we always wore our hair—Never mind." She waved a hand back toward the center. "You've got quite an audience this morning. They're eager to give the set a test drive. My own kids were going crazy after you left yesterday, wanting to come out and play."

"Give me thirty minutes to double-check everything," Dean said, giving the kids a wave. "And clean up any extra items we might've left behind. We still have the platform with the attached fort to store after modifying the tower to take off the extra level."

Sara nodded. "Yes, that was a good idea. My sister and I are planning to hold a 'safety first' lesson right now, but we were wondering if you wouldn't mind saying a few words to the kids? About behaving themselves and playing nice?"

"Ah, yeah, I guess I could."

"Thanks so much. I think it'll hold a bit more weight with them coming from the person who gave us this wonderful gift."

Dean continued with his inspection after Suzie headed

back inside, happy to find everything as perfect as when he'd left last night around sunset.

Dead tired by the time he'd gotten into his truck to head home, he'd purposely avoided driving by the Ace so that he wouldn't be tempted to stop in. In fact, he hadn't been back to the bar all weekend. He'd thought a lot about what Rosey had said to him over the past couple of days.

Maybe some distance was needed.

Being knocked for a loop from the moment he met Shelby was something he'd never felt for any other woman.

The attraction that sizzled between them hammered at his common sense. It'd been seven years since he'd been so enamored with someone.

That relationship had been a slow build, a friend he'd met his first weeks at college who later became his first love, his first lover. Yeah, they'd been young, but he and Jane had three years together before things ended.

She'd made it pretty clear it was over between them when he'd been forced to leave college, but then she'd shown up in Thunder Canyon four months later, pregnant and asking for a second chance.

A chance he'd given her, even falling back in love with her and the idea of being a father at the tender age of twenty-one, until the night before their wedding. Through tears, she confessed she couldn't go through with the sham, that he wasn't her baby's father, breaking his heart and his spirit.

An ache in his chest had Dean pressing his fingers hard against the scar from his long-ago surgery. It'd taken him a long time to get over her deception with dates being few and far between.

He just hadn't been willing to risk it all again.

None of which explained why he felt the way he did now for a woman he'd known for only a week and a half.

The happy cries of the children spilling into the backyard yanked Dean from his thoughts. They raced toward him and the play set, but then stopped short when their teachers insisted they first thank Dean for his generous gift.

He accepted their enthusiastic gratitude with a smile and then gave a quick talk, using their attention to repeat what he guessed was the same basic safety measures the sisters had handed down. Their smiling faces told him he was right. Then they let the kids loose on the play set.

He stood back and watched as they swarmed over the set, a warm feeling settling in his chest. Checking his watch, he saw it was closing in on ten o'clock. Time to head out and meet up with Nick at the job site. He was going to get a kick out of hearing the kids' reactions.

It was then Dean felt a slight tugging on his pant leg. Looking down, he found a little girl, dressed from head to toe in pink from her hair band to her sneakers. Even her pint-size backpack was covered in pink flowers.

"Hi, there."

She craned her head back to look up at him. "Hi, Mr. Pritchett."

Surprised she knew his name, then he remembered the sisters had used it when introducing him to the kids. "So, what do you think of the new play set?"

She looked over at the other kids playing, but her deep sigh told him she wasn't all that impressed. "It's nice."

"Just nice?" Dean fought back a grin.

"The *boys* like it."

Dean looked across the yard. Sure enough, a fight was underway between warring clans of what he guessed were pirates from the pretend swords and the "Argh, mateys" being tossed back and forth across two different levels. Clans that included quite a few female pirates.

Curious as to why she wasn't with the rest of the kids, Dean bent on one knee so they were face-to-face. "I think everyone is having fun. How come you're not over there?"

Her tiny shoulders hitched upward in a quick shrug. "I

don't know. I like to run around and stuff, but sometimes I like being outside and doing my favorite thing."

Not sure if he should even ask, Dean couldn't resist. "Well, what is your favorite thing to do?"

Her blue eyes shone with excitement. "Read!"

He grinned. A girl after his own heart. "Oh, yeah? That's cool. Do you have a favorite book?"

Her head bobbed up and down in a quick nod, sending her blond curls flying around her face. She slid her backpack off one shoulder and unzipped it, causing several books to tumble to the ground at their feet.

Dean eyed the colorful assortment, noting the titles covered everything from a magic tree house to princesses. "Wow, you've got some great ones here."

She bent down and grabbed the book about a princess. "This is my favorite. She likes pink."

"So do you."

The girl giggled and nodded, clutching her book to her chest. "We have reading time inside, but it would be fun to have a place out here where we could read, too."

Dean immediately thought of the unused platform and fort with its canvas cover roof. It was big enough for three or four kids about this girl's size with room left over for plenty of books. The large shady tree in the far corner of the yard would be a perfect spot and the platform would keep it off the ground but not too high. He could even picture a pint-size railing across the front to create a porch and a readers-only sign out front to keep the other kids from commandeering it.

Dean helped her gather the books and put them back in her bag. "You know, I think you're a pretty smart kid. How about I build a special place just perfect for reading?"

The girl's eyes grew round. "Really?"

"Really." Dean figured he'd need only a couple of hours to put the pint-size house together. "But remember, it's important for you to run around and get some exercise, too. Don't let those boys keep you from using the play area."

"Oh, I won't!"

"Okay, I need to make sure your teachers agree with me building this here—"

"Can I help? I've never built anything before."

Unable to say no to that sweet face, Dean mentally added another two hours to his time estimate. "Only if Miss Sara and Miss Suzie say its okay and you promise to do everything I tell you."

"Oh, I promise, Mr. Pritchett."

Dean held out his hand. "Okay, first things first. You can call me Dean."

She placed a tiny hand in his. "You can call me Caitlin."

Chapter Six

"Did you have a good time?"

Shelby waited, but only silence came from the depths of the walk-in freezer. She knew her boss was in there, so why wasn't she answering?

"Did you make it all the way to Calgary?" She tried again. Still nothing.

Shelby had spent Monday morning double-checking the receipts from the weekend and then the last hour reviewing them with Rosey, along with everything that had happened at the Ace while the owner was gone.

It was now almost four o'clock and the two cooks were busy prepping for the dinner crowd, and other than the occasional waitress coming back to grab an order, it was just Shelby in the kitchen.

And Rosey, who apparently thought she could hide in the freezer until Shelby headed home.

Shelby stuck her head inside the unit and was met with

the sight of her boss bent low to reach a bottom shelf, nothing visible but her backside.

"You can't keep ignoring me." She leaned against the door frame, crossing her arms to ward off the chilly air. "This is so unlike you, Rosey. Usually you're all sunshine and smiles and sex talk when you get back from a road trip. Did something happen between you and Sam?"

Rosey backed out of the shelf, got to her feet and propped her hands on her hips. "No. Did something happen here while I was gone?"

"Didn't we already go over everything that went on here this past weekend?"

"So, how about the weekend before that?" Rosey walked past her, hands notably empty, exiting the freezer. "Did anything happen then? Anything *outside* of the bar?"

Rosey knew about her date with Dean.

Shelby was surprised it'd taken the woman this long to find out about her afternoon on the mountain. Even more so that she'd managed to wait until now to bring it up.

After closing the freezer door when her boss disappeared back into the closet-size room that served as her office, Shelby followed. Rosey sat at her desk, reviewing the weekly supply orders.

She perched on the edge of the desk and gently pulled the paperwork from her boss's hand. "Okay, who told you?"

"Dean."

"Dean?" That was the last name she expected to hear. A thread of anger went through her as she wondered how many other people he'd told. "When did he talk to you?"

"Last Thursday, just before Sam and I hit the road." Rosey dropped the pen in her hand and turned to face her. "After I told him the two of you were spotted in his truck heading down Falls Mountain."

Relief filled her that it wasn't just idle talk, but that Rosey had pried it out of him.

"What I want to know is why you didn't say anything before I left?" Rosey continued. "You've always shared things with me."

Head low, Shelby studied the paperwork, the words written in her boss's neat handwriting melting into one big blur. She opened her mouth, but her typical wisecrack died on her tongue.

"Did I ask that tough of a question?"

"I guess…" Shelby pushed the truth past her lips. "I guess I didn't want anything to tarnish the best time I've had in… well, in forever. Not that telling you would do that," she added. "I just wanted to keep it to myself for a little longer."

"Oh, honey." Rosey leaned forward and laid a hand on Shelby's knee. "You shouldn't feel that way."

"But I do and with good reason, right?" She pulled in a deep breath and let it out. "And I'm sure you're not the only one who's said something to Dean about me by now. What exactly did you say to him?"

"Don't worry, I was discreet."

Shelby offered her friend a long stare. Discretion wasn't exactly Rosey's strongest attribute.

"I was," she protested, taking her paperwork back from Shelby. "All I said was that you two were seen together."

Dread filled Shelby. "Who told you that?"

"Sam, of all people. He was out on his bike and spotted you in a stranger's truck. Dean was the one who told me about the picnic. Did you have a good time?"

Shelby smiled, then said, "Yes, I did. He cooked a great meal and we talked about all kinds of things. I tried not to have a good time, as crazy as that sounds, but he's just so… nice." She traced an imaginary line on her jeans. "I let down my guard, Rosey. So much so that I almost let him kiss me."

"Almost? Why almost?"

"Because I panicked, of course, so the kiss never happened. But again, he was nice about my stupidity." A pang of longing swept through her as she remembered his certainty that kissing her would be worth the wait. "Not that it matters now."

"Why would you say that?"

"Because Dean never came into the bar all weekend."

"Maybe that has something to do with the fact that you kept turning him down when he asked you for another date."

"He told you that?"

Rosey nodded. "So, why won't you go out with him again?"

"Because I had to work, filling in for you this past weekend, my mother's schedule got changed due to another hairdresser taking vacation, I have my daughter—" Her phone buzzed from inside her back pocket, cutting off her list. Shelby looked at the screen. Another text from her mother. "Besides, you can bet Dean pulled his vanishing act this past weekend because someone else, or a few someones, took great pleasure in telling him all about me."

"Shelby, those stories about what happened back when you were a teenager are not who you are now. Hell, they're not about who you were back then. Zach Shute was stupid and mean and that posse of hangers-on he ran around with was even worse for spreading lies about you. But that's all in your past."

"Is it? It's been five years and there are still people in this town who repeat those nasty stories, as if they're reliving some old high school memories." She hit the button to read the text, then pushed off from the desk. "What happened back then is part of my life now because of my daughter. And you know what? That's the way I want it. It's the way I wanted it from the moment I found out I was pregnant. If Dean can't handle that, then good riddance to him."

"I don't think you're giving him enough credit." Rosey stood, as well. "Have you even told him about Caitlin?"

Shelby shook her head as she grabbed her purse from a nearby chair and headed for the door. "No. Sunday afternoon and the couple of times he stuck around after hours here at the bar was just a little me-time with a nice guy. Nothing more."

"A nice guy who likes you."

That got her attention. She stopped and turned back. "He told you that, too?"

Rosey nodded.

"Well, those few times with him wasn't the real me. They were just a fantasy. Look, I've got to go. Mama is running late at the beauty shop."

"Don't think for one moment we're done talking." Rosey sat again, waving the pen at her. "About any of this."

"Or about your weekend away?"

"Great ride, great friends, great food and great sex. What else is there to say?" Rosey quipped minus her usual smile. "But Sam is gone now, zooming his way back to sunny San Diego after a stop in Spokane to visit his daughter."

Shelby sent her mama a quick "Be right there" text message before sinking into the chair opposite her boss, knowing she couldn't leave just yet.

"Did he propose again?"

Rosey sighed, then yanked open the center drawer. Pulling out a black velvet jeweler's box, she tossed it onto the scattered paperwork of her desk.

Shelby started to reach for it, then asked, "May I?"

"Sure, why not?"

She picked up the box and opened the lid, gasping softly at the large, rectangular ruby surrounded by diamonds that trailed off into the white gold band. "Oh, this is beautiful." She looked up. "Was this all? I mean, it's more than enough, but usually there's something more to his proposals."

Rosey shook her head. "Just him down on one knee. You'd think the man would know better by now."

"You two have been together for over ten years now and you've known him since you were kids." Shelby closed the lid and pushed the tiny box back across the desk. "You once told me Sam was the love of your life. Maybe you should say yes one of these times. Before it's too late."

"Oh, honey. Sam and I are one beer short of a six-pack between us when it comes to the ol' ball and chain. The majority of those marriages being mine." Rosey swept the box back into the drawer. "That ship has sailed."

"What was it you were saying about letting go of the past?" Shelby asked. "Maybe you're not giving Sam enough credit. Or yourself."

"Isn't there some place you need to be?" Rosey pointed toward the door. "Like five minutes ago?"

"Yes, there is," Shelby said, rising again. "But can I add, we'll be talking about this again later, too?"

"My office, my rules. Now, git!"

Shelby did as she was told, checking the time on her phone as she left the bar. She couldn't believe Rosey had said no to Sam for the fourth time. The first had been back when they were teenagers. At the insistence of her parents, Rosey had chosen college instead. They'd lost touch for years until the internet led them back to each other.

Shelby had met Sam for the first time three years ago when he came to her daddy's funeral with Rosey. A few months later, during a late night of girl talk and take-out wings, Rosey told her the whole story, including Sam's second proposal the week before when he'd attached a diamond ring to the ignition of a Harley-Davidson motorcycle.

Rosey had accepted the motorcycle, but again turned down his proposal.

The next time a different diamond had been attached to keys to his beach house in San Diego. She again returned the ring, but kept the keys when Sam insisted. They continued to see each other every couple of months, with Sam traveling to Montana to stay for a few weeks at a time in the warmer months while Rosey went to him during the winter.

What must that be like? To be loved so fully by someone who refused to give up.

After she climbed into her car, she headed for Bee's Beauty Parlor. Popping in for a moment, she waved at her mother who was busy with a customer, then grabbed her daughter's child seat from the truck and headed off again.

A few minutes later, she pulled into the crowded driveway at Country Kids. Caitlin wasn't a regular at the day-care center, but Sara and Suzie Johnston allowed her to come whenever Shelby or her mother's schedules clashed.

Shelby liked that it gave her daughter a chance to play with other kids on a regular basis. As hard as it was to believe, Caitlin would be starting kindergarten next month, and as much as she seemed to enjoy being with other children, she tended to enjoy her own company best, especially when surrounded by her books and stuffed animals.

Shelby headed up the front walk, but was drawn to the backyard by the sounds of happy kids playing outside. She walked through the new fence and found a group of parents standing with Sara, one of the owners, but the sight of an oversize play set in the center of the yard drew her attention.

Caitlin had been here just last week for a couple of days and neither she nor Shelby's mama had mentioned anything about this beautiful maze of slides, swings, towers and bridges. The wood structure was light oak in color, sitting on a sea of brown wood chips and even came with a tire swing and a fireman's pole.

She tried to find her daughter among the crowd, realizing she didn't have any idea what she was wearing today. Caitlin had been in her pajamas when she'd left this morning. Of course, she was probably wearing—

"Mama! Mama! Over here!"

Several women reacted, a typical occurrence when those words were called out, but Shelby recognized her daughter's voice immediately. She turned, noticing for the first time an-

other new play structure similar in design and color to the
larger set. Only a couple of feet off the ground, it resembled a
mini pergola except for its angled canvas-covered roof, front
porch and railing. Her daughter sat perched on the porch,
waving madly at her.

And Dean stood nearby, a stunned expression on his face
as he stared at her.

Oh, God, the fantasy was officially over.

Shelby automatically stiffened in defense mode. Fight or
flight. Because flight wasn't an option, fighting for her next
breath was all she could manage. Of all the places in town
where she might have run into Dean again, this was the last
on the list.

"Mama, come see what I did!"

Drawing in a lungful of air and grateful for winning that
small battle, Shelby forced her feet to move when Caitlin
excitedly beckoned her again. Her daughter wasn't willing
to wait, however. She jumped to her feet and started down
the steps.

Dean instinctively turned and easily lifted Caitlin to the
ground, as if he'd done it so many times before.

Surprised at the tears biting at the corners of her eyes,
Shelby blinked hard, dropping to one knee to wrap Caitlin
in her arms when her little girl reached her.

"Hey, baby." She buried her face in her daughter's neck
and stole a minute in an attempt to gather her out-of-control
emotions. "It looks like you had a fun day."

"Oh, yes! Look what I did!"

Caitlin wiggled out of her arms and clutching her hand, she
pulled Shelby to her feet, leading her toward the play area.

Toward Dean.

Work boots planted wide and arms crossed over his chest,
muscles testing the seams of his light blue T-shirt, he watched.
His unblinking gaze was focused solely on her, his features
now looking as if they were carved from granite.

"Sweetie, slow down." Shelby tore her gaze away to focus on her daughter, trying to grab a few more moments to stabilize a world that had suddenly gone cockeyed, but Caitlin had already let go, racing back to the playhouse.

"Hi, Shelby." Suzie Johnston greeted her and then she realized there were others standing in the yard, as well. "We've had quite a day here, as you can probably tell."

"Yes, I see that." She looked at the group of ladies, recognizing one who had been with Darlene that night at the bar when she'd been drunk and mouthy. Ignoring the slight narrowing of the woman's eyes, Shelby continued, "Your backyard has certainly changed since the last time I was here."

"All thanks to this man." Suzie waved in Dean's direction. "This is Dean Pritchett. He's part of the volunteer crew from Thunder Canyon and our generous benefactor. Have you two met?"

Shelby finally looked at him again. The hard line of his mouth told her he wasn't going to answer for her, even as a slight tinge of color crossed his cheeks at the teacher's words.

"Ah, yes. We've met a couple of times," she said. "It's nice to see you again."

"Hello, Shelby."

There was a hint of irritation in his eyes despite the calmness in his tone. She guessed from his reaction to seeing her that he hadn't known about her daughter until this very moment.

And if Caitlin was a surprise, then he must not be aware of the stories that surrounded Shelby's teenage pregnancy.

Amazed that no one in town had felt the need to share their version of her story, Shelby felt a sliver of guilt at keeping that part of her life from him. Past history had taught her that once men found out she came as part of a package, they wanted nothing more to do with her.

Then again, a few conversations and one date didn't mean she owed this man anything.

"How did you two meet?" This came from Darlene's friend, her smile a bit too innocent. "At the bar?"

"Yes, at the bar." Shelby tightened her fist, welcoming the press of her keys into her skin as she stepped away from everyone, including Dean. She needed to get out of here before anyone said…anything. She didn't think she could handle that. Not now. "Caitlin, honey, we have to go now."

"Mama, come see our special reading place," Caitlin called from inside the playhouse. "It's so neat!"

Wanting nothing more than to leave quickly, she walked to the structure, noting the same wood chips, actually pieces of chopped rubber, surrounded the playhouse. Peeking inside, a smile came to her face as her daughter gushed about the furniture that had been moved here from the day-care center, including a rug, miniature table and chairs and lots of fluffy pillows.

"And I was the helper because it was my idea," Caitlin said proudly as she stood next to the railing, the platform making her tall enough to look Shelby in the eye. "I carried the nuts and bolts and washers and handed them over whenever Dean asked for them."

Shelby's smile grew as she brushed her daughter's bangs out of her eyes. "I'm sure you were a great help."

"She certainly was."

Caitlin beamed at Dean's words as his voice carried over Shelby's shoulder. He was standing beside her, so close she could almost feel the soft brush of his shirt against her arm.

"And we talked about our favorite books." Caitlin offered a bright smile at her new friend. "Mama, Dean likes to read, too!"

"Something you already knew about me." Those words were purposely kept low so no one else could have heard them but Shelby. "Isn't that right?"

"Yes, well, I'm glad to hear that—"

Her voice caught and she had to press her lips together for

a moment. This wasn't like her. She didn't get unnerved, not after honing her survival skills over the past five years. And *never* around men. Not anymore.

What was it about this man that threw her off her game?

"I'm glad you had a good time today, honey," Shelby managed to get the words out. "But we really need to get home."

"Running away?"

That got her to look at him, and still, she made a quick survey, relieved to find everyone else had moved away. It was just the three of them here. Then she got mad. "Excuse me?"

"You heard me. Don't you think we have a few things to talk about?"

"Not that I'm aware of," she said the words aloud, refusing to react to the disbelief that filled his gaze. Her gut told her she was wrong, but she didn't care.

Thankfully, her daughter listened to her this time, gathering her backpack and her books before scrambling down the steps. She stepped around Dean and took Caitlin's hand. The two of them headed for her car, and Shelby swore she felt Dean's heated gaze on her back the entire time it took to cross the yard.

"Mama, I have to go to the bathroom."

Knowing her daughter wouldn't last the fifteen minutes it would take them to get home, Shelby tamped down her need to escape and released her hand. "Okay. You go inside and I'll be waiting right here by the car."

She watched Caitlin skip into the house, then turned to unlock her car.

"Shelby, wait."

Closing her eyes, she yanked open the back door before turning around. "What part of no don't you understand?"

"What I don't understand is why you didn't tell me you have a child."

"I just met you. There are a lot of things you don't know about me."

"Apparently." He braced one arm on the roof of the car and leaned in close. "And a three-hour picnic just wasn't the right time or place to share something so important?"

"My daughter is the most important thing in my life."

"Then why keep her a secret? Is she the reason you wouldn't go out with me again? Did you not want me to meet her?"

"Look, when I turned you down and said I was busy, that was the truth. Being a single mother means I am the only one Caitlin has to rely on, besides her grandmother," Shelby shot back, her defensive instincts in full gear now.

He was going to hurt her. She knew it. If not now, then later, once he heard the full story of her past.

"You and I have talked a few times at the bar, shared a slow dance and went out once. That's casual, and my daughter doesn't get introduced to casual."

A muscle jumped along Dean's jaw as he stared down at her.

They stood there for a long moment before he finally gave a quick nod of his head, then pushed away from the car and walked away.

Chapter Seven

Shelby was a mom.

Correction, Shelby, at the age of twenty-two, was a *young* mom.

Dean still didn't know what shocked him more: discovering the cute kid at the day-care center belonged to the girl he'd taken on a picnic, or that the same girl had never bothered to tell him she had a daughter.

The shock still hadn't worn off twenty-four hours later.

Unable to do much other than replay the events of yesterday over and over again in his head, Dean had finally gotten sick of listening to his brother's complaints over his inattentiveness and left the job site early. He had a meeting anyway with the owner of the local lumber mill to discuss the next project—a meeting that forced him to concentrate as they discussed costs and materials.

Now that his workday was done, he needed to eat and there wasn't one iota of edible food in the trailer's fridge. Dean pulled open one side of the double doors that led into Crawford's General Store, a place that carried everything from hardware to toys to food, and stepped inside.

He hadn't made a trip down to Kalispell over the weekend for food shopping, and his cupboards were getting pretty bare. Boxes of mac and cheese, cold cereal and a few cans of soup would hold him until the weekend.

Or he could just go to the Ace tonight and grab a burger.

But that meant probably running into Shelby.

Casual.

Yeah, hearing her label the time they'd spent together that way had smarted a bit. Who was he kidding? It burned like a fire in his gut the three beers in his fridge hadn't been able to put out.

By the time the sun rose after a sleepless night, Dean figured he understood why someone like her—a single mother—would say what she said. Do what she did. Or what she didn't when it came to telling him about her daughter.

When he thought back to the things they'd talked about—both at the bar and on their date—he had been sharing bits and pieces of his life. Not her.

Obviously, on purpose.

Did she think he would hold the fact that she had a child against her?

He hadn't avoided dating single mothers in the past—hell, maybe he did, now that he stopped to add up the women he'd been with since those few months he'd been engaged seven years ago.

A list he could check off with one hand.

Ever since his brush with marriage and fatherhood years earlier, he hadn't been eager to get seriously involved with anyone. He'd purposely kept the time he spent with the opposite sex...

Casual.

He shook his head and started for the frozen foods section in the rear of the store. He was almost out of Popsicles.

As warm as the nights had been the past few weeks and the lackluster performance of the trailer's window AC unit, he could easily eat a half dozen of the frozen treats in one sitting.

Especially last night after he'd run out of beers.

He stood there, debating between getting two or three boxes of the variety pack when a familiar voice called out.

"Dean! Hey, Dean!"

He turned, managing to lift the basket out of the way before the pocket-size blonde barreled into him. "Whoa! Slow down there, Miss Caitlin."

She looked up at him and beamed. "What are you doing here?"

"I'm shopping." He bent slightly at the waist, easily returning her infectious grin—something he'd learned yesterday was impossible to resist. "What are you doing here all by yourself?"

"I'm not by myself, silly."

He knew that, of course. He took a moment before he followed the direction of her tiny pointed finger.

"My mama and nana are right there. See?"

Yes, he did see.

Rising to his full height again, he released Caitlin's shoulder, his gaze now firmly locked with Shelby's. He was surprised to find a mixture of uncertainty and concern in her large expressive eyes as she and the woman beside her walked up. He found himself longing for the humor and intelligence he'd seen before in those blue depths.

Or even the fire that crackled and snapped at him as she defended her actions yesterday.

"Ah, hi." *Real smooth, Romeo.* "Hello."

Shelby reached for her daughter, tugging her back to her side. "I'm sorry about that. She saw you from across the store and—"

"It's okay." He cut her off, hating to think she would have walked on by if not for her daughter.

"It's okay, Mama." Caitlin's words overlapped his. "We're friends. Right, Dean?"

"Of course we're friends," he answered the little girl, but kept his gaze locked on her mother.

Shelby looked away, but a slight smile came to her lips.

"What did I tell ya, Nana?" Caitlin folded her arms over her chest, seemingly very proud of herself for being right.

"Oh, boy, where are my manners? This is my mother—" Shelby gestured to the woman with her "—Vivian Jenkins."

Noticing how both her daughter and granddaughter shared her pretty features, Dean offered his hand. "Dean Pritchett, ma'am. It's nice to meet you."

"It's nice to meet you, too." She returned his handshake. "Caitlin has been chatting nonstop about you and the new playground since she came home yesterday."

So Shelby still lived with her mother. Made sense. He wondered if she had talked about him, as well. "Well, Caitlin was a lot of help to me."

"That was a very nice thing you did for the kids," she continued. "Not to mention volunteering your time to help us rebuild the town."

"I'm glad to do it. Rust Creek Falls is a beautiful place. I'm enjoying being here."

Shelby's mother looked him over for a long moment and then reached for her granddaughter's hand. "How about we go see if Miss Nina has gotten any new books for the children's section? That was on our things-to-do list today, wasn't it?"

"Yes, it was," Shelby added. "We should let Dean get back to his shopping—"

"No, you stay and visit for moment." Vivian's gaze darted from her daughter to him and back again. "This is a grandma thing."

"Let's go, Nana!" Caitlin led her grandmother away without a backward glance at her mother or Dean. "I love new books!"

Dean could read the indecision on Shelby's face as she watched her mother and daughter walk away. He wasn't going to let this chance get away from him, but where to start?

"Who's Nina?"

Shelby pulled in a deep breath, then faced him again. "Nina Crawford. Her family owns the store, but she's the one who runs this place. She's created a great area for kids with lots of old-fashioned toys, games and books, of course. Caitlin loves coming here."

Dean took a step closer, angling his food basket out of the way. "I didn't get a chance to tell you what a terrific kid you have there. She really did help a lot with putting together the playhouse. When I ran out of things for her to do, she sat and read me stories while I worked."

"I'm not surprised." A warm glow came over Shelby's features. "Caitlin has been reading since she was three. I guess she saw me with my nose buried in books all the time thanks to…"

"Thanks to…what?" Dean prodded gently.

"Studying for my college classes," she finally said. "It took a lot of day and night classes scattered here and there, but I earned my degree this spring."

Wow, the surprises kept coming. Not that a lot of twenty-two-year-olds weren't college graduates, but to be a single mother, as well? "How old is Caitlin, if you don't mind my asking?"

Shelby opened her mouth, but before she could speak, a sweet Southern voice floated from around the corner.

"She's five, the same as my sweet Maggie. Isn't that right, Shelby?"

Shelby stilled.

Her complexion blanched, her fingers tightening on her basket's handles as a woman appeared, the height of her teased hair matching the high heels she tottered on. She had obviously been eavesdropping on their conversation.

"I graduated a few years ahead of Shelby," the brunette continued as if she was speaking to no one in particular while inspecting the frozen selection behind the glass doors. She then picked out a carton of ice cream, turned to them and Dean would've sworn her smile was as icy as the dessert she held in her hand. "Of course, I waited until I was married before I had my daughter. Shelby was only seventeen when she had her baby, bless her heart."

Angered by the woman's insolence, Dean had to bite back the powerful need to call her back and demand she apologize after she gave a little wave and sauntered off.

Surprised at how protective he felt toward Shelby, he turned to her, the red slash of embarrassment on her face as she studied the contents of her basket tore at his heart.

"Wow, talk about a witch with a capital *B*—"

"Ah, I should go find my mother and Caitlin." She cut him off as she abruptly backed up a few steps. "I'll—I'll see you later."

"When?"

She stilled. "When what?"

Single mother or not, Shelby was all the same things he'd said to Rosey that day in the town hall. Smart, pretty, easy to talk to...especially when he was doing all the speaking. This time he wanted to keep her talking. Hell, he just wanted to spend time with her.

"When will I see you again? I'd really like to get to know you better."

Another step back. "There isn't much more to me."

"I find that hard to believe."

"I'm sorry. I've really got to go."

She whirled and disappeared around the end of the aisle.

He wanted to go after her, wanted to see if she was okay, but he wasn't sure if he should. Wasn't sure if that was what she wanted.

Suddenly, he wasn't sure of anything.

He turned his focus back to the freezer, trying to remember what he'd come here for in the first place. Popsicles. Yep, definitely a three-box night. He filled the basket and continued shopping, trying hard not to look for Shelby and her family among the crowd.

"Psst."

Dean stopped and looked down, not surprised to see Caitlin peeking out from a circular display of summer T-shirts.

"Boy, you sure like Popsicles, huh?"

He glanced at his basket. "Yes. Why aren't you with your mom or grandmother?"

"It's okay as long as I don't leave the store. Besides, my nana is close by." Caitlin curled her finger, beckoning him closer. "Do you like ice cream as much as you like Pops?"

Having no idea where this was headed, Dean leaned in closer. "Who doesn't?"

"Mama doesn't have to work tonight, so I'm gonna ask her to take me to Cherry Hill after dinner." Her words came out in a hushed whisper. "They have the best ice-cream sundaes. Do you know where that is?"

Dean didn't have any idea where or what Cherry Hill was, but in a town this small, it shouldn't be too hard to find out. "I'm sure I can find it, but only if you head straight back to your nana right now."

Caitlin giggled, then disappeared back into the rack of clothing. He stood guard, waiting until she popped out the side and headed for Vivian Jenkins, who stood at the end of the next aisle.

Damn if Shelby's mother didn't just wink in his direction.

Bless her heart, indeed.

Shelby wanted to tell Wanda Jefferson just where she could stick her Southern idiom.

She was mortified by how easily that gossip-loving busybody had just jumped right into the middle of her conversation with Dean. Mortified that she'd just stood there, frozen, with no idea what to say.

Not that he hadn't figured out she'd been a teenager when she'd gotten pregnant with Caitlin, but to have someone else blatantly toss out her personal information... So typical of this town. Everyone loved being the town crier of everyone else's business.

Running away from Dean had been the cowardly thing to do, but she just couldn't talk about her private life in such a public place. Not that Dean had tried to ask her anything or that she owed him any explanations, but he'd been so sweet to Caitlin, both yesterday at the day-care center and again in the store.

She wondered if he would be so sweet once he knew the whole story.

Which he probably did by now.

"We're here! We're here!"

Caitlin called out from the backseat as Shelby turned onto the dirt road that led up a small hill to a barn-shaped building with a giant wooden ice-cream cone perched on the roof.

Cherry Hill Farm was a working farm, the ice cream made fresh daily all summer long thanks to the cows that called the rolling hills home. Built back in the seventies to give the owners something to do with an overflow of dairy products, the ice-cream stand had been a popular hangout for years.

Which meant it was the last place she wanted to be right now, but Caitlin had caught her while she'd been distracted working on the computer after they got home this afternoon. And well, here they were.

She squeezed her car into one of the few empty spaces and cut the engine. Closing her eyes, Shelby blocked the sight of the crowds gathered around the nearby picnic tables.

"Wow, look at all the people." Her daughter was already busy unbuckling her car seat. "This is going to be so fun!"

Fun was the last word Shelby would use, but she refused

to let any of the town's gossiping meddlers spoil her daughter's evening. Sliding out from behind the wheel, she made it to the rear passenger door before Caitlin opened it herself. "You stick close by, okay?"

She nodded and hopped to the ground. "Oh, look. There's Miss Sara and the kids! Can we go say hi?"

"How about we decide what kind of ice cream we want first?"

"But I want to see who's here."

Of course she did. Her daughter, the social butterfly. "After we get your treat, okay?"

Caitlin didn't seem happy with that, but she nodded and they joined the long line waiting to order. Shelby listened as her daughter debated the merits of strawberry or chocolate ice cream and whether rainbow sprinkles tasted better than the plain chocolate ones, but she'd swear she could feel everyone staring at her. It probably wasn't true, but after that run-in today at the store…

"Mama, the twins are waving at me," Caitlin said, tugging on Shelby's hand. "Can I please go over and see them?"

Sara Johnston, the day-care provider, and her daughters were indeed waving at them, so Shelby relented and let Caitlin skip over to join them. Sara and her sister were good people and they'd always been nice to Shelby and Caitlin.

She watched as Sara greeted Caitlin with a smile and then signaled she'd keep an eye on her as the children played on the grass nearby. There were still a couple of hours until sunset and the place had gotten busier just in the short time they'd been there.

"Hey, there, Shelby."

Turning, Shelby found Paige Dalton and Willa Christensen, or she guessed it was Willa Traub now, standing next to her. Both were teachers at Rust Creek Falls Elementary and Shelby had enjoyed working with them last month during the summer school program.

Back when she'd foolishly thought she had a chance at joining their ranks at the school in the fall.

"Hi, Paige." Curbing the seething resentment she felt when she thought about the rejection letter she'd received from the school took some doing, but Shelby succeeded and forced a smile. "Hey, Willa. How's married life treating you?"

Willa glanced over her shoulder and Shelby followed her gaze to where Collin Traub stood talking with a group of men. "It's good. I like being Mrs. Traub," she said, turning back with a big smile. "And it should be easier for my students to pronounce when classes start in the fall."

Just what she needed, a reminder of her own failure, but she pushed that animosity aside. "Well, perhaps they'll be calling you Mrs. Mayor instead if Collin wins the election in November."

Willa blushed. "I think Collin would be a terrific mayor, but I think I'll stick with being Mrs. Traub."

Shelby noticed Paige had continued to stare at the group and she followed her gaze, seeing that Sutter Traub now stood next to his brother. She'd heard Paige and the horse trainer from Seattle shared quite the history before Sutter left Rust Creek Falls to move west. He'd returned for his brother's wedding and it looked like he might be spending more time in town since he was his brother's campaign manager.

Paige pulled in a deep breath and made a point of turning her back to the men before she spoke. "I'm glad we ran into you tonight, Shelby. I tried to speak with you the other night at the bar. I wanted to tell you how sorry I am about the job at the school."

Shelby wanted to believe the sincerity in the woman's tone, despite the fact that she must have heard the news through the local gossip chain. Then again, wasn't she just thinking about the gossip surrounding Paige and Sutter? "Yes, well… I guess they didn't think I'd be a good fit."

"Oh, no, that's not it at all," Willa said.

"I don't understand."

"Shelby, no one was hired." Paige reached out and laid a hand on her arm. "There were three openings when the school year ended and we've lost two more teachers because the flooding has caused people to relocate. As of right now we're combining some of the grades to make do because a hiring freeze was put in place thanks to the damage to the building."

Willa took a step closer, her voice low. "I caught a look at the new hires list and you were right at the top. But until the school gets a better idea of how much it's going to cost to re-build, they just aren't hiring any new staff."

"We both thought you did a great job last month," Paige added and Willa nodded in agreement. "The school should keep your name on the list of potential hires, but if they start again from scratch, we hope you'll consider reapplying once we're ready to fill the open slots."

Shelby didn't know what to say. The letter she'd gotten had said nothing about a hiring freeze. She'd been so sure the rejection had been based on her personal history. After that awful encounter today at Crawford's with Wanda, she'd gone straight home and applied for half a dozen open teach-ing positions, all far away from Rust Creek Falls.

"Ah, I'm not sure," she finally said to the questioning looks on the women's faces. "I'm actually looking elsewhere in Montana for a teaching position."

"You're leaving town?"

The low and deeply masculine question carried a hint of disbelief as it came over her shoulder. Shelby whirled around. Dean stood behind her, looking impossibly handsome in faded jeans, a well-loved Stetson and a button-down shirt worn un-tucked and loose around his hips.

Her eyes were immediately drawn to his stubble-covered jaw and the corded muscles of his throat, visible because the top three buttons of his shirt were undone thanks to her daughter, who he carried piggyback-style, her tiny hands fisted in the cotton material.

"Hi, Mama! Look at me!" Caitlin peeked at her over one muscular shoulder. "Dean is giving me a piggyback ride!"

Dumbfounded, Shelby didn't know where to look. Her gaze darted from her daughter's happy grin to Dean's puzzled expression to Paige and Willa who managed to look surprised, amused and appreciative of the man's magnificent shoulders.

"Dean's going to have ice cream with us, Mama," her daughter continued. "He's never been to Cherry Hill before, so I told him we would show him how to order and where to get the napkins and stuff."

"O-okay." She finally found her voice. And her manners. "Paige and Willa, do you know Dean Pritchett?"

"No, I don't think we've met." Paige smiled and held out her hand.

Dean easily supported Caitlin with one arm while shaking hands with Paige first and then Willa. They chatted for a few minutes before the ladies excused themselves with promises to check in with Shelby again about the situation at the school.

After they walked away, she couldn't help but notice the three of them—her, Dean and Caitlin—were drawing quite a few stares.

Of course they were. Everyone probably thought they were on a date, and for a moment, Shelby was consumed by a familiar need to run away.

The last thing she wanted was to give anyone the impression they were together. Like a couple. Or worse, like a family.

Why not? Who cares what they think?

Shelby could almost hear Rosey's voice as the words filled her head. She hadn't had a chance yet to talk to her friend about Dean finding out about Caitlin, but she'd bet her boss would give her the same advice she'd gotten from her mother earlier today.

So, he knows? So what? He seems like a nice guy. Have some fun.

Oh, if it were only that easy.

Then again, at times having fun in the small gossipy town was easy. Hadn't she had a relaxing and incident-free night when she and Caitlin had attended the impromptu street party downtown the night the power had been finally restored after the flooding? Her mother had joined the two of them, along with the rest of the town, at Willa and Collin's wedding reception and again, no snide remarks about the past.

Of course, she hadn't been on a date on either of those occasions.

Not that she was on a date now.

She wasn't.

Dean just happened to show up and, of course, her daughter had latched onto her new friend the moment she saw him.

"Shelby, are you serious about getting a job outside of—"

She turned back to Dean, her words coming out in a low whisper as she gestured at Caitlin, "Not now. Please."

He looked at her for a long moment, then nodded once and gave her daughter a boost to lift her back in place, bringing forth a squeal, then giggles. "Okay, ladies. I don't know about you, but I'm ready for some ice cream and I think it's our turn next."

Caitlin leaned to one side, her hair falling in a shiny curtain over one shoulder as she tried to look at his face. "What kind of ice cream are you gonna get?"

Dean turned to her, looking very serious. "Hmm, spinach surprise?"

Caitlin wrinkled up her tiny nose. "Oh, yuck!"

"Okay, what about Brussels sprouts swirl?"

Shelby tried to hide her smile at the look on her daughter's face, who didn't seem too impressed with Dean's suggestions.

"Mama." Caitlin's tone was solemn as she looked at her. "I think you better order for him."

Both Dean and Shelby burst out laughing, and Shelby decided at that moment, just for tonight, she was going to let go of her worries and…have fun.

"How about a sundae we can split three ways?" She stepped up to the counter, suddenly conscious of the fact that she was wearing a homemade miniskirt from an old pair of jeans. The double row of eyelet ruffles she'd added brought the length down to midthigh, but still…

She glanced back over her shoulder in time to catch Dean's gaze snapping up to meet hers. Had he just been ogling her? "Ah, I should warn you that sundaes to Caitlin are pretty simple. Ice cream, lots of whipped topping, sprinkles and a couple of cherries on top."

He grinned and tugged the brim of his hat low over his eyes. "Sounds perfect."

Lost in the warmth of his smile, she jumped when something brushed against her hand. Looking down she found Dean had slipped a folded twenty-dollar bill into her palm.

She wanted to argue that she could afford to pay for the ice cream on her own, but the girl was there asking for her order. Turning back around, she made their purchase, returned his change and the three of them sat at the end of one of the picnic tables enjoying scoops of chocolate, vanilla and strawberry ice cream.

Caitlin's endless chatter didn't allow for any conversation between her and Dean, but that was fine with Shelby as she relaxed and enjoyed his company.

She still sneaked a few glances now and then at the crowd, and yes, there were some openly staring at them, but for the most part, people were involved with their own friends and families.

After Dean went to get a handful of wet wipe packets, they cleaned up and tossed away their trash. A lot of the families were leaving and a younger crowd, mostly teenagers, started to show up.

Not wanting to relive any old memories, Shelby looked at her watch and then at Dean. "I think I should get going. It's almost *b-e-d-t-i-m-e*."

"But I'm not sleepy," Caitlin protested, despite a big yawn.

Dean laughed and stood, and Shelby did, too, quickly lifting her daughter into her arms before he had a chance to reach for Caitlin.

He only motioned for her to go ahead of him toward the parking lot. They walked in silence to her car and Dean waited as she got Caitlin strapped into her car seat before he leaned in and spoke softly to the little girl for a moment.

Did he just say thank you to her daughter? And what had Caitlin done in return that caused his low rumble of laughter?

Then he moved out of the way and Shelby closed the car door. Standing there, looking up at him, she realized they were in the same positions as they'd been yesterday afternoon at the day-care center.

Dean must have realized it as well because he took a step back, a look of uncertainty on his face. "Thanks...for letting me tag along on your ice-cream outing. I had a good time."

"So did I."

The words came easily to her because they were true. She'd had a good time tonight and she didn't want it to end. Pulling in a deep breath, she slowly released it while her gaze stayed glued to his.

Could she do this? Could she just open her mouth and ask a simple question?

"Would you like to follow me back to my place?"

Chapter Eight

Surprised by her invitation, Dean had entertained any number of possible scenarios during the drive to Shelby's house—and being a red-blooded male, there were many. Still, he knew she lived with her mother, and obviously, her daughter, so he tried to keep the more lust-filled fantasies at a minimum.

But even he had to admit this scenario never occurred to him.

"Read this book first, please. It's my favorite." Caitlin stood in front of a crowded two-tiered bookshelf that lined one wall in her bedroom. Dressed in a pink nightgown that didn't quite reach her ankles, she leaned over and pulled out two picture books. "Then this one. It's my second favorite."

She raced to her bed and grabbed more books from the bottom shelf on a bedside table. "Oh, and this book! Mama got it for me for my birthday and we just bought this one yesterday at the store."

The pile in his hands steadily grew. Not that he minded. As Shelby stepped forward to corral her daughter from the corner, he stopped her with a quick wave of his hand. Her angelic smile and the slight shaking of her head hit him right in the gut.

She silently mouthed *"You're in trouble now"* over her daughter's head before retreating back to the open doorway.

In more ways than one, Dean feared.

When he'd first spotted Shelby in line at the ice-cream stand in a body-hugging T-shirt and a short jean skirt that showed off her smooth, tanned legs, he'd nearly tripped over his size-eleven boots.

In turn, he'd almost lost his grip on her daughter, who'd asked very politely if he'd give her a piggyback ride. He'd complied and then followed her directions to where her mother was waiting to place their order, arriving in time to hear Shelby say she was looking for a teaching job out of town.

He hadn't even known her degree was in education. Then again, he'd only learned she was a college graduate earlier today.

Inviting him to stick around for ice cream had been her daughter's idea, the little schemer she was, but Shelby could have found a way to get rid of him.

All she had to do was make it clear he wasn't wanted and Dean would have walked away, especially after picking up on what a novelty it seemed to everyone that the three of them were together.

But they ate and chatted, mostly about whatever subject Caitlin jumped to from asking why grass was green to the new puppy a friend at day care got for her birthday. When Shelby said it was time for them to head home, he'd walked her and Caitlin to her car and thanked the little girl for telling him about Cherry Hill with a wink. That resulted in Caitlin squinting and blinking back at him a few times before he realized she was trying her best to return the gesture.

His heart had crawled right up into his throat and he'd

tried to laugh, hoping the action would dislodge it, but then Shelby's invitation had kept it firmly in place.

They'd arrived about twenty minutes ago and a front porch swing had been offered as a place to sit while Shelby got Caitlin ready for bed. He still hadn't seen Shelby's mother anywhere, but the pickup truck was here, so he'd guessed she was home. He'd been enjoying the streaks of red, yellow and pink that made up another spectacular Montana sunset when Caitlin had suddenly appeared at the screened door.

And asked him to read her a bedtime story.

Stunned, he hadn't known what to say. He stood and walked to the door, leaving his Stetson behind on the swing, but didn't reach for the handle. Then Shelby appeared behind her daughter and said he was welcome to come inside.

"Okay, I think that's enough," Caitlin announced. She raced over to give her mom a quick kiss before crawling into her bed and scooting beneath the covers. She turned on her side to face him, a stuffed bear tucked in next to her and patted the edge of her bed. "You can sit here, Dean."

Realizing he had at least a dozen books in his hands, he took a step forward, then paused and looked back at Shelby. It was still light outside, but the room was dim thanks to the pulled curtains. Leaning against the door frame, her face was hidden in the shadows, but she folded her arms over her chest and gave him a quick nod of approval.

He sat on the edge of the bed, pulled out the first book the little girl had given him and started to read. "'Once upon a time, in a kingdom far away, there lived a princess who loved the color pink…'"

Caitlin listened with rapt attention, at times reciting the words along with him. It wasn't until the third book that her eyelids started to flutter, and by the middle of the fourth, they were down for the count.

Without turning around, Dean instinctively knew when Shelby left the doorway, but he kept on reading until he finished the last page, set the books on the nightstand and pushed to his feet. He looked down at the sleeping angel and couldn't stop himself from tugging the light blanket up over her small shoulders.

Exiting Caitlin's room, he figured Shelby was waiting for him in the hallway. He pulled up short when he found her mother standing there instead, looking at the framed photographs lining the wall.

"It's been a long time since we've heard a male voice reading fairy tales around here."

Not quite sure what Vivian meant by that or where Shelby had disappeared to, Dean remained silent. Was she talking about Caitlin's father? He wondered how the man fit into the picture as neither Caitlin nor Shelby had mentioned him yet.

"Caitlin's grandfather, my Ricky, used to love to tell her stories when she was just a baby," she continued, one hand tracing the outline of a framed image. "Either from books or whatever he made up himself."

Dean stepped forward to get a better look, realizing she was talking about her late husband. The man in the picture was 100 percent cowboy, from his hat to his worn boots. It wasn't just the clothing, though. He stood tall next to a horse, his posture relaxed. A saddle sat braced against one leg, as if he'd just removed it from the animal's back. His eyes were hidden beneath his Stetson, but there was a slight grin on his face, as if he'd been surprised to find a camera pointed at him.

"He looks like a good man."

"He was. Swept me off my feet the first day we met, even though it took some time for me to believe his declaration of true love. Shelby arrived nine months from the day we were married." Vivian turned to face him and sighed. "When Shelby told us she was pregnant, we supported her decision to keep the baby and were determined to be the kind of grandparents who let Shelby be the parent. But many times it was Ricky who heard Caitlin first during the wee hours of the morning, which was when he was usually heading off to work at the Triple T. He would change her, get her a bottle and talk to her until she fell back asleep."

Keeping his gaze forward, Dean heard the love and sorrow in the woman's voice as he saw images of a young family during holiday and birthday celebrations, one of Shelby dressed in her cap and gown, holding Caitlin and flanked by her parents and another of Vivian, her hands on her husband's shoulders as the man easily held a tiny newborn in his large hands.

"You miss him very much."

"Sometimes more than you could ever know. He's been gone three years now and there's still a hole in my heart that just won't heal. He always worked hard to provide for his family. He'd been the one who insisted on a hefty life insurance policy. Goodness knows, I hated writing out those checks every month, but when he was taken so suddenly from us…"

Dean looked at her when her voice trailed off.

She pressed her lips tightly together for a long minute, then continued. "We were able to pay off the house, most of the bills and per Ricky's wishes, Shelby, who'd just finished her freshman year in college, continued her education."

"She told me she got her degree this past spring."

"It's been hard for her. Life has been nothing but studies, working at the bar and caring for that little girl in there. Taking all that on at such a young age…I don't know how she does it. I am so proud of her."

"She had you to help her," Dean said. "I think your husband would be very proud of his family."

"Thank you." Vivian dropped her hand. "Please forgive my ramblings. I don't know why I just spilled all that to you."

"That's all right, ma'am. I enjoyed listening."

"Well, I'm going to head to my room to get caught up on my daytime dramas. You'll probably find Shelby out on the front porch if she's not wrestling with that darn leaky faucet in the kitchen again."

Dean headed back to the front of the house, but found the kitchen empty. He retraced his steps to the front porch. The sky was a dark purple now and the air had cooled a bit. He made sure the screen door closed softly behind him. The snick of the latch caused Shelby to look up at him from where she sat, one leg tucked at an angle beneath the other, her foot gently pushing the swing back and forth.

She started to rise, but he quickly crossed the porch, grabbed his hat off the cushions and sank into the empty spot next to her. Planting his boots flat on the porch, he took over the swaying motion. They sat in silence, Dean kept his gaze straight ahead, mimicking Shelby's as dusk took over. Darkness crept into the yard and onto the porch as the outside light next to the door stayed unlit.

He figured he should say something, but it was nice just to be here next to her, the feel of her knee pressed into his hip and the air filled with a flowery scent he knew was hers.

Did she feel the same way or was she trying to think up a way to tell him to hit the road? That her invite had been a mistake?

"How many books did she make it through?" Shelby's soft words were almost a whisper.

He looked at her now, noticing for the first time she'd changed out of her skirt and into a pair of jeans. She still wore the same T-shirt and her body's reaction to the night air was clearly visible.

And his body reacted to hers.

"Dean?"

Oh, right. Books. Grateful he still held his hat in his hands, he laid it casually across his lap. "Four. Well, more like three and a half."

"Oh, I thought maybe she lasted longer. It took you a while to come back out here."

"I ran into your mom outside Caitlin's room. We talked for a few minutes."

Shelby groaned and rolled her eyes. "Oh, that can't be good."

"Actually, she spoke mostly about your father."

"She did?"

Dean nodded. "About how much she misses him. I guess he used to read to Caitlin a lot."

"Yeah, he did. He was always great with her."

"And she told me how proud she is of you, considering everything you've been through."

"Yeah, well…you know, what's the saying? Life is like a box of chocolates. You never know what you're going to get. Funny, how I never seem to get the caramel-filled ones."

Shelby sighed and rose from the swing. She walked to the porch railing and leaned against one of the tall columns supporting the roof, facing him. "Can I ask you something?"

Dean stretched out one arm along the back of the swing, trying to appear relaxed, even though he had no idea what she might say.

Why did he show up tonight at Cherry Hill? Why did he come back here tonight? Did he want to kiss her?

You. You. Yes, desperately.

Pretty simple answers, all things considered. He started pushing the swing again just to keep from putting that last thought into action, whether she asked it or not.

"Sure, go ahead."

"Back in June, Sara told me about the playground equipment she and her sister wanted for the center as part of their overhaul of the backyard. When they told us they weren't going to charge any fees for the rest of the summer, I knew that meant the remainder of the work would be on hold. How did you convince the town to pay for it?"

Dean never planned to advertise where the money came from for the play set, but he wasn't going to lie about it either.

He didn't have to.

Shelby's mouth formed a silent O when she quickly figured it out for herself. "You? When Sara said they had you to thank, I thought that was because you'd built the set. You paid for it, too?"

"It's not that big of a deal."

"Yes, it is. Those things run a couple of thousand dollars each."

"The kids need some normalcy in their lives right now, something that doesn't involve rebuilding, cleaning and all the other fun stuff that comes with a natural disaster." Dean shrugged. "I just wanted to give them a place where they can get away from the reality of losing their school, and possibly their home. A place where a kid can be a kid again. Even if it's just for a couple of hours."

She blinked. "Are you for real?"

"I'm not sure what that means. I'm just a man, like any other man."

"Not the men I've known." Shelby waved off his words. "Not by a long shot."

She wasn't talking about her father. He thought back to the pictures in the hallway. There was none of her or Caitlin with a young man. "It must have been tough, being a teenage mother."

"Being a teenager ended when I became pregnant." Shelby looked him in the eye, her words strong. "A choice I made easily."

A choice, it sounded like, she'd made alone. Besides her parents, that is. So, how did the guy who got her pregnant figure into all of this? "Is Caitlin's father around?"

"No, he left town a few months after Caitlin was born."

She didn't seem too upset about his asking or the fact that the man wasn't around, but Dean knew how tough being pregnant and alone could be.

"It's his loss." His sister, Holly, had had an unplanned

pregnancy, although she'd been a few years older than Shelby when she'd found herself having a baby alone. "My sister went through something similar a few years back and the jerk walked away from her, too," Dean shared. "It's a long, crazy story, but she's now married to a great guy who loves their little girl, Sabrina, with all his heart."

"Oh, I doubt it was in any way similar to what I went through. At least, I hope it wasn't." Her words were flat and detached. "She sounds very lucky. Not everybody finds their happily-ever-after."

"I don't believe that." He stopped the swing, hating the lifeless tone to her voice. He waited until she looked at him again before he went on. "It can take some searching and for some, being happy might be a long time coming, or just a leap of faith. But it's possible. For everyone."

Shelby stared at Dean, surprised more by the certainty in his voice and the honesty in his gaze than his words. He truly believed in the good guy saving the day, the damsel being rescued and everyone getting their heart's desire.

She'd realized earlier tonight at Cherry Hill that for whatever reason, no one had pulled him aside yet to warn him off about her. That was a surprise, too.

Usually she spent her time clearing up people's preconceived opinions or she just let them believe whatever they wanted.

For the first time, with someone she could really care about if she let herself, she had the chance to lay everything out there…before he up and walked away.

"Let me tell you a story, okay?"

"Sure."

"Once upon a time there was a girl who decided that getting straight A's in school wasn't doing enough for her social life. She wanted to be part of the popular crowd in the worst way." It sounded weird, talking about herself in the third person, but somehow it made it easier. She wrapped one arm around the porch column and gazed out over the yard, unable to look at Dean while she spoke. "So, she got herself on the cheerleading squad her sophomore year of high school, but she knew the true key to popularity was having the right boyfriend. It took almost the whole school year, but she finally got her Prince Charming, Zach Shute, the captain of the football team, to notice her."

"Zach Shute. Why does that name ring a bell?"

She turned back, watching as Dean tried to place the name, not surprised that he'd heard of him. She nodded when the recognition came into his eyes. "Yes, the same Zach Shute—the darling of Rust Creek Falls—who plays football for the New York Jets."

Dean nodded but remained silent. He was probably thinking how she must be swimming in child support.

"And just like in all those teenage romance novels, he dumped his picture-perfect girlfriend and asked out this former nerd turned cheerleader," she continued her story, her words softer now. "She was in heaven. Zach was every girl's dream come true. Tall, dark and handsome and already the recipient of a full athletic scholarship to play football in college. Everything was perfect...for a few months."

Shelby looked past Dean again, lost in memories from that long-ago summer.

She'd turned sixteen that June and after a whirlwind summer filled with parties, trips to the nearby lake and many late nights of heavy making out in Zach's car, he began pressuring her to sleep with him. She wasn't sure, but by the end of August she finally gave in. Sex hadn't been all she'd hoped it would be, but it seemed to make Zach happy—at least until the day the at-home test showed two lines.

"I found out I was pregnant that fall when what I thought was a stomach flu wouldn't go away. I don't think I've ever been so scared in my entire life. Of course, the first person I ran to was Zach. His reaction was…was to get 'rid of it,' but I couldn't. I wouldn't. Then I told my parents, who insisted on meeting with Zach and his folks. When we did, Zach lied and said the baby wasn't his. He insisted I was sleeping around with other guys on the team and the baby could be anyone's. Of course, his minions actually had the nerve to back him up."

Dean's swift intake of breath pulled her back to the present. She realized then she'd been speaking aloud and in the first person. Not that Dean hadn't already figured out she'd been talking about herself.

Forcing her gaze to his, she saw his relaxed stance was gone and his green eyes had turned narrow and hard. "That bastard. How could he do that to you?"

"Oh, it gets better." Shelby tried to laugh, but it came out gruff and humorless. "Or worse, depending on your point of view. School was a nightmare, but I refused to let him or his lies keep me away. Of course, my friends were Zach's friends and they sided with him once the news came out. Especially when they were egging our home or flattening the tires on my car."

She wrapped her arms around her middle, suddenly very cold. "I finally accepted that I was on my own with the baby, but by midwinter my father was enraged that Zach still refused to come clean about what happened. He'd talked to the sheriff, wanting him arrested for statutory rape, but the law was in Zach's favor. Despite that, my dad had a temporary order of protection issued to keep him away. An order he violated, but that was my fault as much as Zach's. I was set up to believe he wanted to talk to me by someone I thought was a friend. When we were found together, Zach was arrested. His father's lawyer fought the charges and won, but he lost his scholarship."

"Good. He deserved at least that much."

"Yes, I thought that, too, at first, but then everyone in town started blaming me for ruining the future of their star quarterback. After Caitlin was born that spring, a DNA test proved Zach was her father, not that the results mattered to him or his folks. He signed away his parental rights in exchange for not having to pay child support and was done with me and the baby. By fall he'd been accepted at another college, out of state, and his family left town. But the bitterness and the lies stuck around. Even now. I think those jerks from high school have been telling their stories for so long now that they actually believe them.

"Of course, a couple of mistakes with a couple of cowboys in town on temp jobs hasn't helped my reputation either." Shelby pulled in a deep breath and released it in a rush as she ran her hands through her hair. Tucking the strands behind one ear, she then dropped her hands to her sides. "I'm really surprised no one told you all of this already. Too many in this town believe I should have a scarlet letter permanently tattooed on my forehead."

Dean stood, his hat in his hands.

Her heart sank. He was leaving. Of course he was leaving.

She braced herself, refusing to lean against the porch column again despite the exhaustion that now flowed through her limbs. "I understand. Getting involved with a single mother who is also the town harlot—even for someone only in town temporarily— Anyway, I'm sure you want to head out now—"

"Is that what you want? For me to leave?" He cut her off. "Because I'm telling you right now, nothing you just said makes me think you are anything other than an amazing woman who faced incredible odds and came out stronger because of it."

She should tell him to go.

Before she said something even more stupid than suggesting they were involved. Maybe they could be friends. Sure, they could do that, which was probably for the best anyway.

Her plan was still to leave town, to start a new life for herself and Caitlin, the sooner the better. Anything more than friendship would only be asking for trouble....

"Shelby?"

"Ah, I think you should do what you want—"

Dean tossed his hat to the floor, his long strides easily eating up the distance between them. His hands closed gently over her upper arms as he pulled her close to him. Stunned, she didn't fight him, but placed her hands against his chest, the pounding of his heart created a tight ball of awareness deep inside her. She closed her eyes when his lips moved against her hairline.

"What I want more than anything right now is to hold you in my arms. No, that's a lie." His words were ragged and rushed. "What I want more than anything is to kiss you. It's what I've wanted since we first met."

His declaration took the remaining strength from her, causing her fingers to curl into the soft material of his shirt. A gentle shift and his hands moved, one warm and strong skimming down her spine to her hip while the other cupped the back of her head.

Featherlight kisses brushed her forehead, past her temple and along her jaw. His fingers tightened on her hip for a moment before he released her and lightly caressed his fingertips along her cheek.

His gentleness should have been sweet and innocent, but instead it caused that awareness to morph into a desire that unfurled and spread to every inch of her body.

She'd never experienced a man's touch like this before. The tenderness in his hold that she could easily break free from if she wanted contradicted the restrained passion that emanated from his long and muscular body.

"Can I, Shelby?" he spoke in a low murmur. "Can I kiss you?"

Chapter Nine

She felt more than heard his request as the pounding of her heart echoed in her ears. Her head fell back, cradled in his palm, her lips opening in an unspoken invitation.

Dean looked at her from beneath hooded eyes, lowering his head until his mouth was inches from hers. Still, he waited, until she breathlessly gave him the permission he sought.

"Please…"

He kissed her, soft and unhurried, his lips brushing against hers. The pleasure brought forth a moan she didn't recognize as her own until Dean repeated the sound.

She returned his kiss then, wanting, needing more as she rose on her toes, stretching upward to press her body more fully against his.

As if her actions convinced him more than her words, he deepened the kiss when his tongue slid past her lips, seeking hers.

Oh, this is what she wanted, what she allowed herself to dream of late at night as she lay alone in her bed. Instead of a fantasy, though, she was in the arms of a real man. A good man.

A man who'd didn't judge her by her past.

Right now she wasn't someone's daughter, someone's mother, best friend or employee. She was simply a woman, wanted by this man.

She never wanted this moment to end.

Their kisses became wild and rushed, the coarseness of his beard stubble chafing her skin in the most delicious way. She slid her hands upward until her arms encircled his neck, molding their bodies even closer together.

He dropped his hands to her waist, his fingers burning her skin as they burrowed beneath the edge of her shirt. Holding her tight against him, he lifted her until their bodies were perfectly aligned and he was right where she wanted him to be and she felt as if she were burning from the inside out.

The need for her next breath had her breaking free. He let her mouth go, but then she directed him back, wanting the heat of his lips on hers again.

With a low groan, Dean eased back and lifted his head, breaking their connection at the same time as he set her feet back on the porch.

Her arms eased from his neck until she clutched at his biceps. Cool air rushed between them and she ached from the loss of his warmth.

He pressed his forehead to hers, his breathing coming in fast, uneven gusts that swept against her cheeks. "Shelby... we can't... We have to..."

His words chilled the air between them even more. She tried to back away, but her backside pressed against the porch column. "Isn't this...isn't this what you wanted?"

Dean groaned and captured her hands in his when she slid them down the length of his arms to his wrists. "Let's not start again about what each of us wants or doesn't want, okay?"

She nodded, her throat suddenly tight, making it impossible to speak.

"We aren't exactly alone here." He lifted his head and looked down at her, his eyes bright.

Her brows furrowed.

"I know it's dark out here, but your family is right inside," he continued, his voice low. "Your daughter or your mom could appear in the doorway at any minute."

Of course. How stupid of her.

She caught her bottom lip with her teeth, but that only brought another groan from Dean. "Please, don't do that."

Okay, she wouldn't, but where did they go from there?

"I'm going to be smart and say I should be heading home." Dean stepped away from her, leaned down and grabbed his hat. "It's getting late."

Was it? Shelby didn't have any idea of the time. She didn't have any idea what was going to happen after tonight. Was this a one-time thing?

Dean had said he wanted to kiss her and he had, thoroughly and perfectly. But now what? Did she dare ask him for a date? Or maybe playing it cool and casual was the way to go.

Darn, she was so inexperienced when it came to these things!

"Ah, okay. How about I walk you to your truck?"

He grinned and shook his head, stepping down off the porch. "No, I don't think that's a good idea."

She followed, moving down one step until they were almost eye to eye. "Why?"

"Because it's even darker over there, much more private and I've got a big bench seat inside the cab." He jerked a thumb in the direction of the driveway. "Wouldn't take much to bring to life the high school make-out fantasy I've already got going that includes you, me and the inside of my truck."

Shelby jerked her head in a quick nod, trying not to let the sting of his rejection show on her face.

"Ah, hell, I'm sorry." He slapped his hat against his thigh. "I didn't mean to bring up—to remind you of anything bad—"

She stopped his apology by pressing her fingers to his mouth. "You didn't. Don't think that. What just happened between us now is nothing like back then, nothing like I've ever experienced before."

His smile was slow and easy and when she removed her hand, it slid right into oh, so sexy. "That's good to know. Are you working tomorrow?"

She nodded, a familiar knot returning to her stomach. "Four to closing."

"Okay, I'll come by and see you."

A long familiar defense mechanism kicked in. "Oh, we get pretty busy on Wednesday nights. It's payday for some of the ranches and the bar is usually very crowded."

He took her hand in his and gave it a gentle squeeze. "Shelby, I don't care what other people think or say. I like you. You asked me what I wanted? Well, I want more of what happened between us tonight and I don't mean just in the last half hour. I want to spend time with you and with Caitlin. You're smart and pretty and fun and I want us to get to know each other better."

His words went straight to her heart, but it was easy to say those things now, here when it was just the two of them. And when the town gossips got ahold of the news that she'd grabbed the attention of a nice guy like Dean Pritchett?

What happened today in Crawford's would be repeated again and again and next time the comments and innuendos might not be veiled in faked sincerity.

"Shelby, say something."

"I don't think—"

"Don't think. Just say whatever is in your mind right at this very moment."

"I'd love to spend more time with you, too." The words came from her heart, not her head.

Dean leaned forward and captured her mouth with his, the kiss bone-melting and mind-blowing and over way too fast.

"I'll see you tomorrow."

He turned on his heel and headed toward his truck.

Shelby grabbed the railing, waiting for the strength to return to her knees as he disappeared into the darkness.

She watched as the driver's-side door opened, the cab's interior light slipping out onto the grass and staying there for a long second. Then the door shut again and crunching footsteps brought him back in front of her again.

"By the way, I was right."

Now she was confused. "Right? About what?"

"Kissing you." Dean wrapped his fingers around her nape, his thumb playing havoc with her senses as he dragged it back and forth across her lips. He gave her another quick, hard peck, then said, "It was definitely worth the wait."

"You know, it was just three weeks ago that I had to drag your butt to this place." Nick leaned over the pool table and lined up his shot. "Now, you're here just about every night. Number two in the corner pocket."

Dean leaned against the wooden counter attached to the back wall of the Ace in the Hole, his pool stick held loosely in one hand. "Not every night."

The ball easily went into the pocket. Nick straightened and shot him a grin. "Okay, then every night a certain blonde bartender is working."

"Something you know only because you *are* here every night." Dean grabbed his beer and took a long swallow. "How you manage to make it to the job site every morning is beyond me."

"Skill and grace, little brother, skill and grace."

"How early did you have to get here tonight to grab a pool table?" Dean looked around. The other two tables were crowded, and a couple of heated dart games were going on as well, despite it being almost midnight. Shelby had been right last week when she said the bar was packed on Wednesday nights. "These puppies are always busy."

"Hey, if you're winning, you keep the table." Nick studied the remaining balls, deciding his next shot. Not that he had much to choose from. There were only two solids left on the green. "And you're playing like crap, by the way."

"I've got other things on my mind."

"Yeah, I'll bet."

Dean returned his brother's grin, his reply forgotten when he caught a glimpse of Shelby with a tray full of drinks out in the main part of the bar. His gaze followed her, enjoying the view as she maneuvered in between the tables, her hips swinging hypnotically back and forth.

She looked up and caught him, sending a quick smile before she went back to work.

He liked that she seemed to be smiling more and more lately.

He'd come by the bar a week ago to see her, just like he told her he would. Showing up at midnight after catching a few z's on the couch, he'd stayed until closing time.

Shelby had barely given him a second look as he sat at the bar and talked with a couple of guys from his crew. It'd taken him a while to figure out the reason that kept her at the other end of the bar was more than being busy.

Despite the fact that they'd basically agreed they were dating the night before on her porch, she'd been nervous about him being there. Dean understood, especially after the way she'd blown his socks off—first from what she'd shared about her past and then the power behind just one kiss.

Yeah, it'd been more than one kiss and if they'd been at the trailer or if Shelby was a typical twentysomething who'd lived on her own, they would have moved inside and found the closest horizontal surface.

Only she wasn't.

And Dean was okay with taking things slow.

Their schedules made it difficult to find the time, but they'd managed to be together every day over the past week, even if it was just a few slow dances to Rosey's oldies after the bar closed or watching a movie back at her place after Caitlin was in bed.

It also meant a couple of their dates had included a five-year-old who was a natural-born chaperone.

Dean didn't mind having Caitlin around at all. She was as smart and funny as her mother and as he found out last Sunday, a whiz at miniature golf. He also knew she preferred to dip her French fries in applesauce instead of ketchup when he'd stayed for dinner Monday after fixing the kitchen faucet for Shelby and her mother.

"Hey, lover boy, it's your turn."

Dean looked at the table and realized his brother had missed his last shot. He circled the table once, mentally planning his next move and easily dropped the ball. And the next one. And the one after that.

"What? You suddenly remembered how to play?" Nick moved up to the pool table, a beer in his hand, and stood in the spot Dean needed.

"Move it," he said, tapping his brother on the shoulder with the stick. "Or lose it."

"I'll get out of your way if you tell me why you're keeping your house hunting a secret."

Dean stilled. He'd only gone out to look at the inside of the place down the road from Shelby's at lunchtime yesterday. "Who told you about that?"

"Jon, from our crew. He mentioned his wife, Hallie, who runs the local real estate office, had an appointment to show you a house yesterday." Nick kept his voice low but leaned in close to be heard over the music and the noise. "You really thinking of making this move permanent?"

He was. Working on the reconstruction of the buildings

and homes of Rust Creek Falls filled him with a sense of satisfaction he hadn't felt working in the family business in a long time.

"I know you've really enjoyed the work we've been doing here. Remodeling and building homes for a living is a step up from making furniture, I guess."

Dean didn't buy the wide-eyed look of innocence his brother tried to pass off. Probably because Nick hadn't been innocent since he was a kid. "You and Matt Cates have been talking, too?"

"So, what's the place like?" Nick asked, without answering him. "I'm guessing it didn't suffer any damage from the flood last month?"

"No, it didn't. It's nice. It sits on more acreage than I first thought, located at the base of Falls Mountain. Has four bedrooms, two and half baths and a front porch whose best feature is the patch of yellow roses growing wild at one end. There are a couple of outbuildings, including a barn. I was thinking one of them could be used as an office—"

"*Four* bedrooms?" Nick cut him off. "That's a family home. You thinking of more than just moving to town and starting a new business?"

Now it was Dean's turn to ignore his brother's question. He returned his attention to the pool game, deciding to walk around to the other side of the table for his next shot.

Yeah, it probably was too early for him to be thinking about taking things to the next level with Shelby, especially because she'd mentioned more than once that she was looking for a teaching position out of town, but he couldn't help it.

He'd admit losing his mom and Jane's deception over a child he'd thought was his made it easy for him to hold back from risking his heart over the years. So why now? Why this woman? He didn't know, but his feelings for Shelby and Caitlin were growing deeper by the day.

Dean had to wait until a guy who seemed more interested

in downing his beer and laughing with his buddies to move out of the way. He finally did but graced Dean with a long look as he stepped aside. Having no idea why, Dean shrugged it off and lined up his shot but missed.

"And his luck runs out," Nick said, then chuckled. "Or maybe not."

Dean looked up to find Shelby heading their way.

She balanced a tray with fresh beers and another order of the bacon-wrapped jalapeño poppers his brother devoured like candy.

He moved to the counter, meeting her there as she set out the drinks and food before cleaning up the empty bottles left behind. "Hey, there."

"Hey, yourself. Your brother signaled for another round a while back, but Courtney is busy, so I grabbed it for you guys."

She took a step back when Nick reached between them to grab a popper; but even after Nick set aside his pool stick and headed for the men's room, she maintained a distance between them.

Dean wasn't surprised.

Other than being together at the Ace after hours or at her place, they hadn't spent any time out in public other than when he'd given her a ride to work on Saturday, at his suggestion, so he could bring her home afterward.

When they'd gone out for dinner and a movie in Kalispell the night before that, he'd noticed right away how much more relaxed she was away from Rust Creek Falls. So much so that he'd suggested they return and spend Sunday afternoon at a local fun center with Caitlin.

But when he mentioned hooking up at the local wings place over on North Broomfield during the workday for lunch, she'd been too busy.

"Well, I better get back behind the bar." Shelby took another step backward and bumped into one of the other pool players, messing up his shot. She whirled around, already apologizing. "Oops, so sorry! I didn't see you back there."

The cowboy straightened, his anger slipping into an expression of creepy interest as his gaze raked over Shelby, an interest that set Dean's teeth on edge.

"That's all right, darling," he said, his words showing the effects of the beers he'd been drinking. "You can bump up against me anytime."

Shelby stiffened for a moment, then she offered him that practiced, customer-service smile Dean had seen her use often at the bar. "I apologize anyway."

She started to move past him, but he grabbed her by the wrist. "Hey, now, where youz going?"

Dean tightened his grip around the pool stick and took a step forward, but Shelby easily slipped free of the guy's grasp with a twist of her wrist.

"I'm going back to work," she said, her voice firm while her gaze quickly shot around at the crowd that had gathered to watch. "And you should be getting back to your pool game."

Her eyes landed on Dean for a moment, warning him off with a slight upper jut of her chin. He figured she'd been in situations like this before. She'd told him that dealing with drunks was part of her job when they'd talked about their work, but anger still burned hot in his gut.

That slimeball had no right to touch her.

But touch her he did, sliding his hand over her backside when she walked by him.

Dean didn't know if Shelby had even felt the physical violation as she'd continued walking back to the bar, but there was no way he was going to let that go.

"The lady made it clear she's not interested." He closed the distance between them and made a show of reaching past the guy for the chalk cube sitting on the edge of the pool table. His words were low but filled with resolve. "You'd best keep your hands to yourself from now on."

"Yeah?" The drunk spun on his heels, forced to take a few side steps to stay upright. "What's it to ya?"

"Let's just say, she's a friend of mine."

"Yeah, well, from what I've heard from the boys over here—" he waved one hand at the group standing nearby "—that pretty filly is ready, willing and able to ride any cowboy she can get her hands on."

A haze of raw fury filled Dean's chest. He fought against the urge to wrap his pool stick around the loser's neck. "Those boys are liars. They don't know her and neither do you."

"Well, I plan to change that real quick."

"Leave her alone."

"You gotta be a football player, Smitty, to get her attention," one of the crowd called out. "I heard tell she prefers the offensive line."

Laughter broke out among them. The fury exploded, almost choking Dean. He kept ahold of his common sense long enough to lay the stick gently on the table next to him. He had a feeling where this was headed and he wanted no part of it. Dean figured he'd better head up to the bar and sit there until closing time.

He never saw the punch coming that landed on his jaw.

"Hey!" Nick was at his side in seconds, glaring at the dude who'd hit him. "That was a lousy sucker punch!"

Dean tried to rub away the pain radiating along the side of his face with one hand while planting the other flat against his brother's chest. Keeping him from surging forward into the melee wasn't easy. Nick was all brawn and he was ready to show a bit of Pritchett family unity.

"Nope, you're wrong, bro. That wasn't a sucker punch." He spun back around, his right fist landing exactly where he intended with a satisfying crunch that sent the drunk sprawling to the ground. "*That* was a sucker punch."

The drunk's friends surged forward, fists flying. Dean and Nick divided and conquered, but soon others joined in.

Whether they were defending Shelby, the jerks who'd talked trash about her or just wanted to be part of the fun, Dean didn't know or care. The jerk who harassed Shelby wasn't going down easy, though.

They battled back and forth, crashing into tables, chairs and Dean even had to duck a dartboard that the fool had yanked off the wall and tossed at his head. He looked up in time to see Shelby and Rosey staring at him, mouths agape, but before he could say anything, he had to brace for the full force of the man coming at him. They both ended up against the rear entrance door in a bone-jarring thud that sent them sprawling into the night air.

· The wrestling match in the dirt and gravel of the crowded parking lot went on for several minutes, but then it got old. He didn't know what was happening inside, but it was time for this to end so he could get back inside and make sure Shelby hadn't gotten hurt.

Out of breath, Dean used two quick blows to send the cowboy into the front grille of a nearby pickup truck. He landed hard with a sickening thud and slid to the ground, cradling his left arm just as the sheriff's car arrived, red and blue lights flashing.

"Okay, freeze right there, Pritchett." Gage Christensen exited his cruiser. "What the hell is going on?"

"I think that guy is hurt."

Gage kept his gaze on Dean as he headed for the drunk still on the ground. "Yeah, I can see that. Rosey, what's happened? I haven't had to visit here in a couple of months."

Huffing, Dean turned to find Rosey standing behind him. Nick was in the doorway, none the worse for wear, especially for someone who'd been in a barroom brawl.

"A difference of opinion from what I can tell," Rosey said, moving forward until she stood next to Dean. "I'm afraid a lot of my customers took off when things started to get crazy. How is he?"

Gage looked over his shoulder. "I think we better get Emmet here. Looks like this guy's got a broken arm."

Dean's stomach turned over.

"We're in luck. Emmet stopped by for a quick bite. He's checking over the injured inside."

"There's more?"

"Oh, please." Rosey waved a hand in the air. "Have we ever had a fight at the Ace that stayed just between two people?"

She turned to go back inside, but Dean reached out and laid a hand on her arm, stopping her. "How's Shelby? Is she okay?"

"A little upset, but she's fine. Things calmed down inside as soon as the two of you headed out here. Which I really wish you'd done from the beginning. My bar is a mess."

Despite her wry complaint, relief washed over him. "I'll cover any damages. Both physical and medical."

Rosey looked at him for a long moment, then nodded. "Lucky for you, the worst of the injuries seem to be that guy. Everyone else who joined in seems to be nursing black eyes and sore ribs."

She went back inside and Emmet came out a few minutes later.

Followed by Shelby.

"You okay, Dean?" Emmet asked.

"Yeah, I'm fine." Ignoring the pain in his side and the stinging of his bloodied knuckles, he kept his gaze firmly on the woman who now stood a few feet away from him. "The guy over there is the one who's hurt."

Emmet joined Gage and determined that indeed the man's arm was broken. The sheriff agreed to take them both back to Emmet's clinic. Dean repeated his request that the man's medical bills be forwarded to him and promised Gage he'd be here when he returned.

"Are you out of your mind?"

Dean turned back after watching the sheriff's cruiser depart and found Shelby staring at him, her eyes blazing.

He was right. She was definitely pissed.

"What in the world made you hit that guy?" she demanded, tossing the water bottle she held at him with just a tad more force than necessary. It bounced harmlessly off his chest.

"Hey, that ass clocked Dean first," Nick called out.

Dean looked past Shelby to where his brother still stood in the doorway. "Thanks, bro. I think I've got this."

"I think your ass is in big trouble."

Yeah, Dean sort of figured that out already from the storm brewing in Shelby's eyes. He motioned for his brother to leave them alone.

"Shelby—"

"I'd handled things in there, Dean." Pointing back at the bar with one hand, Shelby advanced on him. "What happened tonight was nothing new. Ask any of the waitresses. When you work in a place that serves booze you have to be ready to deal with jerks who think alcohol magically transforms them into studs, or gives them courage or permission to say or do the stupidest things."

Dean sighed. He grabbed the water bottle from the ground, opened it and took a long swallow, bathing his dirt-coated throat. He hated to tell her this, but she had the right to know. "That guy, and the losers with him, kept trash-talking you after you left."

She dropped her arm, but then folded both over her chest. "Let me guess. It was about some sort of team sport?"

He only nodded, refusing to repeat what they'd said about her.

"I tried to tell you, this is what it's like for me. This is what it's going to be like if you are with me. As long as I live in this town, there will always be someone—man or woman—who will have no qualms about sharing their opinions of my past."

"That's crap, Shelby."

"That's the truth. You need to think long and hard if you want whatever—" she waved one hand between them "—this is that's happening between us to go any further."

"Can we talk about this later? After you finish—"

His heart stopped when Shelby shook her head.

"No. I think you should go home after the sheriff is done with you. I'm sure once you tell him you were just trying to protect my honor, he'll let you off with a warning. Well, here's *my* warning. Stop fighting my battles for me. They are mine, not yours, and if you can't accept me and all the baggage I come with, then we're finished."

Chapter Ten

Shelby peeked in on Caitlin after realizing she'd been napping solidly for the past two and a half hours. Of course, the tantrum she'd thrown earlier today had taken all the fight out of her.

Apparently her little girl missed Dean, too.

She'd asked when Dean was coming back to visit too many times to count today and wasn't happy with the only answer Shelby could give.

I don't know.

After making her little speech Wednesday night to him, she'd turned around and gone back inside the bar without giving Dean a chance to say anything in return. Nick had asked about his brother and then left, to join him she guessed, after she'd told him Dean was waiting to talk to the sheriff.

She hadn't seen or talked to Dean since.

It'd taken all of Shelby's strength not to join her daughter on the kitchen floor in a flurry of tears. Some days the only way to get rid of the uglies was to cry it out.

Or sleep. Or clean.

Opening the blinds behind the curtains to allow filtered sunshine to fill the room, Shelby left again after Caitlin stirred a bit and then settled back into her pillows. Because she tended to be a bit moody after her naps, it was best to allow her to wake slowly to curtail any return of the morning's attitude.

Walking back into the living room, Shelby looked around, glad she'd opted for tackling household chores instead of a nap.

Dishes done, kitchen floor washed, living room dusted and two loads of laundry folded and put away. Hot and sweaty, she'd jumped into the shower, then pulled on a T-shirt and shorts before a scheduled telephone interview with a school district down near Helena that had gone pretty well.

But now, she'd run out of things to do on this beautiful Friday afternoon, which meant she was inches away from giving in to the temptation to call Dean.

Two days had gone by. Well, closer to thirty-three hours and yes, she was counting.

She still couldn't believe he'd come to her defense against those jerks Wednesday night in the bar. Then again, considering his good nature, scenes like that would probably happen over and over again.

As for what she'd said to him in the parking lot…

Shelby groaned and dropped into the leather recliner. She'd tried to re-create the conversation inside her head lying in her bed that night. All she could remember was the warning she'd given him that he better accept the things he heard people say about her.

Goodness knows that might have been the first time he'd heard that crap, but it wouldn't be the last if she stuck around in this town.

But did she have to be such a witch?

The vibrating of her cell phone from inside her pocket

had her jumping to her feet. She dug it out, fumbling as she hurried to unlock the screen, whispering a silent prayer that it was him.

It wasn't.

She thumbed the screen, connecting the call. "Hey, Rosey."

"Hey, honey." Her boss's voice carried over the din in the background that told Shelby she was at the bar. "How are you doing?"

Leaving the inside door wide-open, she stepped out onto the front porch, her gaze immediately going to the spot near the stairs where Dean had kissed her for the first time.

Was that just ten days ago?

"I'm fine," she said, heading for one of the pair of wicker chairs at the other end of the porch. "How are things at the Ace?"

"Picking up, can't you hear? We're only a couple of hours from the end of the workday and the regulars are already claiming their barstools. I'm sure it'll be another typical Friday night around here."

Did that mean Rosey wanted her to come in? Working tonight was the last thing she wanted. "If you need me, it's going to have to wait until after seven. My mom is working late at the beauty shop."

"I'm not asking you to come in. I called to see how you're holding up."

Shelby frowned. "I told you yesterday I'm—"

"Fine." Rosey cut her off. "Yeah, I heard you the first time. And the three times after that when you gave me that same answer during your shift last night. Now, how about telling me the truth?"

Frustration curled deep inside her. "I miss him as much as you miss Sam, okay? Is that what you want to hear?" Shelby slapped a hand over her mouth, surprised at the snarkiness of her tone. "Oh, Rosey, I'm sorry. That was a lousy thing to say."

"Damn, girl, you've got it bad." The background noise dropped considerably and Shelby guessed her boss had moved into her office. "At least Sammy isn't here in town where I might run into him."

"Or not run into him." Her voice dropped to a whisper. "I was doing errands before work yesterday and I didn't see Dean's truck anywhere."

"You told him to do some thinking about the two of you, right? So, let the man think."

Rosey was right. But deep inside, Shelby was afraid that the longer Dean stayed away, the more he was figuring out what it really meant to be with her.

And that she wasn't worth it.

"What if he decides…being with me is just too much trouble?"

Rosey snorted. "Then he's dumber than he looks and I'm a poor judge of character. Neither of which is true."

"But people just won't stop talking—"

"Honey, people talk! And not just about the past. Do you really think no one in this pissant town knew you and Dean had been spending time together before Wednesday night?"

Surprised at Rosey's question, Shelby was at a loss for what to say.

"I never said anything because I didn't want to diminish that glow you've had going on for the last week," Rosey continued. "Believe me, your current love life has been making the rounds, probably because he's the first man you've dated in years."

"But how? We haven't been out locally. I mean, other than going for ice cream and that was before… I mean, we hadn't even kissed yet…" A thought came to Shelby and she didn't want to believe it, but she blurted it out anyway. "Do you think Dean's been talking about me? About us?"

"What? Of course not. You need to get rid of that fool notion right now. Don't you think sharing an ice-cream sundae was enough to start lips flapping? Come on, Shelby, you know how this works. You should also know you aren't the only game in town."

"What's that mean?"

"It means, I've heard talk about a betting pool that's going on as to how long it will be before Willa and Collin announce another Traub is on the way and if our sexy sheriff is ever going to find himself a girl."

Okay, so maybe her love life, both past and present, wasn't the topic of *every* conversation. "You've made your point."

"Look, I've got two cooks glaring at me so I better run. You're off the clock for the weekend, but I expect a full report when you get back here Monday. And just so you know, I won't be allowing you to leave out any of the juicy details."

Shelby laughed, feeling much better. "How do you know there will be any details—juicy or otherwise?"

"Because I saw the way that man fought for your honor."

Shelby's good humor faded, heart jumping into her throat, but she managed to squeak out a goodbye and ended the call.

Seeing Dean fight, knowing it was because of her, and the possibility of him being seriously hurt scared her in a way she'd never felt before.

Maybe it would be better if things did end between them now.

Her stomach clenched so hard it hurt at that thought, especially after all the great times they'd had over the past week.

But it wasn't just her.

Caitlin loved having Dean around, too.

She'd had a great time at mini golf, surprising both Shelby and Dean with her amazing skills, popping a hole in one more than once as they made their way through the course.

When Dean had stopped by Monday and found her wrestling with the ever-present leak beneath their kitchen sink, he'd taken over the chore and put up with Caitlin squatting next to him, peppering him with questions as he worked.

And she'd gotten him to read to her again when it came time for bed.

Was she setting her daughter up for major disappointment when whatever this was between her and Dean ended?

Even if he decided he wanted to be with her, it had to end when she got a job and left town. Or until Dean finished his part of the rebuilding and headed back to Thunder Canyon.

Oh, she was so confused!

One minute she was convinced that nothing good would come of their being more than just friends, and the next she was applying for a teaching position in a town located not too far away from Thunder Canyon.

A cloud of dust and the crunch of tires told her someone was coming down the road. Before the wish could form deep inside her, she saw the vehicle was a vintage Jeep Wagoneer with a U.S. postal sticker on the driver's-side door.

Rising to her feet, she headed across the yard as Martin Grubbs slowed to a stop near their mailbox at the bottom of the hill.

Martin still insisted on doing the daily mail run out to the rural customers despite celebrating fifty years with the U.S. Postal Service last year at the age of seventy-two. His son ran the office in town, and the senior Grubbs helped there as well, but it usually took him most of the day to make his rounds as he visited with every delivery.

"Good afternoon, Miss Shelby."

"Hello, Mr. Grubbs." She walked up to the driver's side. "How are you doing?"

"Finer than frog hair." He handed her their mail through the window. "Hard to be anything else on such a beautiful day as this."

She smiled. "You are right about that."

"Heard there was a little excitement down at the Ace a few nights ago." He peered at her from behind his gold wire-framed glasses. "Don't be too hard on that young man of yours, you hear? Sometimes we men act first and think second."

Oh, small towns. Shelby nodded, then said, "Yes, sir."

"Tell Miss Caitlin I said hello."

She promised she would, then stepped away to allow Mr. Grubbs to turn his Jeep around and head back down the road.

Flipping through the catalogs, bills and letters, she started back toward the house. Halfway across the yard, she heard a vehicle approaching again from behind. Turning back, she wondered if Martin had forgotten to give her something—

Dean.

His truck slowly made its way up the long driveway until he pulled in behind her car and stopped. He turned off the engine, got out and walked around the front end carrying something in his hand.

Stopping in front of the passenger door of his truck, he paused there, looking downright sexy in his work-scarred jeans, white T-shirt and his ball cap pulled low on his forehead.

She swallowed hard as his gaze traveled the length of her. Her skin grew hot and she wanted nothing more than to run and jump into his arms. Instead, she curled her bare toes into the grass, hoping the action would anchor her enough to keep her from making a fool of herself.

At least until she knew why he was here.

"Hey, there," he finally said.

"Hey."

"I didn't see your car at the bar, so I was hoping I'd find you here." He glanced back at his truck for a moment, then looked at her again. "I've been doing some thinking, like you asked, and the thing is, I'm not going anywhere."

The air rushed from Shelby's lungs. "Oh, Dean, I'm sorry for the way I spoke to you Wednesday night—"

"I'm the one who's sorry." He waved off her words. "You were right. That fight was stupid. I was lucky the sheriff let me off with just a warning, probably because I didn't throw the first punch. Still, I should have walked away. I will next time, if there is a next time."

Unable to stand the physical distance between them for another second, she moved across the yard to where he still stood, not caring about the pebbles biting into the bottoms of her feet. "You can count on there being a next time."

"I don't care about that, about what anyone says about you. I'm right where I want to be." He held out a flat box. "My mama always said an apology was best said in person and that a gift never hurts. Seeing as how I already gave you flowers…"

She took the gift, glancing down at fancy scrolled font across the box top before looking at him again. "You brought me chocolates?"

He pushed up the brim on his cap and gave her a smile. "Look again."

She did, her eyes widening before she had to blink hard against the sting of unexpected tears. "You brought me a box of caramel-filled chocolates?"

One step and he was right in front of her. Gently pressing a finger to her chin until she raised her head, he looked down at her. "No matter which one you pick, you'll always get exactly what you want."

Right then, her heart took a step toward an unknown and scary chasm she'd never experience before.

For the first time in her life, Shelby was falling in love.

Dean lowered his head until his mouth was inches from hers, then he paused and asked, "Is Caitlin around?"

"She's taking a nap. In fact, she should be getting up any minute."

"Can I steal a quick kiss first?"

"I really wish you would."

He grinned, his mouth inches from hers when he pulled

back. "Damn it, I forgot. Ah, before she wakes up there's something else I need to talk to you about."

"Okay."

"Well, I brought a gift for Caitlin, too."

Oh, that chasm just got another step closer. "You didn't have to do that."

Dean shrugged and reached for the door to his truck. "Yeah, you might really feel that way once you see it."

Puzzled, Shelby watched as he opened the door. She spotted a cardboard box on the cab's floor but couldn't see what was inside. Dean leaned in and scooped up something, cradling it to his chest before he turned back around.

A tiny ball of black fluff with pointed ears and white whiskers rested in his large hand.

"Oh, how sweet!"

"We found six kittens holed up in one of the houses that has been uninhabitable since the flood last month. The mama cat was nowhere to be found for two days, so we took them to the vet to have them checked out." Dean gently ran a finger across the kitten's fur. The tiny creature purred and nuzzled deeper into his chest.

Shelby totally understood the animal's attraction and actually felt jealous.

"We checked with the homeowner, but he said they didn't have any pets. In fact, all the missing pets have been accounted for, so the vet figured they must be strays," he continued. "He said the kittens looked to be about six weeks old. They've been given a clean bill of health and the other five were adopted by the guys on my crew, except for this little one. I thought she and Caitlin would be perfect together. No pun intended."

She laughed, but then sobered again as she studied the orphaned kitten. "It's a very nice idea, but I don't know…"

"I got everything she needs right here." He gestured back to his truck. "From a litter box to food, even a few toys. If you decide you can't take her, I plan to keep her with me, but I figured she'd get more love and attention living here. You told me about the cats you had growing up and the one you lost not long after your dad died. Maybe you're ready to have one in the family again?"

Touched that he remembered her stories, Shelby stroked the kitten's soft fur, noting the patch of white on its chest and two front paws. Oh, boy, she was losing the internal battle that told her this was the last thing she needed to add to her life right now.

"Mama?" Caitlin's sleepy voice called out from the direction of the front porch. "Oh, Dean. You're here! I thought Mama said you didn't know when you were coming back to see us."

Shelby looked up to Dean's questioning gaze. She sighed, losing the battle. "Go on, give her the kitten. I'll get the stuff from your truck."

Dean's smile was wide as he gave her a quick wink and headed for the porch. Shelby grabbed the box and the bag of supplies and walked up to the house in time to watch Dean instruct her daughter how to sit so he could place the little fur ball in her lap.

"For me?" Caitlin's eyes grew round. "Really?"

"Yes, really, but you need to listen to your mama and your grandmother when it comes to taking care of her," Dean said. "Can you do that?"

Caitlin nodded, her bedhead-styled curls bouncing as she kept her gaze glued to the bundle. "What's her name?"

"We'll have to think up something to call her," Shelby said, setting the armload she had down on the porch just as some of the mail slipped free from her grasp. "Oh, shoot."

"Here, I'll get it." Dean grabbed the envelopes off the grass and handed them back, his gaze lingered on a long, thin envelope lying on top. "The Miles City Elementary School District. Wow, that's quite a ways from here."

Shelby took a step back, keeping her voice low. "It's a reply to a job I put in for, but I already got the email. Thanks, but no thanks."

Dean nodded but remained silent.

"Hey, would you like to come back for dinner tonight? You can help us figure out a name for the kitten."

"Ah, I can't."

Shelby tightened her grip on the mail. "You already have plans?"

"Actually, Nick and I are heading to Butte to get a load of supplies. In fact, I'm late in picking him up, so I have to run." Dean glanced at Caitlin for a moment, then took Shelby's hand and drew her away a few steps.

"It'll be late by the time we get back and I've got a full day tomorrow, but I didn't want to leave town without making sure we got things settled between us." He'd leaned in close. "You know, I wish I'd kissed you when I had the chance."

"I wish you did, too."

"How about I make it up to you tomorrow night?"

The parts of her that were reserved for just being a woman stood up and cheered at the heat in his gaze and the seductive caress of his words. "You've got a deal."

"So, everything is better between you and Dean now." Her mother's voice cut into Shelby's thoughts. "And he got Caitlin a kitten?"

Shelby looked up from where she sat in the waiting area in Bee's Beauty Parlor. She'd brought Caitlin in for her scheduled haircut an hour after Dean had left.

Her daughter was chatting excitedly about her pet with anyone who would listen while showing off pictures taken with Shelby's cell phone. It was better than bringing the kitten along with them.

Thankfully, the still-unnamed newest member of the family had been asleep when they'd left, and they'd made sure the litter box, food and fresh water were all set up in the spare bedroom, even though Caitlin insisted the kitten was going to sleep in bed with her at night.

One battle at a time.

As for her and Dean, were things settled between them?

She had no idea. Impossibly happy that he'd decided he wanted to spend time with her, Shelby had no idea what that really meant—for any of them.

"Yes," she answered her mother, "things between us are… good. And as you can tell, your granddaughter is thrilled with his gift."

"Well, I've got something to tell you that might make you just as happy." Her mother gestured for Shelby to join her at her station located at the far end of the beauty parlor.

Shelby spotted her daughter who, thanks to Beverly, the owner of the beauty parlor, was sitting contently at the main counter, sorting hair curlers by color and size. She stood and followed her mom. "What are you talking about?"

Vivian waved her closer, her voice a hushed whisper. "Thelma McGee was in here earlier getting her hair done. We were chatting about all the progress the volunteers have made in the last month in the rebuilding. Of course, the fight that Dean and his brother were involved in at the bar came up—"

"Mom, please." Shelby cut her off. "You know how I feel about the Rust Creek Falls gossip chain. Thelma is a terrific lady who's been through a lot, but I'm not interested—"

"Not even if rumor has it that Dean is making plans to stick around Rust Creek Falls—" her mother grabbed her hand and gave it a quick squeeze "—permanently?"

Chapter Eleven

Dean was planning to move to Rust Creek Falls?

Stunned, Shelby was positive she hadn't heard her mother correctly. "What are you talking about?"

"Thelma said she was at the town hall when she overheard one of the owners of Cates Construction talking after the weekly rebuilding meeting." Vivian's words came out in a rush. "He said one of the volunteers from Thunder Canyon has been discussing the possibility of opening a satellite office of Cates Construction right here in town."

"Mama, do you have any idea how many volunteers are here from Thunder Canyon? He could've been talking about anyone."

"With talents in woodworking?"

The tightening in her gut that began when her mother first started talking took a hard twist. "Woodworking?"

Her mother nodded with excitement. "That's what Thelma said. Matt Cates was very excited because this person is doing so great with the reconstruction, but he also specializes in custom woodworking."

Okay, so that could be Dean, or his brother Nick or... "There are still a lot of skilled people who are sharing their talents in refurbishing and rebuilding the homes and businesses."

Vivian's bright smile diminished a few watts. "So, Dean hasn't said anything to you? About moving here?"

"Of course not." Shelby crossed her arms over her chest. "I mean, yes, he's mentioned how much he likes Rust Creek Falls and how it reminds him of what his town was like when he was a kid, before the gold, the ski resorts and the tourists..." Her gut squeezed even tighter.

Everything Dean said during their picnic at the lower falls replayed inside her head. His degree in structural engineering and how he was enjoying putting his knowledge and skills into practice. The reasons he'd listed for liking the town—everyone taking an interest in the lives of the others, the degree to which they dug deep and stood side by side—were the same reasons driving her to start over somewhere else.

Oh, my, could this rumor be more fact-based than the normal chitchat that circulated via the local gossip busybodies?

"Shelby, are you okay, honey?"

"Just because Dean likes the town doesn't mean he's going to uproot his entire life. He's only been here six weeks. He barely knows anyone."

"He knows you."

"Mom, we just met the beginning of the month and it took me until last week to find the courage to tell him about... well, about everything." Shelby glanced over her shoulder. Caitlin was still having fun with the curlers and everyone else was busy working and carrying on their own conversations. Still, she kept her voice low as she turned back. "He told me this afternoon he's accepted that certain people will always talk about me, about my past, and there's nothing he can do about it—"

"What about you? Why don't *you* do something about it?"

"I am. As soon as I get a teaching position, I'm out of here."

Her mother's smile disappeared completely. Shelby knew this topic upset her, which was why she didn't talk about it anymore. "I know you don't like the idea, but I want to teach. You know that."

"But those teachers told you why you were turned down by the school. Surely, once the town rebuilds—"

"Mom, it could take months just to get the financing set up, never mind the actual reconstruction of the building. I owe it to myself and all those years of studying to put my education into practice now."

"What about what you owe your daughter?"

Her mother's question surprised her. "What does that mean?"

"I understand you have to act a certain way when it comes to customers at the bar, especially when defusing situations that are, more times than not, alcohol-fueled. Believe me, I know. I waitressed when I was putting myself through beauty school, but when people like Wanda or Darlene or any of those jerks you went to school with feel they can be nasty to you for no reason, why don't you say something back?"

"Like what? Please don't be mean to me?"

"For starters, yes. You have spent the last five years accepting ridicule and blame for a situation you handled with nothing but dignity and grace."

Her mother placed her hands on Shelby's shoulders and turned her to face the center of the beauty parlor. "Look at what you got as a reward," she continued, her words soft in Shelby's ear. "That precious little girl is smart and loving because of you. You have every right to be proud of your life, of your accomplishments and it's past time you stood up to those bullies, tell them that high school is long gone and for everyone to grow up already."

"Do you really think if I just say that...that everything will end?"

"If you say it often enough and mean it every single time, yes."

The simple truth of her mother's words stole the breath from Shelby's lungs. The view in front of her became a blurry mess thanks to the tears welling in her eyes.

She spun back around. "Why are you telling me this now?"

"Because I realized very recently the three of us—you and me and Caitlin—have been living in a fog since your father died. You've been consumed with your studies and raising your daughter. I've been doing everything I could to support you while we all grieved." Vivian gently wiped the wetness from her daughter's cheeks. "It's time for all of us to stop living in the past and move forward."

"That's what I'm trying to do."

"By running away?"

Shelby opened her mouth to protest, but the words wouldn't come. Her mind whirled as she tried to put her bewildered thoughts into place.

Grabbing tissues from a nearby box, Vivian handed them to Shelby while keeping one to dab at her own wet eyes. "Even if your teaching career ends up taking you away from Rust Creek Falls, this is always going to be your home. This is my home and I'm not going anywhere. Believe me, having my family come back and visit is something I am going to insist upon. You know that, right?"

Wiping at her eyes, Shelby smiled and nodded.

"Look, I need to get to work on my granddaughter's hair. Why don't you take a walk and just think about what I said."

"You mean about standing up for myself?"

Her mother smiled and shook out a vinyl hairdresser's cape decorated with cartoon characters. "Yes, that, too, of course, but maybe you can figure out a way to see if that rumor concerning a handy guy moving to town is about anyone you know."

Fifteen minutes later, Shelby exited Crawford's Store with a paper bag stuffed with all the necessary fixings to make her mama's famous meat lasagna and two bottles of wine.

She had a feeling she and her mother would be cracking open one of the bottles later tonight after Caitlin was asleep. The other bottle and the lasagna were for tomorrow night.

With Dean.

She didn't have any idea what he might have planned for them, but the idea of surprising him with a home-cooked meal at his trailer had come to her while wandering around the store.

Her mama was right.

Instead of trying to ignore her past by running toward the future, she was determined to live in the here and now. And that meant facing head-on all things good—or not so good— in her life from now on. To stand up for herself and enjoy her life. To take a few chocolates out of that box knowing that every single one was going to be her favorite.

All the crazy feelings Dean stirred to life in her had Shelby thinking of things she'd never allowed herself to think about before.

Things like falling in love.

Would sleeping with Dean send her completely over the edge? Was it too early for such a big step? Would he turn her down if she dared to try to take things further between them tomorrow night?

And what would it mean to their still-fledgling relationship?

Was she leaving… Was he staying?

Who knew how long it would take for her to find a teaching position. Maybe she would get one right here in Rust

Creek Falls if—no, scratch that— The school board and the teachers were determined the elementary school would be rebuilt, and Willa and Paige had told her she'd been at the top of the new-hires list. Maybe she should see if there were any openings in Kalispell, which was only thirty minutes away.

Or maybe one of the other school districts would make her an offer.

Then she would have to make a decision.

But not now. Not tomorrow.

Determined to take things one day at a time, Shelby pushed her worries about the future to the back of her mind as she neared the beauty parlor. Peeking into the front window, she saw her daughter still being fussed over by her grandmother.

The heavenly smells coming from Wings to Go, the takeout place next door to Bee's, were too hard to resist. A dinner of spicy buffalo wings for her and Mama, and chicken tenders for Caitlin, was exactly what they all needed tonight.

She reached for the door handle, but it suddenly opened and a body walked right into her.

Juggling to hold on to her bag from Crawford's with one hand while grabbing for the door with the other, she didn't see who was in such a hurry until she heard the breathy words, "My goodness! Please pardon me. I didn't see— Oh, it's you."

Shelby mentally cringed as the apology transformed into mocking contempt. Schooling her features into a bland expression, she looked Darlene Daughtry straight in the eye.

Boy, when she decided her life needed to change, the gods must've decided there was no time like the present to test her.

"Don't worry, Darlene, no damage done."

The woman stilled for a moment, then shoved her dark sunglasses down onto her face, but not before Shelby got a look at her red-rimmed eyes.

"You are the last thing I need to deal with today." Darlene's tone was rigid, but her words lacked their usual sharpness.

Shelby wondered what was going on with the woman, but refused to let her nemesis walk all over her like she usually did.

Time to put Mama's advice to the test.

"Now, that's funny. I was thinking the same thing about you."

That got Darlene's attention. The woman's head jerked in shock. Her lips moved as if to respond, but nothing came out.

Refusing to back down, both symbolically and physically, Shelby kept her feet planted right where she stood until the blonde bombshell finally snapped her mouth shut, stepped to one side and continued on her way.

Enjoying the small victory, Shelby continued inside and placed her order at the counter. After paying, she sat at an empty table to wait, surprised when Darlene reappeared and dropped into the seat directly across from her.

"Zach Shute is a real jerk."

Shelby looked quickly around the place, but it was empty except for the two of them and the young girl working behind the counter.

"Yes, well, that was a long time ago."

Darlene shook her head, the dark glasses still in place. "No, I mean he's a jerk now."

"I'm sorry, I don't understand."

Darlene braced her elbows on the edge of the table and leaned forward. "I just got back from New York. Well, New Jersey, actually. I'd decided because you weren't still pining for Zach, judging from that hunky carpenter you've been spending time with, then I was free to see if there were still some old sparks there."

Pining for Zach? After all this time? Was she crazy?

Ignoring the reference to Dean and amazed that the two of them were having such a civilized conversation, Shelby only said, "You must have realized long before now that despite our history, I haven't been interested in Zach Shute in over five years, Darlene."

She seemed to mull that over for a long moment. "Yes, well…I used my position at Daddy's bank and being from Zach's hometown to get in to see him at the Jets training facility. He remembered me, of course, and signed over a big fat check to the town's rebuilding efforts."

Was she supposed to be angry about the money? "The town will appreciate his donation, I'm sure."

"He took me out for a fancy dinner in New York City and then back to his luxury condo. We talked about high school and relived some good times, very good times, if you catch my drift.…"

Darlene let her voice trail off, leaving Shelby even more confused by this whole conversation.

Was Darlene hoping she'd be upset? Jealous even? Was she expecting Shelby to stomp her feet and make a scene?

If so, why not wait until they were someplace where they would draw a crowd. Like the Ace or Crawford's?

"However, when I woke up this morning, he was gone," Darlene continued, her voice much softer. "All I got was a lousy note thanking me for a good time and the number of a local cab to get me back to my hotel."

This was it. Darlene was handing her a moment on a silver platter and a number of nasty comebacks sprang to life in Shelby's mind. But then she realized she wasn't interested in sparring with her old nemesis despite the still-lingering sting from their encounter a few weeks ago.

So much had changed in her life since that night.

Thanks to her mama's good advice and one very special guy.

"I'm sorry you went through that."

Darlene tossed her head, sending her blond curls flying. "I bet you think I deserved every second of it. Karma and all that."

"Honestly? At one time I would have said yes without hesitation." Shelby looked right at the woman even though she could only see her own reflection in the sunglasses. "But now, we should just let the past go. It's time for everyone to get on with their lives, don't you think?"

The girl behind the counter gestured that her food was ready.

"Ah, I need to get my order and head out." Shelby eased from her seat, taking her bag with her. She didn't have any idea what else to say, so she stood there and waited, letting Darlene know the ball was in her court with her silence.

Darlene continued to stare straight ahead, her lips pursed for a moment before she gave a quick nod, pushed away from the table and hurried out the door.

Okay, that was really strange. Maybe Darlene wasn't ready to let the past go yet. At least where Zach was concerned. But that didn't matter to Shelby.

She was thinking only about the future now.

The rain that had been threatening all day started to fall the moment Dean parked his truck next to the trailer. He shut down the engine and heaved a deep sigh, watching the large drops hit the windshield with a splat.

Damn, he was tired.

The clock on the dashboard told him it was almost seven, much later than he'd wanted to end his workday. He hadn't slept well the past couple of nights since the fight at the bar and the disagreement with Shelby.

Things were better between them now, thanks to a box of chocolates and that cute little kitten, but he'd been late getting back from Butte last night and other than exchanging a couple of text messages with Shelby around midnight to let her know he was back in town, he hadn't seen or spoken to her.

They'd agreed he'd give her a call tonight once he was free and they'd decide what to do then. A phone call he planned to make in less than thirty minutes because damn, he really needed to shower before he did anything else.

Today had been a long one, filled with dirty, backbreaking demolition work. The last of what was left of the row of burned-downed homes on South Pine Street were finally leveled. The wreckage had been carted away and Cates Construction was already working with three of the families who planned to rebuild in those very same lots.

And in even better news, Collin Traub had stopped by the job site with the structural inspection on the elementary school.

The building, or what was left of it, was found stable and the decision made to start the rebuilding process, even though the funds earmarked for the project were limited at the moment.

Still, it would be enough to get a new roof in place.

Then Matt Cates had pulled Dean aside and officially offered him the lead on the project as Cates Construction had been awarded the job of rebuilding the elementary school.

He'd thanked him, said he'd seriously think about the position and get back to him soon. His plans to make a new life in Rust Creek Falls were coming together. A job he wanted and a house that would take a healthy chunk of his savings, but it was a place he could grow into, a place big enough for the family he wanted.

And Shelby was exactly the woman he wanted that family with.

Her and Caitlin.

Accepting he was falling in love with someone after knowing her for less than a month had been surprisingly easy. What to do about those feelings? That was much harder to figure out, especially because there were three hearts involved here instead of just two.

That sweet little girl had come to mean as much to him as her mother over the past couple of weeks. Both Shelby and Caitlin had found their way into his heart and he wanted them in his life.

Forever.

But Shelby had made no secret of her need to get away from this town, away from her past. He guessed from the letter she'd gotten yesterday that she hadn't received a job offer to teach anywhere yet.

What would happen if they took this relationship to the next level and she decided to move, leaving him behind?

What if he actually put down roots and Shelby decided to up and walk away from him…from the town?

He hadn't allowed himself to get close to anyone since Jane. He'd loved her, and the child she was carrying that he thought was his, with all of his heart. Her deception over the baby's father had left a hole in his heart that was finally healing. Thanks to Shelby and Caitlin.

Could he take the pain of loving and then losing them?

Not willing to answer that question yet, Dean got out of his truck. Ignoring the fact he was getting wetter by the minute, he yanked his phone from his jeans pocket as he headed up the steps to the tiny porch outside the trailer.

Dirt and rain be damned, he wanted to hear Shelby's voice.

Juggling his phone, the small cooler that held the remains of his lunch and his keys, he unlocked the trailer's front door— Wait, was that music?

He twisted the key, pushed open the door and stepped inside.

The first thing he noticed was the window air conditioner working overtime, and yes, the radio in the kitchen was tuned to the local country music radio station he liked, loud to be heard over the chugging AC unit.

Had he left them on this morning?

Quickly closing the door behind him, he spotted the small round dining table, which was set for dinner with fancy dishes, a white tablecloth, unlit candles, an open bottle of wine and an old mason jar filled with yellow roses.

And to his left, Shelby's very shapely backside bending over in front of the stove.

"Hey, what's going on here?"

"Oh!" Shelby jumped, slamming the oven door closed, and spun around. "Dean, you surprised me!"

"Sorry. How did you get in here?"

"Nick…your brother…he met me here…an hour ago." Holding a hand to her chest, Shelby spoke between scattered breaths. "I called him…earlier today…wanted to surprise you…with dinner."

"Mission accomplished." He grinned, enjoying her explanation. "I'm definitely surprised."

"Looks like we both were." She pulled in one final deep breath and released it. "I didn't hear you come in."

Placing the cooler on the counter, he turned down the radio a bit. "Yeah, I figured that. This looks nice. Flowers, too."

"Thanks." She waved at hand in the direction of the table. "I didn't know what you had in way of dishes, so I brought stuff with me from home, including the flowers. Actually, they grow wild at the old Shriver place just down the road from us. The house is empty now, so I guessed no one would mind if I picked some."

He quickly put two and two together, figuring the roses must the same ones he'd seen when he went to look at the house, but he didn't say anything.

Instead, he gave the air a deep sniff and took a step deeper into the kitchen. "Wow, something smells amazing."

"Lasagna." Shelby now gestured to the oven. "Made with Italian sausage, ground beef and three kinds of cheese, so I hope you're hungry. I've also got fresh bread and a bottle of wine, but I noticed you've got beer in your fridge, if that's what you prefer. I mean, I don't even know if you like wine."

He took in her simple, pink sundress as he moved closer. The short skirt showed off her tanned legs while the sandals on her feet gave her enough height that she was even with his Adam's apple, which was where her eyes were locked as she babbled.

Now that he stood directly in front of her, his mind registered the deep flush of her skin, from the heat of the stove or the warmness inside the trailer, he didn't know. What he did know was that the deep scooped neckline allowed a peek at her untethered breasts and it would only take a couple of easy tugs on the skinny straps at her shoulders to ease her out of that dress.

"I like wine." He used light pressure with his finger beneath her chin to do two things: stop her prattling and force her to look at him. "Everything sounds perfect."

Their gazes locked and both knew the gesture was a repeat of what he'd done yesterday in the front yard, but this time he didn't stop as he lowered his mouth to hers.

The pink tip of her tongue darted out to wet her bottom lip just before he kissed her. A groan escaped and he chased it back inside her mouth, loving the wet heat he found there. They angled their heads in a silent, mutual agreement and he got lost in the soft demand of her mouth.

So much so that it took the feel of her hands on his sweat-soaked T-shirt before he remembered how grubby and disheveled he must look.

He ended the kiss and backed away, her husky moan of protest going straight to his gut and all points south. "Ah, I shouldn't— I really need a shower. I'm a mess from work and wet from the rain."

The heat in Shelby's eyes as they ran the length of him made the fly of his jeans very uncomfortable. When she bit down on her bottom lip and he noticed the faint outline of her nipples pressing against the silky material of her dress, he was sure he felt the top button give way.

"Yes, I can see that." Brushing past him, she walked to the dining table and grabbed the bottle of wine. The liquid splashed into the two glasses as she poured, thanks to the slight shaking of her hand. "Sure, go ahead and shower."

He moved in behind her, raising his hands to cup her shoulders until he saw the dirt on his skin. Dropping them back to his sides, he kept his words gentle. "Shelby, you don't have to be nervous. Not here. Not with me."

She turned to face him, her smile a bit more forced than usual as she offered him one of the glasses. "Go take your shower. We've got at least another hour while the lasagna cooks."

An hour. Oh, what he could do with an hour.

Starting beneath the hot spray of his shower.

Afraid she'd see the relentless desire surging inside of him, he took the glass and headed down the short hall to the bedroom.

Pushing open the door, the sorry state of the room caused him to groan. He took a quick swallow of the wine and set the glass on the dresser. Grabbing two piles of clothes off the floor, he shoved them into the closet and closed the folding doors.

It only took a minute to make up the queen-size bed as the bedding consisted of dark blue sheets, thankfully put on fresh this morning, and a light comforter that usually ended up tossed on the nearby chair.

Not that he thought Shelby would see this room—

"Yeah, who are you trying to fool, buddy," he muttered under his breath. "The shower, kitchen counter, living room sofa, bed…"

Not helping the uncomfortable jeans issue!

Pulling out clean briefs, jeans and a T-shirt from the dresser drawers, he then grabbed the wineglass and headed for the bathroom before he did something really dumb.

Like whip out the emergency candles and scatter some of those yellow rose petals…

He did a quick straightening of the bathroom, too, finished

off the rest of the wine, stripped and got in the shower. The water started hot and soapy, but he twisted on a blast of cold at the end as a reminder that tonight was just about dinner.

Then maybe they'd curl up to watch a movie. Or take a walk over to the park. Hmm, a walk would be out unless the rain had stopped.

Still, they needed to talk.

He needed to share his plans, to see what she thought about him being here on a more permanent basis. Maybe they'd head over to Cherry Hill and grab some ice cream for dessert.

Exiting the shower, he dried off and took a moment to drape the towel neatly over the wall rack. He dressed, but when he reached for his shirt he realized the damn thing was an old gag gift from one of his brothers and there was no way he was wearing it out of this room. He'd grab another before going back out into the kitchen.

Peeking at the mirror, he shoved his fingers through his still-wet hair, sending water droplets to his chest and shoulders. He eyed his surgical scar, wondering what Shelby would think if she saw it, but quickly reminded himself not to head down that road.

He brushed his teeth, but decided if he took the time to shave it'd look like he was trying too hard.

"She came here," he spoke to his reflection. "Remember that. The decorated table, the wine…this was all her idea."

And anything else that might happen here tonight, other than sharing a nice dinner, would have to be her idea, too.

Dean grabbed the shirt and yanked open the door, but came up short, bracing one hand against the door frame to keep from plowing right into Shelby.

"Wow, you keep surprising me."

Humor lit her eyes and laughter spilled from her lips, innocently charming and seductive at the same time. She moved closer, her hands dancing over his chest as she rose up on her toes and pressed the length of her body against his until her arms curled around his neck.

"Well, I decided to take your advice."

"Oh, yeah?" The shirt fell silently to the floor before he curved his hand around her waist, fingers spread wide against her lower back, right above the swell of that gorgeous backside. "What advice was that?"

"Not to be nervous."

Chapter Twelve

A powerful longing to pull Shelby hard against him raced through Dean's veins. To lose himself in the perfection that was everything about her. Her touch, her scent, her body.

The fantasy of having her naked beneath him was moments away from coming true. He wanted to believe she knew what she was asking for, what she was offering, but he had to be sure.

"Shelby, are you—"

She swallowed his question with her kiss, slanting her mouth over his. Not doing anything more than holding her in place with one hand, he let her be in charge of this moment.

When she tugged his head lower, he went willingly. When she licked the seam of his lips, he relented and opened his mouth. When she scraped her nails against his scalp, his only concession was his hand slipping down to fully cup her backside.

She crushed her curves to his body, the soft material of

her dress absorbing the moisture from his still-wet skin that dripped from his hair.

When she raised one leg, her thigh pressing hard against his, he allowed his hand to move. To slide off the silky touch of her dress until he met the heat of her flesh and he held her there, opening her to fit perfectly against him except for the barrier of their clothing.

Her hips rocked and he went harder, if that was even possible.

Damn, she was killing him. But still, he dragged his mouth from her. "This doesn't have to happen now, you know. We can wait."

"Wait for what?"

Hell if he knew. "Shelby, you do know where this is going."

Her mouth moved along his jaw. "Yes."

"What about—"

"The food?" she panted the words in his ear. "It's fine. I turned down the heat."

Maybe out in the kitchen, but he had an inferno building right here and any moment he was going to explode. "Food is the last thing I'm thinking about," he said with a low groan.

She nipped at his throat. "Good, then we're on the same page."

Same page? He was ready to read the whole damn book, cover to cover. To answer this siren's call to adventure, to seek the reward. Hell, just to be lost in the wonders and passions and charms of this woman.

But first things first.

He'd planned to share with her tonight his ideas—making the move to town permanent, finding a place to live, starting a new business—to find out if any of that mattered to her.

"We need to talk." He forced the words past his lips. Releasing the doorjamb, he cupped her jaw, raising her face to look at him. "You're leaving."

"Not tonight."

She wiggled her leg, signaling she wanted her freedom. He let her go, but the action caused her fabric-covered breasts to rub against his chest. It wasn't enough. For either of them. Only skin on skin would be perfection.

"I'm staying," he said.

"Yes, please." She dropped her chin and he released his hold on her jaw. "Stay."

The feel of her lips as they found the thin seam of puckered skin from his surgery fourteen years ago, and the trail of kisses that followed as she traced the line south toward his belly button left him weak in the knees.

"That's not what I mean." He half growled, gripping her shoulders to keep her from going any farther. "Oh, woman, you're killing me."

"But in a good way, right?"

Shelby straightened and looked up at him, her eyes round with sudden shyness. She obviously wasn't a virgin, he knew that, but she hadn't mentioned any relationship, long-term or otherwise, since the guy in high school.

How long had it been since she'd slept with a man?

"I haven't…" Her gaze flickered away to land in the center of his chest. "It's been a while since…well, I've done this."

She must have read the question in his eyes and her answer caused the widening chasm in his heart—a breach she was seeping more fully into with every moment they spent together—to open even further. "How long is 'a while'?"

She closed her eyes, took a breath and then tipped her head back to look straight at him. "Six years."

His heart stopped for a moment before it went into overdrive. She'd waited all this time, either by design or because of the crazy way life had of playing out while a person was making other plans. But to be the first man she had sex with after such a long time…

"Shelby, maybe we should think about this—"

Her fingers halted his moving lips. "I have been thinking

about this, in ways I never allowed myself before I met you. But since we met…you, being with you, being like *this* with you seems to be all I can think about lately. Please tell me I'm not the only one."

He nodded, his throat too constricted to allow him to speak.

Of course she wasn't the only one.

How many times had he woken up, reaching across his empty bed, wanting and wishing she was there?

"No thinking about the past or the future, okay?" Her voice was soft, gliding over his skin while her hands did the same from his chest to the too-tight waistband of his jeans.

Still, she kept her gaze locked with his. "Not tonight. Tonight is about right here, right now…you and me. That's enough."

He turned slightly to allow the bright light of the bathroom to shine on her face. "Is it? Is what's about to happen here enough for you?"

"It's everything."

The certainty in her gaze humbled him. She then reached past him, found the bathroom light switch and clicked it off, leaving them in the shadows.

Grabbing his hands, Shelby took a step backward, angling toward the bedroom. He followed, reaching over her head to push open the door, but she bumped it instead with her hip.

He followed her inside and found the room glowing thanks to the half dozen flickering candles on the dresser and bedside tables.

"I did tell you I came prepared, right?"

He nodded again, his voice failing a second time when he should be finding a way to tell her what she was doing to him.

How much he wanted her. How he would do everything in his power to make this perfect for her.

That he understood what a big step this was for her.

Dean walked her to the edge of his bed and then cradled

her face in his hands. His thumb rubbed back and forth across her full bottom lip, loving how her eyes, skin and hair looked golden and radiant in the candlelight.

"And I'm on birth control," she whispered, "so you don't have to worry about that."

"I'll protect you, Shelby." He thought about the box of condoms he'd purchased just yesterday tucked into the bedside drawer, but his words were a solemn promise that meant so much more. "I'll always protect you."

She pressed a kiss against the pad of his thumb before he moved on, stroking her skin from her neck to her shoulders, his fingertips passing back and forth over the delicate straps of her dress.

He wanted her with a desperation that threatened to take the strength from his limbs, but he had to make certain she knew who was truly in control.

"You can tell me no," he said. "At any time, just say the word and we'll stop."

"I don't want to stop." She captured his hands with hers and together they drew the thin pieces of silky cording away from her shoulders. "Make love to me, Dean."

"*With* you, sweetheart. With you."

He lowered his mouth to hers, kissing her deeply, before drawing away to follow the same path his hands had taken moments before.

She dropped her arms, limited by the way the straps held her captive, leaving only her hands free to curl at his hips. Her fingertips slipped inside the waistband of his jeans and the material pulled even tighter as she held on.

His lips moved slowly, gently, across her skin leaving behind soft, wet kisses as she arched her neck to give him room to taste her.

Slowly. He vowed to take this moment slowly.

Pulling the dress straps down the length of her arms, he forced her to let go of him but he released her from their confines, and then did the same with her breasts. A simple push sent the material over her hips and floating to her feet.

Then he cupped her breasts, loving the weight of them as his lips moved even lower until he drew one tight point into the heat of his mouth.

"Dean...Dean..."

Shelby repeated his name, her hands moving to the back of his head, as if she wanted to make sure he stayed right where he was. No need to worry, he had no desire to go anywhere as he tweaked and tugged the tender bud with his lips and tongue.

He only paused long enough to move from one breast to the other, wrapping one arm around her to hold her upright when he felt her knees give way.

Finally, he straightened, then gently lifted her and laid her on his bed. His hands drifted over her hips and the length of her legs to remove her shoes, letting them drop silently to the floor.

He looked at her, a bright spot of light against the dark sheets. She smiled shyly and grabbed at the top sheet, pulling the corner of it to cover her breasts.

He was about to tell her it didn't work—she still looked so damn sexy, even more so now—but then his attention was captured by her other hand and the way her fingers were lightly trailing back and forth across her flat belly.

They slowly moved lower until they came to the edge of the scrap of pink lace that still hid the most intimate part of her. She slipped one finger underneath the band at the edge of her hip bone, but he smiled and then captured her fingers, stopping her.

"Oh, no...not yet."

Her smile matched his, but then she tugged free and reached out to lay that same hand against the rigid flesh behind his zipper.

"I think you're a bit overdressed, don't you?"

Her words, a hushed whisper that caught in her throat, had Dean reaching for the top button of his jeans before she even finished speaking.

Slowly.

Yeah, that mantra was going to be tough to follow no matter how many times he repeated the word in his head.

He lowered the zipper, then pushed the material past his hips, taking his briefs with it until both items pooled around his ankles. He kicked them to the side and stood there naked as her hungry gaze roamed over every inch of him.

She then crooked her finger, beckoning him to join her as she scooted farther onto the bed. "It's a bit chilly in here."

Chilly? Was she kidding? He was about to explode from the intense fervor that engulfed him.

Then she shivered and he stretched out beside her, propping his head on one hand while the other rested flat over her stomach. "We could get under the covers."

"Hmm, yes, but I was hoping maybe you could keep me warm?"

Yeah, he could that, too.

Covering her body with his, their mouths met in ravenous kisses that went on and on. At times powerfully raw, then slow and teasing, the low mewling sounds from her as she matched his passion, stroke for stroke, consumed him.

Moving the sheet aside, he caressed every inch of her body, loving how she trembled from his touch. He returned his mouth to her breasts, unable to satisfy his need for the sweet taste of her.

The gasps, the way her nails dug into his shoulders, the natural rolling of her hips calling to him.

"You like that, Shelby?" he asked.

"Yes...very much...oh, please..."

Moving lower, his hand curled at her hip as his mouth followed. He breathed deeply, loving the mixture of spice and floral and musk that rose from her skin.

He trailed his fingertips over the dainty material that covered her sex before slowly pulling the scrap of lace away and down over her hips. When the material reached her knees, Shelby kicked it free.

Dean eased between her open thighs, planting kisses from her hip bone to her bikini line, the soft wetness that clung to the dense curls drawing him closer.

He looked up the length of her body as he gently parted her, first with his fingers, easing one, then two inside. She watched him at first, but then arched against the pillows, her breasts thrusting into the air. Then he lowered his mouth to her, tasting and teasing, loving how she rose up to meet him when he would move away.

Slow. Slow and easy.

Time faded to nothing as he brought her to the edge again and again, only to deny her what she wanted, what he wanted for her.

"Dean...I've never... I mean no man has ever...made me..."

A primal sense of possession came over him as he realized she was about to experience something for the first time, with him, made him stroke her softer, drawing out the pleasure that was about to come, dipping into her wet heat again and again.

Then she was there, her slender body tight with need, arched high with expectation before she shuddered beneath him, her climax coming with dizzying speed.

He wanted to be there with her, to feel her tighten around him as he thrust deeply inside her, but he waited, put off his own desires as she started her descent. Then he was back again, offering her more, rebuilding the need, the desire, the wanting until she was panting, pleading for him to come to her....

Rising to his knees, he leaned over and yanked open the drawer on the bedside table to grab one of the foil packets.

Suddenly she was there, sitting before him, grabbing at

his hips as her mouth pressed hot, open kisses along his abs. He groaned, loving the feel of her warm tongue on his heated skin.

Then she took him firmly in one hand, exploring the length of him from base to tip. A heart-stopping jolt raced through him, his breathing now harsh when he felt a cool waft cross over his erection.

He wanted, oh, man, he wanted...

But it'd been a while for him, too. Not six years, but if she touched him there, with her lips, he would...

His fingers gathered a fistful of her honey-blond hair and gently tilted her head back until she looked at him. "Next time," he choked out the words. "Let's save something for next time."

She slowly lowered her body back to lie against the sheets, her fingers still stroking him. "Next time."

He gently pushed her hand away, loving the saucy grin on her face as he quickly ripped open the packet, surprised at the shaking of his own hands as he sheathed himself.

"Dean..."

"Shelby..."

Their words overlapped as he stretched out on top of her again, forearms pressed to the mattress as he framed her face with his hands.

He brushed her hair back off her face so he could kiss her again as he nudged against her wet heat. "Slow, baby, let's take it slow."

She smoothed her hands from his underarms to his hips, pulling him closer, arching as he began to slip inside. "Now, I want you now..."

"I'm here. I'm right here."

He ignored his body's demands to thrust forward, straining his muscles to obey his mental command to move with care, inching deeper and deeper until he was fully into her.

Holding still, he waited, wanting to give her body time to adjust, but she was already rocking against him.

"Shelby, I—"

"Love me, Dean, oh, please, just love me."

His body was hot and hard and he wanted nothing more than to take the pleasure she was surrounding him with and give more in return.

She whimpered into his mouth as he started to move, retreat, then thrust deep, over and over. This was heaven, perfection, an ecstasy he'd never felt before with any woman. He gave her everything that was in him. Their lips met and held as she grabbed his hips, her fingers pressing into his skin as she clung to him.

He was close, so close, he couldn't hold back any longer. She broke free from his mouth, gasping for air as she came apart in his arms. Then his ragged groan of release filled the air as she took him with her.

A warm heaviness she'd never felt before weighed her down.

Shelby tried to move, but muscles she hadn't used in years, had never used properly before, protested. She smiled at that thought, then groaning softly, tried again, but all she could do was stretch out with her legs, pointing her toes, then releasing to fall, feeling boneless, back to the mattress.

Ah, that felt good.

Trying with her hands this time, she succeeded with the left one finding the cool air from beneath the bedcovers, but the other hand landed on warm body heat and taut muscles.

Dean.

Her smile grew as her fingertips danced at the indent at his waist, and because she couldn't help herself, down over his very fine backside, as well.

She brought her other hand back beneath the covers realizing it was his arm, and the defined muscles she now traced there, that angled across her rib cage, holding her in place.

Burrowing deeper into the pillows, she kept her eyes closed as the memories came rushing back to her.

How she'd made the decision to wait for him outside the bathroom door as he showered, so sure she was doing the right thing.

So afraid he'd tell her it was too soon, ask if she knew what she was doing and try to convince her they could wait.

He did all those things, of course, but even after she'd practically come out and told him how little experience she'd be bringing to his bed, he'd still wanted her to be sure about being with him.

She'd never been surer of anything in her life.

Then the powerful rush of experiencing the perfection of his lovemaking. He'd been slow, seductive and sweet, putting her needs and desires ahead of his own that first time, every time.

The night had only gotten better from there as they ate a very late dinner of reheated lasagna while the rain that had started to come down in earnest hours earlier danced atop the trailer's roof.

They then finished the bottle of wine here in his bed while he'd used a single rosebud, with its velvety soft petals, to caress every inch of her body, an amazing prelude to making love a second time.

Afterward Dean had insisted on her taking a shower, telling her the hot water would help her soreness, but when he'd come to check on her, teasing that she was using up all his hot water, she'd been bold enough to pull back the curtain and invite him to join her.

His sexy smile as he'd reached for the waistband of his sweats had gone straight to her heart and she'd taken great pleasure in finally returning the favors he'd shown her many times as she kissed and caressed him beneath the hot spray.

Then he showed her that yes, people really did have sex standing up before they'd dried each other off and fell back into bed again.

As she lay there in his arms, her head resting against his chest listening to the steady beat of his heart, she'd asked about the scar.

He'd told her about his childhood illness, the pain and loneliness of being different from the other kids, yet the love he'd found for books and reading back then stayed with him still today.

Happy to know he was perfectly healthy now, she understood better his connection to children, why he played referee for kids in the park and why it was so important to him that Caitlin's day care have a place for the—

Caitlin.

Shelby groaned and squeezed her eyes tight. The last time she'd checked, it'd been almost two in the morning.

She needed to get home despite her mother's assurances that she was okay with Shelby staying over. Last night, she didn't have any idea how the evening would go, but she promised her mom she'd be there when Caitlin woke up, having never been away from her daughter overnight before.

Meaning to grab her clothes and get dressed, she'd promised herself just a few more minutes with Dean. She'd closed her eyes, knowing they hadn't talked at all yet about what would happen tomorrow—today—how their relationship changed now that they were sleeping together.

Sleeping…

She must have fallen asleep.

Opening her eyes, Shelby looked around the room, blinking several times. The light in the room was different. Grayness edged the blinds telling her daylight was almost here.

Oh, no! What time was it?

"Morning."

Dean's deep voice sent shivers over her body, but when he

tried to tighten his hold on her and pull her closer, she wiggled out from beneath his arm.

"Shelby?" He sat up, scrubbing his hand over his face and then pushed his fingers through his hair. "What... Where are you going?"

She rounded the end of the bed, grabbing her dress and underwear from the chair where Dean had neatly placed them. "Ah, home. I've got to get home."

"What time is it?" He twisted, pulling the sheets tight across his body and reaching for his watch from the bedside table. "It's only eight-fifteen."

"I didn't plan on— I thought I'd be gone by—" She held her clothes to her chest and backed up toward the door. "Bathroom. Can I use?"

"Yeah, sure. Go ahead."

He started to get out of bed, but Shelby hurried from the room.

She'd never experienced the morning-after awkwardness she'd heard others talk about, but suddenly her ability to put together a complete sentence was gone.

Feeling foolish and at a complete loss as to what to do next, she quickly dressed, borrowed a comb to use on her hair and brushed her teeth after spotting an unopened toothbrush in the top drawer.

Offering a quick prayer that Dean was in the kitchen getting his morning coffee started, or whatever it was he did in the mornings, she opened the door.

He stood there wearing nothing but those low-riding sweats.

Oh, boy.

"Shelby, it's okay."

She squeezed past him. Shoes. She needed her shoes.

"I have to use the bathroom. Please don't leave while I'm in there."

Looking up from where she sat, fumbling with her wedge

sandals, she found Dean watching her, an unreadable expression in his eyes.

She nodded and relief crossed his face as he moved inside the bathroom and closed the door.

Eyeing the candles in the room, noting most of them had burned down to nothing, she gathered them and walked out to the kitchen. She tossed the candles, along with the used one from the dining table, into the reusable shopping bags she'd brought with her.

Spotting the dishes from last night still soaking in the sink, she debated for a moment, but then quickly washed and dried them, packing them away, too. Lifting the jar of flowers, she pulled the tablecloth free and rolled it into a ball hiding the cheesy mess that had dripped off the fork when Dean had leaned over to feed her....

"You going to take the flowers, too?"

Dean's voice had her fingers tightening around the soft material for a moment before she shoved it on top of the candles. She turned and found him dressed in jeans and a plain black T-shirt.

"Not if you want them. Ah, if you want to keep them."

"I'd like them to stay." Dean walked to her and gently ran one hand over her hair, pushing it back from her face. "I'd like you to stay."

His simple touch sent shivers through her. "I really should get home."

"Your mom is there."

She nodded. "I know, and depending on how many movies they watched last night, they're probably still asleep, Caitlin with that darn kitten curled up right next to her."

"So why are you breaking the speed record to get out of here on such a dreary morning?" Dean asked, then grinned, easily pulling the bag from her hand. He set it in the chair and then wrapped his arms around her, pulling her close. "To get away from me?"

"Well, as you probably figured out from my lack of experience, I don't know how to act…in a situation like this." Shelby sighed, laying her hands against his chest. "I've never been in a situation like this."

"Like what?"

"Oh, the whole morning-after-great-sex situation."

Dean chuckled. "Great sex? I like the sound of that."

Despite the heated blush on her cheeks, Shelby forced herself not to look away from the warmth of his gaze. "I don't know what happens next."

"I had a great time last night."

A rush of emotions flooded her. "Really? I didn't know what to expect…other than dinner, I mean." The words spilled from her mouth before she could stop them. "Of course, I thought… I hoped we'd…well, considering it was my idea to ambush you right after your shower… Oh, I'm so dumb!"

"No, you're not. You're lovely."

He lowered his head, his mouth inches from hers. He smelled minty and manly and Shelby found herself wanting this kiss even more than the first time he'd kissed her on her front porch.

She sighed and closed her eyes at the first gentle brush of his lips against hers. Once, twice and then a quivering hum filled her ears, anticipation of him deepening the kiss, but instead, Dean stepped away.

"Shelby, is that your phone?"

She opened her eyes. "Huh?"

"I hear a buzzing and my phone is still on the charger in my room, so I'm guessing it's yours." Dean walked over to the counter, grabbed her leather purse and handed it to her.

Realizing he was right, Shelby dug around inside and found her phone. She looked at the screen and groaned. Her mother. "I need to answer this."

"Okay."

She thumbed the connection and put the phone to her ear.

"Hey, there. Look, I know what I said last night, but… Wait, wait, Mom. Slow down. No, I haven't been home yet. Why would you think…"

Shelby tried to piece together her mother's jumbled words as she listened and when she finally understood, unimaginable pain sliced straight to the center of her.

"Gone? What do you mean Caitlin is gone?"

Chapter Thirteen

Dean watched the taillights of the two cars ahead of them turn down the road that led to Shelby's house.

They were from the sheriff's office.

After overhearing her one-sided conversation with her mother, he'd quickly pulled on socks, boots and a zippered sweatshirt. The moment Shelby had ended the call after saying she was coming straight home, Dean grabbed his keys.

Then he quietly suggested she call the sheriff.

Her face had paled, but she made the call, fighting to get out the words about her missing daughter. When the phone slipped from her trembling hand, Dean caught it before it fell.

Wrapping one arm around her shaking shoulders, he pulled her to his chest, his throat constricting at the way she clung to him. He quickly explained what little he knew about the situation, asking the lawman to meet them at Shelby's home.

He glanced over to see if Shelby noticed the sheriff's vehicles, but she was still staring out the passenger window, one hand clenching her purse in her lap while the other was curled into a tight fist, pressed to her mouth.

He eyed the clock. It wasn't even nine in the morning.

Where in the hell could a five-year-old have gotten to this early?

He pulled into the drive just as Sheriff Christensen was getting out of his car while two deputies exited the second vehicle.

Vivian Jenkins came out onto the front porch and Shelby was out of his truck before he came to a complete stop, racing across the yard and into the house, her mother following her back inside.

Dean climbed out as well and waited until the sheriff finished talking with his deputies before he and Dean walked across the still-damp grass and followed the women inside. For a late-August day, it was surprisingly gray and chilly.

"How did this happen?" Shelby cried, her voice coming from deep inside the house. "Are you sure she isn't here? Caitlin!"

"I've checked everywhere, honey." Vivian stood in the middle of the living room, still dressed in her bathrobe, her arms folded tightly across her chest. The older woman's eyes were red, cheeks stained with fresh tears. She looked at Dean and the sheriff. "The attic, the basement. I don't know what's going on, but she's not here."

"Caitlin!" Shelby called for her daughter again, coming back down the hallway and into the room. "Caitlin!"

"Shelby, sweetie, your mom said she's not in the house." Dean reached for her, but she skirted around him.

"I know what she said, but it doesn't make sense."

"Why don't we sit for a moment," Gage said. "I need to ask you a few questions."

"Questions? You should be out there looking for my daughter."

The sheriff removed his Stetson. "I've got two deputies already working in the backyard—"

"The backyard?" Shelby ran to the kitchen window that looked out over the expanse of woods that stretched as far as one could see. "Ohmigod, do you think she— Do they have any idea how much land is out there?"

Dean could tell the panic and fear Shelby had managed to hold inside was beginning to make it through the cracks in her resolve.

He, too, had held out hope that somehow this wasn't real, that Caitlin would pop out of a hiding spot as soon as her mother arrived home, but obviously that wasn't going to happen. To be told devastating news over the phone was one thing, but to actually be here and see that somehow that precious child had disappeared into thin air was a reality no parent should ever have to face.

"Shelby, come on." He walked up behind her, his gaze picking up the two men in the distance as he placed his hands on her shoulders. "Let's sit down with the sheriff."

Again, she avoided his touch, spinning around and walking back into the living room. Gage sat in one chair while Shelby and her mother claimed either ends of the sofa. Dean remained standing, taking a spot near the front door.

This way he could see Shelby and steal glances out at the yard, praying for a miracle.

"Okay, when was the last time you saw Caitlin?" Gage asked, pulling a small notebook and pen from his shirt pocket.

"I put her to bed last night around ten—"

"Ten?" Shelby interrupted her mother.

"Yes, we watched a couple of movies and after the second one I got her into bed. She was asleep before her head even hit the pillow," Vivian continued, her voice shaky. "Then I made sure the house was locked up and went to my room. I read for a while and then fell asleep. When I woke this morning I heard cartoons coming from the television in the living room and figured Caitlin was up."

"Do you know what time that was?"

Vivian bit hard on her bottom lip and shook her head. "I don't remember looking at the time. It was just getting light, so maybe six or six-thirty."

"Does she often do that—come into the living room and turn on the television?"

Vivian and Shelby nodded in unison.

"She usually brings out a few stuffed animals and curls up beneath one of the quilts," Shelby said, rocking back and forth, her hands rubbing at her bare arms. "At least until she gets hungry. Then she'll come looking for one of us...."

Realizing Shelby was still wearing the same sundress she had on last night, Dean quickly took off his sweatshirt. He walked to her and without asking, simply laid the fleece around her shoulders.

Shelby jerked the moment the material touched her skin, looking up at him with wide eyes.

"I thought you might be cold." Worry that Caitlin was feeling the same way, wherever she was, knifed through him.

Shelby nodded, pushing her arms into the sleeves and wrapped the jacket across her middle. "Thanks," she whispered.

"I must have fallen back asleep," Vivian said, "because when I woke again, I went looking for her and the living room was empty."

"What time was that?" Gage asked.

"Around eight. I called out for her, checked all the rooms and nothing. When I saw that Shelby wasn't home either, I just prayed—" Vivian choked back a sob. "I prayed she and Caitlin had gone out somewhere, maybe to town to get doughnuts or to pick up the Sunday paper. So I called Shelby and... well, here we are."

"Obviously, your daughter isn't with you." Gage turned to Shelby. "When was the last time you saw her?"

"Yesterday afternoon, around five. My mom was making her dinner when I left."

"So you weren't in the house last night at all?"

Shelby shook her head, cheeks turning pink. "I...um...I was..."

"She was with me, Sheriff," Dean spoke up. "Shelby and I were together last night, at the trailer I'm staying at in town."

"All night?"

Dean nodded. "Yeah, we came right here after talking to you."

"Okay. I noticed some fresh tire tracks on the driveway when we arrived, but none when we pulled up next to the house." Gage looked at Vivian. "Did you notice any vehicles driving by, either last night or this morning?"

Vivian shook her head. "No, I don't remember any. We don't normally get any traffic out here unless someone is coming to the house or the mail delivery."

"You don't actually think someone took Caitlin." Shelby rose to her feet. "That's crazy!"

Dean closed his eyes for a moment; the idea that someone might have kidnapped Caitlin made him physically ill.

"I'm sorry to say but it's not as crazy as you might think and we need to cover all the bases." Gage made a few more notations in his notebook, then asked, "I know Caitlin's father doesn't live here in town anymore, but have you had any contact with him recently?"

"No, of course not." Shelby got up and started to pace. "I haven't seen or spoken to Zach Shute in almost five years."

"So, he doesn't have visitation rights with his daughter?"

"Zach signed away his rights when Caitlin was just a few months old."

"Which also meant you couldn't request any financial support from him, as well?"

Shelby stopped and looked at the sheriff, her chin jutting out in a familiar way. "That's right. I've never needed anything from Zach Shute, money or anything else. Caitlin is my child."

Gage returned her stare for a moment, then nodded. "Okay. I'm assuming Zach is living on the East Coast because he's playing football out that way. We'll verify his whereabouts just to be sure." He turned his attention to Shelby's mom. "What was Caitlin wearing the last time you saw her?"

"Ah, pajamas. Two pieces, a top and pants."

"Color?"

"Green, different shades of green."

"Would she have changed her clothes when she got up?"

Vivian looked at Shelby, confusion on her face. "I don't know. I don't think so."

"If anything, she probably put on her slippers and housecoat when she got out of bed," Shelby said. "We just got them last week and all the pieces are the same design, but I can check her room."

Shelby turned and went down the hallway. Dean exchange glances with the sheriff, knowing exactly what the man was thinking. If the little girl had gone into the woods her clothing would make it hard for her to stand out against the lush vegetation. And a housecoat wasn't going to keep her very warm. If she'd even wandered off. Hell, the alternative was just too awful to think about right now.

Shelby returned, fear for her daughter clearly visible on her face as she clutched a stuffed bear in her arms. "Her b-bed isn't made up and her pajamas aren't lying around anywhere."

Gage rose to his feet. "Does she normally go outside by herself?"

Mother and daughter again shared a look before Shelby spoke. "Yes, she does, but she knows not to leave the yard. I don't know why she would've gone outside so early in the morning. Unless she went to my room and saw I wasn't here and she went to look for my car which wasn't there either...."

Shelby's voice faded, giving way to tears and Vivian leaped from the sofa, tried to take her daughter into her arms, but Shelby stepped away from her mother's embrace, shaking her head.

For whatever reason, Shelby didn't want anyone to touch her. Not him, not her mother. Torn between wanting to be here for Shelby and a desperate need to get outside and join the deputies in their search, Dean took a deep breath and tried to remain calm.

He glanced at his watch. Almost nine-twenty. "Where do we go from here?" he asked Gage. "Caitlin's been gone at least an hour, probably longer."

"A search was conducted last month after the flooding using the volunteer firefighters as team leaders. That same grid pattern style can be used now, only I think we'll add horses and all-terrain vehicles because we will be looking primarily in wooded areas." Gage looked at Shelby and her mother. "I'm heading back into town and with your permission, I'd like to stop by the church and address those gathered for Sunday services."

"Why?" Shelby asked, scrubbing hard at her cheeks.

"The more people we have looking for Caitlin, the better. I'm going to ask for volunteers. Your home is going to be our central command location and we'll be coordinating all efforts from here."

Shelby and her mother nodded in agreement while from the corner of his eye Dean saw the two deputies had returned.

Empty-handed.

He fought the nausea that climbed into his throat and gestured with one hand. "Sheriff?"

Gage turned and saw his men.

Shelby did as well and pushed past them to slam open the screen door. Dean followed her, but she was already down

the steps, her voice calling out, "Did you find her? Please! Did you find my little girl?"

The deputies stopped and so did Shelby. Before Dean could get to her, she fell to her knees and her gut-wrenching cries sliced right through his heart.

Eight hours and forty-three minutes.

That was how long Caitlin had been missing and Shelby didn't know how she could handle one more minute of not knowing if her little girl was okay.

She stood in the middle of the backyard and watched, her eyes trained on the woods, praying that any moment she would see Caitlin emerge from among the trees.

Her mother had tried to get her to eat, but Shelby wasn't hungry. The sheriff had left shortly after Shelby broke down in the front yard, finally accepting the reality that her little girl, for a reason known only to her, had walked away from their home.

Had she gone into the woods? Why? What could have possibly drawn her attention? Or had she followed the road and someone—a stranger—picked her up?

Her thoughts leaped frantically away from that possibility, but as the minutes ticked past, each offered their own terrifying conclusion....

No! No! No!

She couldn't...she wouldn't let her mind go down that road. If she did, she would spiral into a chilling madness that she'd never be free of.

Shelby had scrambled to her feet the moment Dean tried to help her after her collapse in the front yard. Backing away from his outstretched hands, she could see the hurt in his eyes. Deep inside she knew he only wanted to help, but she'd been afraid to allow him—or even her mother—to comfort her for fear of doing exactly what the sight of those two deputies standing in her driveway had done. Brought her to her knees.

As soon as the sheriff left, she'd hightailed into the house and taken a hot shower, using the privacy to rid herself of any more tears. Of course, standing beneath the hot spray had reminded her of the joy she'd experienced just hours earlier with Dean, but she pushed all thoughts of last night from her head.

Nothing was more important right now than finding her daughter.

She'd dressed quickly, determined not to wait to see how many people—if anyone, other than the firefighters—might come back to help.

She was going out there to look for Caitlin herself.

Dean had stopped her, insisting they needed to wait for those who knew what they were doing to get back here. The deputies backed him up, but when he found her a few minutes later, inching closer and closer to the woods that edged the grassy yard, Dean said he would go out and look for Caitlin as long as Shelby promised to stay here.

To be here when her daughter came home.

"Girl, you really need to eat."

Shelby sighed and turned to find Rosey standing there with a plateful of food. "I'm not hungry."

"Of course you're not. This has nothing to do with hunger." Rosey grabbed what looked to be a chicken salad sandwich, a favorite of Shelby's, and held it out to her. "This has to do with you keeping up your strength. For your daughter's sake."

She took the sandwich, forcing herself to take a bite.

Rosey had been one of the first to show up earlier today, less than an hour after the sheriff left, even beating the search-team leaders to Shelby's house. Behind her came a caravan of cars and trucks, most of which still sat lining the long drive from the main road to the house.

Shelby had been stunned at the amount of people who responded to the sheriff's plea for help.

Rosey had shut down the bar and all of her coworkers were here. Nathan Crawford and his siblings came and so did the Traub family en masse and on horseback. Fathers who knew Caitlin from the day-care center, women from the ladies church group, many of whom looked down on Shelby for years, were here, as well.

Even Darlene came with her girlfriends. Shelby hadn't said a word to them, but watched in amazement as they were assigned to a team.

The biggest surprise had been when Sam had roared into the yard on his Harley motorcycle around one o'clock, having made the trip from Spokane in just over three hours after getting Rosey's phone call. He'd given Rosey a big kiss, Shelby a tight hug and then jumped right into the search putting his years of Navy SEAL training to work.

Ellie Traub and Thelma McGee took over the garage, setting it up as a second kitchen for all the food that was arriving, making sure the volunteers had plenty to eat and drink as they rotated shifts.

The house kitchen had been turned into a central grouping area where all the communications for the search for Caitlin were centered. Maps were tacked to the walls, the base station for the two-way radios being used by the team leaders was on the dining room table and a network of privately owned cell phones were being tracked, although the coverage was often spotty out here.

Dean had returned after his brother Nick reached him on his cell phone, but Shelby had avoided him, as well. In fact, she avoided all the volunteers except for, Rosey who refused to leave her alone.

The fact was, she couldn't face anyone as guilt ate away at her for staying away last night. Yes, she didn't mean to and yes, her mother had been home, but still…

"You can't give up hope, sweetie."

Shelby nodded, forcing the last bite of the sandwich past the lump in her throat. "I know. It's just that it's almost five o'clock. It'll be dark soon. She has to be so hungry by now. We have all this food…"

"At least the weather is cooperating," Rosey pointed out. "There's not much sun, but the temperature warmed up."

"Yes, for now, but what about when the sun goes down?" She turned to face her friend. "You know how dark it gets out here. What about wild animals? What if something got to her?"

"Shelby—"

"Where is she, Rosey? Why haven't they found her by now?" A sickening fear that she'd been fighting all day unraveled deep inside her, sending out a pain so sharp and jabbing that Shelby had to fight for her next breath. "There aren't that many homes out this way. I mean, how far can a five-year-old get when almost the whole town is out there looking for her?"

Her friend grabbed Shelby and pulled her into a strong embrace, her words blistering against Shelby's ear. "They will find her. No one is going to stop looking until they do. Not the sheriff, not your friends, not Sam and especially not Dean. They are going to keep searching, just like they've been doing all day. And when night comes, they will use searchlights or flashlights or candlelight if necessary, but no one is giving up."

Rosey leaned back and took Shelby's face in the palms of her hands. "That includes you, too. You can be scared, you can be mad, but you can never, never give up."

The tears flowed down Shelby's cheeks, but she nodded. "Never give up," she whispered.

Dean stopped to check the map he carried again, noting he and the rest of his search team, Gage as the leader, Sam Traven, Collin and Dallas Traub, both on horseback, and about a half dozen volunteers, were still on Traub land.

Their family ranch, the Triple T, was huge and Shelby's house sat in the northwest corner. Most of the acreage was open pastureland for cattle, but up here, the land ran right into the hills and then the mountains beyond. They had been in dense woods for the past hour, coming in from access roads on the ranch, then leaving behind a couple of pickup trucks and ATVs. Walking spread out, at least half a football field between them, they looked behind every fallen tree, rock formation and timber cluster.

The ground was wet, thanks to last night's rain and it made for slow going, but Dean wasn't giving up.

His last rotation back at Shelby's had just about killed him.

He'd come back with his team for a meal break around five o'clock, even though it was the last thing he wanted. Nine hours and not one sign of Caitlin anywhere.

Gage had even gotten in touch with the child's father who confirmed everything Shelby had said about his relationship with the child, including that he was traveling with his football team in Florida and that his folks were with him, as well.

Dean had almost hoped that for some crazy reason the man had come back to town and taken Caitlin. At least they'd know where she was and he wouldn't have had to listen to the edge of hysteria in Shelby's voice as he eavesdropped on her and Rosey's conversation.

He was amazed at how well she'd been holding herself together. Yeah, it bothered him that she didn't seem to want to have anything to do with him.

Who was he kidding?

It just about killed him every time she turned away whenever he managed to catch her eye, but if that was what she needed to do to get through this, to hold on until her daughter was home again…

Dean saw the bobbing shafts of light dancing through the woods, the men's voices as they called out Caitlin's name echoed through the trees. He looked at his watch. Just after eight and the light of the day was fading fast.

Twelve hours now since Vivian had called to tell them Caitlin was missing.

Shelby's question about how the little girl would manage out here in the pitch-dark resonated in his head as he switched on his flashlight. A decision about keeping the search going all night hadn't been made yet, but Dean and Sam had already decided between them that no matter what, they weren't stopping.

Keeping his gaze to the ground, Dean continued his search. He walked about fifty yards, then noticed he seemed to be on some sort of road. It was overgrown, but the bones of what used to be could still be seen. He followed it, even though the direction led him off his designated section of the map.

He moved faster, calling out for Caitlin, suddenly thinking if there was once a road here, perhaps there was a house or abandoned buildings. The other searchers' voices grew dim as he continued farther down the dirt path. Soon he came to a clearing of sorts, the remains of a home clearly outlined by the debris left behind. He moved onward, deeper into the woods.

"Team One, check in."

The two-way radio he carried on his belt came to life. The men on his team each did as requested. "Dean, check in." The sheriff's voice came in strong over the radio. "Where are you?"

"I'm off my map grid about a hundred yards west," Dean said, thumbing the button that would allow him to be heard. "I've found an old homestead. No buildings yet. Still checking."

"There's no homestead out this far." Collin Traub's voice came over the air. "No roads even."

"Well, I found one." Dean pushed on, the beam of his flashlight bouncing off the thick juniper trees. "An old one that's not much more than an overrun path now. I'm about thirty yards off the road—"

There in the beam of light, still at least twenty yards away, stood a dilapidated barn. "I've found something. An old barn or a shed."

"Wait for backup," Gage ordered. "That thing could come down around your ears and we'll be rescuing you. Estimated time of arrival—twenty minutes."

"Ditto." Sam's voice came over the radio next. "Coming in from the other direction. ETA for me—twenty-five."

Dean acknowledged his team, but couldn't stop himself from approaching the building. More shed than barn with one wall caved in, the rest of the structure remained upright.

"Caitlin?" Dean paused at an opening that used to be a door, waving his flashlight. "Honey, are you in here? It's Dean. I've come to take you home."

He waited, greeted by silence.

Knowing it was wrong, Dean followed his gut anyway and slipped inside. He looked up and found most of the roof gone, its large hand-hewn beams lying scattered across the floor.

He aimed his light at the corners and beneath the beams. "Caitlin? If you're here, please answer me."

Please.

There was no reason why, no clue or explanation, but Dean kept looking, kept calling out, but not a sound. He checked his watch. Gage and Sam should be here any minute. The sky was darkening fast. If she wasn't here, they needed to move on, they needed to keep looking—

A soft scuffing noise caused Dean to go perfectly still.

He waited, sure he'd heard something.

There it was again and then a tiny cry, almost like a kitten's mew.

It came from the far corner. Dean raced over, spotting an opening beneath one of the oversize beams. He shone the flashlight down there but couldn't see anything.

"Caitlin, is that you?" He leaned against the aged wood but the beam didn't budge. "Are you down there?"

Then the crying grew louder, but it still sounded like an

animal. Dean flattened his body to the floor and wedged his head and the hand holding the flashlight down into the hole. The beam landed on a black kitten looking up at him with its mouth open as another lusty cry came out of its small body.

And right next to the pet were the small pale fingers of a child.

"Caitlin!"

He moved the flashlight's beam over her, taking in her crumpled form, her pajamas covered in dirt, as she lay fewer than three feet below him.

His heart froze as a fear-laced sweat broke out over his entire body. "Caitlin, answer me! Caitlin!"

When she didn't move, Dean knew he had to get her out of there now. Wiggling back out of the tight space, he lunged at the beam, putting all his strength into moving the piece of wood, but it scooted across the floor only a few inches.

He tried again, bracing his feet against one beam and using his upper body strength. A low groan escaped his lips, but the beam moved, giving him plenty of space to get down to Caitlin. However, when he relinquished his hold, the wood started to slide back into place.

"Dean, what in the hell are you doing?" Gage's voice called out. "Are you in there?"

"Yes! I've found her!" He called out to his team. "Get in here and help me!"

Both Gage and Sam appeared at his side, the former SEAL immediately copied Dean's stance. The older man was probably pushing seventy, but he was holding his end of the beam with ease.

"She's down in that hole, along with her cat." Dean jerked his head toward the opening. "I only found her because the animal was crying. As you can hear, no response yet from Caitlin."

Gage nodded and moments later he was crawling out of the hole with both Caitlin and the kitten. By silent agreement,

Dean and Sam lowered the beam back into place as Gage sat nearby, cradling Shelby's daughter in his arms.

Dean hated to ask, hated to even think it, but he had to know. "How is she? Is she—"

The tiny blond head turned and beautiful blue eyes stared back at him.

"I got lost," Caitlin said in a soft whisper.

Relief flowed through him as Dean knelt beside her. "You sure did, little one. Are you okay?"

She scrunched her tiny nose. "I'm thirsty and my arm hurts real bad."

Dean shared a look with the sheriff who then handed off the animal to Sam and quickly checked her out from her head to her toes. "She's got some scrapes and bruises and a good-size bump on her head. Her lower right arm is swelling."

"I'm cold, too."

Gage smiled, but Dean could read concern in his eyes. "Well, let's get you warmed up." He looked at Dean again. "I've got a blanket in my backpack."

Dean got the blanket, watching as the sheriff gently wrapped the precious girl in the warm material, taking extra care with her injured arm. The sheriff then handed her over to Dean's waiting arms.

"I want my mama," Caitlin said, her face turned into his chest, right over his heart. "And my nana. And my kitten."

"We're going to take you to see your mama right now," Dean promised, pushing the words past the lump in his throat.

"We best get out of here," Sam tucked the cat inside his jacket and zippered it. "And I'll take care of your critter for you, Miss Caitlin."

Dean nodded and the three men left the building just as Collin and Dallas Traub arrived.

"You found her!" Collin called out as the two brothers dismounted from their horses. "I swear, we never knew this place was even out here. It's not on any of the current land maps for the Triple T."

"What's important is that she's safe," Dean said. "Right now we need to contact her mother and get Caitlin to a hospital."

Everyone agreed that the best way back to the vehicles was to head the way they'd come because no one had any idea where the road led in either direction.

Dean started walking, his steps quick and sure as Sam and Gage flanked him, their flashlights making a bright path to follow. His gaze darted between the woods in front of him and the little girl lying so still in his arms.

"You want to tell her?" Gage held out his radio.

Dean only fought the battle for a moment and then shook his head. He didn't want to let go of Caitlin. Not for a moment. "Go ahead and make the call. Should we get an ambulance to meet us?"

"By the time they get out to the Triple T we'll be headed south to the hospital in Kalispell, but we'll keep in touch and see if our paths cross." Gage pressed the button on the radio, "Sheriff Christensen to base. Come in, base. We've got great news."

Chapter Fourteen

Shelby paced in front of the hospital's emergency room entrance, waiting for the headlights of the ambulance with her daughter to appear in the cool night air.

Where were they?

When the driver had called in they were less than fifteen minutes away, she'd left the noise of the crowded waiting room. It seemed like half the town had made the drive down to Kalispell in support of her, her mother and Caitlin. She was deeply touched, more than she thought she would be—but she needed some peace and quiet, needed to be right here when her daughter arrived.

When the sheriff had radioed in that they'd found Caitlin, safe and alive, a loud cheer had gone up from the crowd gathered in their kitchen. The news quickly spread to those getting ready to go out on the next rotation and was radioed to the teams still looking.

She was found.

Then he said they were calling for an ambulance.

Shelby's blood had run cold, but both her mother and Rosey told her that Caitlin had to be checked by a doctor after spending so much time out in the elements.

She had calmed down a bit and told the sheriff she was on her way to the Triple T ranch, but he'd said for her to head straight to the hospital in Kalispell and they would meet her there. Once she and her mother had gotten in Rosey's car and left the house, she got on the radio she'd taken with her and asked about her daughter's condition and the details of how she'd been found.

The interference and static that had plagued the search teams at times during the past twelve hours had happened again, making it impossible to understand what the sheriff was saying. It wasn't until she'd arrived at the hospital that she learned the ambulance had met up with the pickup truck they were transporting Caitlin in and the EMTs had taken responsibility for her daughter.

That was all she knew.

The hospital staff would only tell her that the technicians were stabilizing Caitlin and their estimated time of arrival. She'd tried the radio again, but there was no response. She then used the phone at the nurse's station to call Dean, after realizing she'd left the house without her cell phone, assuming he'd been there when Caitlin was found. But her call had gone straight to voice mail, meaning his phone was turned off or had run out of power.

Or they were keeping her in the dark.

She tried to fight off that feeling, but a low hum of anger was slowly building inside her. Caitlin was her child and she had a right to know what was going on, damn it!

Why wouldn't anyone tell her?

Why was Dean—of all people—not contacting her?

He must be heading to the hospital with her daughter. Didn't any of those people have a cell phone on them?

Determined to find out the truth, she whirled around and

headed inside when a siren and flashing red lights filled the air. She turned back just as an ambulance pulled up to the sliding glass doors of the E.R., a battered pickup truck with three large bodies squeezed in the cab right behind.

Caitlin.

Racing to the vehicle, she got there the same time as two hospital personnel. When the rear doors swung open, Shelby finally saw her daughter, looking impossibly small and pale, lying still against the large white surface, IV tubing attached to one arm.

She gasped, moving forward, but a pair of strong arms grabbed her shoulders and held her back.

"Let go of me." She broke free of his hold and spun around, already knowing it was Dean.

"You need to let them do their jobs, Shelby."

"What is going on?" she demanded, her gaze darting between him, the sheriff and Sam, both of whom stood behind Dean. "What's wrong—"

"Caitlin was unconscious when we found her, but she did come to and talked to us," Dean said. "The biggest concern is the bump on her head and the swelling in her right arm."

"Why didn't you tell me all of this before?"

"I wanted to, but the decision was taken out of my hands. We didn't want you in a panic—"

"You think being kept in the dark wasn't enough to cause me to panic?"

Her head was pounding and her voice sounded shrill, but her grasp on the terror that had consumed her for the past twelve hours was fading fast. Pressing her hands to the sharp throbbing at her temples, she started to turn away when a bundle of black fur crawling out of the top of Dean's zippered sweatshirt caught her eye.

"What in God's name?"

"She was with Caitlin." Dean pulled the zipper down and palmed the kitten in one hand. "She said the kitten had gotten out of the house this morning and Caitlin went after her. By the time she caught it, the house was long gone and she was lost."

"All of this—" Shelby couldn't believe it. "All of this was because of a *kitten*? A kitten you gave her?" All the pain, fear and horror of this nightmare poured through her, the uncertainty of what could have happened clogging her emotions and clouding her brain. "If you'd never brought *that* into our lives…if *you'd* never come into our lives…"

"Shelby, please listen to me."

Dean took a step toward her, but she scurried backward, holding out her hands. "No…don't…I have to get to my daughter."

She backed away even more, turning away when she heard her name being called. A nurse was gesturing for her to follow him and she did, allowing the sliding glass doors to close behind her without a look back.

"It wasn't your fault."

Nick's low voice filled Dean's head. His brother sat with him in the crowded E.R. waiting room. Leaning forward, hands clasped between his knees, he mirrored Dean's posture as they sat opposite each other in the far corner.

"I know."

"You say that, but do you believe it? I got here in time to see your expression when Shelby spouted off," Nick said. "She didn't mean it. All that…crap came from a dark place, from fear and anger after a long day of holding it together in front of a crowd of people who probably expected her to go ballistic at any moment."

"I know that, too."

Dean understood where Shelby's words had come from, even though each one had hit him like body blows from a prizefighter.

He'd seen the pain and bewilderment swirling in a stormy haze that filled her eyes, the rigid way she held her body.

She'd needed a reason for what had happened. He and the tiny kitten he'd gifted to her daughter had been a convenient answer at a moment when she needed it most.

But that didn't mean she was wrong.

"Maybe I never should've pursued a relationship with her." His heart ached as he spoke the words aloud, but they had to be said. "I knew from the start she was planning to move away and what do I do? Saddle her daughter with a pet. That was real smart. Some parent I'd make."

"Are you kidding me? If there's anyone who was made to be a father, it's you. Jeez, you even made sure someone would take that kitten home tonight and care for it until Shelby and Caitlin are ready to— Hey, what's going on over there?"

Dean followed his brother's stare to see Nathan Crawford standing among a crowd of townsfolk from Rust Creek Falls who had caravanned to the hospital. The high school kids, who Dean found out just today had taken on rebuilding the bridge out at the lower falls to cowboys from the local ranches to the church ladies who had provided enough food to feed an army—all here to support Shelby and her daughter.

At least that was what he'd thought when he, Gage and Sam had first come inside to find the waiting room filled with people. Now he wasn't as sure because the discussion had turned to the mayoral race between Collin Traub and Nathan Crawford.

"…and I'm telling you we need to make sure the children of our town are safe," Nathan spouted, having pulled on a suit jacket and tie, looking every inch the candidate.

Dean did have to give the man credit as he'd been a member of one of the search teams today, but was now the time and place for a campaign speech?

"Just because you own private land doesn't mean you aren't responsible for all the buildings on that property," Nathan continued. "If we need regulations to ensure that structures are maintained for the safety of all its citizens, then that's something the town council, and the new mayor, will have to tackle."

"It's being tackled right now," Gage Christensen said, having just walked through the doors that led to the E.R., his Stetson in his hands. "Yes, the barn where we found Caitlin was on Traub land. The reason you don't see Collin or Dallas Traub here in this waiting room with the rest of you is because they stayed behind to make sure that barn was taken down. Tonight. Actions, instead of words, carry a lot more weight with me, and I would hope with all of you."

A murmur went through the crowd as the sheriff departed again to answer his cell phone. Dean had heard that Gage wasn't always Collin Traub's biggest fan, especially when the man had become involved with his sister in the days after the flood last month, but it seemed the sheriff was firmly in his brother-in-law's corner now.

"Well, that was interesting." Nick turned back. "But back to that nonsense you were saying before. And it was non-sense."

"I don't know." Dean sighed and ran a hand through his hair. "Maybe I should just forget about my plans to relocate and go home to Thunder Canyon."

"Look, if anyone should be heading home, it's me. Cade called last night. It seems Dad's horse got spooked and threw him." Nick waved him off when Dean started to speak. "A week ago. He's okay, even though he did break his collarbone. He refused to let Cade or Holly tell us until now because, well, he's stubborn. The thing is, the business just picked up a big order of designer furniture for a ski resort near Edmonton. Cade is going to be full-out busy for the next year, especially with Dad's recovery time being unknown." Nick pointed a finger at him. "You, on the other hand, belong here. You belong with Shelby and her little girl."

"I used to think so. Maybe this thing with Dad is a sign—"

"Sign? What sign? Caution, stupidity ahead?" Nick demanded, cutting him off. "Look, the family business is going to be fine and you still love the town. More important, you want Shelby and Caitlin to be in your life, right?"

"She made her choice."

"What choice? You're letting her push you away without a fight."

Dean opened his mouth to argue, but at that moment the doors that led back to the E.R. opened again and this time Vivian stepped into the room. She was immediately surrounded by people and questions were coming at her from all directions.

She smiled and held up a hand. "Please, Shelby asked me to share with all of you the news that Caitlin is going to be just fine."

A cheer went up from the crowd and Dean's heart pounded in his chest, as if it was coming back to life for the first time since he'd spotted the little girl lying in that dark hole.

"Caitlin is awake and talking, answering simple questions and asking for macaroni and cheese." She smiled at the laughter, then continued, "She does have a broken arm and the doctors want to keep her overnight for observation, but that's all."

Vivian paused, laying a hand over her heart. She looked around the room and stopped when her gaze caught and held Dean's. "I don't have the words to thank all of you for everything you did for my family today. Shelby and I will be forever grateful for your time and efforts, your love and support."

Dean and his brother stood when Vivian headed in their direction, stopping to accept hugs and well wishes of many in the crowd before most started to gather their belongings to return to Rust Creek Falls.

When she finally reached them, she tried to wrap her arms around Dean's shoulders. "Thank you, thank you, thank you for saving my grandbaby."

He stooped to return her embrace. "I was just in the right place at the right time."

"The sheriff told us that you were the one who found her and the kitten, how you lifted that beam—"

"It was a team effort." Dean cut off her praise. "Sam and Gage were just as involved in getting Caitlin home to you... and to Shelby."

Vivian stepped back, concern in her eyes. "Shelby is trying so hard to be strong back there, but her emotions from today are churning just below the surface and I'm afraid..."

"You don't have to explain," Dean said when the older woman's voice faded. "Shelby has every right to think and feel exactly as she does."

Vivian nodded, pressing her lips together in a hard line. "I need to get back in there. Oh, Caitlin is asking about Princess, her kitten."

"Bert, one of the cooks at the Ace, agreed to take her home earlier. He said he'll take care of her until you all are ready for the kitten to come home."

Vivian nodded again, gave Nick a hug as well and then crossed the room to talk to Rosey and Sam, who sat with the sheriff. The room had emptied fast, but quite a few people remained, including the two ladies Dean had seen talking with Shelby that day at the ice-cream place.

Nick took his seat again, but Dean waved a hand at him. "How about giving me a lift home?"

"You sure?"

Dean nodded, forcing the words, his voice miserable. "Yeah, I think it's best if I'm not here. You know, in case Shelby comes out to talk with her friends."

"You don't think she's going to want to talk to you?"

Sadly, he didn't.

It was nearly midnight when Shelby finally found the courage to leave her daughter's bedside.

And that was only because her mother slept curled up in the chair next to her, her hand resting on Caitlin's hospital bed. Shelby knew exactly how she felt. She didn't know when either of them would allow Caitlin out of their sight again.

Her precious little girl slept soundly at the moment, but the staff was waking her every half hour or so to perform another test. Thankfully, one of the nurses had given her a stuffed bear the last time as Caitlin was getting a bit cranky.

She'd also been asking for Princess.

Caitlin had told them that the kitten had scurried out the front door when she had gone looking for Shelby's car after finding her bed empty. She'd followed, scared her new pet would be lost. Only the two of them got lost. So she kept walking, carrying Princess, until she came across the old barn.

Thankfully, her daughter didn't remember how she'd ended up falling down in the hole, only that she'd been tired, so she'd lain down to take a nap.

Then the sheriff had come back and given Shelby and her mother the details of how, thanks to the kitten's cries, Dean had found Caitlin.

Dean.

Pausing at the doors that would take her out into the E.R.'s waiting area, Shelby leaned against the wall, the strength gone from her legs. Shame filled her as she thought back to those awful moments when Caitlin at first arrived at the hospital.

Boy, when she had told Dean on their first date that she could be a witch with a capital *B*...well, she'd certainly lived up to that statement last night.

How could she have actually blamed—blamed!—Dean and a helpless kitten for Caitlin being lost in the first place?

Then she made it worse by telling him this terrible thing had happened because he came into their lives. That was wrong. She was responsible for all of this, not Dean.

The truth was, because of him her girl had come to know what it meant to have a good man in her life.

As for Shelby...

In just a few weeks, Dean had shown her it was possible

to overcome a past that had made her suspicious of a strong, caring and honest man…and she'd fallen in love for the first time in her life.

Pulling a deep breath, Shelby pushed away from the wall and squared her shoulders.

Her mother had told her repeatedly that many of the towns-people had stuck around and were still in the waiting room, even after they'd learned Caitlin was going to be okay.

It was time for Shelby to thank them for everything they'd done.

And to apologize to Dean for her foolish words.

She pushed open the doors and stepped out, surprised to find at least a dozen people still here that she recognized from Rust Creek Falls despite the late hour.

The first person her gaze landed on was Rosey, curled up in Sam's embrace. He nudged her and she awoke with a start, then jumped up and hurried across the room to Shelby. Sam rose to his feet as well and followed.

"Oh, honey!" Rosey pulled her into in her arms. "She's going to be okay! Your mom told us the wonderful news a couple of hours ago!"

Shelby accepted her friend's warm hug, then said, "Yes, we're very lucky." She then moved to give Sam a hug of his own. "Thank you so much for coming back to help us, for being there when my daughter needed you most."

"I wouldn't have been anywhere else," Sam said. "But it was your friend Dean who found Caitlin."

Shelby nodded, suddenly feeling very nervous. She stepped back, her gaze darting around the room, searching for him. "Yes, I know. Have either of you seen him recently?"

Sam and Rosey joined her in looking around the waiting area. "I could've sworn he was just here, but honestly, this place was wall-to-wall people for the longest time," Rosey said, then hid a yawn behind her hand. "It just thinned out in the last twenty minutes or so. Maybe he went down to the cafeteria for coffee."

Holding on to that slim hope despite the thought racing through her head that he wasn't here at all, Shelby forced a smile. "You should be heading home, as well. Both of you must be exhausted."

"I tried to get her to leave, but Rosey wanted to talk to you first," Sam said with smile, wrapping one arm around the woman's shoulder.

"Talk nothing! I wanted to show you this!" Rosey held out her left hand and it took a moment for Shelby to notice the oversize ruby ring her boss had shown her that day in her office was now in place on her finger. "I finally said yes!"

Shelby blinked back the tears biting at the back of her eyes. "Oh, how wonderful for both of you."

"She was wearing the thing when I found her in the waiting room," Sam said, then smiled. "At first I didn't know what to think."

"Until I told him that today taught me life is too short not to grab all the happiness one can get." Rosey aimed her sharp gaze at Shelby. "Don't you agree?"

She nodded, unable to speak. She was thrilled for her friends, but as the minutes ticked by and Dean still didn't appear...

"We'll have to plan a spring wedding," she said.

"Spring?" Rosey said in mock horror, then winked. "I'm thinking more of hopping on the bikes and zooming down to Vegas!"

"Speaking of zooming, if you need us to stay to give you a ride home, we will," Sam said. "Seeing how Rosey was your ride here."

"Oh, please don't worry about that. My mom and I are going to be here until the doctors release Caitlin. Ellie Traub stayed behind to make sure our place was cleaned up and she had someone bring us the truck about an hour ago." Considering her car was still parked at Dean's trailer. "Besides, you have a business to open tomorrow, er, today."

"You bet I do!" Rosey grinned. "I promised all the volunteers a free beer for helping in the search. We're going to be busier than a mosquito at a nudist colony."

Shelby laughed and hugged her friend again. After Rosey and Sam left, Shelby made her way around the room, taking a few moments to thank each person for their help while trying not to notice that Dean still hadn't made an appearance.

In fact, she didn't see him or his brother, causing her stomach to twist into a painful knot that she tried but failed to blame on hunger.

When she reached a group of ladies sitting in the far corner, she was surprised when two of them led her to one side after she'd let them know how much she appreciated their still being here.

"Oh, you sweet thing, we just have to talk to you. In private." An older woman said in a hushed whisper, her gray curls bobbing as her gnarly fingers held tight to Shelby's arm. "It just isn't fair."

"Certainly not, especially after all you have been through." The other woman stood close by, a determined gleam in her eye as she crossed her arms over her ample breasts. "Not fair at all."

"I'm sorry, I don't know what you're talking about." Confusion filled Shelby. These ladies were familiar to her from the church, but other than that connection, she had no idea why they wanted to speak with her.

"Auntie Louisa, Auntie Lauren, I moved the car closer. In fact, I'm parking in a handicapped spot, so we need to go—" Wanda Jefferson walked up, her jaw dropping in surprise when she saw Shelby standing there. "Shelby. I'm… How's your daughter?"

"She's fine."

"Oh, I'm so happy to hear that. My family and I were at

the church when the sheriff spoke and my heart just sank when he told us…." She blinked and Shelby was stunned to see tears in the woman's eyes. "Being a momma myself, I just can't imagine if my sweet Maggie were to… Oh, how awful today must have been for you."

"It's not anything I'd wish on my worst enemy." Shelby paused, the truth of her words settling deep inside her.

The way the town had responded today, taking the unknown of her daughter's whereabouts into their hearts and giving back in any way they could—searching for hours in the woods, supporting with food and beverages, coming down here and waiting until they heard Caitlin was going to be all right—it made her see Rust Creek Falls in a way she hadn't in a very long time.

"Shelby, I know this probably isn't the time or the place, but I want to apologize." Wanda kept her voice low but looked her straight in the eye. "I was rude to you that day in Crawford's store for no cause. I never should've butted into your private conversation and the things I said…well, they were just wrong. I'm sorry."

"Thank you for that." Surprised, Shelby didn't know what else to say. "And thank you for being here. Were you at my house earlier today?"

"We stopped by with a few casseroles for the volunteers." Wanda waved a hand at the two women. "My aunts and I wanted to do what little we could to help. They also insisted on coming here after your daughter was found."

"And we're going to insist on telling her that despite that young man being a hero, he's turning into a cad."

"Auntie—"

"What young man?" Shelby asked, turning her attention back to the older woman.

"Why, Dean Pritchett, of course." Wanda's aunt pulled her tiny body up straight, even lifting her nose in the air. "And how he's leaving town. For good."

Chapter Fifteen

The hospital had released Caitlin with a clean bill of health and no residual effects from her ordeal in the woods. Shelby, her mother and Caitlin had arrived home Tuesday around dinnertime to find the house spotlessly clean, the refrigerator fully stocked and Shelby's car parked in front of the garage.

All thanks to Rosey.

Her friend had left the bar in Sam's capable hands for a couple of hours on Monday to come to the hospital with fresh clothes and other essentials for Shelby and her mother and a stuffed kitten that looked exactly like Princess for Caitlin.

The only thing missing had been Dean.

As Rosey shared that many people were still asking what else they could do to help Caitlin and her family, Shelby's mind had kept wandering to the same question she'd been asking for the past several hours.

Why had he changed his mind about staying?

Shelby had somehow found the willpower to wait until she'd walked Rosey to her car to ask about Dean's whereabouts. Despite what the local gossip mill had reported when she'd gone to the waiting room looking for him in the wee hours of Monday morning, she hadn't wanted to believe he was really planning to leave town.

He *wasn't* planning…he was already gone.

Rosey had hemmed and hawed but finally admitted that all she knew was that Dean and his brother Nick had gone back to Thunder Canyon sometime early that morning.

Heartbroken, Shelby had only nodded and then asked Rosey to get her car from Dean's trailer and leave her keys on the kitchen table. She'd gone searching for her phone in the bottom of her purse when she got back to Caitlin's hospital room, but realized she must have left it at home in her mad dash to the hospital.

She didn't want to ask Rosey to make another trip, so she forced herself to concentrate solely on her daughter when the doctors insisted she stay another night thanks to a high fever.

Besides, she didn't think she'd have the courage to call Dean and ask why he'd left.

But now they were home and after a quick meal, they'd put a sleepy Caitlin to bed, her mother and Shelby stumbling over the little girl's questions about Dean and when she was going to see him again.

She wanted him to sign her cast.

Her mother had given her shoulders a quick squeeze as Shelby had blinked back tears and gave only the answer she could—she didn't know—and that was when Caitlin had simply told her to call him and ask him to come over. Vivian had smiled and whispered that the best advice often came out of the mouths of babes.

Her mother went off to bed, but Shelby, cell phone in hand, had chickened out and had gone to take a shower instead.

Now, dressed in her silky cotton nightgown and matching bathrobe, with her hair wrapped turban-style in a towel, she checked on Caitlin again—something she'd be doing a lot of for many nights to come—and found her daughter sound asleep.

She stood at the doorway, awed by the ease with which the little girl seemed to be recovering from her harrowing ordeal. Shelby, on the other hand, wasn't faring so well. She missed Dean so much that her stomach hurt.

Grabbing her phone, determined to at least give him the apology he deserved, even though she'd much rather do it in person, she thumbed in her password.

Twelve voice mail messages.

She didn't think twelve different people had her number. Okay, there was Rosey, her mother of course, her coworkers at the bar, Dean…

Could one—or more of them—be from him?

Almost forty-eight hours had passed since they'd last seen each other, a day and a half since she'd learned he had indeed left town.

She punched in the code and listened, pacing back and forth across the kitchen floor. One from Rosey, and two were from waitresses at the bar the morning Caitlin went missing. Not wanting to relive those moments, Shelby deleted them. The next thing she heard was Dean's deep voice in her ear.

Shelby…it's Dean…look, I know I'm probably the last person you want to talk to right now…

Oh, how wrong he was! She gripped the kitchen counter as a long pause filled the air. She wondered if he'd hung up, but then his voice returned.

This isn't how I wanted to tell you…I mean, please know I'm thinking about Caitlin…the thing is, I need to go…

Her heart seized in her chest.

A knocking at the kitchen door made Shelby jump and her phone slipped from her hands to land in a pile of dirty dishes in the sink.

Damn! Shelby reached for the phone, hitting the button to exit from voice mail by mistake as the knocking came again.

Marching across the room, she peeked through the curtains, her frozen heart jump-starting back into action when she saw the wide shoulders and close-cropped blond hair.

Then he turned and looked directly at her.

Fumbling with the door, Shelby finally got it open and stared through the screen as Dean stood there looking wonderful in his familiar outfit of jeans and plain T-shirt.

She opened her mouth to speak, but nothing came out.

"You're surprised to see me," Dean said.

"Yes—" she nodded at her phone still in her hand "—I am. I was just listening to my messages, as a matter of fact."

He heaved a deep sigh and braced his hands on his hips, her eyes drawn to the single yellow rose he held in his fingers.

"Can I come in?" he asked.

Shelby unhooked the door and scooted backward. "Of course."

He stepped into the kitchen, his gaze immediately taking in the masses of flowers on the table and counters.

"Those are from…well, everyone. The day-care center, Rosey and Sam, the Traubs. Caitlin's hospital room was so full we ended up leaving some flowers to be enjoyed by the other patients."

"I planned to call the hospital to check on her, but then I saw Rosey and she told me Caitlin had been released today."

"Just a few hours ago. She's sound asleep now, perfectly healthy except for a selective memory of her adventure, which is probably a good thing, and a bright pink cast on her arm." She was babbling, but she couldn't help it. "I didn't hear your truck pull up."

"That's because I walked."

She blinked. "All the way from Thunder Canyon?"

He turned and looked at her. "From the Shriver place just down the road." Then he thrust the rose in her direction. "This is for you."

"It's beautiful. Thank you."

"It's not much, considering all this." He waved at the colorful arrangements.

"It's perfect." Shelby lifted the flower to her nose, the velvety soft petals and fragrant scent taking her back to Saturday night at his trailer.

Looking up, she found his gaze on her.

Was he remembering, too? Did it matter?

No, what was important now was that she had the chance to tell him what she'd wanted to say, what she needed to say.

"You know, I'm glad you stopped by. I tried to find you that first night at the hospital. Actually it was very early in the morning, but you'd already left."

He crossed the kitchen toward her. "Shelby—"

"No, Dean, please let me say this. I reacted terribly when the ambulance arrived with Caitlin. To blame you for what happened was stupid and thoughtless and I'm so sorry." Her fingers tightened around the stem of the rose, the tiny thorns pricking her skin. "You've been so sweet and wonderful. My God, you saved my daughter's life and I never even said thank you."

"You were upset." Dean took a step closer. "I understood that—"

"That's no excuse." Shelby shook her head and backed away, her backside bumping into the counter behind her. "I've heard… I know that you've decided to return home—" Her voice broke and she had to take a moment to swallow the sudden lump in her throat, but she forced herself to keep talking. "I'm sad that what we shared is ending. Caitlin will miss having you around as much as I will, but I'm grateful that my last words to you won't be ones of anger."

Two more steps and Dean was right in front of her, bracing his hands on the counter, caging her in with his body. He leaned in close. "Can I talk now?"

"Um, sure." She jerked her head in a quick nod. "I guess—"

He crushed his mouth to hers, cutting off whatever she'd

planned to say next with a kiss that consumed her. The first swipe of his tongue against hers took her breath, but it was the passion and intensity that had her responding with the same urgency.

She angled her head, the towel falling from around her hair to land on the kitchen floor, but she didn't care. Her muscles tightened as liquid yearning raced through her.

Then slowly he gentled his kisses, now soft and unhurried and achingly sweet. Finally he dragged his mouth away and she found herself leaning forward, reluctant to end the connection between them.

Because once it was broken, she feared he would tell her what that kiss had really meant.

Tears threatened, forcing her to keep her eyelids closed. "I thought you were going to say something," she whispered.

"I just did."

Goodbye.

He was saying goodbye.

She squeezed her eyes tight, but a single tear escaped anyway and trailed down her cheek.

"Oh, Shelby, please don't cry." Dean brushed at the wetness with his thumb. "I'm not going anywhere."

"What?" Her eyes flew open and then she blinked as more tears escaped. She reached to wipe them away, but Dean gently erased them for her. "What are you talking about?"

"Don't you listen to your voice mails?"

Stunned, Shelby shook her head. "I just started to... I didn't have my phone at the hospital. How many did you leave me?"

"I don't know, seven or eight? I hate talking to those things. I sound like an idiot every time."

"But I thought—"

He placed a finger against her lips, stopping her words. "I can figure out what you thought. You listened to town gossip." He smiled and dropped his hand. "Don't you know better than that, Miss Jenkins?"

Shelby thought she did, but now the hope swelling inside her at his declaration had her asking, "So what did you say in those messages?"

"That I had to go home because my dad got hurt—"

"Oh! Is he okay?"

"Yes, he's fine. I also said I had some thinking to do, but that I'd be back by the end of the week."

"But it's only Tuesday."

"I couldn't stay away from you." Dean brushed back her wet hair, his hands cradling her face. "Being away from Caitlin, away from Rust Creek Falls… I love you, Shelby. I've thought about moving here and starting my own contractor business and I'm almost as much in love with that old house down the road as I am with you, but the most important thing is being with you and Caitlin. No matter where that might be. You'd talked about moving away. So if you do, I want to go with you, because any place will be perfect as long as we're together."

Tears filled her eyes again, but this time they came from a place of unbelievable joy. For too long she'd been lost in the past, unable to move forward, too worried that she'd make another mistake.

She didn't have to worry anymore because life wasn't about the mistakes she'd made in the past; it was about living the life she wanted and being lucky enough to find someone to love who wanted to share that life with her.

Dean was the man she loved. The one she wanted to be with. Right here in Rust Creek Falls.

"Could you say that again?" she whispered, winding her arms around his neck, the rose still in her hand.

"Which part?"

"The part about loving me?"

Dean's hands skimmed down her back, landing at her hips

before he pulled her close. "I love you, Shelby Jenkins, and I promise I will for the rest of my life."

"Oh, Dean, I love you, too."

"Okay, no peeking now."

Shelby smiled. "How can I peek with this cloth tied over my eyes?"

Dean returned her grin, even though she couldn't see it. He'd picked her up around noon, glad when she'd told him her mother and Caitlin were out running errands.

That wasn't true. Actually, they were already here. Everyone was here, except for him and Shelby.

"Are you sure I can't take this off yet?" She'd looked a bit hesitant when he'd presented the blindfold, but had finally agreed to wear it when Dean told her it was part of her surprise. "You've parked the truck, so I'm guessing we're here?"

"Not yet." He shut down the engine and then raced around to the passenger side and helped her out. Eyeing the rocky incline before them, he made a split-second decision and scooped her into his arms.

"Hey!"

"Shh, it's just easier this way."

Dean cradled her close and dropped a quick kiss on her lips. She relaxed in his embrace, much like she'd done four days ago when he told her how much he loved her.

And she'd said the same to him.

Since then, they'd both been busy with work and he went over to her place in the evenings for dinner and to spend time together, but Shelby was still uneasy about leaving Caitlin for long periods of time. He understood that and hoped he wasn't taking things too fast with his surprise for her today.

"So, I know we're outside because the sun feels wonderful and the air smells so fresh and clear and… Wait, is that water I hear?" Shelby turned her head. "Are we at the falls again?"

Dean remained silent as he walked up the last rise, easily

spotting the small crowd gathered around a picnic lunch. He smiled at everyone and sent Caitlin a wink as he walked past her. The little girl blinked back at him and giggled.

"Okay, I know that giggle." Shelby started to squirm. "What is Caitlin doing here?"

"Relax, Mama," she called out. "It's a surprise!"

"Yeah, it's a surprise," Dean repeated, his voice low. "And we're almost there."

"Almost where?"

Moments later, Dean planted Shelby's feet to the ground, making sure she was steady before he reached behind her and loosened the covering and eased it away.

She blinked in the bright sunshine and looked around, her eyes growing round with surprise once she realized where she was standing. "Oh, Dean! The bridge! You rebuilt Daddy's bridge."

"Actually a group of kids from the high school wood shop did the work with a little help." Dean took her hands in his, loving the expression on her face. "Thanks to photographs, they were able to re-create the original design. They've been working hard to get it finished before school starts next week."

"Oh, it's beautiful!" She lightly trailed her fingers across the waist-high timber railing. "What a wonderful surprise. Thank you."

"Wait, we're not done yet." Dean turned and motioned for the people behind him to come forward. "There are some folks here I'd like you to meet."

It took a few minutes to introduce Shelby to his family as everyone had made the trip up from Thunder Canyon. His father, his left arm in a sling to support his recovering collarbone; his brothers, Nick, whom Shelby already knew, and Cade; Cade's wife, Abby; his sister, Holly, and her husband, Bo Clifton, and their daughter, Sabrina, who already seemed quite taken with Caitlin as the two girls stood together and chatted.

Shelby's mom admitted that she'd found out about the picnic just last night from Dean but agreed to play along to surprise her daughter. Soon, everyone was enjoying a picnic lunch and it meant the world to Dean to see Shelby and her family embraced by his.

"Did I throw you into the deep end of the pool here?" He nudged Shelby's shoulder with his own as they sat together on one of the blankets. "You know, with my family?"

"Sort of," she said, then smiled in return. "I thought maybe we'd take a trip down to Thunder Canyon—you, me and Caitlin—in the next couple of months so we could meet everyone, but this was very sweet. Everyone in your family is so nice. Thank you for a wonderful day."

"Do you think you can stand a bit more wonderful?"

"What do you mean?"

Dean got to his feet, held out his hand and helped Shelby up. He led her back to the bridge, enjoying her delight at being able to stand there as the rushing creek flowed beneath them.

"I love you, Shelby." He took her hands and stood right in front of her. "I want to spend the rest of my life with you, and be a proper father to Caitlin and any other children who might come our way."

"Dean, what are you saying?"

He reached into his pocket and pulled out the small velvet box. Dropping to one knee, he held tight to one of Shelby's hands as the other had flown to cover her mouth when she gasped. "I'm saying, I know this is awfully fast, maybe too fast, but this summer love between us is a forever love and I want you to be my wife." He opened the box and showed her the solitaire diamond inside. "Will you marry me?"

"Oh, Dean, yes! Of course! Yes!"

As their families clapped and cheered behind him, Dean slipped the ring on Shelby's finger, then rose and took her into his arms. The promise of love and happiness he saw there told him they'd found their happily-ever-after at last.

Together.

* * * * *

"She's your daughter."

His mouth snapped shut, his face paled. "Why would you concoct such an outrageous story?"

"It's not a story—it's the truth." Kelly should have known telling him would be a mistake. She stood up. "I thought you—and Ava—had a right to know. But I'd rather she didn't know the identity of her father than know he doesn't want her."

Jackson pushed away from his desk as she reached for the handle of the door. "Wait." He slapped his hand against the frame. "You can't drop a bombshell like that and just walk out."

He stood so close that he breathed in her hauntingly familiar scent. Memories of that long-ago weekend teased his mind, and something stirred low in his belly. Even now, when she was making accusations that could turn his life upside down, he couldn't ignore the heat thrumming in his veins.

"We're done here," she said.

He moved closer. "We're not even close to being done."

HIS LONG-
LOST FAMILY

BY
BRENDA HARLEN

MILLS
BOON

First published in Great Britain 2013
by Mills & Boon, an imprint of Harlequin (UK) Limited,
Eton House, 18-24 Paradise Road, Richmond, Surrey TW9 1SR

© Brenda Harlen 2013

ISBN: 978 0 263 90133 7
ebook ISBN: 978 1 472 00516 8

23-0813

Harlequin (UK) policy is to use papers that are natural, renewable and recyclable products and made from wood grown in sustainable forests. The logging and manufacturing processes conform to the legal environmental regulations of the country of origin.

Printed and bound in Spain
by Blackprint CPI, Barcelona

Brenda Harlen is a former family law attorney turned work-at-home mum and national bestselling author who has written more than twenty books for Mills & Boon. Her work has been validated by industry awards (including an RWA Golden Heart Award and the *RT Book Reviews* Reviewers' Choice Award) and by the fact that her kids think it's cool that she's "a real author."

Brenda lives in southern Ontario with her husband and two sons. When she isn't at the computer working on her next book, she can probably be found at the arena watching a hockey game. Keep up-to-date with Brenda on Facebook or send her an email at brendaharlen@yahoo.com.

This second book in my series about brothers is dedicated to my brother, Jim, who was part of my inspiration for Jackson Garrett—and who will no doubt experience much of the same angst as this story's hero when his beautiful daughters get to be Ava's age…

With special thanks to Emily Baker for proofreading Ava's scenes to ensure that I wasn't completely out of touch with the current teen generation. Someday you will find a romantic hero worthy of you—in the meantime, enjoy the journey, YOLO

Prologue

Kelly Cooper glanced at her watch as she slipped her feet into a pair of navy blue pumps and bit back an exasperated sigh. Every day, it was the same. No matter what time she woke her daughter, it seemed they were always running behind schedule.

"Come on, Ava. We're going to be late."

The twelve-year-old raced down the hall, her backpack in one hand and a piece of paper in the other.

"Sorry, Mom. I forgot that I need you to sign something."

Kelly dug into her bag for a pen. Her daughter was famous for holding on to trip permission and lunch order forms until the morning that they were due, usually when they were already late getting out the door.

Ava flattened the page out on the table by the door so that Kelly could scrawl her signature on the dotted line. But something about the way her daughter's hand was splayed over the top of the page triggered Kelly's maternal radar. She tugged the page out of Ava's grasp, caught the headline at the top—CONSENT FOR BODY PIERCING OF A MINOR.

When she was sure that she could speak calmly, she turned to her daughter and said, "Nice try, Ava."

"Come on, Mom. *Please.*"

"No." She tore the paper in half, then in quarters, and opened the door. "Let's go."

Ava's deep green eyes, the mirror image of her father's, filled with tears. "It's just my belly button."

"It's not *just* anything," Kelly argued. "Which I told you last week when you came home raving about Rachel's sister's hips being pierced. I am *not* letting you permanently disfigure any part of your body with holes or ink."

"Why not?"

"Because you're twelve years old." She locked the door and headed down the hall to the elevator.

"I'm almost thirteen," Ava said.

Actually, she'd only celebrated her twelfth birthday a few months earlier, but that wasn't the issue. "Still nowhere close to eighteen," she pointed out. "If you want a belly button ring when you're eighteen, I won't be able to say no. But until then, that is the answer."

"You're *so* mean."

"You've mentioned that once or twice before," she acknowledged as they exited on the ground floor.

"Miranda and Corinne have belly button rings, and Rachel's getting hers pierced on her birthday." Ava climbed into the passenger side and latched her belt. "Because her mother's cool, and because she believes it's a way for Rachel to express her individuality."

"How can it be an expression of her individuality if she's having it done to be like everyone else?" Kelly countered.

Ava huffed out a breath. "Why do you always have to treat me like a baby?"

"Because you are my baby," she reminded her.

Her daughter was silent for a long minute, but Kelly knew better than to think that she'd given up. It wasn't in Ava's nature to back down on anything. As she proved when she said, "I bet if I had a dad, he'd let me get my belly button pierced."

It was a familiar argument. Whenever Kelly didn't give

her daughter what she wanted, Ava played the no-father card. And while Kelly didn't let the arguments sway her, she couldn't deny the guilt that inevitably swamped her. Because Ava *did* have a father, but she'd never met the man who had contributed to her DNA—and that man had no idea that he had a child.

She tried not to think about him, but she'd never forgotten him. Not since the night of her sixteenth birthday, when he'd kissed her. In that first moment that his lips touched hers, he'd also taken hold of her heart. It was several years later before their relationship progressed beyond that single kiss, before the one weekend they spent together changed her whole life.

He was the only man she'd ever really loved, and when he'd chosen to be with someone else, Kelly had taken her shattered heart and her unborn child and moved as far away as possible. But it turned out that halfway across the country still wasn't far enough to outrun the memories, guilt and regrets.

"This isn't negotiable," she said firmly.

Ava fell silent again, pouting.

On her way to her daughter's school, Kelly tried to remember what she'd been like as a twelve-year-old girl. She'd been shy and withdrawn through most of her childhood, cautiously trying to find her way in the world. Thankfully, she'd had Lukas Garrett to guide her. Maybe it was because her best friend was a boy, but she'd never thought too much about clothes or makeup. She'd never worried about keeping up with fashion trends or trying to attract boyfriends; she'd never dyed her hair or worn black nail polish. And she certainly hadn't been thinking about body piercings or tattoos.

Of course, she'd grown up in a different time, and Pinehurst, New York, was definitely another world. Though fifteen years had passed since she'd first gone away to college and the population of the town had increased exponentially, she knew that not much else had changed. Pinehurst still was, and probably always would be, a small town at heart. It was a place where neighbors talked to one another on the street, where the residents baked cookies to welcome newcomers, and where traditional values continued to be revered. Recently Kelly had found herself thinking that it would be nice to raise her daughter in a town like that.

As she pulled up in front of the school to drop Ava off, her thoughts drifted back to the email Lukas had sent to her the previous day, and she cursed him for tempting her with the link to a job posting at Richmond Pharmaceuticals. Because she *was* tempted and she didn't want to be; because going back to Pinehurst would inevitably mean revealing the secret she'd kept throughout her daughter's entire life.

If she stayed in Seattle, on the other hand, everything would remain status quo. Unfortunately, the status quo was no longer as satisfying as it used to be. And while a cross-country move wouldn't make Ava happy in the short term, Kelly believed it would be the best thing for her—maybe even for both of them—in the long term.

A new start in a new town, a new school, new friends… and maybe even a chance to finally meet her father.

Chapter One

Four months later—

"Sorry I'm late." Jack Garrett slid into the vacant seat across from Gord Adamson, a former law school class-mate and occasional courtroom adversary, at The Winking Judge, a small pub across the street from the courthouse.

"I was surprised to get your call," Gord admitted. "I thought you'd given up criminal law."

"So did I," he agreed. "But every once in a while, there's a client I can't turn away."

"Because you believe in his innocence?"

"Because I believe that he deserves a break."

The waitress came over, momentarily disrupting their conversation. Gord ordered a scotch, neat, and Jack asked for a bottle of the locally brewed Millhouse beer.

"I reviewed the file, Jack. And I'm sorry, but I don't see probation for Travis Hatcher."

"Come on, Gord. He's just a kid."

"A kid who took a baseball bat to a Mercedes that is worth more than twice my annual salary," his colleague pointed out.

"It was his father's car," Jack told him, though even he wasn't sure if that was a mitigating or an aggravating factor.

"With incidental damage to two other vehicles."

"Restitution has already been made to the owners."

Gord sighed. "What's your connection to this kid?"

"I handled his parents' divorce a few years back," Jack admitted.

"Rough one?"

"I don't seem to get any other kind, but this one was particularly difficult. A ten-year marriage that fell apart because the husband couldn't keep his pants zipped and the wife couldn't keep looking the other way. They fought over each piece of artwork and every stick of furniture, but mostly over who was going to get stuck with their ten-year-old son."

Gord, a father with two sons of his own, winced. "Damn, Jack. You're yanking on my heartstrings here."

"He isn't a bad kid," Jack insisted. "He just got caught in a bad situation."

"Give me some background," the prosecutor suggested.

"A few months back, Travis was invited to a weekend camp to try out for the national amateur all-star tournament. There wasn't anyone at the camp who doubted he would make the team. But instead of being offered a roster spot, he was sent home."

"I can understand that he would be disappointed and upset," Gord acknowledged. "But that doesn't justify his actions."

"That's not the end of the story," Jack told him. "About two weeks before the tournament, the number-one center fielder breaks his collarbone. There's no way he can play, so Travis calls the national team coach, asks him to give him another chance to prove that he can fill the vacancy. And the coach bluntly tells him, 'You're good enough, but you're never going to play on any team that I'm coaching. If you want to know why—ask your father.'"

"The kid's dad screwed the coach's wife," Gord guessed.

Jack nodded. "Which he finally admitted when Travis confronted him after baseball practice."

"Jesus." His friend lifted his glass, swallowed a mouthful of scotch.

"There was no premeditation—he had the bat in his hand, and he simply reacted," he explained. "Under the circumstances, can you blame him?"

"Actions have consequences, and he has to be responsible for those consequences."

"Absolutely. But the consequences should be commensurate with the action. He had *a moment* where he acted impulsively and recklessly, but a criminal record will stick with him *for life*."

"You stay up late last night working on that spin?"

"The truth doesn't need spin."

Gord considered that for a moment. "Is he remorseful?"

"Very." Jack passed a handwritten note across the table.

His colleague skimmed the page; he scrubbed a hand over his jaw. "Damn you, Jack."

"You're repeating yourself, Gord." He passed over several more pages. "Character references from his teachers, guidance counselor, principal, high school baseball coach, his boss at the grocery store where he works part-time, and supervisor of the homework club where he volunteers twice a week."

Gord sighed. "You really think you can get probation?"

"With a joint-sentencing recommendation, I do," Jack said.

"I'll go joint if anger management is one of the terms of probation, but the final decision is still up to the judge."

"Of course," he agreed.

Gord took another sip of his drink. "You still dating Angela from the registry office?"

Jack shook his head. "That was over a long time ago."

"No thoughts about settling down and starting a family at this stage in your life?"

"Hell, no." His failed marriage might be in the past, but it wasn't so distant that he'd forgotten. And how could he when he spent almost every day in meetings and motions with husbands and wives who had once promised to love, honor, and cherish their spouses and were now hating, dishonoring, and spurning them?

His friend chuckled. "Are you sure you don't want a minute to consider your response?"

Jack shook his head. "I was married once," he confided. "When I was young and stupid."

"Was it that girl you were with in Chicago?"

Jack paused with his bottle halfway to his lips. He'd forgotten that Gord had been at the same law conference he'd attended more than a dozen years earlier in Chicago. "No," he said now. "That wasn't her."

"So who was she?" Gord asked curiously. "Because I seem to recall that you had some pretty intense chemistry with her."

He frowned, as if trying to recall the details of those three glorious days that were still indelibly imprinted on his mind, then shook his head. "I don't remember."

His friend snorted. "Yeah, and I took a job in the district attorney's office for the extravagant salary."

"Why did you leave private practice?" Jack asked, because it seemed like an opportune moment to shift the topic of conversation.

"Because when Sheila and I got married, she understood that I wanted to get my practice off the ground before I took any time off for a vacation. On our third anniversary, she reminded me that we still hadn't had a honeymoon."

"And yet, you're still married," he mused.

"Because I was smart enough to realize that I needed to balance my personal life and my professional life. Five years and two kids later, it was the smartest move I ever made—even if it means that my kids will have to go to public school."

"Thankfully not something I have to worry about."

"Never say never," Gord warned.

But Jack wasn't worried. He was thirty-seven years old and happy to be on his own. And while he dated—albeit a lot less frequently than he had in the past—he always said goodbye without any regrets. The sole exception was the one unforgettable weekend he'd spent in Chicago with Kelly Cooper.

Yeah, he had a boatload of regrets where she was concerned. He regretted walking into The Four Brothers pub for a drink—and not walking right back out again when he realized the gorgeous bartender who'd snared his attention was none other than the girl who'd lived next door when they were kids.

He regretted giving in to the irresistible urge to taste the sassy mouth that had tormented him for more years than he wanted to admit; he regretted succumbing to the need to explore every inch of her soft, silky skin with his hands and his lips; he regretted losing himself—over and over again—in her warm, willing body. Mostly he regretted ever letting her go.

"Speaking of family," Gord said, drawing Jack's attention back to the present, "I should get home to Sheila and the boys."

He started to call for the waitress, but Jack shook his head. "You go ahead. I've got the bill."

"Thanks." Gord slid out of the booth, offered his hand. "I'll bring your client's case forward for a plea on Wednesday, when Judge Parrish is sitting."

"I appreciate it," he said, confident in the knowledge that Judge Parrish had never overruled a joint recommendation.

After his colleague was gone, Jack sat alone, nursing a

second beer. He was grateful for Gord's cooperation with
Travis's case—and annoyed that just the mention of Chicago had brought memories of Kelly Cooper to the fore-
front of his mind.

Not that those memories were ever very far away, especially not since his brother had informed him that she
was coming home.

He didn't understand why she was the one woman he
couldn't forget. They'd spent one unforgettable weekend
together, but neither of them had mentioned the possibility of anything more. So when Kelly called a few months
later—shortly after Sara had decided she'd been too hasty
in ending their engagement—he'd been completely caught
off guard. Just the sound of her voice had the memories
flooding back and desire stirring. Then Sara had walked
into the room and pointed to her watch, and he'd admitted
to Kelly that he had an appointment with a wedding planner. After a brief moment of awkward silence, Kelly had offered a quick congratulations and an even quicker goodbye.

Six months later, he'd married Sara. About two years
after that, Kelly married some guy out in Seattle. Now
they were both divorced, and despite all the years that had
passed, he hadn't forgotten about her. For some inexplicable
reason, memories of one long ago weekend still stirred his
blood more effectively than most of the flesh-and-blood
women he'd dated in recent years.

Maybe it was because he still felt guilty about the fact
that he'd slept with the girl who had been his brother's
best friend since childhood. Yeah, it was the guilt, he assured himself.

Because Jack refused to consider that he might have
had feelings for Kelly that ever went any deeper than that.

* * *

The knots in Kelly's stomach tightened as the plane touched down on the runway.

This was it—there was definitely no going back now.

Not that she wanted to go back. Although she'd made the decision to move back to Pinehurst quickly, it hadn't been impulsively. Which made her realize she'd been thinking about it for a lot longer than she'd been ready to acknowledge. Because no matter where else she might have lived, Pinehurst was still home.

She'd had such grand plans when she'd moved to Seattle. A new city, a new job, a new husband. Even when she and Malcolm had gone their separate ways, she hadn't wanted to leave Seattle. Of course, Malcolm's mom—the only grandmother Ava had ever known—had still been a big part of their lives. Kelly knew she wouldn't have made it through those first few years without her former mother-in-law, and when Beverley Scott had passed away, she'd been at a loss. Not only because Bev had willingly stepped in whenever Kelly needed someone to watch her little girl, but because the older woman had been Kelly's best friend in Washington.

Now it was time for a fresh start again. After more than a dozen years on the West Coast, she had no regrets about leaving. But she wasn't entirely sure she wouldn't regret coming home.

The plane pulled up at the gate, and the knots multiplied.

Okay, she was more than a little nervous, but she reminded herself that she was doing this for Ava. This decision, like every other decision she'd made since she'd learned that she was pregnant, had been focused on what was best for her daughter. Even if Ava didn't agree.

And the words she spoke, as they made their way off the plane, confirmed that she didn't. "I can't believe you made me leave Seattle to come here," Ava grumbled.

Kelly hadn't expected that her daughter would be overjoyed by her decision, but she had hoped that she would have accepted it by now. "You know, if you weren't so determined to hate it, you might actually like it here," she told her.

"I doubt it."

She didn't argue. The choice had been made and their new life was about to begin, so all she said was "Grab your suitcase."

They'd packed only what they needed for a few days, with the rest of their clothes and household items being shipped.

Ava hauled the bag off of the conveyor belt. "How are we getting to Pinecone?"

"Pine*hurst,*" she corrected automatically. "And Uncle Luke said he would pick us up and take us to our new place."

"When are we getting a car?"

"Before August fifteenth," Kelly assured her, because that was the date she was scheduled to start her new job as an in-house accountant at Richmond Pharmaceuticals.

Ava rolled her eyes. With the purple streaks she'd added to her hair during her last sleepover at Rachel's house and the gloomy expression on her face, she looked too much like a typical sullen teenager—and she was still only twelve. As much as Kelly desperately hoped this move would help turn things around with Ava, she knew that any change would take time.

"I'll probably start looking tomorrow," she said, hoping to appease her daughter. "I just wasn't keen on picking up a rental and then driving to Pinehurst after spending all day on airplanes."

"How far is Pinetree?"

"About an hour from here," she said, not bothering to correct her on the name of the town again. Instead, she grabbed the handle of her own suitcase. "Let's go find Uncle Luke."

Kelly headed out of the baggage claim area, then stopped so abruptly Ava plowed right into the back of her.

"Geez, Mom," her daughter grumbled.

Kelly didn't—*couldn't*—respond.

Because standing at the car rental counter, where Lukas said he would be waiting, was his brother, Jackson, instead.

"Mom?" Ava prompted, sounding genuinely concerned. "What's wrong?"

Kelly had to remind herself to breathe, and she exhaled slowly. "Nothing's wrong," she lied, not wanting to alarm her daughter. "I just lost my train of thought for a moment."

"Well, put brake lights on next time," Ava suggested. Then, after looking around, "I don't see Uncle Luke anywhere."

"Apparently there's been a change of plans," Kelly noted, trying to keep her tone light while she inwardly cursed Lukas Garrett all the way to hell and back.

"Does that mean we're going to rent a car?" Ava asked.

"No, it means you're going to meet Uncle Luke's brother."

A lot sooner than I had planned.

She stood for another minute, still rooted to the spot, and just looked at Jackson. She hadn't seen him in thirteen years, but she'd recognized him immediately. But it was more than the dark brown hair that was always immaculately trimmed, more than the exquisitely shaped mouth that had inspired so many of her teenage fantasies, and more than the green eyes that were as dark and clear as emeralds. It was even more than the fact that he was six feet of solidly built male, with broad shoulders and strong arms that ensured any woman would feel secure and protected in his embrace. It was, more than anything else, the way Kelly felt when she looked at him—all hot and tingly and tongue-tied.

Sternly reminding herself that she wasn't still sixteen years old—or even twenty-one—she took a step toward him.

He glanced up from the book he was reading—a legal journal of some kind—as if he sensed her approach. She'd noticed that the book was in his left hand, and that the third finger was bare. But the fact that he'd been divorced for quite a few years now didn't make him any less off-limits.

As he closed the cover of the journal, his gaze skimmed over her, from the top of her head to her toes in a quick, cursory perusal that nevertheless caused heat to flare low in her belly and spread through her veins. She hadn't counted on this, and that was a definite miscalculation on her part.

But how could she have known that, after so many years, he would still have this effect on her? Because even from a distance, even after so much time, she couldn't deny her body's instinctive response to him. Or the ache in her heart.

She pushed her bangs away from her face and silently reprimanded herself for even noticing that her hair was as flat and tired as the rest of her. She'd dressed comfortably for travel in a pair of faded jeans and an ancient University of Chicago sweatshirt and had put on the barest touch of makeup before heading out to the airport more than ten hours earlier. As a result, she felt not just unprepared but ill-equipped to come face-to-face with Jackson now.

When she'd decided to return to Pinehurst, she'd known it was inevitable that she would see him. But she hadn't planned on seeing him when she was looking like *this*. She knew it shouldn't matter, but when a woman was facing an ex-lover, she wanted to look her best. Unfortunately, she wasn't even close.

Those green eyes lifted to her face again. "Hello, Kelly."

Two simple words, but after so many years of silence, the achingly familiar voice was like a warm caress.

Her heart was pounding inside of her chest, but she inclined her head and responded in a similarly casual tone. "Jackson."

His lips curved, just a little, and she suddenly remembered that no one else, aside from his mother, had ever called him "Jackson." At least not more than once. But he'd never been Jack to Kelly—that name was too common, and Jackson was anything but. She had, occasionally, shortened his name to Jacks, but that seemed too familiar now.

He shifted his attention to her daughter again. "You must be Ava."

The girl nodded, her gaze darting from her mother to Jackson and back again, as if she sensed the strange undercurrents between them.

Kelly held her breath, waiting for any sign of recognition. But there wasn't any. And why would there be? Unless Lukas had shared the occasional photos that she'd sent to him, Jackson had never seen her daughter before. But she'd thought he might see some of the familial resemblance that Kelly saw whenever she looked at her little girl.

"I'm Jack Garrett, Luke's brother." He offered his hand.

Kelly fought an almost irresistible urge to cry as she watched them shake hands. It broke her heart to see the distance between them, but what had she expected? It was her fault that neither of them knew the truth of their connection.

Thirteen years ago, Jackson had been focused on his career above all else. He'd been clear that he had no interest in having a family, at least not any time in the near future. That was one of the reasons why Kelly had honestly believed she'd made the right decision. But she didn't know what was right for any of them now.

She wanted Ava to know her father, but only if Jackson

was prepared to *be* a father. And she was afraid to finally reveal the secret she'd kept for so long because she knew that when she did, it was quite possible he would hate her—either for keeping his child from him for so many years... or for bringing her into his life now.

"You seem surprised to see me," Jackson said, speaking to Kelly again as they made their way toward the exit.

Surprised was barely the tip of her emotional iceberg, so she only said, "I was expecting Lukas."

"He said he'd let you know that I'd be meeting you instead."

"Maybe he tried," she admitted, taking her cell out of her purse. "I turned off my phone when we boarded the plane."

She powered it up now and heard the familiar chime that indicated a text message. But since it was written in Luke's unique form of shorthand and without any punctuation, she had to read it twice before she figured out what it said.

Srry kel ER at clinic cant meet u sending j instead will stop by ur plc if not 2 late

Gee, thanks for the warning, Lukas.

"I'm guessing that's his message," Jackson said, his voice tinged with humor as he popped the trunk of his car to load their suitcases.

Of course he would find this amusing. He wasn't the one who'd been blindsided by the change of plans.

"You guessed right," she agreed lightly, then slid into the soft leather passenger seat of his luxury sedan.

Ava was already in the backseat with her mp3 player plugged in, leaving her mother to make conversation with Jackson. But Kelly didn't know what to say. She'd known that she would see him again—but she hadn't expected that he would be the first person she saw at the airport, and she mentally cursed Lukas again.

Of course, he couldn't know what he'd done. After all, he didn't know that his brother was the only man she'd ever really loved.

Well, this is more than a little awkward, Jack thought, as he pulled out onto the highway heading toward Pinehurst. He'd suspected that it would be, considering that the last time he'd seen Kelly, they'd both been naked. Which was definitely *not* something he should be thinking about right now—not under any circumstances and certainly not with her daughter in the backseat.

He tightened his grip on the steering wheel, but the smooth, warm leather beneath his palms made him itch to feel the much softer, warmer texture of Kelly's skin. Not that he really knew what her skin felt like—it was ridiculous to think that he could recall those kind of details after so much time had passed. So why was he convinced that her skin was softer than silk? Why did he remember that her body had responded not just willingly but eagerly to his touch? And why couldn't he forget that, throughout that one weekend they'd spent together, he'd wished it would never end?

Of course it had ended, and they'd gone their separate ways. Since then, they'd both married and divorced other people. The main difference being that Kelly had come out of her marriage with a child. He frowned, trying to remember the age of her daughter. For some reason, he couldn't recall Luke ever mentioning that she was pregnant or that she'd had a baby. He'd just one day mentioned Kelly's daughter as if the little girl had always existed.

He glanced in his rearview mirror, confirming that Ava was tuned in to her music and tuned out to everything else.

"She's tall for her age, isn't she?"

Kelly seemed surprised by the comment—and a little wary. "How old do you think she is?"

"Well, considering that you got married just over eleven years ago, I figured she couldn't be more than ten."

"That's a reasonable guess," Kelly agreed, without actually confirming the accuracy of it. But before he could question her further, she spoke again. "Lukas said that the house I'm renting is next door to Matthew's new place."

Jack nodded. "In fact, the house is owned by his mother-in-law, Charlotte Something-Something Branston."

"Something-Something?"

"There might be a few more 'somethings,'" he told her. "She's been married a few times."

"Where does she live?"

"Montana."

He smiled in response to her quizzical look. "Long story."

"It's a long drive," she reminded him.

She was right, and since talking about Matt and Georgia was easier than trying to manufacture another topic of conversation, he filled her in on some of the details.

"Georgia had three-year-old twins and was pregnant with her third child when her husband died, so Charlotte suggested that she leave Manhattan and move to Pinehurst to live with her. A few months after Pippa was born, Charlotte headed off to Vegas for a couple of weeks with some friends, fell in love with a cowboy from Montana, and married him. So Georgia was in an unfamiliar town and on her own now with three kids, and then Matt moved in next door."

"And the young mother suddenly had a white knight riding to her rescue," Kelly guessed.

"Actually, he's an orthopedic surgeon," Jack reminded her teasingly.

"But no one does the white-knight routine better than your big brother."

"True," he agreed. "But in this case, I think it might actually have been Georgia and her kids who saved him. Matt had a really hard time after the divorce."

Kelly's nod confirmed that she was aware of those details. "Sounds like Matt and Georgia were lucky to find one another, that each was exactly what the other was looking for, even if neither of them realized it."

"They do seem perfect for one another, and Matt absolutely dotes on her kids." Of course, Jack's oldest brother had always wanted a family of his own.

"He would," she agreed. "Although a lot of men wouldn't want to take on the responsibility of someone else's child."

He didn't miss that she'd said child and not children, and he suspected that she wasn't thinking of Matt and Georgia now but of another situation—possibly even her own. And he wondered if she spoke from experience, if she'd been alone since her divorce, reluctant to get involved again for fear that another man wouldn't accept her daughter.

But he didn't ask, because it was none of his business. They'd had a brief fling that was ancient history—he had no right to pry into her personal life now.

Except that the history between them continued to haunt his dreams, even after thirteen years. And even more so since he'd learned of her intention to return to Pinehurst.

He still didn't know what had precipitated the move, or what Kelly's daughter thought about her decision. He couldn't imagine that it was easy for a kid to be uprooted from everything that was familiar and moved clear across the country.

He glanced in the rearview mirror again. Kelly's daughter was a beautiful girl, with long, dark hair just like her mother—aside from the purple streaks, of course. Her eyes were a similar shape, too, and fringed with long, sooty lashes. But the color of her eyes was different. Kelly's eyes were the warm, golden color of aged whiskey; Ava's were a clear, emerald green.

He stole another glance, trying to figure out what it was about the child that made him uneasy.

"I guess Ava will be attending Parkdale," he said now.

"That's the plan," Kelly agreed. "I just hope she's lucky enough to make the kind of friends that I made at school there."

"It must have been difficult for her, leaving Seattle."

"It would have been more difficult if we'd stayed."

It was a surprising revelation from a woman who had previously volunteered no information about her reason for the move across the country. But she didn't say anything else, and though he was curious, he didn't press for any details.

Instead, as they passed the elementary school, he said, "You'll be happy to know that Mrs. Vanderheide finally retired a couple years ago."

She smiled. "That is good news—at least for Ava."

"And for all future generations of seventh graders," he agreed. "Which was proven by the fact that almost all of Pinehurst turned out for her retirement party at the school. She thought they were all there to celebrate her forty years of teaching, but I think everyone just wanted to make sure that she really was retiring."

The sensuous sound of her soft chuckle heated his blood. *Ancient history,* he reminded himself again.

He tightened his grip on the steering wheel and turned onto Larkspur Drive, grateful the journey was almost at its end.

"This is it," he said, pulling into a wide asphalt driveway beside the two-story saltbox-style house. He noticed that there were lights on at both the front and back doors—

no doubt Matt's wife wanted the place to look warm and welcoming, and it did.

"Georgia said she would leave a key in the mailbox," he told Kelly now. "She also wanted you to know that they had a cleaning company come in yesterday to give the whole house a thorough once-over and that she was in today to inspect and put clean sheets on the beds."

"I'll have to remember to thank her for that," she said. "Because right now, I'm tired enough to fall face down on any horizontal surface."

He shifted into park and glanced in the rearview mirror again. "Apparently your daughter doesn't need to be horizontal."

Kelly turned to look at Ava, who had fallen asleep with her head against the window. Since the days when she could carry her slumbering child were likely long gone, he wasn't surprised when she reached back to tap the girl's shoulder. "Wake up, Ava. We're home."

He was surprised by her use of the word *home,* and he frowned as it echoed in his head. It seemed strange to him that, after being gone for more than fifteen years, Kelly would still refer to Pinehurst as home. He hadn't known if this was a temporary relocation or a permanent move, and he refused to admit that it mattered. He could have asked Luke, of course. No doubt his brother was privy to all of the details of her plans. But asking Luke anything about Kelly when he'd been so careful not to mention her name for so long would undoubtedly trigger more questions that Jack wasn't prepared to answer.

There was little he didn't share with his brothers, but the fact that he'd spent a wild weekend with Kelly Cooper was a secret he'd kept for thirteen years—and one that he had no intention of revealing now.

Chapter Two

While Kelly roused her daughter, Jack retrieved their luggage from the trunk. He took the suitcases upstairs, setting the one with Kelly's name on it in the biggest room and her daughter's in the room directly across the hall. A quick glance at the tag gave him pause.

He couldn't remember the name of the guy Kelly had married, but regardless of whether or not she'd taken his name, he would have expected their child to have it. But the tag read *Ava Cooper*—and it made him think again about the reasons for Kelly's divorce and her decision to move Ava so far away from Seattle.

Reminding himself that it was none of his business, he headed back down the stairs and, following the sound of voices, into the kitchen.

"You're only asking for mushrooms because you know I don't like them," Kelly said.

"I'm asking for mushrooms because I *do* like them and that's what I want on my pizza," her daughter insisted.

"Well, no one else does, so we're not getting them."

He knew he shouldn't get involved and he had no intention of staying, but Jack heard himself say, "I like mushrooms."

Ava looked at her mother, her smile more than a little smug. Kelly didn't look annoyed; she looked…unnerved. Which didn't make any sense to him at all.

"And bacon?" Ava queried.

"And bacon," he confirmed.

"Fine, I'll get half with bacon and mushrooms," Kelly relented. Then she looked at Jack. "Which means that you're staying for pizza."

"If you'd told me you were hungry, I could have stopped somewhere on the way from the airport," he told her.

"I didn't realize how hungry I was until now."

"Then you should order from Marco's—they deliver and they're quick."

He gave her the number, and while Kelly made the call, Ava ventured upstairs to check out her new room and start unpacking. After pizza was ordered, Kelly took a look around. She'd seen photos and even videos of the house before signing the lease, but she wanted to see everything up close. Jack opted to respond to some email messages on his BlackBerry while she explored.

She was back in less than ten minutes, and obviously pleased with everything she'd seen. "Lukas told me the place was furnished, but I didn't expect it to be so well equipped. There are pots and pans and dishes and cutlery in the kitchen—and even toilet paper in each of the bathrooms. Something else I'll have to thank Georgia for, because I didn't think to pack any of that in my suitcase."

"I'd be surprised if you had room," Jack said. "Considering that you each only brought one suitcase and one carry-on."

"I prefer to travel light, but there's a lot more to come. It just seemed easier—and cheaper—to ship the rest rather than pay the airline fees for extra baggage."

"Makes sense," he agreed.

But he still had questions about her sudden decision to return to Pinehurst after so many years away. And he had an uneasy suspicion that nagged at the back of his mind. He hadn't wanted to ask it while her daughter was in the backseat of his car—even if she had seemed oblivious to their discussion—but it was a question that needed an answer.

"I just hope it arrives on schedule," Kelly continued her explanation about the luggage. "Because my work clothes are in that shipment and I start my new job on the fifteenth."

"Was it the job that lured you back to Pinehurst?"

"It was the deciding factor, but I've been thinking about coming back for a while," she admitted. "I wanted a fresh start for Ava and myself."

Jack tipped her chin up, forcing her to meet his gaze.

The contact was casual, but he would have sworn that sparks flew at the brief touch of his fingertip against her skin. Judging by the way Kelly's eyes widened, she'd felt them, too.

He dropped his hand, forced himself to remember the question he needed to ask. "Was he abusive?"

She blinked, clearly startled by the inquiry. "What? Who?"

"Your ex-husband," he said. "Because I've been wracking my brain, and that's the only reason I could imagine for taking a child three thousand miles away from her father."

Kelly dropped her gaze and shook her head. "No, Malcolm wasn't abusive."

He wanted to feel relieved—he *was* relieved. And yet, he couldn't let go of the suspicion that there was something more Kelly wasn't telling him.

A suspicion that was confirmed when she looked up again and said, "And he wasn't Ava's father."

Kelly held her breath, waiting for Jackson's response to her revelation. But before he could say anything, the doorbell rang and Ava was racing down the stairs in response to the summons. "Pizza's here!"

And that quickly, any chance of taking the conversation further was gone.

Her daughter flung open the door without first looking through the peephole to confirm that it was their food delivery. Of course, in Seattle no one could gain access to their door without first being buzzed into the building, so now that things were different they would have to have a discussion about basic safety precautions.

Or maybe not, considering that this was Pinehurst, where many of the residents didn't even lock their doors during the day. And wasn't that one of the reasons she'd brought her daughter here? To give her the benefits of living in a small, close-knit community. Of course, an even bigger reason stood right beside her.

As it turned out, it wasn't their pizza at the door—it was Lukas with his arms full of grocery bags. Setting the bags down inside the door, he swept Ava up for a big hug. "There's my favorite girl."

The girl in question would have been absolutely mortified by such an overt display of affection from her mother, but her cherished "uncle" got away with a lot. And Kelly suspected that the prospect of living in close proximity to Lukas was the one reason that Ava hadn't kicked harder and screamed louder about the move.

He ruffled her hair. "What's with the purple streaks?"

"Mom wouldn't let me have a belly button ring."

"Makes perfect sense to me. And speaking of your mom…"

He turned to wrap his arms around Kelly, squeezing her so tight she could hardly breathe, but it felt so good—so right—to be in his arms that tears filled her eyes.

"I missed you," she told him now. "I never realize how much I miss you until I see you again."

"I'm just glad that you're finally home." He released her

with obvious reluctance and looked at his brother. "Thanks for doing the airport run."

"When have I ever objected to picking up a beautiful woman?" Jackson asked.

Lukas chuckled. "Never."

The knots in Kelly's stomach returned. Was Jackson's comment just brotherly banter or a statement to her—a reminder that she'd never meant anything more to him than any other casual pickup? And why did she even care? She hadn't come back to Pinehurst to rekindle her relationship with Jackson but for Ava to establish a relationship with her father.

Now his words gave Kelly pause. Was he still a relentless flirt and unrepentant playboy? Because that was hardly the type of male role model that she wanted for her impressionable daughter. Or was she just looking to find fault, to justify her own actions? Since that was a question she couldn't answer right now, she shifted her attention to Lukas instead.

"I should have figured you'd be here in time for pizza," she said, as the delivery car pulled up in front.

"Am I?" He turned to follow her gaze and grinned. "My timing is impeccable as usual."

As Kelly dug in her purse for money to pay for their dinner, she couldn't help thinking his timing would have been much better if he'd been able to meet them at the airport. But she could breathe a little easier now, confident that she'd survived her first face-to-face with Jackson relatively unscathed.

She knew they had to finish their interrupted conversation at some point, but not today. Not when her heart was already feeling battered and bruised by the callous remarks of a man who probably had no idea how much he could hurt her. Instead, she gestured for Jackson to follow Ava—and the pizza—into the kitchen.

He shook his head. "I need to get going."

"I thought you were going to stay for pizza," Kelly said.

"I've got files to review for court tomorrow."

Lukas retrieved the bags he'd dropped. "The files will still be there in half an hour," he pointed out to his brother.

"I'm sure you guys have lots to catch up on," Jackson said. "You don't need me hanging around."

"Your choice—and more pizza for me," Lukas said with a shrug and a grin as he headed toward the kitchen.

Kelly wished she could be so nonchalant, but she wasn't sure if she was relieved or disappointed that Jackson was leaving. She followed him to the door. "Thanks again for meeting us at the airport."

"It wasn't a problem," he assured her.

Her heart was pounding so hard and fast, she was surprised he couldn't hear it, and she had to moisten her suddenly dry lips before she could speak. "What I started to say, when we were in the kitchen, about Ava's father—"

"It's not really any of my business," he said.

Actually, it is, she wanted to respond. But aloud she only said, "I *want* to talk to you about it. There are some things you should know."

He frowned. "Do you have legal questions about custody?"

She wondered how he could be so oblivious—or maybe she expected too much of him. After thirteen years, he had no reason to suspect that she had news that would turn his whole life—*all of their lives*—upside down. And instead of being exasperated, maybe she should be grateful that he had no clue, because it meant that she could keep her secret a little bit longer.

Except that coming face-to-face with her daughter's

father, she was forced to acknowledge that thirteen years was already too long. Jackson needed to know the truth, and she needed to deal with the consequences of that revelation—whatever they might be.

"It's nothing like that," she said to him now. "I don't want to talk to you as a lawyer but as a…friend."

"Okay," he finally said. "Why don't you give me a call when you're ready to talk?"

If she waited until she was ready, she knew that the conversation might not happen for another thirteen years. But she nodded. "I will. Thanks."

"Okay," he said again, and then he was gone.

Kelly stood for a moment, staring at the back of the door and feeling much like she imagined Pandora had felt when she'd lifted the lid of a box that should never have been opened.

Lukas and Ava were both on their second slices of pizza by the time Kelly made her way to the kitchen. They also had cans of soda, which Lukas had obviously brought in one of the grocery bags. Beside Kelly's plate was an open bottle and a glass of her favorite Shiraz.

"Okay, you're forgiven for not meeting us at the airport."

He smiled. "I figured you'd had a long day and might need some help to unwind."

"Food and good company would have sufficed, but the wine is a definite bonus." She picked up the glass and sipped.

"Eat." He nudged her plate toward her. "If you drink that on an empty stomach, you'll fall asleep at the table."

Kelly dutifully picked up a slice of pizza and took a bite.

"I brought a few essentials for the morning, too," Lukas told her. "Bread, milk, eggs, juice, coffee."

"Coffee?" She nearly whimpered with gratitude. "Now you're definitely forgiven."

Ava polished off her third slice and wiped her fingers on a paper napkin. "Can I go now?"

"'Thanks for dinner, Mom,'" Kelly said, mimicking her daughter's voice. "'You're very welcome, honey.' 'May I be excused now?' 'Of course.'"

Lukas lifted his can of soda to hide his smile. Ava, predictably, rolled her eyes, before she dutifully intoned, "Thanks for dinner, Mom. May I be excused now?"

"Of course," Kelly said agreeably. "*After* you put your plate in the dishwasher."

Lukas reached for another slice as Ava clomped up the stairs. "So," he said, when she was out of earshot. "How does it feel to be back?"

"I'm not sure," she admitted. "It's been such a long time. I don't know if this is the right thing—for Ava or for me."

"She's not happy about the move?"

"That's the understatement of the year."

He shrugged. "She's twelve. She'll get over it."

"I hope so."

"So—belly button ring?" he prompted.

She just shook her head. "Can you believe it?"

"I'm having a little difficulty reconciling my memories of the cute little second-grader who clutched my hand so tightly with the brooding purple-haired preteen-ager who barely looked up from her plate."

"The purple streaks aren't so bad. You should have seen her a few months ago—her hair was Pepto-Bismol pink. Her best friend's older sister put the color on for her one afternoon when I had to work late." She sighed. "The first tangible evidence that my formerly docile angel had developed a rebellious streak."

Lukas winced sympathetically. "How did you handle that?"

"I took a deep breath and reminded myself that hair color is easily undone—unlike a piercing or a tattoo. And I knew that it was, at least in part, my fault. I'd been so preoccupied with my job that I didn't realize how much distance had grown between us," she admitted.

"When rumors of cutbacks first started circulating around the lunchroom at work, I crossed my fingers and prayed that I wouldn't lose my job. And when those cuts were made and I was spared, I was so grateful I didn't balk at all the extra hours I had to work.

"And then I realized that I'd given up my life to keep my job. And I'd somehow lost the close connection I used to share with Ava." Her daughter's recent willful behavior was proof of that—and reminded Kelly uncomfortably of the impulsiveness that she herself had occasionally exhibited before motherhood had taught her to consider the consequences of her actions.

"And because I was working so many extra hours," she continued her explanation, "Ava was hanging around with her friend Rachel—and Regan, Rachel's sixteen-year-old sister—a lot."

"Then I'd guess that you made this move at the right time."

"I hope so," she said again.

"What aren't you telling me?"

Kelly lifted her glass and took another sip of wine as she considered how much she should say.

"Because I know there's more to this cross-country move than that," he prompted when she failed to respond.

She nodded. "I wanted a career change and a change of scenery for Ava, but I also hoped that coming back to Pinehurst might provide a chance for her to meet her father."

His brows rose. "Then he does live in Pinehurst."

"He does live in Pinehurst," she confirmed.

"Someone I know?" he asked.

The undercurrents in his tone were exactly why she'd never revealed the identity of her daughter's father to him. "Doesn't everyone know almost everyone else in this town?" she countered.

"Who is it?"

She touched a hand to his arm. "Please—let me tell him before I tell you."

He frowned. "Are you saying that this guy doesn't know he has a twelve-year-old daughter?"

"I couldn't tell him," she reminded Lukas. "By the time I knew I was pregnant, he was already with someone else."

She'd wanted to tell Jackson that she was going to have his baby. Although she'd had no expectations of a future for them together when he'd left Chicago, she'd hoped that the revelation of her pregnancy would make him want to be a father to their child. But as much as she didn't want to do it alone, she'd had no doubt—even then—that she was going to keep her baby.

Except that when she'd finally gotten up the nerve to call, he'd told her that he was once again engaged to Sara Ross—the daughter of one of the senior partners at his firm. And while Kelly didn't believe he would get married solely for the purpose of advancing his career, she didn't doubt that dumping the boss's daughter would jeopardize his future at the firm. And nothing had mattered to Jackson as much as his career. So she'd only offered congratulations and ended the call with her heart in pieces and the news of her pregnancy unrevealed.

"Yeah, you told me what happened," Lukas admitted now. "But you didn't tell me who the father was."

"No, I didn't," she agreed. "And I'm not going to tell you now. Not until I've told him."

She could tell by the muscle that clenched in his jaw that Lukas wasn't finished with his interrogation, but she also knew he wouldn't press for more details. At least not yet.

Jack was distracted, and he'd never been the type to let anything—or *anyone*—interfere with his concentration, especially when it came to his work. He was a well-respected and generously compensated family law attorney because he was diligent and focused. He paid attention to details and he made every client feel as if his or her case was the only one that mattered.

And yet, in the middle of a cross-examination during a custody hearing that morning, he'd actually lost his train of thought. Sure, he'd recovered fairly quickly, and it didn't seem as if anyone else in the courtroom had even noticed that he'd faltered. But he'd noticed. And he knew that it was Kelly Cooper's fault.

"Hello, Jackson."

He blinked, half-suspecting that her appearance in the open doorway of his office was an illusion, and more than half-hoping that she would disappear again. But when he opened his eyes, she was still there—and looking even hotter than the woman who had starred in his dreams the night before. And the night before that. In fact, every one of the five nights that had passed since she'd come back to Pinehurst.

She made her way across the carpet, putting one sexy foot in front of the other in the way that women had perfected to make their hips sway and men drool. And as much as he wished it weren't true, he was very close to drooling.

Damn, she looked spectacular. In the slim-fitting burgundy skirt, silky white V-neck blouse and peep-toe shoes that added close to three inches to her five-foot-seven-inch frame, she looked professional, confident—and dangerous.

He frowned at the thought, but he couldn't deny it was true. For too many years, Kelly Cooper had threatened his peace of mind. It had been easy enough to ignore the girl next door when she was a kid. Then adolescence had turned her bony, sticklike figure into a woman's body with subtle but undeniable curves. And he'd started to have very inappropriate fantasies about his little brother's best friend. Thankfully, he'd gone away to school and had managed to put her out of his mind. Mostly.

"You told me to call you, but you haven't returned any of my calls. I was beginning to think I would have to schedule an appointment to see you."

"I'm not hard to find, but I am busy," he said pointedly.

"I can appreciate that," she said. "And I promise you, I wouldn't be here if it wasn't important."

"How did you get past my secretary?" Colleen was usually a pit bull when it came to protecting her boss's time and space.

Kelly just smiled. "Your secretary was my eleventh-grade lab partner."

Having lived in Pinehurst his whole life, he understood that personal connections frequently trumped protocol. "Okay, that answers the how," he admitted. "But not the why."

She settled into one of the client chairs on the other side of his desk, and crossed one long, shapely leg over the other. "I just wanted to talk to you without my daughter or your brother interrupting, so I asked Colleen if she could squeeze me into your appointment schedule."

"Now you've stirred my curiosity," he admitted. And certain other areas as well.

"Your brother was, and still is, my best friend," she reminded him. "And while you and I were never close friends, we used to be friendly. And then, for one incredible weekend, we were a lot more."

Whatever he'd expected when she'd walked through his door, it wasn't a walk down memory lane. Not that he was unwilling to take the journey, but he knew it was unwise. His past with Kelly was the past—no way would he risk starting anything up again with his brother living in the same town. Luke had always been protective of his friend and if he ever suspected that Jack had been naked with Kelly—well, Jack didn't even want to think about what he might do. It was smarter, and safer, to keep the past in the past. "Why are you bringing this up now?"

"Because I'm hoping, now that I'm living in Pinehurst again, that we can get back to being friendly."

"Have I been unfriendly?"

"Not exactly," she admitted. "You've been…distant."

"I've been busy," he said again.

"Your brother and sister-in-law invited Ava and I over for burgers last night and while we were there, one of Georgia's sons asked Matthew why 'Uncle Jack' hasn't been around to visit in so long. Matt told him you had a big court case coming up, but the way he looked at me before he responded made me think he was making excuses."

"He wasn't."

"I don't want you to feel uncomfortable visiting your brother and his family just because I'm living next door."

"I don't."

She shifted forward in her chair, enough so that he could see the slightest hint of cleavage in the V-neck of her blouse. "You're not worried that the chemistry that exploded between us thirteen years ago might still be simmering?"

"No," he lied.

"Well, that's good then," she said, but her easy smile didn't reach her eyes.

"Thirteen years is a long time," he said, in an attempt to convince himself as much as her.

She nodded. "It always boggled my mind that I could be such good friends with Lukas, that I could snuggle up with him to watch a movie, hold his hand as a gesture of comfort or support, and never feel anything remotely like the zing that I felt whenever I was in the same room with you."

"Chemistry is a personal thing," he noted.

She tilted her head to look up at him. "Have you ever felt that zing with anyone else?"

"Too many times to count," he lied.

She seemed disappointed—and maybe even a little hurt—by his casual response. But Kelly being Kelly, she didn't try to deny her feelings or hide behind a flippant response. She was, as always, brutally and painfully honest.

"I haven't," she told him. "From the first time you kissed me, on my sixteenth birthday, I've never felt that zing with anyone else."

"Not even your husband?" he challenged.

She shook her head. "No, not with anyone else."

Knowing how incredibly passionate she was, he was surprised that she would settle for comfort and companionship. On the other hand, it might explain why her marriage had failed.

"I think you're romanticizing the memory," he told her.

"Maybe," she allowed. "But it wasn't my first kiss. And you weren't my first lover—but you're the one I've never forgotten."

Even if what she was saying was true, he wouldn't let it matter. Because rekindling a romantic relationship with Kelly wasn't an option. Getting involved with a woman who was also his brother's best friend could only lead to a whole lot of grief, not to mention the fact that she had a kid to think about.

So instead of admitting that he'd never forgotten her either, he only said, "Is there a purpose to this reminiscence?"

"I wanted you to know that I had some concerns about coming back to Pinehurst now."

"Because of what happened between us so many years ago?" he asked skeptically.

Her smile was sad. "Is that so unbelievable?"

"Yes," he said.

"Did you never think of me after that weekend?"

"Sure," he said easily. "But I didn't think that one weekend changed anything."

"It changed everything—at least for me," she told him. "But when I called, you were already back together with Sara."

"It's not like you called a few days later," he felt compelled to point out in his own defense. "It was more like a few months."

Actually, two months, three weeks and five days, and during that time, not a single day had gone by in which he hadn't picked up the phone to call her. But he'd never actually dialed her number, because he knew it would be a mistake. Because after only three days with her, he'd known that he could fall fast and hard for Kelly Cooper, and that was a complication neither of them needed at that point in their lives.

She nodded in acknowledgment. "I know."

"And Sara and I had a history together," he continued. "So when she said she'd made a mistake in ending our engagement, I agreed that we should try to work things out."

"Because you loved her," she said softly. "And I was

just the girl who helped you forget—for a few days—that she'd broken your heart."

He heard the vulnerability in her tone and he knew that, even after so many years, his reconciliation had hurt her. But the truth was, he'd never thought about Sara—not once—throughout the weekend that he was with Kelly. So instead of nodding and letting her believe it was true, he said, "I wanted you to believe that."

She frowned at his admission. "Why?"

"Because we'd both agreed, at the end of the weekend that we'd spent together, that it couldn't ever happen again. And then you called, and I could hear in your voice that you'd changed your mind, that you wanted more." And in that moment, as much as he'd wanted *her*, he knew there could be no future for them together. Not at that time and definitely not in light of the conversation he'd had with his brother.

"And you didn't want more," she guessed. "Not with me."

"What I wanted didn't matter," he told her. "You were still in school and barely twenty-one years old."

"You're right—I was twenty-one years old." She paused to draw in a deep breath before looking up at him. "And I was pregnant."

Chapter Three

Jackson stared at her for a long moment, as if he couldn't quite comprehend what she was telling him. When he finally spoke, his tone conveyed as much confusion as his words. "You were…pregnant?"

She nodded.

He frowned but didn't say anything else.

"On the way from the airport, you asked how old Ava was. She turned twelve in February."

"Are you saying…?" His question trailed off, as if he couldn't bear to speak the words out loud and acknowledge the possibility.

But Kelly had been holding on to the secret for too many years and she wasn't going to hide the truth for even a minute longer. "She's your daughter."

His mouth snapped shut; his face actually paled. But after another pause, which was probably only a few seconds but felt like hours, his gaze narrowed and he shook his head. "Nice try, Kelly."

She felt her back go up. "What is it you think I'm trying to do?"

"Suck me into paying twelve years of child support."

"Child support?"

"I know you came back here to work at Richmond Pharmaceuticals, but losing your job in Seattle must have—"

"I *chose* to leave my job in Seattle," she interjected.

He shrugged. "Regardless of the reason for your financial difficulties—"

She couldn't help but laugh at the absurdity of his allegation. Because the truth was, between the inheritance left to Kelly by her grandmother and the trust set up for Ava by her former step-grandmother, she had no immediate financial issues. "You really think this is about money?"

"I can't imagine any other reason that you would concoct such an outrageous story."

"Maybe it seems outrageous to you," she acknowledged. "But it's not a story—it's the truth."

He snorted derisively. "Are you willing to submit your daughter to DNA testing to prove it?"

"Absolutely."

Her immediate and unequivocal response finally seemed to give him pause.

"Trust me, Jack, if I got to choose a father for my daughter, I wouldn't have chosen someone who's made it more than clear that he doesn't want to be a father."

He considered that for a moment, then asked, "You really do think I'm her father?"

"You really think I had so many lovers I don't know who fathered my child?"

"I wasn't your first," he said, in an echo of her own statement.

"No," she agreed. She hadn't been innocent, but she had been inexperienced. "You were my second."

He winced. "How the hell was I supposed to know something like that?"

"You weren't," she admitted. In fact, she'd done everything she could to ensure he didn't know. Afraid that her naïveté might put him off, she'd tried to make up for her lack of experience with enthusiasm. She'd been in love with him for so long, nothing had mattered to Kelly except that she was finally going to be with him.

"You told me you were on the pill," he said now.

"No." She felt her cheeks flush at the memory of that awkward conversation. "When the condom broke, you asked if I was 'safe' and I said yes."

"But you weren't," he said accusingly.

"I thought you were talking about the risk of sexually transmitted diseases."

Jack scrubbed a hand over his face. "It would have been nice to have clarified that little misunderstanding thirteen years ago."

"I was young and naive, but even if I could, I wouldn't change anything that happened back then because it gave me my daughter."

"Except that you're now claiming she's my daughter, too."

She should have known this would be a mistake. She'd suspected that he would be shocked, and probably more than a little angry. But his disbelief cut her to the quick. She had *never* slept around and there was *no* possibility that anyone else was the father of her child.

Of course, Jack had no way of knowing that—especially considering that she'd had no direct contact with him over the past thirteen years. But that didn't make his accusation hurt any less. She stood up. "I thought you had a right to know. I thought *Ava* had a right to know. But I'd rather she didn't know the identity of her father than to know that he doesn't want to be her father."

"*If* I am her father—"

Kelly cut him off with a sharp expletive and turned away, but not before he saw her eyes fill with tears.

Jack tried to ignore the twist of guilt. He hadn't barged into her place of work with outrageous accusations. Why should he feel guilty just because he wasn't willing to accept her claim unequivocally? Well, he wasn't. He had questions, and he damn well wanted answers to those questions.

And now she was just going to walk out?

The phone on his desk buzzed. "Donald Winter is here for his two-thirty appointment," Colleen announced.

He pushed away from his desk as Kelly reached for the handle of the door. "Wait."

"No." She shook her head, refusing to look at him. "I'm done here."

He slapped his hand against the frame. "You can't drop a bombshell like that and just walk out."

"You have a client waiting," she reminded him.

But right now, Donald Winter and his legal issues were the least of Jack's concerns. In fact, standing so close to Kelly, breathing in her hauntingly familiar scent, he could barely remember the client's name. He tried to focus his thoughts on the here and now, on Kelly's revelation and his response to it. But memories of that one long-ago weekend teased the back of his mind, and he felt something begin to stir low in his belly.

He dropped his hand from the door, curled his fingers into his palms so that he didn't give in to the urge to touch her. Because he'd lied. When she'd asked if he'd ever felt the same zing with anyone else, he'd blatantly and unapologetically lied. It was true that he'd been attracted to other women—probably too many other women—but never had he experienced an attraction as compelling or intense as his desire for Kelly.

Even now, even when she was making wild accusations that could turn his entire life upside down, he couldn't ignore the heat thrumming in his veins. And because he was standing so close to her, he could see the pulse point pounding at the base of her jaw, and he knew that she was feeling that zing, too.

"The client can wait," he said to her now.

She finally looked at him, and he was relieved to see that her golden eyes were clear again, with no hint of the tears that had twisted knots in his belly. "There's no reason to make him wait—we're done here."

"We're not even close to being done."

"I said everything I wanted to say and you've made your feelings on the subject more than clear."

"Dammit, Kelly, I don't know what I'm feeling," he admitted. "But as an attorney, I'm finding it difficult to accept the word of a former lover without any concrete proof when I know there's no way in hell I would let any client of mine do the same."

"We used to be more than lovers, Jack. We used to be friends."

"We used to be," he agreed. "But I haven't heard a single word from you in thirteen years."

"Why would I lie about something that is as easy to disprove as it is to prove?" she challenged.

It was a good question, and one he probably should have considered. But his mind had been reeling since he'd heard her say "I was pregnant"—and frantically trying to reject the possibility that her child could be his.

Because kids weren't anywhere in his plan. Sure, he'd considered the possibility when he was married, but when his marriage had fallen apart, so had the expectation that he would someday have a family. Now Kelly wanted him to believe that he was the father of her twelve-year-old child? His brain simply refused to wrap around the possibility.

"So you really want to do a DNA test?" he asked her now.

"No," she said. "What I really want—and probably what

you want, too—is to forget we ever had this conversation. Unfortunately, I know that's not going to happen."

He shook his head. "No, it's not. And if—"

Her steely glare had him biting back the words and frantically seeking another direction for his thoughts.

"*If* you have some time tonight," he said quickly, "I could stop by and we could discuss this in more detail."

She shook her head. "I'm not talking about any of this around my daughter."

"Don't you mean *our* daughter?" he challenged.

"Make up your mind, Jackson. You can't deny paternity in one breath and use it as a weapon in the next."

"I just want the truth."

"And you need a DNA test for that? Did you even look at her?"

"She looks like you," he said dismissively.

And though it was undeniably true, there was something about the girl that had—even at a first glance—nagged at him. "If that's all you saw, maybe that's all anyone else will see," she said.

"So you're just going to walk away?"

"I told you, Jacks—I thought you had a right to know. But I have no desire to force you into a role you don't want to fill."

"You can't blame me for being suspicious," he said. "It's my job to ask the tough questions."

"And you've obviously done well enough at your job to get your name on the door," she noted. "Or was that a wedding present?"

His gaze narrowed. "I don't remember you having a nasty streak."

"We spent three days together more than thirteen years ago—there were a lot of things you didn't know, never mind remember."

And then she yanked open the door and walked out.

* * *

Jack met with Donald Winter, but he cancelled the rest of his afternoon appointments after that. Actually, he told Colleen to cancel his appointments on account of a family emergency—a request that had her jaw falling open. Because Jack Garrett never cancelled appointments for any kind of personal reasons, because nothing had ever mattered more to him than his career. But right now, he couldn't focus on anyone else's legal problems. He couldn't think at all with Kelly's words still ringing in his ears.

She's your daughter.

He still had trouble believing it could be true. And yet, as much as he wanted to continue to deny even the possibility, deep in his heart he knew Kelly wouldn't lie about something so monumental. Nor would she have made the claim unless she was one-hundred-percent convinced that it was true.

Which meant—Lord help him!—that he was the father of Kelly's daughter. He had a daughter. And not a chubby-cheeked infant or even a wide-eyed toddler but a twelve-year-old. For God's sake, the kid was practically a teenager!

And to Jack's mind, that was definitely a family emergency.

When he left the office, he did so without any kind of plan. He only knew that he needed some time and space, so he got into his car and drove. Since the death of his parents, family had been himself and his two brothers. Now that Matt was married to Georgia, that family had grown to include his new sister-in-law and her three children. And considering that Luke was a lot like Matt with respect to his ideals about hearth and home, Jack figured his younger brother would also hook up with one woman and have a family of his own someday.

But that wasn't Jack's future. When his marriage ended,

he figured any chance of someday having a family had ended with it. And truthfully, he hadn't been too disappointed. The whole wife-and-kids thing had never been his life's ambition. But now it seemed he had a kid, whether he wanted one or not. And right now, he was leaning in the direction of "not." He wasn't proud to admit it, and he knew it wasn't what Kelly wanted to hear, but it was true. He was thirty-seven years old, content with his life. Adding a child to the mix now would turn everything upside down.

Not that it was his choice to make. The fact of Ava's paternity wasn't something that could be debated. A test would either prove that he was her father or—dammit, he knew there wasn't any "or." In his gut, he knew that Kelly was telling the truth. The fact that she hadn't faltered or flinched when he'd demanded proof of paternity convinced him that she had absolutely no doubt that he was the father of her child. Which meant that he had to accept not just the possibility but the probability that her twelve-year-old daughter was also his daughter.

He knew his responsibilities, at least in so far as the law was concerned. Despite Kelly's claim that she didn't want financial support, he understood that a father had a legal obligation to contribute toward his child's maintenance— to ensure that she had food, clothing and shelter. And he would do so.

It was his rights more than his responsibilities that gave him pause. He was more than willing to write checks, but did he want to play any more of a role in the child's life beyond that?

His practice in the field of family law had demonstrated to him time and time again that some people instinctively knew what it took to be good parents, and some people didn't. And he'd often wished that those who didn't would realize it before they made the mistake of procreating.

His brother, Matt, had always wanted to be a father, and when his girlfriend of only a few weeks told him she was pregnant, he hadn't hesitated to marry her. He'd been a doting husband, catering to Lindsay's every want and need—and thrilled beyond belief when Liam was born. Three years later, Lindsay admitted that Liam wasn't really Matt's son, that she'd already been pregnant when she seduced him. She'd chosen Matt because she knew he would want to be a father to her child, but once Liam's real father was back in the picture, she wanted to be with him. Considering his brother's experience, was it any wonder Jack was skeptical of Kelly's claim?

Not that the experience had sidetracked Matt from his ultimate goal of having a family of his own. Not for too long anyway. Once he got over Lindsay's betrayal and the loss of his son, he'd jumped with both feet into a relationship with his beautiful neighbor—a widow with three kids. In fact, Jack had stood up for Matt at his wedding to Georgia only a few weeks earlier, and though Shane and Quinn and Pippa weren't Matt's biological children, Jack knew his brother couldn't love those kids any more if they were.

Which only proved to Jack how different he was from his brother. When faced with the news that he was a father, he didn't feel the least bit paternal, just panicked. After his divorce, he'd accepted that fatherhood wasn't in the cards for him and moved on. And he'd felt no twinges of loss or regret. In fact, he'd been grateful that he and Sara hadn't had any children to fight over during the divorce. Not that they'd fought over much of anything. By the time she'd filed for divorce, it was obvious to both of them that whatever passion they'd once shared had long since burned out. Neither of them cared enough to take issue over anything.

Before she moved out, Sara had accused him of being cold and unfeeling, and Jack had accepted that she might

be right. He figured the numbness was a natural conse-
quence of having been witness to the breakdown of so
many marriages and the nastiness that often accompanied
the splits. Except that he only had to spend five minutes
with Kelly Cooper to be feeling all kinds of emotions he
didn't want to feel.

But the one that rose above all others, at least right now,
was anger. He was furious that she hadn't made any effort to contact him at all over the past thirteen years. He'd
been divorced for more than eight years and he was sure
Luke would have advised her of the fact. Not because he
suspected the news would have any significance to her, but
just because he told her pretty much everything. But Kelly
still hadn't initiated any contact. She hadn't even called to
tell him that she was planning to move back to Pinehurst.
And though it was a free country and she certainly didn't
need his permission to change her residence, it would have
been nice if she'd given him some kind of heads-up that
she was planning to turn his entire world upside down.

He'd actually worried that she'd moved halfway across
the country because of difficulties with her ex-husband.
He'd assumed that she had some reason for taking her
daughter away from her father. Now he learned that she
was actually moving the child *to* her father. *Him.*

He yanked at his tie, unfastened the button at his throat.

He hadn't paid too much attention to Kelly's daughter
when he'd met them at the airport. In fact, he'd tried not
to pay too much attention to Kelly, either. He'd only been
there because Lukas had asked him for a favor. But he had
noticed—it was impossible not to notice—how much the
girl looked like her mother.

She had the same willowy build, the same dark hair. But
even when he was trying not to notice, the daughter's eyes
had nagged at him. The shape and color of her eyes was

very similar to Lukas's—a coincidence that he'd immediately disregarded because the idea of Kelly and Lukas in a romantic relationship was one he didn't like to contemplate.

He hadn't thought about the fact that his brother's eyes were very much like his own, which meant that the child's eyes were like his own. But apparently, even at that first meeting, his subconscious had recognized the possibility his mind still didn't want to acknowledge.

And he knew now that his life was never going to be the same.

Kelly had expected to feel relieved after telling Jackson about Ava, but when she left his office, she was more angry than anything else. She was hurt by his accusations, infuriated by his questions. She wanted to rant and scream, except there was no one she could rant to or scream at. Desperate for an outlet for her turbulent emotions, she decided to clean.

Despite the fact that she and Ava had moved in less than a week earlier, she attacked the furniture with a polishing cloth and an enthusiasm born of anger and frustration. Dust was viciously annihilated, smudges ruthlessly obliterated, but nothing wiped the memory of Jack's skepticism from her aching heart.

She plugged in the vacuum and turned her attention—and fury—to the carpets, hopeful that the whirring of the motor might drown out the thoughts in her head. And she nearly jumped out of her skin when a hand came down on her shoulder.

She stepped on the power button and pressed a shaky palm to her heart. "Lukas—you nearly gave me a heart attack."

"I called out, but you obviously didn't hear me."

"Obviously." She tucked a stray hair behind her ear. "What are you doing here?"

"You're not happy to see me?" he teased.

"I'm always happy to see you. I was just wondering why you stopped by."

"Because I can—because you're no longer three thousand miles away."

She managed a smile, but he frowned and touched a fingertip to the shadows beneath her eyes. "What's going on with you?"

"I'm just tired," she hedged. "I've been going nonstop over the past few weeks, in preparation for the move, and I haven't really had a chance to catch my breath."

"So put the vacuum away and give yourself a break," he suggested.

"I wanted to get this done before Ava came home," she said, but tucked the vacuum into the corner.

"Where is she?"

"She went to the park with Georgia and the kids." Kelly led the way to the kitchen, set up the coffee maker to brew a fresh pot.

"She must really be bored if she's hanging out with a couple of four-year-olds," Lukas noted, following her out to the back deck.

"She gets a kick out of the twins—and she absolutely adores Pippa."

"Typical only child," Lukas noted, settling into the Adirondack chair beside her. "If she had brothers and sisters of her own, she wouldn't be nearly as tolerant."

"Probably," she agreed. "But not something I have to worry about."

"But you're worried about something," he guessed.

She traced a finger over a knot in the wooden arm, avoiding his gaze.

"What's going on, Kel?"

"Can we just chalk it up to a really bad day?"

"Do you want to tell me about it?"

She did, but she couldn't. She shook her head.

Lukas frowned. "How is it that you talked to me more when you were living on the other side of the country?"

"I know there isn't anything I can't talk to you about— except this."

"Then it's about Ava's father," he guessed.

She hesitated, then nodded.

"You've seen him?" Lukas pressed.

She nodded again.

"Did you tell him?"

"I told him," she admitted. "And he didn't believe me."

His hands curled into fists on the arms of the chair. "Do you want me to talk to him?"

Kelly reached over and covered his fisted hand with her own. "Thanks, but I don't think that would help."

"What about Jack?"

Her breath caught in her throat. "What about Jack?"

"Why don't you talk to him?" Lukas suggested. "He could outline your legal options, suggest a course of action."

She shook her head, let her hand drop away. "Talking to Jack is not going to fix any of this."

"He's good at his job, Kel. He could—"

"No!" Her response was a little too vehement, a little too loud, and she winced even before Lukas frowned.

She pushed up from her chair, walked across the deck and tried to figure out a way to untangle the mess that she'd made. She wanted to tell Lukas everything, but it was harder than she'd imagined to find the words to reveal a secret that she'd kept closely guarded for so long. Especially when Jackson didn't believe it was true.

She should have been prepared for his questions, braced for his skepticism. But aside from having paternity results in hand, she didn't know what she could have said or done to convince him. And she wasn't going to pretend that he wasn't Ava's father just because he didn't want to be.

Because the simple truth that she'd learned from her visit to Jackson's office was that he didn't want to be a father—at least not to her daughter. Just like her mother and father hadn't wanted to be parents to Kelly. And Jackson's disinterest hurt more than his disbelief. He had every right to be angry with Kelly, but he had no reason to reject the daughter he didn't even know.

"Kelly?" Lukas prompted.

And she found herself trying to guess how he might react to the news—if Lukas would refuse to believe that Jackson was Ava's father, too. She didn't think she could bear it if he questioned the veracity of her claim. But even if he did believe her, he would be hurt by her silence, by her deception.

"I've made a mess of everything," she admitted softly.

She'd thought she was doing the right thing, but really, what had she known? She'd been twenty-one years old, pregnant and in love with her child's father, who was planning to marry someone else. Not the ideal scenario in which to make any kind of life-altering decision. But what alternative did she have? Because as scared as she was to have a baby on her own, she'd had too much pride to want to be with someone who didn't want to be with her.

Pride goes before a fall, her grandmother had been fond of saying. And Kelly knew that her actions in this situation might prove that adage to be true, especially if the decision she'd made ended up ruining her friendship with the one man who had always stood by her.

But even if she could turn back time, she didn't know that there was anything she would have done differently. Jackson had been in love with Sara. She didn't know any of the details of how or why their marriage failed, but she knew that he would never have made plans to marry her if he didn't love her. He and Kelly, on the other hand, had never made any plans.

She certainly hadn't planned to get pregnant, and she had no intention of using her baby to trap him. But she knew him well enough to know that if she'd told him she was pregnant, he would have broken off his relationship with Sara to marry her. He would have done "the right thing"—and he would have hated her for it. And that's why she'd never told him about the baby.

He hated her now, anyway, and she knew that was probably no less than she deserved. She only hoped she could somehow get through this without Lukas hating her, too.

When she heard the doorbell ring, she jumped at the reprieve, grateful for the interruption. Grateful for any excuse to escape Lukas's scrutiny and the inevitable confrontation that would follow her revelation.

Of course, that was before she opened the front door and found his brother standing on her porch.

She didn't realize Lukas had followed her to the door until he said, "Speak of the devil."

"Lukas." Jackson seemed even more surprised to see his brother than Kelly had been to see him at the door.

He glanced at her, a silent but desperate plea for help. But she didn't know what to say or do to extricate them from the suddenly awkward situation.

In that brief moment of charged silence, Lukas's gaze

bounced from Jackson to Kelly and back again. And Kelly knew the exact moment when all of the pieces clicked into place for him because he said, "You sonofabitch."

And then he hauled back a fist and punched his brother.

Chapter Four

Jackson's head snapped back; he stumbled.

"Lukas!" Kelly grabbed his arm as he advanced toward his brother again. "Stop!"

He turned around, so abruptly and with so much fury in his eyes that she took an instinctive step in retreat. "God-dammit, Kelly. My own brother?"

Her eyes filled with tears. "Let me explain."

But he shook his head and turned away.

A few seconds later, the back door slammed and she felt a single tear slide down her cheek.

"I wouldn't mind hearing that explanation," Jackson said.

She swiped impatiently at the trail of moisture and turned back to face him. The pithy response she'd intended died on her lips when she saw the red mark on his jaw. "Let's get you some ice," she said instead.

Jackson followed her through to the kitchen and took a seat at the kitchen table while she rummaged through the freezer.

"I told you that I didn't want you coming here," she reminded him.

"And I decided that you've been calling all the shots for too long."

She wrapped a bag of frozen peas in a clean tea towel and handed it to him. "How did that work out for you?"

He wiggled his jaw, winced. "Well, I didn't anticipate

getting sucker punched by my brother," he admitted, lifting the ice pack to his face. "And I didn't realize he had such a strong right hook."

"You haven't ever been on the receiving end before?"

"Not since we were kids."

The coffee that she'd put on for Lukas had finished brewing, so she poured two mugs and set one on the table in front of him. "I'm sorry. The last thing I ever wanted to do was to cause trouble between you and your brother."

The uninjured side of his mouth tipped up in a half-smile. "I knew you were going to be trouble for me the summer you turned sixteen."

She poured milk into her own coffee, and tried not to remember that summer. Or the fact that she'd fallen head over heels in love with Jackson Garrett the night of her sixteenth birthday when he'd kissed her for the first time.

She'd been so young, so naive. Of course, sixteen was only four years older than her daughter was right now—a reminder that brought her firmly back to the present.

"Why are you here, Jacks? Because I doubt very much you came over to take a stroll down memory lane."

"I blocked a lot of memories," he told her now. "Or tried to—until you showed up at my office today."

"I know I dropped a lot on you—I expected you'd need some time to think about things."

"I've done nothing but think since you left my office," he told her.

She wrapped her hands around her own mug of coffee.

"My head is still reeling," he continued.

She nodded.

"But I realize, in retrospect, maybe I didn't handle it as well as I could have."

"Maybe I didn't, either," she admitted. "Ava had an appointment with Dr. Turcotte this afternoon."

"Is she sick?"

"No, she's fine. I wanted her to have a complete checkup before she started school, anyway, and I asked the doctor, as part of his exam, to take a DNA swab."

"I feel like I should say that it isn't necessary."

"But it is." She met his gaze evenly. "I understand why you want proof. I might not like it, but I understand. And maybe when you have the results, you can let me know what you want to do."

Before showing up at Kelly's door, Jack had driven aimlessly around town for more than two hours, trying to figure out what he wanted to do, and he still didn't have any answers. The only thing he'd known for certain was that he needed to see Kelly—and her daughter. "Is…she here?"

"She?" Her brows lifted. "Do you mean Ava?"

He nodded.

"No, she isn't."

Jack was both relieved and disappointed. Part of the reason he'd steered toward Kelly's house was to see her daughter, because he thought that if he saw her again, he would know. The instinctive sense of relief warned that he wasn't yet ready to know.

"Is she still upset about the move?"

"Well, she only told me she hates it here four times today—it was seven yesterday."

"Sounds like progress."

"Monday will be the real test," she admitted. "That's when I start my new job."

"Is she old enough to be home by herself?" he asked.

"Technically, yes. But it's a new home, in a new neighborhood, so I decided it would be easier for both of us if I enrolled her in camp."

"Isn't she a little old for camp?"

"It's a junior leadership camp designed for kids entering grades seven and eight. It promotes goal setting and peer mentoring, and uses role playing to demonstrate responsible decision-making and leadership."

"What does something like that cost?"

"Is it always about money with you, Jackson?"

He turned over the ice pack, reapplied it to his jaw. "I was just curious."

"Don't worry—I'm not asking you to pay half."

"Does your ex-husband pay support?"

"He's not Ava's father," she reminded him.

"But if he acted *in loco parentis*—"

"He didn't. Malcolm was always very clear about the fact that Ava was *my* daughter. She grew up calling him 'Daddy' but she knew he wasn't really her father."

He frowned at that. "Has he had any contact with her since the divorce?"

"Ava," Kelly reminded him again.

"I know her name."

"Then why don't you say it? Does referring to her by pronouns make it easier to keep her at a distance?"

He scowled, because that was exactly what he'd been doing, even if he hadn't realized it. "Has your ex had any contact with *Ava* since the divorce?"

"She used to see him on a fairly regular basis at his mother's house, but she hasn't seen him at all since Bev died, more than three years ago. Since then, it's just been the two of us." She got up to refill her mug, topped up his, too. "That's one of the reasons I wanted to come home—back to Pinehurst. So that Ava could know her family." She looked across the table at him. "So she could know her father."

"You're not sick, are you?"

Her brow furrowed. "What?"

"Wasn't there a movie where the mother tracks down the father of her child because she's dying?"

"I'm not dying," Kelly assured him. "And even if I was, guardianship arrangements for Ava are set out in my will."

"Lukas," he guessed.

She just nodded, and he tried not to be annoyed that she would entrust her daughter to the care of his brother when she hadn't even trusted him with the information that he was her daughter's father.

"You'll change that if the test results prove that I'm her father," he said.

"*When* the test results confirm paternity, it won't be necessary to change it. The rights of a biological father supersede any contrary provisions in a will—as I'm sure you're aware."

Of course, he was aware—he just didn't appreciate the fact that she'd chosen his brother to be the legal guardian of his child. If he thought about it rationally, he knew that Kelly's long-standing friendship with Lukas made him a logical choice. But he wasn't thinking very rationally about anything right now.

"Your peas are thawed," he told her, and handed the bag across the table.

"I've got corn, too, if your jaw's still sore," she offered.

He moved it carefully from side to side. "No, it's good."

She got up to toss the package of peas into the sink.

"What are you and…Ava doing on Saturday?"

If she noticed the slight hesitation before he said her daughter's name, she ignored it. "Back-to-school shopping."

"All day?"

She smiled at that. "You've obviously never shopped with a twelve-year-old girl."

"Obviously," he agreed, and gave himself credit for

not shuddering at the very thought. "How about Saturday night?"

"Why?"

"Because I was thinking maybe we should spend some time together…." The suggestion trailed off when he saw that Kelly was already shaking her head. "Why not?"

"I just think it's too soon. Until you've actually accepted the truth, you're going to be looking for any tiny piece of evidence to support your hope that Ava's not your daughter."

He frowned and pushed away from the table to take his empty mug to the counter. "I don't know what I hope."

"Your instant and vehement denial when I told you about Ava proved, at least to me, that you don't want to be a father."

"Right now, I'm not sure what I want," he admitted.

But when he turned to face her, he realized that she was now trapped between the counter at her back and him at her front. He knew the smart thing would be to step away, but he didn't. Instead, he lifted his hand and brushed his thumb gently over the curve of her bottom lip.

Her breath hitched, her eyes darkened. "Jacks."

He didn't know if she'd spoken his name in warning or request, and he didn't care. Despite their complicated history, there was something about being in close proximity to Kelly that made him forget everything else and simply burn with need. Heat flared in his belly, pulsed through his veins. He might not *want* to want her, but there was no denying that he did.

"Actually, that's not entirely true," he told her. "I do know what I want—at least in some respects."

She put her hand on his chest and shook her head. "Don't do this, Jackson."

"Don't do what?" he challenged, his lips hovering only inches above hers.

"Kiss me."

He ignored the "don't" and, focusing on the "kiss me" part, brushed his lips against hers.

He wasn't the kind of man who gave in to impulse. At least not since that night he'd taken Kelly back to his hotel room more than thirteen years earlier. But being so close to her now, he found he didn't have the willpower to resist what he wanted. *Just one little taste,* he promised himself. Just a sample of her flavor, to prove to himself that she wasn't nearly as intoxicating as he recalled and rid himself of the haunting memories.

But that sample proved otherwise; one little taste wasn't nearly enough. He settled his mouth over hers, and slowly deepened the kiss. Her resistance melted like a double scoop of ice cream in the August sun—slowly and sweetly. And her flavor was even sweeter.

He traced the shape of her mouth with the tip of his tongue, felt her breath shudder out between her lips. The hand she'd laid against his chest was no longer trying to push him away but clutching at the fabric of his shirt.

He'd wanted to do this since he'd seen her at the airport. Not that he would have admitted it, even to himself, but he'd felt the flare of desire in that first moment when her gaze locked with his. And now that he had her in his arms, he wasn't even close to being ready to let her go.

Then the screen at the back door banged against its frame, and she froze.

"Mom?"

Jack was already stepping back before Kelly pushed him away.

"In the kitchen." She picked up a cloth and began to wipe down the already spotless counter.

Ava poked her head inside the doorway. "Can I hang out next door with the twins and the puppies for a while?"

"If it's okay with Mrs. Garrett."

The child rolled her eyes. "She's the one who told me to check with you."

"Then it's okay with me," Kelly allowed.

"Great." She was gone again as quickly as she'd entered, without ever noticing that Jack was standing on the other side of the room.

But he noticed that Kelly's hands weren't quite steady as she carefully folded the cloth and draped it over the faucet. Had she been as shaken as he by the kiss they'd shared? Or was she simply unnerved by the fact that her daughter had very nearly walked in on them together?

He might have initiated the kiss, but there was no doubt that Kelly had been an enthusiastic participant, and he couldn't help but speculate about how far things might have gone if Ava hadn't interrupted. But maybe he didn't want to know. He suspected that the memory of that kiss was going to be more than enough to keep him awake at night without imagining how Kelly's skin would have felt beneath his fingertips, how her body would have responded to his touch.

He forced those thoughts aside to ask, "Does Ava spend a lot of time with Shane and Quinn?"

Kelly took a deep frying pan out of the cupboard and set it on top of the stove. "She likes to play big sister, and the twins don't seem to mind her bossing them around."

"They might not be siblings, but they could be her cousins—by marriage, if not by blood."

She nodded, confirming that she'd already considered the possibility. When she'd told him that Ava was his child, he'd only thought about how that revelation affected him.

He hadn't considered that his daughter would be a niece to each of his brothers.

Obviously the situation was a lot more complicated than he'd realized—and that was before he'd kissed Kelly.

On Saturday, Kelly took Ava shopping. She wanted to make sure that her daughter had everything she needed to start the new school year and, even more importantly, she wanted to spend some time with her. Ava still wasn't happy about the move, and although she kept in frequent contact with Rachel and some of her other friends online, she was feeling a little lonely.

Kelly knew from personal experience that it wasn't easy to move to a new town and start over again. She'd been a couple of years younger than Ava when she'd been dumped at her grandmother's house in Pinehurst because her father was a long-distance trucker who was gone more than he was home and her mother couldn't handle full-time care of a child on her own. What was originally supposed to be a few weeks had somehow turned into months, and then into years. On her first day of school, she'd been absolutely terrified. And it hadn't been so long ago that she couldn't remember the tangle of knots in her stomach that had made her want to throw up the cereal she'd had for breakfast.

She'd stopped at the corner and stared at the crowd of students already milling around outside of Parkdale Elementary School. Other kids moved past her, most of them in groups, talking and laughing, their friendships established over the years that they'd been together. She didn't know how long she stood there, trying to ignore the churning in her stomach and summon the courage to move forward, when she saw Jackson and Lukas coming toward her.

The Garrett brothers lived next door to her grandmother, so she'd gotten to know them a little bit over the summer.

Lukas was her age, Jackson was three years older, and Matthew was two years older than him and in high school already. But she didn't know much more than that, and she was more than a little surprised when Lukas stopped beside her. Jackson scowled and mumbled something under his breath, but Lukas just waved him on.

"Trying to decide whether to go forward or back?" Lukas asked.

Though her cheeks had flushed with embarrassment that he'd been able to read her thoughts so easily, she nodded.

"If we had Mrs. Vanderheide, I'd tell you to go back. I'd even go with you," he said. "But Miss Ellis isn't too bad."

It was all he said, but he stood patiently, waiting until she was ready. And when she was confident that the Frosted Flakes were going to stay in her stomach, she turned toward the school and he fell into step beside her.

She'd lucked out that day, and she was keeping her fingers crossed that Ava might be half as lucky with the friends she made at her new school—or maybe even before then. Though her daughter wasn't looking forward to camp ("summer camp is for babies"), Kelly was hopeful that she would meet some kids there who would be in her class at Parkdale when school started up in a few weeks.

But for now, mother and daughter were focused on shopping. Of course, Ava complained that all of the stores at the mall and even the more upscale shops in the village were completely lame. Despite that fact, however, she managed to find a couple of pairs of jeans, a skirt, several T-shirts, three sweaters, various accessories and a new backpack. The only real dissension occurred when they passed Gia's Salon & Spa and Ava decided that she wanted more streaks put in her hair. Kelly nixed that plan but suggested that, after several hours of shopping, they both deserved to pamper their feet.

By the time they left the spa, it was almost seven o'clock. Since they were already out and just down the street from Mama Leone's, Kelly decided to treat her daughter to dinner out.

As they made their way to the restaurant, Kelly realized she was smiling. It had been a good day, with only a few minor bumps along the way, and she was thrilled that she'd had the time to reconnect with her daughter.

Her smile slipped when the hostess led them to the back of the restaurant and they passed the table where Jackson was seated across from a beautiful blonde with glossy red lips and fingernails to match the spandex dress that emphasized her impressive curves. His gaze never wavered from his companion, for which Kelly was grateful. She didn't want him to know that she was there, and she wasn't thrilled about the possibility that Ava might spot him, either.

So she made sure that Ava was seated with her back to them, which meant that Kelly was facing their table. And while Jackson flirted with his date, she couldn't help but remember that he'd been kissing her less than twenty-four hours earlier.

It was one kiss, but that one kiss had unleashed a tidal wave of memories that kept her tossing and turning through the night. It wasn't fair that he should still be able to affect her. It wasn't fair that he could kiss her like he'd kissed her yesterday and move on to seducing another woman tonight.

But that was Jackson. She'd known his reputation all those years before, but she'd chosen to overlook it. She'd believed—in her youthful naïveté—that once he was with her, he would realize he loved her as much as she loved him. He would forget that he'd ever wanted anyone else, and they would be together forever.

Obviously things hadn't gone according to her plan. For

Kelly, the weekend they spent together in Chicago only cemented her feelings. For Jackson, it was merely a brief interlude in his life—she was merely one of numerous women who had shared his bed.

And here he was again now, with another woman, proving to Kelly that he hadn't changed at all. He was still a player. And so what? That one kiss aside, she had no intention of resuming any kind of relationship with him. His personal life wasn't any of her business, but she did worry about Ava and how she might respond to the parade of women through her father's life.

Right now, though, she was going to put Jackson out of her mind and focus on her daughter. She *wasn't* going to watch Miss Scarlet feed him bites of her cheesecake. She *didn't* care that the blonde then put the fork to her own lips and slowly licked the tines, obviously savoring his flavor even more than the dessert. Instead, Kelly dropped her gaze and stabbed her own fork into a wedge of tomato.

Ava had already finished her salad and dug into her seven-cheese ravioli with enthusiasm. Kelly forced down a few more bites of lettuce and wondered again if she'd made a mistake in coming back to Pinehurst.

She'd been certain that he would have changed in the past thirteen years. But seeing him here tonight, she realized that was her mistake. He wasn't the man she wanted him to be, and the fact that she was disappointed by that realization was her fault more than his. She hadn't been hoping for any kind of reconciliation with Jackson when she decided to come back—but she had hoped that he could be the father her daughter deserved. Now she knew otherwise.

He finished his coffee and signed the check. Then he offered his hand to the blonde, and she stood up, tottering a little on her skyscraper heels. And when she smiled at him, the curve of her lushly painted lips was full of promise.

Jackson momentarily shifted his attention away from his date—and his gaze collided with hers. She saw the range of emotions cross over his face: recognition, surprise, guilt. It was Kelly who broke the connection, deliberately looking away to prove that she didn't care, that his presence didn't matter, that *he* didn't matter.

But as she poked at her angel hair pasta, she knew it was a lie. The truth was, he'd always mattered to her. Too much.

"Mom—is something wrong?"

Kelly glanced up, forced a smile. "Of course not."

Ava gestured to her plate. "You said you were starving, but you haven't even touched your meal."

"I guess I wasn't as hungry as I thought."

"I'm still hungry," Ava told her.

"Did you want some of my pasta?"

Her daughter shook her head. "Can I have dessert?" she asked hopefully.

Kelly was grateful to realize that some things in life were still simple, and her smile came more easily this time. "You can absolutely have dessert."

"Can we get it to go? There's a movie on TV tonight that I thought we could watch."

Her daughter was actually initiating a plan to spend more time with her? Kelly couldn't have been more pleased. "Sounds good to me."

When they got home, they put their pajamas on and snuggled on the couch together. While Ava watched her movie, Kelly's thoughts wandered. Nothing had gone as she'd planned so far. She hadn't expected Jackson to immediately embrace the fact of fatherhood, but she hadn't anticipated an outright rejection of the claim, either. And while he seemed to be coming around to accepting the truth, Lukas wasn't even talking to her.

She had no intention of going back to Seattle. All of

the reasons she had for leaving were still valid. But maybe she should have considered moving somewhere other than Pinehurst, somewhere where she wouldn't be haunted by memories of the hopes and dreams she'd had so long ago. Except that no other place had ever felt like home. Pinehurst was where she wanted to raise her daughter, and she was confident that Ava would make friends quickly and be happy here.

She didn't realize the movie had finished until she saw the credits rolling on the screen. Pushing her questions and uncertainties aside, she nudged her sleepy daughter up the stairs and tucked her into bed.

"Mom?"

"Hmm?"

"Thanks for today. It was kind of fun—hanging out with you."

And with those words, the last of Kelly's reservations was obliterated. Because she knew now that, regardless of what happened with Jackson, she had done the right thing by bringing Ava to Pinehurst. She brushed the hair away from her daughter's face and touched her lips to her forehead. "Me, too."

She and her daughter had each other and that was enough—neither of them needed Jackson Garrett.

Unfortunately, that didn't stop Kelly from wanting him.

Chapter Five

It was a sign of how complicated his life had gotten in the space of a single week that Jack left a willing woman on her doorstep Saturday night and went home to his empty bed to dream about another.

He woke up alone, aroused, and cursing Kelly Cooper.

She'd turned his entire life upside down with the proclamation that he was the father of her child. Actually, she'd turned his entire life upside down simply by walking back into it. Because even after thirteen years, she was the one woman he'd never been able to forget.

If he'd been a romantic, he might have thought she was "the one who got away"—except that he'd purposefully sent her away because he'd believed it was the right thing to do. When she'd been a kid hanging out with his younger brother, he'd sometimes caught her looking at him with something like hero worship in her eyes. He'd been flattered and amused by her attention, but when he'd gone off to college, he hadn't thought too much about her harmless infatuation or her.

And then he'd come home for Christmas that first year to discover that Kelly Cooper wasn't a kid anymore. Somehow in the four months that he'd been gone, she'd grown up. The skinny kid with a mouthful of braces had become a stunning beauty with interesting curves in all the right places. And suddenly that infatuation wasn't quite so harmless anymore, not when he was experiencing feelings he shouldn't be experiencing for his little brother's best friend.

But he'd kept his wayward emotions in check, at least until her birthday the following summer.

Shirley Lawson had hosted a sweet sixteen party for her granddaughter in the backyard, complete with bouquets of pink and white balloons, miles of streamers fluttering in the breeze and a multi-tiered birthday cake. Jack hadn't planned on stopping in at the party. He had other plans for the evening already in place—and he was confident that the evening would end with Leesa Webster in the backseat of his Mustang up at Eagle Point Park.

He was on his way to the car when he glanced over and noticed that Kelly was standing alone on the front porch while music and laughter sounded from the back of the house. He tucked his keys in his pocket and walked over to her.

"Isn't the birthday girl supposed to be at the birthday party?"

She smiled. "I just wanted to take a break from the crowd for a minute."

"It is quite a crowd," he noted, climbing the steps toward her.

"Sweet sixteen is a milestone, according to Grandma."

"Sixteen I believe," he teased. "But sweet?"

She responded with a sassy smile. "I am sweet," she assured him. "But I'm not as innocent as you think."

It was a challenge—and one he couldn't resist any longer. He tipped her chin up. "Let's see about that," he said, and brushed his lips over hers.

Her golden eyes widened momentarily, then drifted shut. Her mouth was soft—softer than he'd anticipated, moist and sweetly yielding. She lifted her arms to link them behind his neck as her body melted against his.

He touched his tongue to the seam of her lips, a question more than a demand, and she answered by opening for him. Her tongue touched his, tentatively at first, then more boldly. She had some experience with kissing, or she was a fast learner, but he would bet the Mustang he'd recently emptied his bank account to buy that she hadn't done much more than that.

The realization should have succeeded in lessening his desire; instead, her innocence had the opposite effect. He wanted to touch where no one else had touched, make her feel things no one else had made her feel. But for now, he contented himself with kissing her, savoring the flavor of her lips and the softness of her curves pressed against him.

She was sweet...and, his conscience belatedly reminded him, only sixteen.

He eased his lips from hers.

Kelly looked up at him, her eyes dark and silently questioning.

"You're still too innocent for me," he said with genuine regret.

She blew out a slow, shaky breath as he took a step back.

"You're not staying for cake?"

He shook his head. "I have to go."

She shrugged, as if she didn't care, but he could see that she was hurt and confused—and more than willing to finish what they'd started. And as much as he'd been looking forward to his date with Leesa, he knew he wouldn't take her up to Eagle Point Park tonight. He couldn't be with her when he'd be thinking about Kelly.

But before he walked away, he brushed his thumb gently over her bottom lip, which was erotically swollen from his kiss. "Happy Birthday, Kelly."

That had been the beginning of the end for Jack. From

that moment, all of his best intentions had gone straight to hell.

He hadn't made another move that summer—he hadn't dared. Because he'd known that if he put his hands on Kelly again, she wouldn't stop him, and he hadn't trusted that he'd be able to stop himself.

And then Kelly had left Pinehurst before the ink was even dry on her high school diploma, heading off to college in Chicago. She'd come back for the summer after her first year, intending to take care of her grandmother while she recovered from a stroke. But a second blood clot interrupted those plans, and after the funeral, Kelly had gone back to Chicago again.

It was two years after that before Jack saw her again, before they spent those three glorious days and nights together.

Three glorious days and nights that had resulted in Kelly having his child.

No wonder she wasn't infatuated with him anymore. In fact, if he had to guess, he would say that whatever she felt for him now was closer to the opposite end of the emotional spectrum. She might not like him, but she wanted him. It wasn't arrogance or delusion that made him think so, but a simple assessment of her physical response to his nearness.

She didn't want to want him, but the chemistry was undeniable. And when he'd kissed her, she'd definitely kissed him back, confirming that she wasn't nearly as disinterested as she wanted him to believe.

It was his frustration with Kelly that had made him amenable to Norah Hennessey Sinclair's invitation to dinner the night before. Frustration combined with determination to not sit at home and think about her—or his still-convoluted feelings about her daughter. *His daughter.*

Those two words still made him break out in a cold

sweat, and although his thoughts had finally shifted from denial to acceptance, he didn't know what would come next. Dinner with a client had offered a welcome reprieve from his own thoughts. He certainly hadn't given Norah any indication he was interested in sharing anything more than a meal.

He'd been more annoyed than enticed by her drunken and obvious attempt at seduction. Even if she hadn't been inebriated, he wouldn't have been tempted. As a client, she was strictly off-limits, and even aside from that, he didn't do casual hook-ups anymore. Hadn't in a long time. But mostly it was because, while Norah's foot had been climbing inside his pant leg under the table, he hadn't been able to stop thinking about Kelly.

Then he'd looked up, and his gaze had locked with hers. And the look in her eyes, the cool contempt in her golden gaze, told him more clearly than any words how she'd interpreted the scene. Although it irked him that he even cared what she thought, he couldn't deny that he did.

Kelly had planned to spend most of the day Sunday reviewing the information Craig Richmond had sent to her about Richmond Pharmaceuticals. Then she woke up to find the sun spilling into her bedroom and decided the review could wait until after the sun went down. It was too nice a day to be stuck indoors and there were gardens to be tended.

She'd tried to persuade Ava to come outside with her, but her daughter had decided to weed through her closet instead. She was sorting through her clothes and discarding those that she didn't want anymore. Kelly had suggested that she do exactly that before they packed everything up in Seattle and shipped it halfway across the country, but of course Ava had resisted.

Kelly didn't mind working alone, and she found the out-door chores surprisingly relaxing. Her twelfth-floor condo in Seattle hadn't boasted any kind of yard, but she'd had a balcony. Every spring, she'd filled it with baskets and pots of flowers.

As it turned out, she wasn't alone for very long. Quinn and Shane and Finnigan and Frederick—the adorable twins from next door and their energetic puppies—ventured over to see what she was doing, and so that Finn could "water" the alyssum. And then, a short while after that, Mrs. Dunford wandered across the street to see how Kelly and Ava were settling in.

She didn't mind the interruptions. In fact, casual drop-ins and easy conversations with neighbors were some of the reasons Kelly was glad to be back in Pinehurst. Or so she thought until Jackson stopped by.

He parked in front of the house and casually strolled up the walk. He was wearing a blue golf shirt that stretched across the breadth of his shoulders and a pair of well-worn jeans that molded to the strong muscles of his thighs, and with each step that drew him nearer, her heart started to pound just a little bit faster.

"I wouldn't have guessed that you had a green thumb," he mused.

"I'm not sure that I do," she responded in a similarly casual tone. "But I like flowers."

He hooked his thumbs into the front pockets of his jeans and gave her a leisurely once-over. "You should have a hat on—your nose is looking a little red."

She rubbed the back of her hand over it, shrugged. "Is that why you're here, Jackson—as a representative of the SPF police?"

His lips curved, just a little. "No, I actually came to see my brother."

"He lives over there," she reminded him, pointing to the house next door.

"*And* I was hoping to see you."

"Why?"

"I wanted to explain."

Kelly didn't ask what he was talking about. In that brief moment of eye contact at the restaurant, too much had passed between them for her to pretend otherwise. Instead, she only said, "No explanation necessary."

"I know what you're thinking."

She hacked at the roots of a stubborn weed with her trowel. "Do you?"

"Yeah. And before you try and execute me, you should know that the woman I was with at the restaurant last night is a client."

She almost laughed out loud. If he was going to insist on offering an explanation, she would have expected something a little more creative than that. Or at least more credible.

And though she didn't want to ask—because asking would suggest that she cared, and she didn't want to care— the words spilled out, anyway, and with enough of an edge to belie the casual disinterest she wanted to project. "Do you usually conduct business with wine and candlelight?"

"No." He took off his sunglasses and tucked them into the pocket of his golf shirt. "But it's not unusual to meet a client outside of the office, so when she called and suggested a meeting at Mama Leone's, I didn't see any reason not to agree."

Kelly hacked at another weed, probably more viciously than was necessary.

"I handled her divorce a few years back," he continued. "She's thinking about getting married again and wanted to talk about a prenup."

"Yeah, she looked like a woman who was in a committed relationship with someone else," she noted dryly.

"She was at the restaurant before me and already halfway through the bottle of wine when I got there. I had one glass, she finished off the rest with her dinner, then I drove her home."

"She was feeding you off of her fork."

"She asked if I wanted to try the cheesecake, I said no thanks. She held the fork out to me, and when I tried to decline again, she stabbed me in the mouth with the tines. I figured sampling the cake was a better alternative than a bloody lip."

Kelly remained skeptical. From her perspective, she hadn't seen any evidence of Jack resisting the woman's advances. But if the woman truly was exploiting their professional relationship to put the moves on him, she could see how that would have put him in an awkward situation. Or maybe she was an idiot for wanting to believe any part of his explanation.

"And the reason she was plastered to your side as you left the restaurant?" She shook her head and held up a hand before he could answer. "You know what? It doesn't matter. It's really not any of my business."

"I think I have some pretty good reasons to be angry with you—but why are you mad at me?"

"I'm not mad at you."

"You sound mad," he noted.

She huffed out a breath. "If I'm mad, it's at myself."

His brows rose. "Care to explain that one?"

"I was…surprised to see you with her," she admitted. "And then I realized I shouldn't have been."

"I'm still not sure I understand."

"I thought you'd changed. I'd *hoped* you'd changed."

She stood up and brushed her hands down the front of her shorts. "That was my mistake."

His gaze narrowed. "You think I was kissing you in your kitchen one day and seducing another woman the next?"

She didn't bother to deny it.

"Dammit, Kelly, I didn't sleep with her."

"I don't care who you sleep with," she finally told him. "But I would appreciate it if you exercised a little discretion—for Ava's sake, if no one else's."

She picked up the basket of gardening tools and started to turn away, but he caught her arm, halting her escape. She didn't try to pull away; she knew he wouldn't release her until he was ready. Instead, she looked at him with what she hoped was casual disinterest.

"I didn't sleep with her," he said again, the icy tone of his voice a stark contrast to the heated fury in his eyes. "And when I do take a woman to my bed, I prefer that her faculties aren't impaired by alcohol."

"Too much of a gentleman to take advantage of an intoxicated female?"

"No," he corrected her. "Too demanding to settle for any less than equal and eager participation." His hand trailed down her arm, slid behind her back to draw her closer. "As I remember it, you were definitely an equal, and very eager, participant."

"That was a long time ago," she reminded him.

"I'm looking forward to having you in my bed again."

It wasn't arrogance in his tone, but confidence, and his absolute certainty made everything inside her tremble. But there was no way she was going to let him see it. She wasn't an infatuated twenty-one-year-old anymore, and she tilted her head back to meet the challenge in his gaze head-on.

"When I take a man to *my* bed, I prefer if he's not inhibited by his ego."

Jackson's lips curved in a slow and devastatingly sexy smile. "Then we understand one another."

But as Kelly watched him cross the grass toward the house next door, she realized that she didn't understand anything, least of all the tangle of emotions inside of her.

After Jackson had gone over to his brother's house, Kelly moved around to the backyard and continued with her gardening as if the encounter had never happened. Thankfully there was no one around to witness her distraction when she yanked a petunia out of the dirt.

What was wrong with her that she could still get tangled up in knots over the man who had broken her heart thirteen years earlier? She'd been so sure that she was over him, that the only connection between them was their daughter. But when he looked at her, when his eyes skimmed over her from head to toe in slow and blatantly masculine perusal, every hormone in her body went on full alert. It was a complication she hadn't been prepared for and definitely didn't need.

Since her divorce almost a decade earlier, she could count on one hand the number of sexual liaisons she'd had—with two fingers left over. And she honestly hadn't felt as if she was missing out on anything.

As far as she was concerned, the whole dating and mating thing was hugely overrated. Especially when most of her time and energy was focused on raising her daughter and building a career. So why was it, after only five minutes with Jackson Garrett, she couldn't think about anything else but him?

"Am I interrupting?"

Kelly glanced up at Georgia. "Yes," she said. "And thank you."

Her neighbor chuckled. "Are the weeds winning the battle?"

"No—it's not the garden but my own wandering thoughts." She dropped her gloves and trowel on top of the basket she'd filled with weeds—and one broken purple petunia. "I just finished."

"The boys and I baked too many cookies." She gestured with the plate she carried. "So I was hoping I could pawn some off on you and Ava."

"Anytime you want to pawn cookies, we're more than happy to help." Kelly headed back toward the house. "I put a pot of coffee on before I came out, if you want a cup."

"Maybe half a cup," Georgia allowed. "I'm still nursing."

Kelly smiled. "I remember those days—and how much I missed my daily jolt of java."

Georgia followed her into the kitchen, set the plate of cookies on the table. "I almost manage to convince myself that I don't miss it, and then I'll walk past the Bean There Café and catch the scent of freshly roasted beans in the air, and I actually get weak in the knees."

"I know what you mean." Kelly took two mugs out of the cupboard, poured half a cup in one for Georgia. "Milk?"

The other woman shook her head. "Matt thinks Pippa is lactose intolerant. She went through a really bad colicky phase that finally eased when I cut milk from my diet."

"I've heard horror stories about colic," Kelly admitted, filling her own cup to the top. "Thankfully, I didn't have to deal with that with Ava."

"The twins were good, too," Georgia told her. "It was just hard because there were two of them. And maybe my memory of those early days has faded, but I know I wasn't nearly as sleep-deprived caring for the two of them as I was in the first few months with Pippa. Of course, I wasn't on my own when Quinn and Shane were babies, either."

"I had a wonderful neighbor who was happy to pitch in whenever I was ready to pull my hair out, and I never felt like I was on my own when she was around." Kelly picked up a cookie and smiled. "Bev liked to bake, too." Then she bit into the treat, and sighed with pleasure. "Oh, these are heaven."

"Chocolate chip are Matt's favorite, and the boys wanted to help make them this time. The plan was for them to take turns measuring out ingredients—instead they each measured everything, so we doubled the batch."

"They should help you bake more often," Kelly suggested.

Georgia smiled. "There's some peanut butter, too, because they're Jack's favorite. Quinn and Shane wanted to thank him for taking them to see *Ted E. Bear's Birthday.*"

Kelly paused with a cookie halfway toward her mouth. "Jackson took your boys to see a kids' movie?"

"Matt was supposed to take them when I went to Megan Richmond's baby shower, but he got called into the hospital, so Jack stepped in."

"Was there bribery or blackmail involved?"

Her neighbor chuckled. "Not that I'm aware of."

"Because the Jackson Garrett I used to know would have run far and fast in the opposite direction of a movie theater full of preschoolers."

"A few months ago, he probably would have," Georgia agreed. "And while I was a little concerned about his reputation in the beginning, I have to admit, I've developed something of a soft spot for Jack."

"Now you've piqued my curiosity," Kelly admitted.

"When I first moved in, even before Matt and I were officially dating, Jack warned me off."

"I can see how that would endear him to you," she said dryly.

Georgia laughed. "What it showed me is that, despite his casual and cavalier attitude, he is close to his family, cares deeply about people and has protective instincts."

Kelly was skeptical, but since she'd been gone for a lot of years, she really couldn't disagree with any part of that assessment. So all she said was, "Even as kids, they were close. The three brothers would—and often did—fight with one another, but against anyone else, they always stuck together."

"They still stick together," Georgia said. "Usually on Sunday afternoons in front of the television, watching whatever sport is in season."

"Is Lukas there today?" Kelly asked, keeping her tone deliberately casual.

The other woman shook her head. "No. He called earlier to say that he was behind on his paperwork at the clinic."

Kelly would have bet that Lukas wanted to avoid another confrontation with Jackson more than he wanted to catch up on paperwork. And she knew that was her fault, but she didn't have the first clue how to fix it.

The clatter of footsteps on the stairs drew her attention back to the present.

"Hey, Mom, can we go— Oh, hi, Mrs. Garrett."

"Hello, Ava."

"Where did you want to go?" Kelly asked her.

"Back to that store at the mall, the one where I got the green top." She smiled coaxingly. "I think they had it in purple, too."

"Maybe tomorrow."

Ava sighed, obviously disappointed. Then her gaze landed on the plate in the middle of the table and her eyes lit up. "Cookies?"

Georgia laughed. "Help yourself."

Ava zeroed straight in on the peanut butter, forcing Kelly to acknowledge that the truth about her daughter's paternity couldn't remain a secret forever.

Chapter Six

By Wednesday night, Jack had spent more than enough time alone with his thoughts and still didn't have any answers to the questions that plagued his mind. He needed to talk to someone. He didn't necessarily want advice so much as he wanted to vent. And since there was no one outside his immediate family who he would trust with the information, his choices were limited.

He didn't even consider going to see Lukas. His younger brother had made his feelings about the situation more than clear when he'd introduced his fist to Jack's face the week before. Though the bruise on his jaw had already faded, Jack wasn't willing to chance a repeat performance. Which is why he found himself dialing Matt's number.

Less than thirty minutes later, his brother was at the door.

"I'm sorry to drag you away from your wife and kids," Jack apologized.

Matt took the bottle of Millhouse his brother opened for him. "The offer of beer and a baseball game aside, I know you wouldn't have asked me to come over if it wasn't important."

Jack nodded. "It's about Kelly."

Matt paused with his bottle halfway to his lips. "Kelly? Or Ava?"

He scowled as he dropped onto the opposite end of the couch. "She told you?"

"She didn't tell me anything," Matt said.

"Then it was Lukas," he guessed.

"No one told me—no one had to," his brother assured him. "The first time I saw Kelly's daughter, I figured she had to be yours."

Jack hadn't been prepared for his brother's simple and ready acceptance—especially when it contradicted his continued denials. "You really think so?"

Matt shook his head. "I can't believe *you* doubt it. There's no mistaking the fact that Ava's a Garrett, even if it doesn't say so on her birth certificate. And since I know neither Luke nor I ever slept with Kelly, that narrows the choice of paternal prospects down considerably."

He tipped his bottle to his lips, giving himself a moment to consider his brother's logic. "Luke is furious with me."

"I'd bet he's even more furious with Kelly right now," Matt told him. "From the beginning, Ava has called him 'Uncle Lukas,' but he never knew that he really was her uncle."

"She never told me that she was pregnant," Jack told him.

"And if she had told you—what would you have done?"

Damn, his brother always asked the tough questions. It was the same one Jack had been asking himself since Kelly had dropped her bombshell in his office. And it was a question to which he still didn't have an answer. "I was engaged to Sara," he reminded Matt.

His brother frowned. "While you were sleeping with Kelly?"

"No. Of course not." His reputation aside, Jack had never been one to juggle women. He might not stick with anyone for very long, but he wasn't a cheater. "What happened with Kelly—it was one weekend, after Sara had given me back her ring."

"I don't need the details," Matt told him.

Jack took a long swallow from his bottle. "I don't know anything about being a father."

"No one does in the beginning, but you'll learn."

Jack wasn't so sure that he would—or even that he wanted to. Almost a week after Kelly's visit to his office, his head was still spinning, and whenever he let himself think *I'm a father,* his heart would start to race with as much apprehension as anticipation. "I had everything I wanted—a successful career, an executive condo, female companionship when I wanted it, and peace and quiet when I didn't."

"And now you have a child to add to the mix."

"Yeah." And Jack suspected it was going to be like trying to mix oil and water.

"She's a great kid," Matt noted.

It was, he knew, the same sentiment Lukas had frequently expressed, and it frustrated him that both of his brothers could speak with such authority about the child with whom he'd barely exchanged half a dozen words. "I wouldn't know."

"So get to know her," his brother suggested, unfazed by the irritation in Jack's voice.

"Do you really think it's going to be that easy?"

"I don't think it's going to be easy at all," Matt acknowledged. "But nothing worthwhile usually is."

He was probably right. The bigger problem was that Jack didn't have the first clue about how to relate to a twelve-year-old girl. Thankfully, he still had some time to figure things out. "Cam said the DNA results would take about ten days."

Matt frowned. "Do you really need some lab report to confirm what you already know?"

"But I don't know," Jack told him.

"Stop being a lawyer for five minutes and tell me what you feel in your gut."

Jack scowled. "What's wrong with wanting proof?"

Matt sat back and studied his brother across the table. "You're not in denial because you don't want it to be true," he realized. "You're hesitant to take the next step because you *do* want it to be true and you're afraid that it might not be."

"Maybe you should have been the lawyer, because that's the kind of convoluted reasoning I usually hear in the courthouse."

His brother ignored the snide comment. "It was more than a fling, wasn't it?" he asked instead.

"What?"

"You and Kelly," Matt clarified. "You never got over her, did you?"

"We spent one weekend together more than a dozen years ago—there wasn't much to get over," Jack assured him.

"And yet…" his brother mused thoughtfully.

"And yet *nothing*."

"So why haven't you ever fallen in love?"

"That's an odd question from the brother who was the best man at my wedding," Jack noted.

"Did you love Sara?" Matt asked him now. "Or were you trying to forget about Kelly when you got back together with her?"

It occurred to Jack that maybe he should have called Lukas, because the impact of his younger brother's fist was less uncomfortable than his older brother's speculation. Unwilling to answer Matt's question, he picked up the remote and turned on the ball game. And breathed a sigh of relief when his brother didn't press him for a response.

He wasn't prepared to admit that he'd reconciled with

Sara not because he wanted to forget about Kelly but because he knew he had to. Because Lukas had called him, seeking advice after Kelly had confessed to her best friend that she'd fallen in love and was thinking about leaving school. And he was tired of being the bad guy for doing the right thing.

Except that, now that he knew about Ava, he wasn't sure it had been the right thing, after all.

Kelly didn't like feeling off-balance, but she hadn't felt steady or sure about anything since she'd stepped off the airplane and seen Jackson at the airport. And he, predictably, enjoyed flustering her. From the mind-numbing kiss in her kitchen to his arrogant assertion that he would have her in his bed again, he continually used the sexual tension between them to undermine her control. But she was determined to take it back.

She decided that the best way to do that was to make the next move—to act instead of react—and to keep the focus of the conversation on Ava. So when she stopped in the village after a meeting at Richmond Pharmaceuticals Tuesday afternoon, she took out her cell phone and dialed the number of Jackson's office.

This time, he took her call.

"I'm just down the street from your office and thought I'd see if you had time for coffee."

"If you're at the Bean There Café, I can make time," he told her.

And he did, arriving at the café just as Kelly was carrying their beverages to a table. She sat down with her decadent caramel macchiato and passed him the oversize mug of dark roast. "I wanted to invite you to come over for dinner Friday night."

His lips curved as he lifted the mug, just enough to

make her heart pound a little bit faster and throw her off-balance again.

"Are you asking me on a date?"

She huffed out a breath. "No, I'm asking if you want to share a meal with me *and Ava*."

He sipped his coffee. "You're no longer concerned that I'll be looking for any tiny bit of evidence that she's not mine?"

"I'm not concerned that you'll find any," she said evenly. "So are you interested?"

His gaze dropped to her mouth, lingered. "Oh, I think you know I'm interested."

Less than two minutes in his company, and she'd already lost control of the conversation—and her hormones. She wrapped her hands around the mug and tried to get a grip on her wayward thoughts. "How do you do that?"

"Do what?"

"Turn everything into innuendo."

"It's a gift," he said mildly.

She shook her head. "I thought you hated me."

"I don't have to like you to want you."

She lifted a brow. "Do you usually have sex with women you don't like?"

"No—liking is usually a minimal requirement," he told her. "But nothing between us has ever been usual."

She couldn't deny that was true. "Getting back to my question—are you interested in coming for dinner? Or do you have other plans?"

"What are you making?"

"Really? That's going to be the deciding factor for you?"

"No, I was just wondering," he said. "I'm definitely interested in dinner and I don't have other plans. But won't Ava think it's strange that I'm coming for dinner? Or do you frequently cook for male guests?"

"Are you asking about my social life?"

"One more thing I'm curious about."

"Well, I can assure you that mine isn't nearly as busy or varied as yours."

"You shouldn't believe everything you hear," he warned.

"Dinner?" she prompted, refusing to be sidetracked again.

"What time?"

"Six thirty."

He nodded and picked up his mug. "That works for me."

Kelly sipped her macchiato.

"Have you told Ava anything about me?" Jackson asked.

"Do you mean specifically about you—or generally about her father?"

"About her father," he clarified.

"Not really," she admitted. "I've never lied to her, but I haven't volunteered much information, either. She went through a phase where she asked a lot of questions, but I managed to deflect most of them, and I think she got used to it just being the two of us."

"That's going to change," he said.

It wasn't a threat or a warning, just a simple statement of fact, and she nodded. She *wanted* it to change. She wanted Ava to know her father, as she'd never known her own. But somehow it had been easier to want those things for her daughter when they were living three thousand miles away and there was little chance of actually getting them. Now that she was sitting across the table from Ava's father, she couldn't help but worry that she'd started on a journey that might not end where she wanted.

"I want to tell her that I'm her father," he said, when she remained silent.

And once again, he'd thrown her for a loop. His statement didn't just surprise her, it left her completely baffled by the change in his attitude.

"I thought you were still in denial about that."

He shook his head. "I've missed more than twelve years of her life already, and I don't want to wait another week for the test results to tell Ava."

"Suddenly you believe that I'm telling the truth? That I didn't give birth to someone else's baby for the sole purpose of hitting you up for child support a dozen years later?"

He winced. "I hope it didn't sound that ridiculous when I suggested it."

"Not just ridiculous but insulting."

"Would it help if I said I was sorry?"

She looked at him over the rim of her cup. "Are you?"

"Yes." His response was immediate and sincere. "You caught me off-guard and it was a totally knee-jerk response."

"Well, the 'jerk' part sounds about right," she said.

"I am sorry," he said. "And I do want to know…my daughter."

The pause before "my daughter" was almost imperceptible, but she suspected that his hesitation this time wasn't because he didn't believe that she was "his" child but because he didn't know how to be her father.

Jackson Garrett—a man who could charm the most contrary female with little effort, who could face off against the most ornery judge without blinking an eye—was worried about impressing a twelve-year-old girl. And this brief glimpse of uncertainty from a man who was usually so overwhelmingly confident touched something deep in Kelly's heart.

"Let's start with dinner," she suggested.

Kelly treated her daughter to a movie Thursday night, hoping that while they watched the previews for coming attractions and munched on popcorn, she might have a chance to casually mention that Jackson would be coming over for dinner the following night. But the opportunity never seemed to arise—or maybe she was just reluctant to say anything that might affect the easy camaraderie they'd recently established.

On their way back home afterward, Kelly found herself driving by Lukas's house. He still lived on Terrace Avenue, in the redbrick back-split where he and his brothers had grown up. While Matt and Jack had each chosen to move out as soon they could afford to, Lukas had never seen any reason to move out of a home that so perfectly met all of his needs. Especially when one of those needs was adequate space for various creatures with fur, feathers or fins that he might be caring for at any given time. When Kelly saw the lights were on, she impulsively pulled into the driveway.

After the confrontation between Lukas and Jackson, she'd thought it was best to give him some time. And she'd been certain that, after a few days, Lukas would contact her. Except that six days had passed and she hadn't heard a single word. He had neither initiated any contact nor returned any of her calls. She knew he was probably still angry and upset, and that he had reason to be, but she wasn't going to let him continue to ignore her.

Ava didn't object to the detour. She'd always adored her uncle Lukas. And though she didn't know Matthew very well, she'd been spending a lot of time with Georgia and the kids, so she felt comfortable around their home and with the family. But there had been an uncharacteristic coolness when she'd met Jackson, and that worried Kelly. She didn't know if Ava sensed that Jackson wasn't at ease around her, or if she simply didn't like him. The latter would certainly make the father-daughter revelation even more awkward. Thankfully, that wasn't something Kelly needed to worry about just yet.

A cacophony of excited yips immediately sounded in response to the peal of the bell, and Ava's face lit up in anticipation of meeting the relation of Quinn and Shane's puppies. When Lukas opened the door, he had the wriggling animal tucked in the crook of his arm and icy reserve in his eyes. But the ice melted as soon as he saw Ava standing beside her mother.

He stepped back so that they could enter, and Ava immediately reached for the puppy. Einstein was thrilled by her attention and showed his enthusiasm by licking her whole face. Daphne, on the other hand, was a spoiled feline who had never been particularly fond of visitors invading her domain, and she stalked off to the upper floor to sulk when her master invited Kelly and Ava into the house.

"Did you want me to put on a pot of coffee—or are you in a hurry to get home?"

The tone of his question suggested to Kelly that he would prefer if she declined the less-than-gracious offer. But she had no intention of going anywhere until they'd reopened the lines of communication. "I'd love a cup of coffee."

Lukas's scowl deepened as he filled the reservoir with water and measured out the grounds. Thankfully, Ava seemed oblivious to his dark mood, and she babbled happily about the movie they'd just seen while she wrestled on the floor with the puppy.

When Lukas was finally pouring the coffee, Einstein headed toward the back door.

"Can I take him outside?" Ava asked Lukas.

"Sure," he agreed.

The door banged shut behind her, but then there was silence—and a whole lot of tension.

Kelly stirred a spoonful of sugar into her cup. "Did you get your paperwork done on the weekend?"

"Paperwork is never done," he told her.

"Then it wasn't just an excuse to avoid seeing me?"

"Believe it or not, not everything is about you. I had a busy life here while you were in Seattle, and it's still just as busy."

"And that's why I haven't heard from you in almost a week—because you've been busy?"

"Yeah."

She frowned at the terse response. "Have you talked to Jackson?"

"I think I said everything I needed to say to him."

Kelly sighed. "If you want to be mad at someone, you should be mad at me, not your brother."

"Don't worry," Lukas assured her. "I'm plenty mad at you, too."

"And you have every right to be," she admitted. "I should have told you."

He just stood with his arms folded across his chest and said nothing.

"I was going to tell you," she said, aware that she sounded more than a little defensive.

"When?" he demanded. "When *my niece* was graduating from college?"

She winced. "I hated keeping the truth from you."

"But you did it, anyway—for *thirteen years*."

"What was I supposed to do?" she challenged. "By the time I knew I was pregnant, Jack was engaged to Sara."

"He still had a right to know that you were going to have his child."

"And he would have been thrilled with me for ruining his wedding plans—and his career—wouldn't he?"

He lifted his brows at her sarcasm. "No, he probably

wouldn't have been thrilled. But he would have done the right thing."

"What was the right thing?"

"Marrying you and being a father to his child."

She shook her head. "And you couldn't guess why I didn't tell you?"

"He would have stepped up."

"Maybe. And then he would have hated me."

"You don't know that," he told her.

"He was in love with Sara."

"He probably thought he was, when he asked her to marry him," Lukas admitted. "But when she broke off the engagement, he told me that he was more relieved than anything, because he'd realized that the whole thing was a mistake."

"And yet he was happy enough to put the ring back on her finger when she changed her mind again."

He frowned at that. "I don't know what was going through his mind at the time, but I do know that he would have done things differently if he'd known that you were pregnant."

"I didn't want him to feel trapped by circumstances neither of us could have foreseen."

"You didn't give him a chance to feel anything."

She blinked back the tears that threatened. "You're right," she admitted. "Because I was pregnant and alone and so terrified I didn't think about his feelings. Or yours."

Now Lukas sighed. "I never understood why you refused to tell me. Now that part, at least, makes sense."

"Are you going to stay mad at me forever?" she asked softly.

He considered the question for a minute. "Probably not forever," he said. "And I wasn't only mad—I felt like an idiot."

"Why?"

"Because I never even suspected the truth. I never picked up on any vibes between you and Jack, and I never saw how much Ava looks like him."

"Jack doesn't see it, either," she said. "Or maybe he doesn't want to see it."

"Matt said he figured it out the first time he saw her, so it probably won't take other people too long to see the resemblance," he warned.

She knew he was right. "I'm going to tell her."

"When?"

"Soon," she assured him. "It's just that Ava's wanted a father for so long, I can't help but be a little concerned that, when she finally gets to meet him, she's going to expect too much."

"And you don't think Jack can live up to her expectations," he guessed.

"I don't know that he wants to." She sipped her coffee. "Maybe coming back to Pinehurst was a mistake."

"Do you really think so?"

"No," she admitted. "It was time to leave Seattle—and there wasn't anywhere else I wanted to go. Besides—" she nudged his shoulder "—I missed my best friend."

He shook his head. "You're making it really hard for me to stay mad at you."

"You have every right to be mad at me," she admitted.

"Even if I could understand why you didn't say anything in the beginning," he allowed, "I can't understand why you kept the truth of her paternity a secret for so long."

"Because I knew exactly how you'd react when you found out that your brother was Ava's father."

She didn't realize that Ava had come back into the house or overheard any part of the conversation with Lukas until her daughter said, "Dr. Garrett's my father?"

Chapter Seven

Jack was staring at his planner and trying to figure out what he was going to do with the four days he'd set aside for a contentious custody hearing that had been postponed. Ordinarily, he would have opposed the eleventh-hour adjournment request as prejudicial to his client, except in this situation, it was not. Because his client had interim custody of her three children and her estranged husband was currently in the custody of the Las Vegas Police Department after a weekend trip with some buddies ended with an ill-advised proposition to an undercover police officer.

He wasn't accustomed to so much unscheduled time. He enjoyed his work and he had no problem with fifteen-hour days or even working weekends. In fact, he sometimes worried that he wouldn't know what to do if he didn't have such a busy practice. And there were other times that he wished he could escape from his clients' problems, just for a little while. Now that he had such an opportunity, he thought he should focus on his own life—and establishing a relationship with his daughter.

He looked up at a knock on his door. "What are you still doing here?" he asked his secretary.

"I'm not still here," Colleen told him. "I went home for dinner, saw a movie with a friend, then came back to pick up some files I wanted to finish billing tonight. You're the only one *still* here."

"Not for long," he told her, shutting down his computer.

"Well, since you are here, you can let me know what to do about Norah Hennessey Sinclair. She called several times this afternoon demanding an appointment for tomorrow."

"And you said?"

"That you were scheduled to be in court all week, which is technically true."

"Your boss should give you a raise," Jack told her.

"He should," she agreed. "But he's way too cheap."

"Or he could demote you to the copy room."

She just shrugged, unconcerned. "If she calls again in the morning, do you want me to book her in for Monday morning? If I schedule an 8:00-a.m. appointment, she should be sober."

"I told you about that dinner meeting in confidence," he reminded her.

Colleen glanced around the empty office, but all she said was, "Monday?"

"The following Monday," he allowed. "I want to keep next week open."

"For what?"

"Personal reasons."

"You usually have to have a personal life to justify personal reasons," she pointed out.

"Ha, ha."

"I wasn't joking."

He closed the lid on his briefcase. "You know how to reach me in case of emergency."

"You're really taking time off?"

"And I have complete confidence that you can handle the office."

She folded her arms across her chest. "Who are you and what have you done with Jackson Garrett?"

He chuckled. "Go home, Colleen. You can do the billing tomorrow."

She was walking beside him to the elevator when his cell phone rang. Jack pulled it out of his pocket, surprised—and pleased—to see Kelly's name and number on the display.

"Maybe I was wrong about you not having a personal life," his secretary mused, punching the button to summon the elevator.

Jack connected the call as the elevator dinged to signal its arrival.

"I hope it's not too late," Kelly said without preamble.

"Actually, I'm just leaving the office," he told her.

"In that case, could you stop by on your way home?"

He couldn't resist teasing, "If this is a booty call—absolutely."

"In your dreams."

She had no idea how very true those words were. And while he had a ready retort on his lips, the underlying tension in her voice prompted him to ask instead, "Is everything okay?"

"Not really," she admitted.

"Ava?"

"She's fine, but—" She blew out a breath. "I'd really rather talk about this in person."

"I'll be there in ten minutes," he promised.

He was pulling into her driveway in less than that, and when Kelly answered the door, he could see the worry in her eyes.

"What's going on?"

She managed a wobbly smile. "Well, you said that you wanted Ava to know—now she knows."

He did want Ava to know, but he'd got the impression that Kelly was a little less eager to share the news, so this revelation coming so soon on the heels of their earlier conversation surprised him. "You told her?"

"She overheard Lukas and I talking." She hesitated, as if she was going to say something else, then apparently changed her mind.

"How did she take it?" he asked cautiously.

"She didn't say too much on the drive home," Kelly admitted. "And then she went to her room and slammed the door."

"Is she mad at you or me?"

"Both, I'd guess, but probably more at me. She thinks I should have told her who her father was a long time ago."

He couldn't disagree, so instead he asked, "Why am I here?"

"I don't know," she admitted. "I probably shouldn't have called. I thought maybe you could talk to her, but I don't think she's in a mood to listen to anyone right now."

When he'd suggested telling Ava about their relationship, he'd assumed that he and Kelly would sit down together and make the announcement. But he hadn't anticipated what kind of reaction Ava might have to the news, and he certainly hadn't expected to be called in for damage control. Or to worry that he might exacerbate the damage.

"I can try," he said, and she looked up at him, her golden eyes filled with wary hope and reluctant gratitude.

He climbed the stairs to the second floor. Even if he hadn't known which room was Ava's, he could have guessed by the firmly closed door. He knocked, but the sound barely registered over the pounding of his heart against his ribs.

"Go away."

He turned the knob, pushed open the door a crack.

She glared at him from her cross-legged position in the middle of her bed. "I said 'go away.'"

"I thought maybe that was code for something else—like how 'sick' actually means 'cool.'"

"You thought wrong."

He shrugged. "Do you want to tell me why you're so pissed off at me?"

Her jaw dropped. "You're not supposed to swear in front of me."

"Why not?"

"Because I'm a kid and it sets a bad example," she informed him primly.

He stepped farther into the room, straddled the ladderback chair at her desk. "I don't have a lot of experience with kids," he admitted.

"Could've fooled me." Her voice dripped with sarcasm, but at least she was talking to him.

"So why are you pi—mad at me?" he asked again.

She held a fuzzy purple pillow against her chest, her fingers raking through the fur as she considered how to respond—or maybe if she should. Instead of answering his question, she asked one of her own. "Did you sleep with my mom and then dump her?"

"Is that what she told you?"

"I didn't ask her," Ava admitted. "I'm asking you."

"You could have started with an easier question," he grumbled.

She hugged the pillow tighter and waited for his response.

Jack knew he could try to slant the truth in his favor, but what would be the point? It seemed as if Ava had already made up her mind about him and nothing he said was going to change it.

"Yeah," he finally said. "That's not a complete summary of what happened, but it's basically accurate."

"Did you know she was pregnant?"

"No." Kelly answered her daughter's question from the doorway before he could. "When we decided to go our separate ways, neither of us knew that I was pregnant."

"Didn't they teach you about safe sex back then?"

Thankfully, Kelly came to his rescue again, adeptly skirting the question as she lowered herself onto the edge of her daughter's bed. "Just because you weren't planned doesn't mean you weren't wanted."

"Maybe you wanted me," Ava acknowledged. "But what about him?"

"That's not a fair question," Kelly chided. "Because I moved to Seattle without telling Jack about you."

"Why?"

"It's...complicated."

"Don't you think I have a right to know why I didn't have a father for the first twelve years of my life?"

"The details don't matter as much as the fact that you have a father now."

Ava looked at him with blatant skepticism. "Do I?"

"I know this revelation came as a surprise to you—it was a surprise to me, too," he admitted. "And I'm not expecting you to embrace me with open arms, but I'm hoping that we can give each other a chance to try and figure this out."

She didn't seem thrilled with the idea, and finally admitted, "I thought Dr. Garrett was my father."

Jack glanced at Kelly in surprise and confusion; she shrugged apologetically.

"Mom told Uncle Lukas that his brother was my father," Ava explained. "And I thought—I *hoped*—she meant Dr. Garrett."

"Matt already has three kids," he said lightly.

"Probably because he likes kids."

He frowned. "I like kids."

She rolled her eyes. "I might only be twelve, but I'm not stupid."

"Ava," Kelly said warningly.

But the child kept her gaze firmly on Jack. "How long have you known about me?"

He cleared his throat. "Your mom told me last week."

"And you were obviously overjoyed."

"I was…overwhelmed," he said cautiously.

"Did you ever plan to have kids?"

He glanced to Kelly for assistance, but she looked as helpless as he felt. "I never thought too much about the possibility," he finally acknowledged.

"I guess I know now why Mom didn't tell you about me," Ava said. "Because she knew you wouldn't want me."

"That's not true," Jack said.

"And not fair," Kelly interjected.

"Isn't it?" She tossed the pillow aside and pushed off the bed to face him more directly. "What did you say when she told you about me?"

"Ava," Kelly said, trying to divert her attention.

She shook her head. "I want to know."

Jack held her gaze. "I didn't react well," he admitted.

Green eyes, so similar to his own, narrowed. "You didn't want to believe it, did you? That's why Dr. Turcotte took that swab—it wasn't a strep test but a DNA test."

"I don't doubt that you're my daughter," Jack said now, because it was true.

"Did you ask for a DNA test?" Ava asked.

He sighed. "Yes."

Her eyes filled with tears. Then she turned on her heel and stormed out of the room and down the hall to slam another door.

Kelly blew out a breath. "Look at us—one big happy family."

"At least now I know where she gets her penchant for sarcasm." He scrubbed his hands over his face. "I completely screwed that up, didn't I?"

"Welcome to parenthood." Kelly stood up and moved toward the door.

Jack followed. "Maybe if you'd said those words twelve years ago, I might have figured out a few things by now," he told her. "Instead, you spring a twelve-year-old child on me and I have no idea what to say or do."

"I was just as unprepared to be a parent when she was born," Kelly reminded him as she made her way down the stairs. "And completely on my own."

"That was your choice," he shot back.

"I never chose to be a single parent," she argued. "I only chose not to tell your fiancée that I was pregnant with your baby. And truthfully, when I realized that you'd jumped from my bed right back to hers, I decided that you weren't the kind of man I wanted as a father to my child."

The accusation wasn't just hurtful, it was wrong. "I didn't jump from your bed to hers," he protested.

"When you came to Chicago, you told me your engagement was over. And when I called you a few months later, *she* answered your phone."

"We weren't together when I came to Chicago." He paced the length of the living room. "God, Kelly, how could you even think otherwise? There's no way I would have spent that weekend with you if I'd still been with Sara."

"So when did you get back together with her?" she wanted to know. "The day after you got back from Chicago?"

"You'd like to believe that, wouldn't you? Because then I'm the bad guy and you can feel self-righteous about keeping my child from me for the past twelve years."

"Are you denying that's what happened?"

"It's not even close to what happened."

She shook her head. "It doesn't matter."

"The only reason I even agreed to see Sara again is that I couldn't stop thinking about you."

"That's your story? That you jumped into bed with your ex because you were thinking about me?"

He heard the scorn in her voice and knew he couldn't blame her for being skeptical. Looking at the situation now, he could see that it wasn't the most logical course of action. But at the time, it was the only option he could see.

"Yeah, because no other woman has ever haunted me the way you did. After only three days together, I couldn't stop thinking about you. Even weeks later, you were my first thought in the morning and my last thought at night. And I couldn't think about you without wanting you. It's never been that way before, not with anyone else. So when Sara called, I wanted to believe that I wasn't missing you specifically, I was just missing being with someone." He pinned her with his gaze. "I was wrong."

"And yet, a few months later, you married her."

"I knew it was probably a mistake," he acknowledged. "But I knew that if I chased after you, I'd be making a bigger one."

She drew in a sharp breath and rubbed a hand over her breastbone, as if to assuage an ache, and he cursed himself for hurting her yet again when that was exactly what he'd tried to avoid from the beginning.

"Well, that's a flattering assessment."

He scrubbed his hands over his face. "It would have been a mistake because the timing was all wrong. Dammit, Kelly, I didn't want you sacrificing your education or your career because you thought you were in love with me."

"I did think I was in love with you," she agreed. "But I fell out of love quickly enough when reality hit."

"You're never going to forgive me for what happened thirteen years ago, are you?"

"On the contrary, I'm grateful to you for what happened thirteen years ago, for giving me Ava."

"But you can't forgive me for not being there for you—even though I didn't know there was any reason to be there."

"And if you had known? If I'd responded to the news of your engagement with 'That's great, Jack—you're getting married and you're going to be a father,' what would you have done?"

"I don't know," he admitted.

"I do," she told him. "You would have freaked because my unplanned pregnancy could have destroyed everything you wanted—not just your relationship with Sara but your name on the door of her father's law firm."

"Maybe I would have," he acknowledged. "I was young and stupid—and no way was I prepared to be a parent."

She just nodded. There was no need for her to point out again that she had been even younger and equally unprepared to be a parent. And yet she'd done what she needed to do.

"What about now?" she asked.

"I don't feel any more prepared now," he admitted. "Why do you think I panicked when you told me about Ava? Maybe part of it was that I wasn't ready to believe she was my child, but a bigger part was because I don't know how to be a father. But...I want to try."

She nodded again. "Thank you."

"You probably shouldn't thank me just yet," he warned.

"You have your faults, Jacks, but I've never known you to give up on something just because it wasn't easy. And Ava really needs a father."

* * *

Kelly didn't push her daughter to make conversation the next morning. After everything that had happened the night before, she figured Ava was entitled to be quiet and introspective, but she was hopeful that a day at camp would improve her mood. That hope was short-lived as Ava barely spoke half a dozen words on the way home at the end of the day, and those were only in response to direct questions.

"How was camp today?"

"Fine."

"What did you do?"

"The usual."

"What was for lunch today?"

"Cold pizza."

"Is Laurel going back next week?"

"Yeah."

Thankfully it wasn't a very long drive from camp to home, so while the silence the rest of the way was awkward, it wasn't interminable. And then she turned onto Larkspur Drive and saw a familiar vehicle parked in front of the house.

Ava apparently recognized the vehicle, too, because her scowl darkened. But she said nothing, only grabbed her backpack and slammed out of the car. Kelly unlocked the house for her, then waited on the driveway for Jackson.

He didn't look like he'd come from the office today. Instead of a shirt and tie, he was dressed in a pair of jeans and a T-shirt. But he still looked good. Too good.

The surprise must have shown on her face, because the first words he spoke were "Did you forget you invited me to dinner?"

"No, I just thought, after Ava's reaction last night, you might not want to come back here."

"I didn't expect it was going to be easy. I hoped it might be," he admitted, with just the hint of a smile. "But I didn't expect it."

"It could be a quiet meal—Ava's barely talking to me."

"She can't give us the silent treatment forever."

"You might be surprised," Kelly warned. "She's stubborn and hardheaded. Which I guess only proves she's a Garrett."

"Yeah, because you're such a pushover," he said dryly.

She had to smile at that. "How do you feel about fajitas?"

"As favorably as I feel about any meal that someone else is making," he assured her.

"It's one of Ava's favorites," she told him. "Tacos are the absolute number one, but we just had those last week."

"And you're still feeling guilty for the way she found out about me," he guessed.

"I've been feeling guilty for twelve years." She opened the fridge to pull out the ingredients she'd chopped earlier that morning.

While she started cooking, Jack opened the bottle of wine he'd brought. "And in those twelve years," he said, "did you ever think about contacting me?"

She nodded. "From the day she was born, and for a long time after, I thought about it almost every day. But you were married to Sara, then I married Malcolm, and then it seemed as if I'd let it go for too long."

He poured the wine into two glasses. "When was she born? All you told me was that it was February, but you didn't mention the actual date."

She added the onions and peppers to the pan. "The twelfth."

"February twelfth," he echoed. And she could tell by his tone that he finally understood why she hadn't reached out to him on that day.

She nodded. "Ava was born the day you got married."

* * *

When they sat down to eat and Ava finally decided to break her self-imposed vow of silence, the first words out of her mouth were "I've decided that I should move in with Jack."

Kelly had to focus all of her effort on breathing. Suddenly there was an unbearable weight on her chest that made it impossible to draw air into her lungs. She didn't know if Ava's request to live with Jack was based on a desire to get to know him better or a plan to punish her mother for keeping the identity of her father a secret for so long; she only knew that her heart was breaking into a thousand pieces.

Maybe she should have anticipated this. Or maybe, subconsciously, this scenario was one of the reasons she'd stayed in Washington as long as she had. Because she'd feared that when Ava found her father, she'd choose to be with him. Because no one had ever chosen Kelly. Not her mother or her father, not even the man she married, and certainly not Jackson. So why should she expect her daughter to be any different?

He seemed to recover from his surprise first. "You want to live...with me?"

Ava nodded.

His panicked gaze flew across the table, but Kelly couldn't help him. She was still too busy trying to process her daughter's statement to know what to do or say.

"Where is this coming from?" Jackson finally asked.

"I was talking to Laurel about the fact that I suddenly have this father I don't even know, and she suggested that the best way to get to know you would be to live with you."

Kelly managed to find her voice. "You talked to Laurel about this?"

"Yeah." Ava lifted her chin. "So?"

"So…I thought we might want to take some time to think about this before we announced it to the whole world."

"I didn't announce it to the world—I told my one and only friend in Pinetar, and you can't get mad at me because I know you've at least told Uncle Lukas."

Which, of course, she couldn't dispute. "You're right. And I'm glad you have a friend in whom you feel comfortable confiding, but living with Jackson is not an option."

"Why not?"

"Because I've only got a one-bedroom apartment," he said.

"I can sleep on the couch," Ava offered.

"Actually, it's an adults-only complex."

"What does that mean?"

"It means that no one has kids."

She frowned. "Why would you live in a place like that?"

"It's a nice building in a good location." He shrugged. "And there was no reason not to live there, because I never had a kid before now."

"I know you're eager to spend time with Jack," Kelly said, trying to keep her tone calm and rational, "but this situation is new to all of us and I think we should, right now, just take it one day at a time."

Ava didn't seem thrilled with this suggestion, but she turned her attention back to her plate. She finished folding her second tortilla and took a bite, and Kelly exhaled a quiet sigh.

"I noticed a picture of you in a soccer uniform in the living room," Jack commented when she was finished eating. "Do you still play?"

"Not this year," Ava told him, with another unhappy look toward her mother. "I couldn't do anything this summer because we were moving."

"You've been playing at camp," Kelly reminded her.

"Like that counts," the girl grumbled.

"There's a school tournament every fall," Jackson interjected. "Tryouts for the team start the second week of September."

"I'm really rusty," Ava said.

"Do you have a ball?" Jack asked.

"Of course I have a ball."

"Then why don't we take it outside and see just how rusty you are?" he suggested.

Ava looked at him as if he'd just offered her the moon on a silver platter. "Do *you* play?"

"Just for fun every once in a while now," he told her. "But I was on the varsity team all through high school and I usually help Adam Webber—he's the fifth-grade teacher and coach of the girls' team—with his practices."

Ava was already pushing away from the table. Then she suddenly remembered the manners that had been ingrained in her and paused to ask, "May I be excused?"

Kelly nodded. "Go wash up."

Ava carried her plate and cup to the counter, then raced up the stairs. Ordinarily Kelly would have called her back to put her dishes *in* the dishwasher, but she was so grateful to Jackson for successfully diffusing the volatile situation that she wasn't going to object to being stuck with the kitchen cleanup.

"She's good," Kelly told Jack as she started carrying the rest of the dishes to the sink. "You won't have to use your personal connection with the coach to get her on the team."

"I expect her to be good," Jack said, with more than a hint of arrogance. "She's my kid."

"Yeah, all I did was carry her in my womb for nine months and give birth after thirty-four hours of labor," Kelly noted dryly.

His cocky smile faded. "Thirty-four hours?"

"Actually, it was only four hours," she admitted, her own lips curving. "But no one ever sympathizes with a woman who only suffers through four hours of hard labor."

He turned her around to face him, his expression serious now. "Was it hard?"

"Not really. It was a pretty routine pregnancy and a blessedly quick birth. But the twelve years since have definitely been a challenge."

Before he could say anything else, Ava was back with her ball in hand.

Kelly tried to focus on the dishes while Jackson and Ava kicked the ball around the backyard, but she couldn't prevent her gaze from occasionally shifting toward the window. Ava's earlier moodiness was completely forgotten, and she was smiling and laughing as she deked around Jack. But he had some pretty good moves of his own for a thirty-seven-year-old, and sometimes their battles for control were pretty intense. Certainly Jack didn't seem to be trying to score any points with his daughter by letting her win.

It was the sound of barking that drew her attention to the window again, and she saw that the game had expanded now to include Matt, Quinn and Shane, with Finnigan and Frederick trying to chase the ball and avoid flying feet.

There didn't seem to be any real purpose to the action, at least not so far as Kelly could tell. But they were all laughing and having a great time, and she felt as if some of the enormous weight had been lifted off of her chest as she watched her daughter playing with her father.

She hadn't been sure it would ever happen. Even when she'd decided to return to Pinehurst, she couldn't have predicted what would happen when Ava and Jack each learned about the other. And although she knew there would inevitably be bumps further down the road, this, at least, had turned out to be a very good day.

Chapter Eight

On Saturday, Jack invited Ava and Kelly to go hiking at Eagle Point Park. He didn't know if either of them was the outdoorsy type, but it was a perfect day to be outside, as evidenced by the numerous other groups and families on the trails. The sky was a brilliant blue and nearly cloudless, and though the sun was high in the sky when they started, the canopy of trees offered some respite from the heat.

There hadn't been much rain in the past couple of weeks, so the trail was dry, the dirt packed hard from all the boots and shoes that had stomped upon it. Sometimes, if he wasn't in a hurry, Jack would look for animal tracks, but he knew they wouldn't find any today.

They started along one of the easier routes with the thought that a less strenuous hike might help facilitate conversation. But after a brief discussion of the weather and an even briefer discussion about the local flora and fauna, Ava plugged in her earbuds. Obviously she preferred her music to the sounds of nature—and conversation with her parents.

After a few minutes, Kelly said, "Lukas never told me that you coached soccer."

"I'm not actually the coach—I just help out."

"Still, I would have thought that a man who'd shared that basic connection with kids wouldn't freak out at the news that he had a kid of his own."

"But they weren't kids to me," he admitted. "They were

soccer players. And if I ever did think of them as kids, there was comfort in knowing they were someone else's."

"Are you still freaked out?"

"No. Just terrified."

She smiled. "Good."

"Why is that good?"

"Because you wouldn't be scared if you didn't care. It proves that she matters to you."

"I didn't expect that she would matter so much so fast," he admitted. "I mean, I barely had my head around the fact that I was a father and suddenly she was *my* child."

To his surprise, Kelly's eyes filled with tears.

"What did I do?" he asked warily.

She shook her head. "You said 'my child' without any hesitation."

"Yeah, well." He wasn't quite sure how to respond to that.

Kelly laughed. "So what have you been doing with your life besides practicing law and helping-but-not-coaching girls' soccer?"

He was grateful for the change of topic. "Work doesn't leave me a lot of time for anything else."

"How long have you been on your own?"

Obviously she knew that he was practicing independently now, because she'd been to his office and the name "Taylor & Ross" wasn't on the door. He thought Lukas might have told her the details of his decision to leave his father-in-law's firm, but maybe she'd never asked about him, as he'd been careful not to ask his brother about her.

"Almost ten years," he said in response to her question.

She stopped in the middle of the path. "You left Taylor and Ross ten years ago?"

"Yeah. About two years before Sara left me."

"Why?"

"Because I did want my name on the door, but I wanted to know that I'd earned it. As long as I was working for my father-in-law, I would never be sure."

"I'm sorry," she said. "For that crack I made about it being a wedding present."

"I'm a lawyer," he reminded her. "You'd have to throw sharper barbs than that to pierce my thick skin."

"I'll keep that in mind."

"How about you? What have you been doing with your life besides cooking books and raising our daughter?"

"Forensic accountants don't cook books," she said indignantly. "They investigate and analyze financial evidence."

"And they have very thin skin." As if to prove the point, he rubbed his hand on her upper arm briskly. He was being playful, teasing her. But then he noticed that her skin wasn't thin, but soft, and warm. And his movements slowed, gentled.

She stepped away, picked up her pace. "But my new job is more managerial than practical, and my hours will be more regular, which means I'll be able to spend less time at work and more time with Ava."

Jack fell into step beside her again.

"But speaking of cooking books," she continued in a deliberately casual tone. "I do have a collection of cookbooks that I haven't cracked open in far too long because I didn't have time for anything more than the basics, and I think I'd like to start cooking again for fun."

"I thought cooking was just for eating," he admitted. "And speaking of eating—why don't we stop for lunch when we get to Summit Falls?"

So they did.

Kelly had offered to pack a lunch, but Jack had arranged for a takeout picnic from the Bean There Café. A pointed look from her mother had Ava tucking her music away while they dined on turkey sandwiches, macaroni salad and potato chips, and washed it all down with bottles of water. But as soon as they were packing up to head back to the trail, the music came out again.

Obviously, Ava wasn't a nature lover, but Jack wasn't too disappointed. His plans for the day hadn't been a complete bust, because at least he and Kelly seemed to be communicating again. He wasn't ready to forgive her entirely—and he didn't doubt that she still had some residual anger of her own to work through—but he was at least confident that they could cooperate for the sake of their daughter.

Based on the experience at Eagle Point Park, Jack suspected that the urban jungle might be more Ava's style. So the following day, he decided to take her to The Fun Warehouse in Syracuse. He extended the invitation to Kelly as well, but he wasn't surprised when she declined, claiming that she had errands to run. As much as he enjoyed spending time with both of them, he couldn't deny that being close to his daughter's mother was more than a little distracting. Especially when he couldn't stop thinking about the kiss they'd shared in her kitchen more than a week earlier.

He picked Ava up at ten o'clock and took her to The Pancake Palace to fuel up on carbs before they went gaming. They played three rounds of laser tag and five games of air hockey (three of which she won), and then spent an hour in the arcade, at the conclusion of which they were both suffering from extreme sensory overload. But when they got back to Pinehurst, it was still only early afternoon.

"Are you ready to go home? Or do you want to check out my condo?"

"Am I allowed?" she asked hesitantly.

"There are no age restrictions on visitors."

"Okay."

He parked in his usual spot and led her into the building. She looked around curiously, but didn't say anything. In fact, as they made their way toward the bank of elevators, she seemed to be tiptoeing.

"It's so quiet," she said, her voice pitched so low it was practically inaudible. "I feel like I'm in a library."

"That's because you're whispering," he said, speaking in a normal tone.

"I don't want to get you in trouble for having a kid in the no-kid zone."

"The official designation is adult lifestyle condominium," he reminded her.

"We lived in a condo in Seattle," she told him. "On the twelfth floor. What floor are you on?"

"Three," he said, and pressed the button for his floor.

She frowned at the panel. "There are only three floors?"

"This isn't Seattle," he reminded her.

"No kidding," she grumbled.

She shrugged and wandered through the living room, studying the art on his walls, the books on his shelf, the CD collection. Then she wandered over to the floor-to-ceiling windows, peered out. "There's no Space Needle, but the view doesn't completely suck."

"High praise," he mused. "Do you miss Washington?"

She lifted a shoulder. "I miss my friends."

"You've already made some new friends, haven't you?"

"Yeah. A few. At camp."

"Are you looking forward to starting school?"

She just shrugged. "I'm thinking of getting some more streaks in my hair before then. Maybe green this time."

Jack shook his head, genuinely baffled. "Why would you cover up such pretty hair with fake color?"

"You think my hair's pretty?"

"It's beautiful," he told her sincerely. "You're beautiful." Because she was, and it absolutely stunned and humbled him to know that she was his daughter, that he'd had any part in the creation of this gorgeous creature. "Did you know you look just like your mother did at the same age?"

"Really?"

He nodded. "In fact, I think she was just a couple of years younger than you are now when she first came to live with her grandmother in Pinehurst."

"Have you known her since then?" she asked curiously.

"Yeah. Although I didn't know her very well. She and Lukas were always best buddies, though."

"When did you start to like her?"

Jack realized, too late, that he'd started a conversation he wasn't sure he wanted to finish. Because he knew that when she asked about him "liking" her mother she wasn't referring to the platonic friendship sort of "like" but the boy-and-girl-get-naked-together-and-make-a-baby sort. For purposes of self-preservation, however, he pretended to misunderstand. "I always got along okay with your mom."

Ava rolled her eyes. "When did you start to date her?"

That one wouldn't be deflected quite so easily, but it was even more awkward for Jack to answer because the truth was, he and Kelly had never really dated. They'd flirted, they'd kissed, and then they'd jumped into bed together without ever having been out on a single date.

"Not until she was in college."

"I thought she went to college in Chicago."

"She did," he confirmed.

She nodded, as if that explained everything. "Long-distance romances never work."

"And you know this—how?"

"Regan—Rachel's sister. Her boyfriend went to UCLA, which isn't even really that far from Seattle. But he said he had to break up with her because missing her was interfering with his schoolwork. Regan said it was sleeping with all the L.A. sluts that was interfering with his schoolwork." Ava shrugged. "Either way, she's got a new boyfriend now."

The matter-of-fact tone in which she'd referenced sex unnerved him as much as the content. She was *twelve,* for God's sake. He tried to think back, to remember what he'd known about sex at the same age, and came up with nothing. Which probably was the answer.

Apparently Seattle was a world away from Pinehurst in more than distance. And what kind of comment was he supposed to make now to follow up that revelation? He didn't have a clue.

"Are you hungry?" he asked, in a desperate and not-at-all subtle attempt to change the topic of conversation.

"Yeah."

"Do you want to go out to eat or help me make dinner here?"

"You cook?"

She sounded so dubious, he had to smile. "Well enough that I don't starve."

"What can you make?"

"Fettuccine, linguine, spaghettini, tortellini."

Ava rolled her eyes. "So basically you know how to boil water and cook pasta?"

"I can also make tacos."

"In that case," she decided, "let's eat here."

While Jack browned and seasoned the ground beef, Ava chopped lettuce and tomatoes and grated the cheese.

"Hard or soft shell?" he asked, setting a plate with both on the table.

"Soft," she replied, automatically reaching for one. "Hard are too messy."

"There's a trick to eating hard tacos," he told her, spooning filling into his shell.

She expertly rolled up her tortilla. "What's that?"

"The grip." He held the top of the shell with his fingers, then brought the taco to his mouth and bit into the end.

The shell broke apart and dumped all the meat and toppings onto his plate.

Ava giggled.

"And then," Jack continued, as if the disintegration of his taco had been planned all along, "you use your fork to scoop up the rest."

"I'll have to try that next time," she said gamely.

Then she neatly bit into her own taco.

It wasn't unusual for Ava to be up early on the first day of school. But this year, Kelly suspected that her daughter's inability to sleep in was as much apprehension as anticipation. It was seventh grade so the whole school thing was hardly new to her, but it was a new school, and Kelly remembered all too clearly how difficult that could be.

Ava was seated at the breakfast bar now, dressed in a new pair of jeans and a peasant-style top, with her purple-painted toenails peeking out of her sandals. She pushed her Cheerios around in her bowl, stirring more than eating.

Yeah, Kelly remembered first-day jitters.

She took a sip her coffee. "Do you want me to take you to school?"

Ava looked up from her cereal with an expression of absolute horror. "I'd rather wear a neon sign flashing 'new kid' over my head."

"That's a better idea," she agreed. "But I don't know where we'd find one this early in the morning."

Her daughter pushed away from the table.

"Brush your teeth," she said, because she'd been saying it for so many years it had become a habit.

Ava rolled her eyes. "Cuz that would never have occurred to me."

Kelly chose to ignore the sarcasm because she knew that Ava was dealing with a lot. Not just her first day at a new school, but settling into a new home in a new town, and getting to know her father. While there hadn't been too many bumps in the road and nothing too major, she had to be feeling overwhelmed. Anxious. Uncertain.

Or maybe Kelly was projecting her own feelings onto her daughter.

When Ava returned from the bathroom and lifted her backpack onto her shoulder, Kelly indulged herself by stroking a hand down her daughter's hair. The purple streaks had almost completely faded and her hair was soft and silky. "You look very nice."

Ava smiled shyly. "Thanks."

Kelly kissed her forehead. "I'll be here when you get home," she promised. "But just in case, you know where the key is, don't you?"

"Yes, I know where the key is."

Kelly kissed her cheek. "Have a good day."

"You, too."

She stood at the front window, watching her walk down the sidewalk and trying not to worry.

A few minutes later, she was on her way out to the car when she saw Georgia making her way down the sidewalk, flanked by Shane and Quinn with matching packs on their backs. Matt was right behind them, with the baby strapped in a carrier on his chest. The twins' first day of school was obviously a whole family event, and Kelly couldn't deny that she felt just a little bit envious as she watched them set off.

Ava's first day had been an entirely different experience, as was the case with most of her daughter's firsts. Kelly had been there, of course, as had Bev, but the little girl's father had been three thousand miles away and unable to share any of those milestone moments with her. And while Kelly sometimes regretted that fact, she'd managed to convince herself that she'd made the right choice. That even if Jack had known about his child, he had hardly been the type to hold her tiny hand in his on that long walk to the first day of school.

Now she wasn't so sure. And she felt a pang of regret that she'd denied him—and Ava—that opportunity.

One of the greatest perks of Kelly's new job was the flexible hours. Craig Richmond might have been the company vice president, but he was also a father of four, and he assured her that she wouldn't have to punch a clock. He didn't care if she arrived late or left early so long as the work got done. Kelly decided to take him at his word and tried not to feel guilty about leaving work at two o'clock so that she would be home before Ava got back from her first day at school.

Apparently Jackson didn't have to punch a clock, either, because he was on her front step when she pulled into the driveway, and her heart automatically did a little skip and jump. She found it as baffling as it was frustrating that he continued to have such an effect on her. After everything they'd been through and in spite of the current tension and distrust between them, just a hint of his smile was enough to make her knees weak.

"For you," he said, handing her a paper-wrapped bundle of roses and daisies and freesia. "To commemorate Ava's first day of school."

"You mean her first day in the seventh grade?"

He shrugged. "Sure."

Though she was still a little puzzled, she brought the bouquet up to her nose and inhaled the fragrant scent of the blossoms. "Thank you."

"I've been thinking about all of the things I missed out on because I didn't know about Ava. And as much as I'm angry and frustrated that I'll never get that time back, I realized that I at least have an opportunity to get to know my daughter now. And although I don't know her very well, I know that she's a good kid. And that's because of you."

She had to blink away tears as she unlocked the door. "That was quite the speech."

"I practiced while I waited for you to come home. I've been here since about ten o'clock this morning."

She smiled at the blatant fib. "Don't you have a job?"

"One of the perks of being my own boss is that I can take a day off if I want to. Unless I'm scheduled to be in court or have a client emergency," he amended.

She filled a vase with water, arranged the flowers in it. "Well, I'm glad you could be here today. I know Ava will be happy to see you when she gets home. But she'll probably be tired," she warned. "She never sleeps very well the night before the first day."

"Do you remember her very first day?" he asked.

"As if it was yesterday."

"Can you tell me about it?"

"I can do a little better than that," she said, and went to the cabinet in the living room to pull out a photo album.

Jackson sat on the sofa and she opened the front cover of the book before setting it on the table in front of him.

"She was as cute as a button, wasn't she?" he said, pride evident in his tone.

"And terrified. You can tell by the way she's smiling— just a little too wide and bright. That was Ava putting on her brave face." She settled beside him. "She picked out her Dora lunchbox, and we packed it together. A cheese sandwich cut into four triangles with the crust removed, homemade chocolate chip cookies, apple wedges and fruit punch.

"Today, she took a couple of slices of leftover pizza, a package of cheesy crackers and a can of lemonade in a brown paper bag."

"What a difference eight years makes."

She nodded and pointed to another photo with a two-story brick building in the background. "That was her school." She turned the page. "And there's Ava with her teacher, Miss Watson."

"Did you stay and take pictures through the whole day?" he teased.

"No," Kelly admitted. "I dropped her off at school and headed to work, but I left my camera with Bev and she hung around for a while."

"She was your daycare provider?"

"As well as my neighbor, one of my first friends in Seattle, and eventually my mother-in-law."

"Is that how you met him…your husband?"

She nodded. "Bev never actually admitted it, but I think she kept setting things up to ensure our paths would cross. Calling Malcolm to come over on the nights she'd invite Ava and I to stay for dinner. Offering to watch Ava so I could attend various school functions with Malcolm."

"And eventually you fell in love," he guessed, keeping his gaze focused on the photo album.

"Yeah. Or close enough that we thought we could make marriage work."

"So what happened?" He felt compelled to ask, though he wasn't sure he wanted to know. Aside from the fact that the details of her marriage were none of his business, he couldn't stand the thought of Kelly with anyone else.

He knew it was completely irrational, but that knowledge didn't negate the feeling.

"He was offered a job in Boston—a very prestigious position at a private school—and I didn't want to leave Seattle."

He lifted his gaze to look at Kelly. "You got divorced because you didn't want to move?"

"I know it sounds ridiculous," she acknowledged. "But our difference of opinion on the job was only a symptom of a bigger problem, starting with the fact that he never asked what I wanted. He never even discussed the job offer with me before he accepted it. I was just supposed to be the dutiful little wife and start packing, never mind that I had a career of my own and a child to think about."

"He obviously didn't know you very well if he expected you to be a dutiful anything," Jack teased.

She smiled, though he could see the lingering sadness in her eyes. "And ultimately that was the truth," she agreed. "We each had our own reasons for marrying, but we didn't really know one another at all."

"That's not so different than what happened with me and Sara," he confided.

"She wanted you to move to Boston?"

He smiled. "No, but we each had our own reasons for marrying, and none of them were what they should have been."

Kelly didn't say anything, and really, what was there to say? What was the purpose in trying to explain what had gone wrong in his marriage when she wouldn't believe it anyway?

Only a complete fool married one woman when he was all tangled up in knots over another, and that's exactly what Jack had done.

"This is a picture of Bev with Ava." She pointed to another photo. "On a class trip to the Museum of Flight."

He flipped through more pages, enjoying more glimpses of Ava's first year at school. Marching in her first Halloween costume parade, creating her first handprint Thanksgiving turkey decoration, singing in her first Christmas pageant.

"Bev took most of those pictures," Kelly admitted. "I tried to be there as much as I could, but when I couldn't, she was."

"You miss her," he noted.

She nodded. "She was a good friend to me, and the closest thing to a grandmother that Ava's ever known." She looked at him now, her eyes filled with regret. "I didn't realize, when I decided to move to Washington, that your parents wouldn't ever have a chance to know their granddaughter. That Ava wouldn't have a chance to know them."

"They would have been over the moon to know they had a grandchild."

"And my parents have as little interest in Ava as they had in me."

He frowned at that. "I always thought…"

"You thought I lived with my grandmother because my parents were dead?"

He nodded.

"Nope. They just didn't want me."

"I'm sure that's not true."

"It is true," she said, in a neutral tone. "Both my parents are alive and well, and I haven't seen either of them in years. My mom lives in Australia with her third husband—she's never even met Ava. And my dad's a long-distance trucker with his home base in Detroit. He's only seen her a handful of times, although he usually remembers to send a card on her birthday."

"What about your birthday?" he asked.

She just shook her head.

I'd rather she didn't know the identity of her father than to know that he doesn't want to be her father.

At the time, her words had made no sense to Jack. Now he realized that she'd been speaking from personal experience, and it gave him some insight into her actions. Not that the neglect of her parents justified what she'd done, but it helped to explain it. Kelly's fear that he wouldn't want to be involved in his daughter's life wasn't so much a judgment against him but a response to her parents' lack of involvement in her own.

He finished thumbing through the album, ending with the little girl's kindergarten graduation, then closed the cover. "Do you have any pictures of Ava as a baby?"

She smiled. "Only about ten thousand."

"Then we should probably get started."

They were still poring over photo albums when Ava got home from school.

The envelope from PDA Labs was in his mail slot when he got home later that night. Until that moment, Jack had actually forgotten that he'd asked for the test. Well, demanded was more accurate, he acknowledged as he tore open the flap. His fingers weren't entirely steady as he pulled out the report and scanned for the result.

Probability of paternity: 99.99999%

He hadn't realized he was holding his breath until all of the air whooshed out of his lungs.

It was the most positive result that could be reported, and it confirmed beyond a shadow of a doubt that Ava was his daughter. Not that he had any doubt. Not after spending time with Kelly and Ava. But it was still a relief to have official confirmation in hand.

And he was relieved. When he'd first asked for the test, he'd been panicked, in denial. Kids were nowhere in his plan. No, thank you. Not interested in going down that road.

But he wasn't the type to shirk his responsibilities, and when he'd started to accept the possibility that he'd fathered a child, he'd resolved to do the right thing. He'd never suspected that he'd get to know the child and *want* to be her father. And he definitely hadn't anticipated that he would start reminiscing about his relationship with the child's mother.

Now, only a couple of weeks after Kelly's first visit to his office, everything had changed. He wanted the world to know that Ava was his.

And he was starting to realize that he wanted Kelly to be his, too.

Chapter Nine

Tryouts for the soccer team started the following week, each day for an hour after school with the first cuts being made on Wednesday. Jack was there every day to help Adam run drills and evaluate the players, as he'd been doing in each of the past few years. But this was the first year he had a vested interest in any of the students who were trying out for the team.

When practice was finished and Ava picked up her backpack, he went over to her. "Adam said there's no tryout tomorrow night because of something going on at the school."

"Yeah, it's a Meet the Teacher thing for parents."

"What's a 'Meet the Teacher thing'?"

"It's where parents go to the school...and meet the teacher."

"Should I go?"

"Do you want to go?"

Apparently they were both playing their cards close to the vest. He decided to lay his hand on the table. "Yes, I would like to go to your school to meet your teacher."

She blinked at the unequivocal response. "Really?"

"Unless you don't want me to go."

"No, I want you to go," she said. "If you want to go."

"What time?" he asked.

"Six o'clock."

"I'll come by around five-thirty so we can walk over together."

"Sure."

As she wandered off with Laurel, he went back to the bleachers, where Adam was making notes on each of the players.

"We've got impressive new talent this year," he said to Jack. "That Cooper kid, in particular, has some good moves."

He nodded his agreement, proud that his own assessment had been accurate, even more proud because Ava was his. And more than a little annoyed that she was "that Cooper kid" rather than "that Garrett kid."

"About her…"

Adam's gaze didn't shift away from his papers. "Don't worry—I know."

"What do you know?"

"That she's yours."

The teacher did look at him now, and grinned at the surprise Jack didn't doubt was evident on his face.

"There was whispered speculation in the teacher's lounge," Adam confided. "But no confirmation. I was skeptical myself, until I saw her. Then I saw her with a soccer ball, and any lingering doubts vanished."

"It's not public knowledge," Jack told him.

His friend laughed. "You only think it's not."

He scowled at that.

"I do have one question, though," Adam said.

"What's that?"

"You and Kelly Cooper—old news?"

His scowl deepened. "Aren't you dating Melanie Quinlan?"

"Not exclusively."

"And isn't there a rule against dating the parent of a student?"

"She's not my student."

Adam's immediate response proved that he'd already given some thought to the ethical implications. A realization that didn't sit well with Jack.

"You're her coach."

"Only for a few weeks."

Jack didn't bother to respond, because he was confident that before the championship tournament was over, no one would be wondering if he and Kelly were old news.

Kelly's worries about Ava's transition to Parkdale Elementary School had apparently been for naught. Her daughter had settled into the routine of seventh grade with little difficulty. At home, they'd also settled into a routine. After school/work, Ava would do her homework—if she had any—while Kelly got dinner ready. Following the meal, they did dishes together and packed lunches for the next day.

"What did you do at school today?" Kelly asked as she chopped up raw vegetables for their snack.

"We had a pop quiz in math."

"How was it?"

Ava shrugged. "I think I did okay. Then we had a substitute in music who didn't know anything about music, so we watched a movie."

"Glad to know my educational tax dollars aren't being wasted."

"And there's a barbecue at the school on Thursday for Meet the Teacher." She pulled the flyer out of her agenda and set it on the counter.

Kelly glanced up from the cutting board and noted the date. "*This* Thursday? As in *tomorrow?*"

"Yeah." Ava grabbed a stalk of celery, bit into it.

"I'm sorry," Kelly told her. "I have an interdepartmental meeting at six o'clock tomorrow night."

"I thought you weren't going to miss any more of my school stuff because of work. Isn't that why we moved here?"

"One of the reasons," she acknowledged. And maybe she could miss a meeting, but she didn't want to miss *this one* because it was the first since she'd started in her new position at Richmond Pharmaceuticals.

Ava shrugged. "Whatever."

"I'm sorry," she said again.

"S'okay," Ava said around another bite of celery. "My dad said he would go."

Kelly had noticed that Ava always referred to Jackson as "my dad" when she was talking to her, but she never actually used the title in his presence. She didn't know if that was because Ava was insightful enough to realize that Jackson was still a little intimidated by the word, or if she simply wanted to emphasize the relationship Kelly had denied for so long.

"When did you see Jackson?" she asked her daughter.

"He was at my soccer tryout after school."

"You were supposed to go to Laurel's house after school."

"I went to Laurel's house after tryouts," Ava said patiently. "And then her mom brought me home after we'd finished our science project."

"Is Laurel trying out for the team, too?"

"Yeah. We both made the first cut. Next tryout's Friday at lunch. Coach Webber said he'll make the final cuts then."

"Are you worried?"

"Not really. My dad said he'd come by later so that we could work on some stuff." Her eyes lit up in response to the ring of the doorbell. "In fact, that's probably him now."

"Apparently I should have been a lawyer instead of an accountant," Kelly grumbled to herself as her daughter raced to the door.

* * *

Shortly after father and daughter had headed off to the park and Kelly had finished packing lunches, Lukas stopped by to take his "favorite girls" for ice cream.

"Ava's not here," Kelly told him. "She went to the park with Jacks to work on her corner kicks."

He shrugged philosophically. "How about you? Are you in the mood for a double scoop of mint chocolate chip?"

"Isn't ice cream appropriate for any mood?"

"Absolutely," he agreed.

They chatted easily on the way to Walton's. Kelly told him about her new job at Richmond Pharmaceuticals and Lukas filled her in on Einstein's most recent antics. Once they had their ice cream in hand—a double scoop of mint chocolate chip in a waffle cone for Kelly and a caramel pecan brownie sundae for Lukas—they sat side by side on one of the picnic tables outside.

They talked some more about everything and anything, but it wasn't until their ice cream was nearly done that Lukas finally mentioned his brother's name.

"It seems like Jack's been spending a lot of time with Ava these days."

"He has," she agreed, and tried not to sound too unhappy about it.

"Isn't that what you wanted? The reason you came back to Pinehurst?"

"I thought so." But she hadn't thought Jackson would make such an effort. She'd thought he might spend a couple hours a week with his daughter, but in the past two weeks, he'd been there almost every single day. And on the days that he didn't see her, he at least made a point of calling. "But it seems as if he's seen more of Ava recently than I have."

"It's not a competition, Kelly."

"I know," she said. "Or I know it shouldn't be."

"But you're used to being the center of her world, and now you're not," Lukas guessed.

"Now I'm not even in the same orbit. Lately all she talks about is 'my dad.'"

"Having a father is a new and exciting experience. Don't worry, the novelty will wear off."

She smiled, because she knew that was what he wanted, but the truth was that she didn't want the novelty to wear off. She sincerely hoped that Ava would develop a good relationship with her father—she just didn't want to lose her in the process.

"I've got competition now, too," Lukas reminded her. "When it was just an honorary title, I was her only 'uncle.' Now I have to compete with my own brother to be her favorite."

"I never thought about that," she mused. "That would be a tough competition."

"But Ava's known me longer, so I figure that gives me a slight edge."

"On the other hand, Matt has a wife, three kids, and two puppies, and Ava's always wanted to be part of a big family."

"I've got a puppy," he reminded her. "And a cat."

She smiled. "Yeah, that definitely narrows the gap."

"And I've got two tickets to the Black Keys concert Saturday night."

"I don't think Ava's a fan."

"I wasn't going to take Ava."

Her spirits immediately lifted. "You're going to take me?"

"Do you want to go?"

"I absolutely want to go," she assured him. Then reality hit, and her excitement dimmed. "But—"

"Ask Jack to hang out with Ava," Lukas suggested, anticipating her concern.

"It's a Saturday night."

"That is what it says on the tickets," he confirmed.

"He probably already has plans."

"I know you don't want to believe that he's changed, but he has," Lukas told her. "Jack's wild ways with women are very definitely a thing of the past."

Kelly did want to believe it, but she was afraid to. Because if she did believe it, she might fall for him all over again, and she wasn't going to let that happen.

"Okay," she relented. "I'll ask him." Then she bumped his shoulder with her own. "Thanks."

"For the ticket?"

"Well, that," she agreed. "And for being here."

"Always."

It wasn't nearly as unusual as Kelly thought for Jack not to have plans on a Saturday night. And if he did go out, more often than not it was with one or both of his brothers. But since Matt had married Georgia, it was next to impossible to get him out, and since the incident with Luke at Kelly's house, Jack had been maintaining a cautious distance from his younger brother.

So when Kelly asked him if he could hang out with Ava on Saturday night, he had no reason to refuse the request. In fact, he was happy to have extra time with his daughter. But he was curious about where Kelly was going. The possibility that she might have a date—

Well, he just didn't want to consider that possibility. So he was relieved to learn that she was going to a concert with Luke. Or so he thought until she said goodbye and walked out of the house in high heels, snug-fitting jeans, and a sexy little top, and he realized it wasn't relief that he was feeling.

Based on a few offhand comments that she'd made, he didn't think she'd done much dating. No doubt because she'd been so focused on raising their daughter. But Ava was almost a teenager now, and it wouldn't be too long after that when she herself would start dating—or at least wanting to date. Since Jack had no intention of letting that happen until she was at least twenty-one, that wasn't anything more than a distant concern. The idea of Kelly dating, on the other hand, was a more distinct possibility. And one that he didn't like at all.

Ava popped a DVD into the player while he put a bag of popcorn in the microwave.

"I was wondering about something," she said, when the kernels had stopped popping.

"What's that?" He opened the bag and dumped it into a large plastic bowl.

"Am I supposed to call you Jack? Or Dad?"

He'd noticed that she didn't tend to use any form of direct address when she spoke to him and he suspected that she hadn't yet figured out how he fit into her life. Which wasn't really surprising, since he was still struggling to figure that out himself. And while there was a part of him that wanted to be Ava's "Dad," another part feared that he wasn't worthy of the name. Aside from contributing half of her DNA, what had he done to deserve the title?

"There isn't any *supposed to*," he said. "It's up to you."

She frowned, clearly dissatisfied with his response. "It feels weird to call you Jack."

"And it probably feels just as weird to think about calling me Dad."

"Except that you are my dad."

He could see her dilemma, because his was similar. She

was his daughter, but he had yet to refer to her as such in conversation with anyone other than Kelly.

"But we're both new to this father-and-daughter thing," he pointed out. "It would probably be easier if I'd been there when you cut your teeth or started to walk or learned to talk. Then we might have naturally progressed from 'da-da' to 'daddy' to 'dad'—but even most babies take a year to get to 'da-da.'"

"Are you saying that you want me to wait a year to call you Dad?"

"No, I want you to wait until you're ready, whether that's a month or a year or even longer."

She popped the top of her soda and took a sip while she considered, then nodded. "Okay."

With that matter decided, at least for the moment, they settled down in the living room to watch the movie. As the action played out on the screen, Jack found himself thinking about everything he'd missed over the past twelve years. And when he started counting all those milestones that had passed without him even being aware that he had a child, he couldn't help but feel angry with Kelly.

But being here with Ava now, just hanging out with his daughter on a Saturday night, was a milestone he'd never thought he would experience. And as she yawned and let her head drop onto his shoulder, he realized that he wouldn't trade this night for anything in the world.

When the movie was over, he picked up the empty popcorn bowl and soda cans while she ejected the disc.

"I have one more question," she told him.

He braced himself. "What's that?"

"Can I have a puppy?"

He laughed. "*That's* a question you have to ask your mother."

* * *

Kelly had a fabulous time at the concert, so much so that she actually stopped worrying about Ava and Jackson for a few hours. And she was happy to spend the time with Lukas. She wasn't sure he'd completely forgiven her for keeping the identity of her daughter's father a secret for so long, but she was confident that their friendship was back on track.

As a result, when she got home Saturday night, Kelly felt as if there wasn't anything she couldn't handle. The feeling lasted only until she sat down at the kitchen table with a mug of peppermint tea and Jackson said, "I've been thinking about what Ava said—about wanting to live with me."

Kelly tried to ignore the knots that tightened in her belly as she picked up her mug. "Even if you had a spare room, I wouldn't let her move in with you."

"I know," he admitted. "And I was actually thinking that it makes more sense for me to move in here."

She was shaking her head before he finished speaking. "Why not?" he demanded.

"There are so many reasons why not, I don't know where to begin."

"I'm Ava's father."

"A status that is independent of your home address."

He scowled. "You could at least pretend to consider it. Or do you hate me so much that you can't stand being in close proximity?"

Kelly wished she could say yes. Unfortunately, her feelings for Jackson had never been that simple. "I don't hate you at all—I just don't want to live with you."

"I want to get to know my daughter. How is that going to happen when I only see her for a few hours a couple of times a week?"

"It will happen," she assured him. "But you've got to give it time."

"We've already waited more than twelve years."

Whether or not the statement was intended to make Kelly feel guilty, it certainly had that effect. It also made her wonder if what he was asking was really so unreasonable.

She was pleased that Jackson wanted more time with Ava, and she knew that their daughter would be thrilled to have more time with her father. But if that time together was under her roof, Kelly couldn't help but worry how that would impact her. It might be selfish, but it was undeniable. There was no way to pretend that she was unaffected by Jackson's presence, and if they were actually living together, as if they were a real family, she feared that she would fall for him all over again.

"I get that you want more time together," she finally said. "But you don't have to move in here...." Her words trailed off when she saw her daughter standing in the doorway.

Ava's sleepy gaze sharpened as it shifted from Kelly to Jackson. "You're going to move in here?"

"No!" Kelly said quickly, firmly. And then, in a more level tone, "I thought you were asleep."

"I was. Then I woke up and heard voices, so I came down."

"And interrupted a private conversation," she admonished.

"About Jack moving in here."

"No one's moving anywhere."

Ava's hopeful smile faded. "Why not?"

"Because..." Kelly looked around for help, but none was forthcoming.

"Please, Mom." Then she turned to Jackson. "Would you want to live with us?"

"I'm willing to give it a try," he said, "if your mother is."

Of course Kelly wasn't willing—and she didn't believe that Jackson wanted to move out of his high-end downtown condo to a house in suburbia with an ex-lover and their twelve-year-old daughter. But he obviously didn't want to disappoint their daughter, so he was going to make her do it.

"Mom?" Ava prompted.

And when Kelly looked at her daughter again, she found that she couldn't. Because she knew that if she refused to let Jackson move in when he'd already said he was willing to do so, Ava would never forgive her. Kelly already felt guilty enough for depriving her daughter of her father for so many years, and she really didn't want to stand in the way of their developing relationship now. She really didn't want to live under the same roof with Jackson, either but how could she worry about protecting her own heart when her daughter's was so vulnerable and needy? And what Ava really needed right now was her father.

"I guess we can give it a try," she finally relented.

Ava rushed over and hugged her. "Thanks, Mom." Then her attention shifted to her father again. "When can you move in?"

"I'll pack some things tomorrow," he promised.

It was a prospect that didn't help Kelly sleep that night. And by the time she'd cleared up breakfast dishes and dropped Ava off at Laurel's house the next day, she'd had second and third thoughts about her decision.

"Please tell me you're not actually packing," Kelly said, when Jack responded to her knock on his door just before noon on Sunday.

"I'm not actually packing," he said obediently.

She exhaled, so visibly relieved he nearly smiled. "I'm glad you came to your senses."

"I didn't know I'd lost them—and I only said that I wasn't packing because that's what you told me to say."

She frowned at that.

"You told Ava that you were willing to give it a shot," he reminded her, stepping away from the door so that she could enter.

She huffed out an exasperated breath as she followed him into the foyer. "Because my back was against the wall. But the more I think about it, the more I know this won't work. It's an impossible situation."

"Actually, it's not just possible but practical."

She shook her head. "I'm asking you to take the lead here and to tell Ava that you've reconsidered."

"But I haven't reconsidered," he said mildly.

"Well, you should. Because the two of us living under the same roof is a bad idea."

He shifted closer, deliberately invading her space. "Afraid you won't be able to withstand the temptation?"

She held her ground and tipped her head back to meet his gaze. "I promise you, Jacks, I'm not the least bit tempted— except maybe to slap you for being such an arrogant ass."

"I don't think you'd be so angry if you didn't still have feelings for me."

"I didn't come here to feed into your delusions but to try to talk you out of this crazy plan. If that's not possible, we need to at least set some ground rules."

Her prim attitude and cool demeanor tempted him to ruffle her feathers, but her statement also piqued his curiosity. "What kind of ground rules?"

She crossed her arms over her chest in a gesture so similar to their daughter's that he nearly smiled. But then he noticed that the movement pushed her breasts together, enhancing his view of the cleavage visible down the V-neckline of her top. He caught a glimpse of the scalloped edging on the cup of her bra, silky peach-colored lace against satiny pale skin. There were five more buttons down the front of her top, round pearl-like buttons that he could have unfastened in about three seconds. Maybe less.

The possibility was tempting…and incredibly arousing. His response to her was baffling, but undeniable. And while he wanted to believe it was purely physical, because sexual attraction was something he understood, he worried that his feelings for her were deeper and more complex than he was willing to acknowledge.

"First, I want a two-week trial, and I want you to tell Ava that we agreed to a two-week trial."

"Three weeks," he countered.

"Fine. Three weeks," she relented. "Second—but most importantly—you're not bringing women to the house."

It took a moment for her words to register, and when they did, he felt as if he'd had a bucket of ice water dumped over his head. He lifted his gaze from the tempting view of her cleavage to her golden eyes. "You're kidding."

"No, I'm not kidding," she snapped. "I don't want a series of your girlfriends in and out of my daughter's life."

"For God's sake, Kelly. I wasn't talking about your so-called rule, but the fact that you actually thought you had to spell it out to me."

"I might have been gone more than a dozen years, but I haven't forgotten your reputation, Jack."

"I'm not the same man I was then."

"I'm sure the blonde in the red dress would beg to differ."

He gritted his teeth. "I told you that she was a client."

"Well, I'd appreciate it if you entertained your 'clients'

away from my home," she said stiffly. And then she continued, almost apologetically, "I'm not trying to interfere with your social life. I'm just asking you to ensure that my daughter isn't a witness to the parade of women through your life."

"*Our* daughter," he reminded her.

"Our daughter," she agreed.

"Can I say something now?"

She eyed him warily. "What's that?"

"Instead of worrying about nonexistent parades of women, you should think about the fact that I haven't wanted any other woman since I saw you at the airport more than four weeks ago." He shifted closer. "But I definitely want you."

Her eyes widened slightly, but she'd never been the type to back down, and she didn't do so now. Instead, she lifted her chin. "No doubt that's because I'm the only woman in town you haven't slept with at least once in the past decade."

As soon as the words were out of her mouth, Kelly wished she could take them back. The intense focus of the gaze Jackson narrowed on her warned that it was already too late. She'd waved the red cape in front of an angry bull. He took a step closer, so close that she could feel the heat emanating from his body, the frustration rising in waves around him.

Yeah, he was angry. But there was something else in the predatory gleam in his eyes, something that looked a lot like arousal. And—heaven help her—his nearness was definitely stirring her up inside.

"It's been a long time," he acknowledged, and though his tone was casual, his gaze was heated, hungry. "But I can still remember how soft your skin felt beneath my hands, how you trembled when I touched you, how you came apart when I was buried deep inside you."

Her knees were trembling now, but she refused to let him know it. She dropped her arms, her hands reaching behind her to grip the edge of the table at her back. "I'm not the same naive girl I was back then."

He dipped his head, so that his lips were close to her ear. "And I'm not the same boy who couldn't think of anything but getting into your pants. What is the same is the desire—I want you just as much as I wanted you back then. Maybe even more."

She knew what he meant. The attraction she'd felt at twenty-one was nothing like the torrent of need raging inside of her now. And when his tongue traced the outer shell of her ear, the slow, sensuous glide turned her bones to jelly and made everything inside her quiver. But she also knew that succumbing to the want that pulsed through her every vein would be a mistake. And she'd already made enough of those where Jackson was concerned.

His breath was warm on her cheek as his teeth tugged gently on her lobe. He'd barely touched her, but her entire body was suddenly hot and achy. She felt tingles in her breasts, between her thighs. She put her hand up, against his chest, and felt his heart thud wildly against her palm. But instead of pushing him away, her fingers curled into the fabric of his shirt.

His lips skimmed across her jaw. "This is why you really came here, isn't it?"

She shook her head. "I came here to *talk*."

"Tell me you don't want me."

She closed her eyes, bit hard on her lip to hold back the moan when his mouth moved down her throat. "I don't want you."

But it was a lie, and they both knew it.

And when his lips touched the frantically beating pulse point below her ear, she shivered.

"I don't *want* to want you," she clarified.

He'd already made quick work of the buttons running down the front of her blouse, and he dipped his head lower, his tongue delving in the hollow between her breasts.

Inside the lacy cups of her bra, her nipples pebbled, aching for his touch. She closed her eyes against the sting of tears. Dammit, she did *not* want this. Because she knew that getting naked with Jackson would be a mistake for so many reasons. But right now, she couldn't think of a single one of those reasons. She couldn't seem to focus on what was smart or reasonable. She couldn't think at all, but she instinctively knew that this was what she needed. *He* was what she needed.

She pulled his head down, nibbled on his bottom lip. He had a fabulous mouth. Lush and tasty, and incredibly talented. And his hands—oh, those hands were moving over her now, teasing and tempting, making her burn everywhere they touched.

She tore her mouth from his to say, "This doesn't change anything, Jacks."

"I'm not trying to change a thing," he assured her, then cupped her buttocks to lift her up against him.

She wrapped her legs around his waist, rubbed herself wantonly against the hard press of his denim as he carted her down the hall. "You have to know this is a bad idea."

"I can't think of a worse one," he agreed, then kicked open the door of his bedroom and tumbled with her onto the bed.

Chapter Ten

He tugged off her blouse and tossed it toward the floor. Kelly yanked his shirt out of his pants and slid her hands beneath the hem. The taut muscles of his abdomen quivered as she ran her palms from his belly to his chest, reveling in the warmth and strength beneath her fingertips.

He straddled her hips and unfastened the center clasp of her bra. As he pushed the lacy cups aside, Kelly felt everything inside of her clench in anticipation. He lowered his head and flicked his tongue over one already taut nipple, then the other, and a low moan sounded deep in her throat.

While his lips nibbled teasingly at her breasts, his hands moved lower. He slid her skirt up and her panties down, and then his hand was between her legs, those clever fingers dipping into the slick folds. This time it was Jackson who groaned, a sound of pure male appreciation. "You're so wet…and ready."

She could only nod as his thumb moved over her most sensitive flesh and everything inside of her began to tighten.

The first time she'd been with Jackson, he'd simply and completely overwhelmed her. He'd instinctively known how and where to touch her, and he'd driven her to distraction with his hands and his lips and his body. No other man's touch had ever affected her the same way. No one else had ever made her want the way she wanted Jackson, and no one else had ever satisfied her so completely.

Now there was no denying that she wanted. And while his fingers continued to work their magic between her thighs, he fastened his mouth over her breast and suckled her nipple, hard. She cried out as fiery spears of desire shot through her system, arrowing toward her center. There was so much sensation, so much pleasure—and still there was more. He continued to touch and taste and tease, until it was finally…too much. And she shattered.

But despite the waves of pleasure that washed over her, she still felt empty, aching for him. "Please…"

"Tell me what you want," he commanded.

"You." She opened her eyes. "I want you, Jacks."

He pulled away only long enough to shed the rest of his clothes. Then he was stretched out on top of her, his naked body against hers, and it felt so gloriously wonderful.

There was still a small part of her rational brain trying to warn that they were approaching the point of no return, but the quiet logic was drowned out by the clamoring demands of her hormones.

He reached into the bedside table for a foil packet and quickly sheathed himself. Then he lifted her hips off of the bed and buried himself inside of her in one hard, deep thrust.

She cried out at the shock—and pleasure—of the invasion, as new waves of sensation began to ripple through her. He began to move, slow and steady at first, giving her a chance to catch her breath. But she didn't want to breathe; she only wanted to feel. She wrapped her legs around him, pulling him deep, deeper, inside.

Her head fell back against the pillow, but she didn't realize she'd closed her eyes again until he said, "Look at me, Kelly."

She didn't want to—she didn't want to experience the intimacy of that visual connection. But in that moment, she couldn't deny him anything he asked. And when she opened her eyes, she found his locked on her.

"You are so…unbelievably…beautiful."

"Jacks…" She didn't know what else to say. This wasn't supposed to be some emotional bonding moment, it was supposed to be sex. Raw and primal and more powerful than anything else she'd ever known.

Thankfully, he didn't seem to expect her to say anything more. Instead, he captured her mouth in a long, slow, deep kiss that made her blood pulse and her heart ache. As the tension built inside of her again, past and present tangled together so that she didn't know which was real. But it didn't matter.

Nothing mattered except that she was in his arms—exactly where she wanted to be. And they plunged into the abyss of pleasure together.

It was absolutely, undeniably the most incredible sexual experience of her life. And he was absolutely, undeniably the last man on the face of the earth that she wanted to share it with.

What was wrong with her that she was still attracted to the man who had once broken her heart into a gazillion jagged little pieces?

She'd dated other men—not a lot, but a few—who were smart and funny and kind. But she'd never felt the same overpowering desire for any one of them that she felt for Jackson Garrett.

No one had ever touched her the way he touched her. No one had ever made her feel the way he made her feel. And no one had broken her heart as carelessly and completely as he'd done. And she wasn't going to let that happen again.

Feigning a nonchalance she wasn't anywhere close to feeling, she pushed herself off of the bed and began to gather her clothes. She'd thought—*hoped*—Jackson was sleeping, but the rustle of sheets as he sat up in bed proved otherwise.

"What are you doing?" His voice was quiet and controlled, but there was just a hint of frustration around the edges.

She didn't—couldn't—look at him. "I'm leaving."

"Sneaking out?" he taunted.

"No, I just have to go."

"Don't you think we should talk about this?"

"No," she said again, and focused on fastening the buttons of her blouse. "I absolutely do *not* want to talk about it."

"What do you want to do—act like it never happened?"

She tugged the hem of her skirt and stepped into her shoes. "It never should have happened."

"It was inevitable." He was out of bed now, too, and tugging on his jeans.

She shook her head. "I don't do things like this."

"I'd say our twelve-year-old daughter is proof to the contrary."

"Correction," she said coolly. "I've done something like this exactly twice in my lifetime."

"And both times with me? I'm flattered."

Her gaze narrowed. "You're a bastard."

"Actually, *my* parents were married." He tugged his shirt on over his head. "Maybe that's something we should consider."

He said it as casually as if he were suggesting a restaurant for dinner. She responded with a blunt and simple, "No."

"Ava told me she's always wanted a real family."

And Kelly had always wished, more than anything, that she could give her daughter what she wanted. But it wasn't going to happen like this. "And I've always wanted to win the lottery."

He shrugged. "It was just a thought."

His casual dismissal was as insulting as his offhand proposal and not even worthy of a reply. She simply stalked out of the room.

It amazed Jack that Kelly always seemed so cool and composed—except in the bedroom. There, she was all fire and passion, eager to give and to take, to please and be pleased. She was his most erotic fantasy and his biggest weakness.

He'd wanted a lot of women, and he'd had a lot of women. But he'd never needed anyone—except for Kelly. And he didn't like the feeling. He wasn't comfortable with the desperate gnawing in his belly. When he was with her, it was as if he needed to touch her more than he needed to breathe.

He was a man who liked to be in control, and he was never in control around Kelly Cooper. That one weekend in Chicago had made the point clear to him, and even when he'd left the city, he hadn't been able to get her out of his mind.

His reconciliation with Sara had been the desperate act of a desperate man, and an unsuccessful one at that. He wasn't going to make the same mistake again. This time, he wasn't going to let Kelly go.

She paused in the hall, probably trying to remember where she'd left her purse. She found it on the table in the foyer, and immediately began fumbling around inside of it. He guessed that she was probably looking for her keys, but she was too flustered to see that they were beside the bag on the table.

"If this was part of your plan to change my mind about

moving in, it didn't work." He picked up the ring of keys that were on the table, dangled them in front of her eyes. When she reached for them, he closed his hand—capturing her hand along with the keys. "If anything, I'm even more committed now. And I'm going to get under your skin the way you've gotten under mine."

"I thought this was about Ava."

"Ava is only part of the whole equation."

"Ava's the only part that matters," she insisted.

He didn't argue. There was no point when he knew she would only give him the cold shoulder and walk out the door. But she wouldn't be able to do that when they were living under the same roof.

"If you're rushing home to get my room ready before moving day, you should know that I only sleep on Egyptian cotton."

"Bring your own damn sheets."

"Language," he chided gently. "You wouldn't talk that way in front of our daughter, would you?"

She tugged the keys out of his grasp, giving him the satisfaction of knowing that she wasn't so cool or reserved right now.

"And I'm going to need a key," he said, his tone mild.

She yanked the door open—and found herself face-to-face with Lukas.

Jack, experiencing an odd and uncomfortable sense of déjà vu, immediately took a step back.

"Well, this is...unexpected," Lukas noted.

"I have to go get Ava," Kelly said to his brother.

Jack waited until she was halfway out the door before he said, "Don't forget about the key."

Her response was an anatomical impossibility that had Luke's eyebrows lifting.

"Do I want to know what you did to warrant such a

reply?" his brother asked when Kelly had stomped off down the hall.

"Probably not." Jack wandered into the kitchen, keeping a safe distance between himself and his brother. He pulled two bottles of beer out of the fridge, offered one to Luke. When it was accepted, their unspoken truce was sealed.

"Any particular reason you stopped by?"

"To drink your beer," Luke said easily.

"Anytime."

"And to find out if the rumors are true. I heard through Matt, because Ava told Georgia, that you're moving in with your daughter and her mother."

"It's true. For a three-week trial period, anyway."

"Whose idea was this?"

"Ava's."

"What does Kelly think of the plan?"

"She wants to do what's best for Ava."

"Is that why she was here?"

Jack sipped his beer. "Can we maybe talk about something that isn't going to make you want to hit me?"

Lukas flexed his fingers. "I'm not going to hit you," he said. "Aside from the fact that your jaw's like a rock and I need my hands for surgery, I'm starting to see that there's more going on here than the simple fact that you knocked up my best friend thirteen years ago."

The words made him more wary than if his brother had clenched his fists. "What are you talking about?"

"You and Kelly. I never saw it way back when, but I realize now that I should have. And I can't help but think that the two of you might have ended up together if I hadn't interfered."

"Nothing that happened was your fault."

"I went to you for advice, because she told me that she was in love and re-evaluating her future plans. She was so close to finishing school, and I was afraid she was thinking about dropping out. I didn't know the guy she'd fallen in love with was you—or that she was pregnant."

"I'd already decided, long before you ever talked to me, that I had to make it clear to Kelly that our relationship wasn't going anywhere."

"Because you didn't love her?" Luke challenged. "Or because you did?"

"Because I was terrified of the way she looked at me, as if I was everything to her."

"And you were afraid you'd disappoint her."

"As I did, in spectacular fashion."

His brother could hardly dispute the point. "So what do you want from her now?"

"Everything," Jack admitted.

"I never could figure out why you became a serial dater after your divorce," Luke said. "I didn't believe it was a side effect of your failed marriage. It wasn't until I saw you and Kelly together that I realized the truth."

"What truth?"

"That you were never able to give your heart to any other woman because you'd already given it to Kelly."

It was a truth that Jack had only recently acknowledged himself. But accepting his feelings for Kelly didn't make it any easier for him to forgive her deception.

"You were in love with her then, and you're still in love with her now," Luke continued.

Jack wasn't sure he was ready to use that particular word, so he only said, "I've never felt about anyone else the way I feel about Kelly."

"They why were you smiling when she walked out of here cursing your very existence?"

"Because it proved that she isn't indifferent to me."

Luke shook his head. "I hope you know what the hell you're doing."

"So do I," Jack admitted.

Kelly fluffed the decorative pillows on the bed and stepped back to survey her handiwork. She'd had more than a few doubts and second thoughts as she'd loaded up her cart at Betty's Boudoir; she'd known her actions were both petty and immature. But she needed to do something, to take back just a little bit of control over a situation that was rapidly spiraling out of her control.

And, in a roundabout way, it *had* been Jackson's idea. That thought made her smile as she poured the rose-scented potpourri into the glass bowl on the bedside table.

As the estimated time of his arrival drew nearer, the doubts and second thoughts came back with a vengeance. But by that time, it was too late to undo what had already been done. Instead, she kept herself busy in the kitchen, stuffing pork chops for dinner.

Ava had offered to help, so Kelly had put her to work peeling potatoes. The relatively simple task took her daughter almost an hour, because every time she finished peeling one potato, she would wander into the living room to look out the front window, searching for her father's car. It was as if she feared he'd drive right past the house if she wasn't watching for him, and realizing how excited her daughter was about Jackson moving in only made Kelly feel guiltier.

When he finally did arrive, Kelly was almost as relieved as Ava—and more than a little worried that she might have started something she didn't know how to finish.

Jack understood that Kelly had reservations about this arrangement. Hell, he had more than a few of his own. But he wanted to make it work, because it was what Ava wanted. And because it meant that he would get to see a lot more of his daughter and her mother.

He didn't expect that Kelly would have rolled out the red carpet in anticipation of his arrival, and that was okay. Especially when Ava's enthusiastic welcome more than compensated for her mother's lackluster one.

"Is that all you brought?" Ava eyed the garment bag and small suitcase with obvious disappointment.

"I wasn't sure how much room I'd have," he explained. He didn't remind her that this was a trial arrangement and that it was entirely possible—probable even—that he would be moving out again in a few weeks.

"You've got two dressers and a walk-in closet," she told him. "Can I help you unpack?"

"Sure."

She skipped ahead of him down the hall and opened the door.

Jack stood frozen on the threshold. "Maybe I should have asked to see the room before I agreed to this plan."

Ava peeked past him, her eyes widening. "I don't think it looked like this before."

His brows lifted. "How did it look before?"

"The walls were pink," she admitted. "Cuz it was Mrs. Garrett's mom's room when she lived here. And there were pink pillows on the bed, but I thought the comforter was chocolate brown."

He could have lived with chocolate brown with pink accents, especially if it was only for a few weeks. But he could *not* live in this, not even for one night.

Pink didn't begin to describe it. The curtains that draped the wide window were sheer and ruffled and the color of bubblegum, and the ruffled shade on the lamp on the bedside table was the same color. The bed itself was covered in a spread of fuchsia satin and piled high with ruffled pillows in more shades of pink than he ever could have imagined.

He blinked once, then again. Unfortunately, each time he opened his eyes, the room remained unchanged.

"I can't sleep in this," he said. "I'll have nightmares about satin ruffles."

Ava's smile faded, her gaze dropped. "You're not going to stay?"

"I'm staying," he promised her. No way was he letting Kelly get rid of him that easily. "But I'm going to make a few changes in here."

"What kind of changes?"

"Do you have any boxes left from when you moved?"

"A whole pile in the basement."

"Let's get some of them up here so we can pack up these perfume bottles and doilies." He looked at the pile of pillows on top of the satin spread and shuddered. "We're going to need some garbage bags, too."

As she'd been cooking, Kelly had decided that she would tell Jackson not to expect a meal on the table every night. She might have agreed to let him move in temporarily, but she wasn't going to be his cook or his maid. But he ate with such enthusiasm, complimenting her on the pork chops, garlic mashed potatoes and buttered beans, that she couldn't get the words out. Besides, whether she was cooking for two or for three, she had to cook, and it was a sincere pleasure to feed someone who obviously appreciated her efforts.

Kelly had always enjoyed creating in the kitchen, but in the past year, she'd had little opportunity—and less time— to prepare meals like this, and she and Ava had eaten more takeout than she wanted to admit.

Now that her schedule was more defined, she'd started

looking in her cookbooks again and making grocery lists with specific recipes in mind. Although Ava would be happy with tacos or fajitas or nachos every night of the week, she wasn't really a fussy eater, and Kelly was pleased to be able to offer different and healthier options.

When dinner was finished, Ava cleared the table and Jackson loaded the dishwasher. They worked well together, and as Kelly scrubbed up the pans, she realized it would be far too easy to fall into the rhythms and routines of a family—and far too tempting.

After her duties were done, Ava went upstairs to email Rachel. Jackson finished drying the pans, then said to Kelly, "There was a brown comforter in the dryer that Ava said I could use."

"Sure, if that's what you want," she said agreeably. "I just thought the new one brightened the room."

"I figured it was new, because it still had a price tag on it. So did the pillows and the curtains."

She shrugged. "Just in case they weren't to your taste and I had to take them back."

"The comforter was on sale for seven dollars."

"I thought I should try to be frugal, since you seem so concerned about my financial situation."

"So you were looking in the clearance section, not the ugly section?"

"You don't like ruffles and lace?"

He pinned her with his gaze. "I have no objection to ruffles and lace—especially if you're wearing them. But I'm not sleeping in a room that looks like it was decorated by Barbie on crack."

She felt her lips twitch. "The sheets are Egyptian cotton, as specified."

"The sheets are fine," he agreed. "It was everything else that had to go."

"You put the idea of redecorating in my head—telling me what kind of bedding you wanted."

"Obviously I didn't realize how completely opposed to this arrangement you are."

She shrugged. "I'll deal with it."

"I'm not often accused of being selfless, but I agreed to move in here because it was what Ava wanted and because it's the only thing she's ever asked of me. Well, this and a puppy," he admitted. "But if it's really a problem for you, I can try to make her understand that it just won't work."

"No," Kelly said. "You're right—we should at least give it a try." And then, as if the other part of his comment had only just registered, she looked up at him. "She asked you for a puppy?"

He nodded.

"What did you say?" she asked warily.

"I told her we'd go to the animal shelter after school on Monday."

Her jaw dropped. "You didn't."

"Okay, I didn't," he agreed. "I told her that she'd have to clear that with you."

"Thank you."

"But now I'm thinking that it's not a bad idea."

"Okay." She held up her hands in mock surrender. "I'm sorry about the pink bedding."

Jack seemed to consider her apology, and find it lacking. "I've always been partial to German shepherds."

"*And* the curtains and doilies."

"Although chocolate Labs are beautiful dogs, too," he continued. "Lukas mentioned that he'd be seeing a litter of those soon."

She sighed. "And I'm sorry about the perfume bottles and the potpourri."

"Of course, a dog is a long-term commitment, and not

one that should be undertaken without careful consideration."

"Is that an offer of a truce?"

"Do you cook anything else that tastes as good as those pork chops?" he countered.

"How do medallions of beef tenderloin in a cabernet reduction sound?"

His smile was just a little bit smug. "Sounds like a truce to me."

Chapter Eleven

The revelation that Jack Garrett was the father of Kelly Cooper's daughter barely caused a ripple, but the news that he'd moved in to the house on Larkspur Drive raised more than a few eyebrows. Having grown up in Pinehurst, Kelly should have known better than to think that her private life would remain private, but she still worried about how the gossip and innuendo might affect Ava.

Not that her daughter seemed bothered by any of it. She was too happy to finally have a father—and two uncles, an aunt and three cousins—to worry about anything else. For most of Ava's life, it had just been she and her mom on national holidays and at family events, and she embraced her new extended family with enthusiasm. Kelly just hadn't yet figured out where she fit into the picture.

When the Parkdale Elementary School senior girls' soccer team played in the championship game, the whole Garrett family was in attendance. Although the Panthers lost three to two in the final and Ava was undoubtedly disappointed that her medal said *finalist* rather than *champion,* her mood quickly lifted when Matt and Georgia invited everyone—including her BFF and Laurel's family—back to their place for a barbecue.

After the meal, Kelly helped Georgia with cleanup. It was the first chance they'd had for some one-on-one conversation since Jack had moved in and Kelly wasn't surprised when Georgia asked, "So how's it going, living under the same roof with your sexy and charming ex-lover?"

"It's...awkward."

"I was hoping for something a little juicier than that."

Georgia's unbridled disappointment made Kelly smile.

"Well, I can tell you that we're both trying to make it work. And maybe we're trying too hard. Our conversations are mostly formal and polite—sometimes painfully polite. I find I'm often biting my tongue when Jack says and does things that I know are intended to annoy me because I don't want to fight with him and upset Ava."

"Couples argue—it's a fact of life."

"We're not a couple," Kelly reminded her.

Georgia's brows rose. "You live together, eat meals together, watch TV together and share parenting responsibilities. I don't know what your yardstick is for comparison, but that says 'couple' to me."

"We're not sharing a bed," Kelly pointed out.

"And whose fault is that?" her neighbor challenged. "Because I've seen Jack look at you, and if you're not sleeping together, it's not because he isn't interested."

"It's because I'm more concerned with self-preservation than sexual gratification."

Georgia shook her head. "Silly girl."

Kelly chuckled, but her tone was serious when she said, "I just can't risk it."

"You're afraid to fall in love with him again."

"I'm not afraid, because I'm not going to let it happen."

Her friend's smile was sympathetic. "I wasn't going to let myself fall in love with Matt, either, but it happened. Almost without me even realizing it."

But Kelly shook her head stubbornly. This time her eyes were wide open and her heart was strictly off-limits.

* * *

Jack had spent the better part of the day in court and gotten absolutely nothing accomplished, so he was in a dark mood and not amenable to any new interruptions to his schedule. And then Kelly walked into his office.

"I didn't realize you'd have a waiting room full of clients at this time of day," she said. "I didn't want to bother you, but Colleen assured me you wouldn't mind."

"I don't mind," he said. "But I am curious. The last time you came here, it was to tell me that I had a child."

She smiled, just a little. "No breaking news today. I was just out running some errands and thought I'd check in to see if you wanted to meet Ava and I for dinner after her basketball practice."

"I want to, but I can't. I got caught up in court, so I'm running behind, and I have at least half a dozen clients to see before I can call it a day."

"That's okay. I didn't really expect you would be free."

"I wish I was," he said, sincerely disappointed to have to decline her impromptu invitation. But he took it as a good sign that she'd even issued the invitation. They were into the second week of the three-week trial period that she'd insisted upon for their living arrangement, and she'd finally stopped marking the days off on the calendar. It gave him hope that she wasn't just getting used to having him around but might actually enjoy his presence, rather than simply tolerating it for Ava's sake.

Although his appointments kept him busy for several more hours, he still found his thoughts drifting occasionally. He was confident that he and Ava were on the right track. He and Kelly, on the other hand, seemed to be on very different tracks. She continued to fight the attraction between them, and he didn't want to fight anymore.

When he finally left the office he was tired and hungry—and surprised that Kelly's car wasn't in the driveway. Ava was home, snuggled up in her pajamas and watching TV in her mom's bedroom, and she told him that Kelly had just popped out to pick up a few groceries.

Since there were no leftovers waiting for him tonight, he pulled out some meat and cheese and bread and made himself a sandwich. Kelly came in the back just as he was sitting down at the table.

"I wasn't sure if I'd see you back here tonight," she said.

"Where else would I go?"

She shrugged and started to put the groceries away. "Maybe back to your condo."

As she opened and closed cupboards, he tried to figure out what was going on. Because there was definitely something going on. She'd been in a friendly mood earlier, now she was distant and cool. He bit into his sandwich. "Why would I go there?"

She turned to face him. "Because I saw Miss Scarlet in the waiting room when I was at your office."

Miss Scarlet?

Jack frowned, and then the pieces clicked into place. She was referring to Norah, who liked to dress in red and paint her lips to match.

He pushed his plate aside, his appetite gone. "You really don't think much of me, do you?"

"I don't know what to think when I see a woman like that climbing all over you. Or when I walk into the hardware store and Annalise Wilson makes reference to your intimate history."

"Jesus, Kelly, you know my relationship with Annalise started and ended in high school."

"Not to hear her tell it."

"And you believe her?"

She blew out a weary breath and turned to get a glass

from the cupboard, then filled it from the tap. "No, I don't believe her," she finally said. "But Cassie Silverstone looks at me like she wants to claw my eyes out whenever I see her in the cafeteria at work, because she thinks I'm sleeping with you and she wishes she was, and Leesa Webster looks right through me if our paths cross in town."

"I have no interest in Cassie Silverstone or Leesa Webster," he assured her. "As for the client you saw me with at Mama Leone's—she fired me tonight because I told her I would never sleep with a client."

"She fired you?"

He nodded. "And then she rehired me when I confided that our professional relationship wasn't the only reason I wouldn't sleep with her."

"Aren't you breaching lawyer-client confidentiality by telling me this?"

"I'm not revealing any privileged information," he pointed out. "And I hope you don't mind that I told her I was living with you and not interested in a relationship with anyone but you."

"Do you really think that will dissuade her?"

"I didn't say it to dissuade her. I said it because it's true. I want *you,* Kelly. Only you."

"You only want me because I'm a challenge."

His lips quirked. "I won't deny that you're a challenge."

"It's a game to you," she clarified. "And you've always been intensely competitive. If I said, 'Okay, let's go do it,' that would be the end—game over."

"You want to test that theory?"

She shook her head. "You're here to build a relationship with your daughter," she reminded him.

"Why can't I build a relationship with my daughter's mother at the same time?"

"Because that's not what you really want."

"Don't try to tell me what I want," he said, his voice dangerously soft. "You've been under my skin, and in my heart, for more than thirteen years.

"Did I try to forget about you? Hell, yes. But it didn't work. No other woman was ever able to erase the memory of your warmth, your smile, or your touch. No other woman's kiss satisfied my craving for yours. No other woman felt so right in my arms.

"So don't you dare try to tell me what I want," he said again. "Because you obviously don't have a clue."

Then he dumped the rest of his sandwich in the garbage and shoved his plate in the dishwasher before stalking out of the kitchen.

Kelly stood with her hands still wrapped around her water glass for several minutes after he'd gone. He hadn't touched her, but he'd still managed to leave her shaken to the very core. The stormy intensity in his gaze had made her heart pound and her knees weak. She knew he had a volatile nature, but she'd never seen him like that, and she hadn't known how to respond when every ounce of fury and frustration was focused directly on her.

He'd looked angry. Dangerous. And incredibly hot.

She took a long sip of water to cool herself.

The words—if he hadn't practically shouted them at her—might have warmed her heart. Certainly they suggested that his feelings for her might be stronger than she'd dared to hope.

Her ground rules aside, she hadn't expected Jack to give up his social life, nor did she want him to. Because as long as he was going out with other women, she would remember to keep her guard up. But when he insisted on hanging around the house, spending time with her and Ava, it was harder for Kelly to remember all the reasons she shouldn't fall for him again.

In the absence of those reasons, she would just have to give him a wide berth.

"I have to admit you were right, Jack."

He paused outside of Judge Ryan's courtroom and turned to face Gord Adamson with a grin. "Those words are magic to my ears. But what, exactly, was I right about?"

"Your baseball player."

Travis Hatcher had been granted a conditional discharge pursuant to their joint recommendation of the judge, but he wasn't completely in the clear just yet. He still had twelve months of probation to complete, including an anger management course and fifty hours of community service.

"I appreciate your cooperation, and the vote of confidence," he told his friend.

"I was at the probation office when he came in to sign the papers," Gord said. "Most of the kids that I've met in court would have looked away, even after I've cut them a break. Your guy crosses the room, holds out his hand, *and thanks me.*"

Jack had to smile at the incredulity in his friend's tone.

"And then he says he's going to make sure he stays out of trouble because he wants a baseball scholarship to put him through college so he can maybe be a lawyer someday. Like you."

"Really?" Jack was as pleased as he was surprised by that revelation.

"I told him to set his sights a little higher," Gord said. "Like the ADA's office."

He chuckled. "I'm sure you did."

As he shook Gord's hand, another thought occurred to

him. "Who came in with him to sign the undertaking—his mother or his father?"

The look on his friend's face gave him the answer before he spoke. "Neither. It was his high school baseball coach."

"Damn."

"Some people were not meant to have kids," Gord noted.

Jack just nodded as the ADA walked away. He used to worry that he was one of those people. Actually, that wasn't even true. He'd never worried about it because he'd never given the matter much thought. And because he'd never aspired to parenthood, he'd assumed that he lacked parental instincts.

The past few weeks with Ava had proven otherwise. He didn't think he was going to be a candidate for Father of the Year anytime soon, but he would make sure that his daughter never had cause to doubt how much he loved her.

Jack's experience in family court had demonstrated time and time again how crucial parental involvement was to a child's success in life. And he realized that the abandonment by Kelly's parents was probably one of the reasons she was so wary about rekindling their relationship. She didn't trust him to stand by her, and why should she? He'd left her once already, after she'd been abandoned by her mother and her father—the two people who should have loved her most. And then her husband had walked out, too, choosing the advancement of his career over his marriage.

He knew it would be an uphill battle, but he was going to prove to Kelly that not only could he stick, he wanted to.

On Wednesday, Jack had a meeting at Legal Aid after work, so it was just Kelly and Ava at the dinner table.

"Did you finish all of your homework?" Kelly asked.

"Except for social studies." Ava made a face as she pushed a piece of cauliflower around her plate. She disliked social studies as much as she disliked cauliflower. "I'm supposed to research European colonization of the Americas."

"That's a pretty hefty subject."

"It's a group project that Mrs. Kellner wants us to work on at the library. She said she wants proper research, not just an internet search."

"Who are you working with?"

"Laurel and Hayley. They want to meet at the library tonight at six o'clock, if that's okay."

Kelly glanced at the clock, saw that it was almost quarter to six already. "You're trying to get out of kitchen duty again, aren't you?"

"Actually, if I had a choice between dirty dishes and history, I'd probably choose the dishes."

"Well, tonight you get a reprieve," she told her daughter. "Go wash up and get your stuff together. I'll drop you off at the library and give you my cell phone so that you can call home for a ride when you're finished."

When the phone rang at eight o'clock, Kelly assumed it would be Ava calling, but it was Jack to say that he was on his way home. Since the library was en route, she asked him to pick up Ava; then she called their daughter and relayed the plan.

Half an hour later, the back door slammed.

Kelly looked up from the book she was reading as Ava stormed through the living room. "How did your research go?"

"I hate him!"

And with that, Ava raced up the stairs and into her bedroom, slamming that door, too.

Kelly set her book aside and followed her path. She tapped on the closed door, then turned the knob. Seeing her daughter in such obvious distress—face down and sobbing into her pillow—made Kelly's heart ache. She cautiously lowered herself on to the edge of the bed and rubbed Ava's back. "Who do you hate?"

"Jack."

The fact that Ava had said "Jack" and not "Dad" warned Kelly of the need to tread carefully even more than the slamming of the doors had done. "What did he do?"

Ava lifted her tear-streaked face. "He told Devin Nicholls that I was in seventh grade."

"I don't know who Devin Nicholls is," Kelly admitted. "But since you are in seventh grade, I'm not seeing the issue."

"Devin's a guy I saw at the high school last week, when we had our class trip to hear the band. He was at the library tonight, and we got talking. He's really cute and smart, and he thought I was in high school."

Kelly mulled over the details for a minute, giving her mind a chance to catch up. She wasn't really surprised that her baby girl was noticing boys—by the time she was twelve, she'd been more than halfway in love with Jackson—but she wasn't ready for those boys to be noticing her back. Especially not high school boys. She pushed aside the unease that stirred inside her and casually asked, "And what were you and Devin doing in the library?"

"Nothing."

She exhaled a slow, unsteady breath.

"Jack *totally* overreacted."

"But what was he reacting to?" Kelly prompted.

"Nothing," she said again. Then she swiped her hands over her tearstained cheeks. "We were upstairs, in the stacks, just talking. And then Devin...well, he kissed me. Sort of."

"He sort of kissed you?"

"His lips *barely* touched mine, then Jack barged in."

"And what did he do?"

"He yelled. In the library." Fresh tears filled her eyes, spilled over. Then she demonstrated. "'Get away from my daughter.' And Devin jumped about ten feet away from me.

"Then he said, 'Let's go, Ava. *Seventh grade* starts early in the morning.'" She buried her face in the pillow again. "He ruined my life."

Kelly winced in sympathy. "I'm sure that wasn't his intention."

"It was the result," Ava responded into the pillow.

Jackson was staring out the kitchen window into the darkness when Kelly came back downstairs.

"Do you want to tell me your side of the story now?"

"She was with a boy in the nonfiction section."

"The nonfiction section?" she said in mock horror.

His gaze narrowed. "Nonfiction is on the upper level. The only time anyone ever goes up there is for privacy."

"Definitely not for research."

"I might not know much about being a father," he admitted. "But I was a fifteen-year-old boy once. If I wanted to be alone with a girl, I would lead her into the nonfiction section, so I know damn well what that kid was thinking."

"And it probably wasn't much different than what she was thinking," she warned him.

He scowled at that. "She's twelve."

"You think only fifteen-year-old boys are ruled by their hormones?"

"Are you saying that I should have left her there with him?"

"No," Kelly said immediately. "I just think you might have handled the situation a little differently."

"She hates me, doesn't she?"

"Let's just say you're not her favorite person at the moment," she told him.

"I saw him lean toward her, and all I could think was, 'Get away from my daughter.' I don't know that I've ever thought of her so clearly and unequivocally as mine to protect."

She smiled. "If you learn not to overreact, you might get the hang of this parenting thing, after all."

"It's scary," he admitted. "Accepting the responsibility, knowing that there will be consequences if I fail."

"There's no pass or fail—it's a learning experience for all of us. And we're all going to make some missteps along the way."

"She reminds me so much of you at that age."

"How would you know?" she challenged. "You didn't pay any attention to me when I was twelve."

"Probably not," he agreed. "But by the time you were sixteen, you scared the hell out of me."

She remembered, all too clearly, how shy and inexperienced she'd been at sixteen, and she couldn't imagine why he would have been afraid. "Why?"

"Because you had no one to look after you." He smiled. "Aside from Lukas, of course."

"Why did I need someone to look out for me?"

"Because you were curious. And I was afraid that if I'd pushed, you wouldn't have pushed me away."

She felt her cheeks flush, because she knew it was true. "Then why did you kiss me?"

"Because I couldn't stop myself. Then you got mad at me."

"I wasn't mad because you kissed me," she told him. "I was mad because you *stopped* kissing me."

"You were sixteen," he said again.

"I knew what I wanted."

"So did I, but I knew that if I let things go any further that night, Lukas would have killed me."

"As if I would have run straight to your brother."

"I wasn't willing to take the chance."

"You didn't worry that I'd tell him we spent the weekend together in Chicago?"

"When I saw you behind the bar at the pub, I couldn't think about anything but how much I wanted you," he admitted.

"The chemistry between us was pretty explosive," she agreed.

"I was never very good at chemistry," he said. "But one of the few things I remember from high school science class is that whatever effect was generated—a bright flash of light or a bubbling liquid—it eventually fizzled out."

"I'm not sure I see your point."

"We never fizzled," he noted. "Which leads me to believe that what's between us is more than simple chemistry."

"Maybe it is," she acknowledged. "But there's too much at stake to play around with it this time."

"Don't use Ava as an excuse. We both care too much about her to let our personal relationship affect her."

"We don't have a personal relationship."

"We have a child together," he reminded her. "I'd say that proves we have a relationship."

"No, that only proves we had sex."

"Great sex."

She blew out a breath. "The details are irrelevant."

"The details keep me up at night—thinking about you, wanting you."

"You're a man," she said dismissively. "Men are always thinking about sex."

"Are you trying to annoy me?" Though his tone was mild, the heat in his gaze was not.

She swallowed. "No."

"You always did know how to push my buttons," he admitted. "And maybe that's what you're doing—trying to push me to make the next move so that you don't have to acknowledge your own feelings. Your own desires."

"Your next move is to talk to your daughter," she told him.

It wasn't quite the direction that Jack wanted to go with their conversation, but he knew Kelly was right.

"Do you want to come up with me?" he asked hopefully.

She shook her head. "You need to do this. She needs to know that she matters enough for you to make the effort."

Because she did, he trudged up the stairs.

"I'm sorry if you think I overreacted," he said, standing in the doorway of Ava's room.

"You *did* overreact."

"I'm just trying to look out for you."

"Why?" she challenged.

Since it was obvious that an invitation wasn't forthcoming, he stopped waiting for one and moved into the room. "Because I'm your father."

"That's just biology."

He settled himself onto the edge of her mattress. "It started with biology," he admitted.

"And then what?" Her tone was derisive. "A parent-teacher barbecue and a few soccer practices somehow developed your nurturing instincts?"

"Don't forget The Fun Warehouse."

She didn't crack a smile.

"Yes, Ava, through those events, I started to get to know you. And the more I learned about you, the more I realized that you are a bright, beautiful young woman. You're caring, compassionate, and more than a little competitive. You've got a soft heart, but you don't like anyone to see your vulnerabilities." He smiled. "You really are more like your mother than either of you probably realizes."

She seemed unimpressed by his analysis. "Do *you* realize I'm almost thirteen?"

"Not until February twelfth."

Ava pouted, obviously not expecting him to know that.

"And even if you were thirteen," he continued. "I still wouldn't have let you sneak off with a fifteen-year-old boy. If you want to hang out with someone—friend, boyfriend, whatever—you should invite him over so that your mom and I can meet him."

"Yeah, cuz that wouldn't be embarrassing," she muttered.

"Probably less embarrassing than me hauling you out of the nonfiction section of the library."

"Maybe," she acknowledged.

"Do we have an understanding?"

She nodded slowly. "But I'm still mad at you."

"I hope, when you get over being mad, that you'll realize I'm setting boundaries because I love you and want you to be smart and safe."

He hadn't practiced a speech. He hadn't known what he was going to say until the words spilled out of his mouth. And though they were probably no different from the words spoken by countless fathers before, they were undeniably true.

When Kelly had first told him that he had a daughter—after the initial shock had faded and the instinctive panic had receded—he'd been curious. As they'd gotten to know one another and slowly overcome their mutual wariness, he'd realized that he genuinely liked her. And then somehow, sometime between that first disastrous dinner and tonight, she'd moved in and taken up permanent residence in his heart. Just like her mother.

Ava blinked damp eyes. "You...love...me?"

"I guess I haven't said that before?"

She shook her head.

"I'm still kind of new at this father thing," he reminded her. "But I do love you."

She sniffled, and though he knew she wasn't yet close to forgiving him, he didn't think she was quite as mad anymore. "There's something Mom used to say to me when I was little, if I was misbehaving."

"I can't believe you ever misbehaved," he said, and earned a small smile.

"Not often," she promised. "But she used to say that she might not like how I was acting, but she always loved me. So I thought I should tell you—I didn't like what you did tonight, but I—I love you, too."

He leaned over to touch his lips to her forehead. "That works for me."

Chapter Twelve

The Pinehurst Fall Festival had been one of Kelly's favorite community events when she was a kid, but not for any of the usual reasons. As much as she'd always enjoyed the rides and the games and the cotton candy, it was the electric buzz of excitement that ran through the crowd that had made the biggest impression on her.

She was curious to know if it would still feel the same or if, as an adult, she would realize that it was the innocence and wonder of youth that had made the event seem much bigger and better than it was. Since she was taking Ava and Laurel, she hoped that they would experience some of the same joy and excitement.

She had planned to be gone before Jackson got home from work. Not that she was avoiding him, exactly. She just found that if she kept some physical distance between them, it was easier to think clearly and remember all the reasons she needed to keep that physical distance between them.

Of course, Jackson seemed to take advantage of every opportunity to invade her personal space and take pleasure in doing so. He liked to touch her, although not in a blatantly sexual way. Just casual, seemingly innocent touches that nevertheless stirred up everything inside her. The briefest stroke made her remember leisurely, lingering caresses; the softest touch inspired memories of hard, impatient demands; the slightest brush of skin made her crave full-body contact.

He was, slowly and relentlessly, seducing her. And Kelly feared that she wouldn't be able to resist him for much longer. And then what? What was his plan? Was it all about the conquest? Or did he want something more?

Until she knew the answers to those questions, maintaining that physical distance wasn't just smart but necessary.

But once again, Jackson thwarted her plans, coming in the back door just as Kelly was spooning leftover rice and stir-fry into a container.

"Dinner," she told him. "If you're hungry."

"You ate early tonight."

She nodded. "I promised to take Ava and Laurel to the fair, and they wanted to get there as soon as possible."

"I almost forgot the fair was this weekend," he said. "Can I tag along?"

She eyed him warily. "It's a Friday night, Jackson. Don't you have a date?"

"You know there's only one woman I want to go out with—" he lifted his hand and skimmed his knuckles gently down her cheek "—and she keeps turning me down."

She swatted his hand away, refusing to let herself be charmed by his easy smile. "Save your charm for someone who's interested."

"You're interested, but you're scared."

"You don't scare me."

"So why won't you go out with me?"

"Because I already have plans," she reminded him.

"I'm just asking to tag along."

"If I let you tag along, it's not a date."

"What is it?"

"It's me letting you tag along."

"What if I buy you cotton candy?" he asked hopefully.

"Still not a date," she said firmly.

"What if I take you on the Ferris wheel?"

Kelly shook her head. "I hate the Ferris wheel."

"Really?"

She glanced away, embarrassed to have admitted to such a weakness. "I'm not fond of heights."

"What if I put my arm around you and held you close?" He slid an arm over her shoulders to demonstrate.

She shook her head. "I don't think that would help."

In fact, she suspected that being in close proximity to Jackson would have the opposite effect. And she knew that she was more willing to risk a turn around the giant wheel than spend thirty seconds in his arms. Because as afraid as she was of high places, she was even more afraid of her growing feelings for Jackson.

"I just want to go to the fair with you," he said, when she remained silent.

"Then you better go get changed. We're supposed to pick Laurel up in half an hour and I doubt you want to traipse through the barn in a designer suit."

"I don't traipse anywhere," he said indignantly.

She glanced at her watch. "Twenty-nine minutes."

He headed for the stairs, already loosening his tie.

Jack did buy her cotton candy, and a glass of cold-pressed apple cider. And he indulged the girls' every wish and whim, buying them tickets for the Zipper, the Ferris wheel, the Tidal Wave, and the Tempest—and then more tickets so they could ride them all again. While Ava and Laurel conquered the midway rides, Jack and Kelly wandered through the barn to check out the livestock exhibits and agricultural displays.

Jackson seemed to know almost everyone in Pinehurst, and every time they turned a corner, they were bumping into someone else who wanted to say hello.

He'd always been popular, but she realized now that

he was also respected and well-liked. As a teenager, he'd earned a reputation for being arrogant, talented and capricious. Now it seemed that he was knowledgeable, successful and steadfast, and Kelly wasn't sure what to think of the apparent changes.

He introduced her to Gord Adamson, a colleague who was at the fair with his wife and their two kids, Pete, his mechanic, and Reginald, a security guard at the courthouse. But it was an exchange with Mrs. Cammalleri that really opened Kelly's eyes.

Kelly had paused to peruse the assortment of fudge for sale when the elderly woman behind the table called out to Jackson. He obediently responded to the summons, and she pulled his head down to kiss both of his cheeks before she asked, "What kind of fudge do you want?"

He looked at Kelly. "What's your favorite?"

"Rocky Road."

The old woman eyed Kelly appraisingly. "She's with you?"

He nodded. "Yeah, this is Kelly. Kelly—Mrs. Cammalleri."

Mrs. Cammalleri smiled at Kelly and rattled off a bunch of Italian as she cut a thick slice of Rocky Road fudge and wrapped it in plastic. Then she added an equally thick slice of Peanut Butter Cup, no doubt because she knew that was Jackson's favorite. Her hands were wrinkled and spotted, but their movements were steady and sure. She put both pieces of fudge in a paper bag and passed it across the table to him. He gave it to Kelly and reached for his wallet.

Mrs. Cammalleri shook her head. "A gift," she said. "Because you're a good man, Jackson Garrett."

He looked around, as if afraid that someone might overhear. "Don't be spreading rumors like that, Mrs. C," he chided.

She chuckled and swatted at him playfully. "He was a bad boy, but he's a good man," she said to Kelly now. "A good man needs a good woman. A family."

"I'm working on that, Mrs. C," Jackson told her.

But the old woman stayed focused on Kelly. "Don't make him work too hard," she advised.

Kelly left the table with the bag of fudge in hand, feeling a little baffled and a lot confused by the brief exchange.

"Are you going to tell me what that was about?" she asked Jackson.

He seemed almost as embarrassed by her quietly spoken question as he'd been by the older woman's exuberant greeting.

"She had a little bit of a legal problem a couple of years back."

"What kind of problem?"

"I can't share the details—lawyer-client confidentiality."

"I bet Mrs. C would be happy to tell me."

He sighed. "It was just a small claims thing."

"I didn't know you did small claims."

"It's not a big part of my practice, but every once in a while, there's a case that piques my interest."

She had a sneaking suspicion that she knew why he was being deliberately vague with the details. "You do *pro bono* work."

He shrugged. "I originally signed up because it sounded like a sexual thing."

But she knew his easy response was a cover. He'd frequently joked that he got into the practice of law because he wanted to make as much money as his brother without the hassle of being summoned to the hospital at all hours. But just last week, she'd woken up in the night and found him pounding away on the keyboard of his laptop at 3:00 a.m. Apparently he'd gotten a call from a client whose estranged spouse had refused to bring the kids home, so he'd been preparing the necessary documentation for an emergency motion the next morning.

"You are a good man, Jackson Garrett," she said, echoing Mrs. Cammalleri's words.

He scowled. "Give me some of that fudge."

They nibbled on the sweet concoction as they wandered through the tables set up to display the wares of the arts and crafts vendors, and they got back to the midway in time to see that Ava and Laurel were joining the Ferris wheel line for the third time.

"I think they would go all night if we let them."

"I have nowhere else that I need to be," Jack assured her.

"I promised Laurel's parents that I would have her home by midnight."

"Then we'll make sure she's home by midnight," he agreed.

"She's a good kid."

"What's the basis for your assessment—the fact that she doesn't have piercings or tattoos?"

"That's a factor," she admitted.

"Newsflash—she has holes in her ears."

Kelly rolled her eyes. "Notwithstanding that fact, I'm glad Ava found her."

"Sometimes we luck out with the people we meet in life," he said, putting his hands on her hips and drawing her closer.

She didn't resist, at least not too much, but her eyes were wide and wary.

"What are you afraid of?" he asked gently.

This time she didn't deny that she was. "I'm afraid that we're both trying to make this into something it isn't."

"I think we both know that it's something," he said, and touched his mouth to hers.

She stayed perfectly still, not leaning in but not pulling away, either. So he kissed her again, softly, slowly, thoroughly, determined to savor the moment. Her lips were warm and soft and sweetly responsive.

He tasted the fudge she'd been eating—dark and rich and temptingly sinful. His hand skimmed up her back, his fingers tangling in the ends of her long, silky tresses, dragging her head back to deepen the kiss. Her tongue touched his, tentatively at first, then again, more boldly.

Desire pulsed through his veins, roared in his blood, drowning out the sounds of the crowd all around them. There was something about kissing Kelly that had always felt so incredibly intimate. As if there was a connection not just between their lips but their souls.

A connection that was violently severed by a three-foot whirling dervish wielding a candy apple like a sword.

Their teeth bumped, their foreheads collided.

"I'm so sorry." The apology was tossed over her shoulder as the child's mother continued her harried pursuit.

Jack swore; Kelly giggled.

He wrapped his arm around her waist and drew her close again, but he only touched his lips to her forehead this time.

"You're driving me crazy," he warned her.

"You know it goes both ways."

"I didn't know." His lips curved. "But I was hoping."

"We have to get Laurel home," she reminded him.

"Sooner or later, we're going to finish this."

She could only nod.

"And my vote's for sooner rather than later," he said.

"I'll take that into consideration."

* * *

When Georgia came to the door in response to Jack's knock, she had a baby in her arms and two puppies at her feet.

"Since when do you knock?" she said, in lieu of a greeting.

He kissed her cheek. "Since my brother doesn't live alone anymore."

"Afraid I might be walking around in the buff or something?" she teased, stepping away from the door so that he could enter.

"Or something." He bent down to pat Finn and Fred so they would stop trying to climb up his legs for attention. "Where's Matt?"

"At the hospital. But he should be home soon."

"That's okay—I wanted to talk to you, if you've got a few minutes."

"I would love some adult conversation," she assured him.

He held up the two bags in his hand. "I brought the boys some kettle corn from the fair."

"They'll be ecstatic," she said. "If there's any left when they get back."

He followed her into the kitchen and put the bags on the counter. "Where are they?"

"Birthday party." She glanced at the clock. "I have almost two hours before they come home to bounce off the walls because they're pumped up on cake and ice cream."

"I won't stay that long," he promised.

"Do you want me to put on some coffee?"

"No, thanks." He was surprised, and pleased, when Pippa held out her arms to him. "Can I?"

"Are you kidding?" Georgia willingly shifted the baby to him.

"Aren't you a pretty girl?" he said, lifting Pippa over his head and earning a beaming smile.

"And aren't you the charmer?"

Jack just grinned. "She looks more and more like her mama every day."

"Do you think so?"

"Absolutely. Matt's going to have to beat off the boys with a stick by the time she starts kindergarten."

"Or duel with them in the stacks of the library."

Jack winced. "Heard about that, did you?"

She nodded. "Yeah, I heard about that."

"It's not easy, trying to be a parent to a twelve-year-old that I didn't even know existed until a few weeks ago."

"I'm sure it's not," she agreed.

Pippa let her head fall onto his shoulder, rubbed her cheek against his shirt. He felt the tug of so many emotions inside his chest: warmth, pleasure, regret. "I missed this part with Ava."

"You missed a lot of parts," Georgia agreed. "Dirty diapers, midnight feedings, projectile vomiting."

"I never thought I wanted to experience any of those things, but now that I know I've missed them, I can't help but feel ripped off."

"I can understand that."

"I know Kelly and I both made mistakes," he admitted. "I don't know if we can get past them."

"Do you want to get past them?" she asked gently.

"*I* do."

"Then I'd say that nothing that happened before matters as much as what you do going forward from now."

He nodded.

"Have you and Lukas resolved things between you?" she asked cautiously.

"Sort of."

"What does that mean?"

"It means that he's decided to forgive me for knocking up his best friend because he's convinced himself that I've been in love with Kelly for thirteen years."

"Is he right?"

"Yeah, but no way am I going to admit that to him."

After spending a long and mostly sleepless night alone in her bed, Kelly awoke feeling edgy and uneasy. The edgy was Jackson's fault. All it had taken was one kiss to get her all stirred up and aching for him. The uneasy was in direct connection to him, too, because she suspected that she might have judged him unfairly.

She thought she knew who he was. True, her opinion had been broadly based on his sketchy reputation layered over her own residual hurt and anger, but she'd had no reason to question that opinion. Not until last night. Now, suddenly, she was starting to question everything she'd ever believed about him.

Since no one knew him better than his brothers, Kelly found herself at Lukas's door. And found Lukas occupied with a pair of unbelievably tiny kittens.

"Someone left them in a shoebox outside the clinic early yesterday morning." He carefully transferred one of the babies to her.

"How old are they?"

"Probably not much more than four weeks, if that."

"Are they going to survive?"

"If I have anything to say about it."

Which was, of course, no less than she expected. Lukas was a dedicated veterinarian who went above and beyond and who, even after more than a decade at his practice, still took it to heart whenever he couldn't save an animal.

"Have you named them?"

"This one's Boots," he said, pointing to the white feet that made the kitten look as if it were wearing boots. "And that one's Puss."

"Puss and Boots," she realized, and smiled.

"So what's got you in a mood?" he asked.

"I'm not in a mood," she denied.

"That furrow between your brows says otherwise."

She sighed. "I'm confused," she admitted, gently stroking the soft fur of the kitten that was tucked in the crook of her arm. "I'm generally a pretty good judge of character and I hate when people turn out to be different than I expected."

"Different—how?"

She huffed out a breath. "He wasn't supposed to have depth."

"Am I supposed to know what you're talking about?" Lukas asked.

"Jackson." She said his name as if it was a curse.

Lukas feigned shock. "He has depth?"

She glared at him. "Apparently."

Her friend chuckled. "What did he do?"

"I don't know exactly," she admitted. "I just know that it was a *pro bono* case in small claims court for Mrs. Cammalleri."

"He took on the contractor who did her roof," he explained. "Shortly after she paid for the repair, Mrs. C went to Syracuse to stay with her daughter, who had just had a baby. While she was away, we had a huge storm and, for three days, water leaked through the roof—around the chimney where the guy forgot to install new flashing—and into her kitchen, severely damaging her upper cabinets."

"The roofer was obviously negligent."

"Obviously," Luke agreed. "But the insurance company wanted to replace the cabinets with a similar—but much more economical—style from the local DIY store, and Mrs. C wanted them professionally stripped, sanded and refinished, which would be much more labor intensive and, therefore, more costly."

"I would think most people would be happy with a new kitchen," Kelly remarked.

"Most people would. But Mrs. C's husband, now deceased, was a cabinetmaker, and he had made them. The insurance company tried to argue that forty-year-old cabinets weren't worth restoring, but it was the sentimental value that mattered to Mrs. C. So Jack took the case to court for her and got the cabinets restored."

"How do you know all of this?"

"Mrs. C has three cats. While she was going through all of this, one of them—Milo—had a bad upper respiratory infection, so she was making frequent visits to the office." He frowned. "That had to have been four years ago at least."

"Well, she hasn't forgotten. She kissed both of Jackson's cheeks and gave him fudge."

Lukas smiled. "She makes really good fudge."

Kelly wasn't thinking about Mrs. Cammalleri's fudge but about Jackson, and she frowned. "And then, when I finally manage to pry the tiniest details out of him, he acts like it's no big deal."

"Because it wasn't to him," he explained. "It's just what he does."

"I thought he just sat behind his glossy desk overbilling heartbroken clients and splitting up matrimonial assets."

"He does that, too," Luke agreed.

"But he cultivates that image," she grumbled. "As if he

wants people to think he's a morally corrupt and heartless shark who finds pleasure, or at least a paycheck, in the pain of others."

"You can't tell me that any of this really surprises you," Luke said. "If you didn't see past the facade, you would never have fallen for him so completely."

"I was young and inexperienced," she reminded him.

"Maybe you were, when you first fell in love with him," he acknowledged. "But you're not quite as young or inexperienced now, and you're still in love with him."

She wanted to deny it, but they'd both know she was lying. She blew out a breath. "I thought I was at least smarter now. Apparently I'm not that, either."

"So why don't the two of you stop pretending that you're tolerating one another and admit how you feel? Then you could get married and give your daughter the family she's always wanted?"

"For a man who's never taken the matrimonial plunge himself, you're awfully quick to recommend it."

"Because I can see that you guys are meant to be together."

"Except that Jackson has never aspired to be any woman's Mr. Right—he was always focused on being 'Mr. Right Now'—and I have no intention of getting involved with another man who can't stick."

"You thought he was shallow, and you were wrong about that," Lukas pointed out to her. "Maybe you should consider that you might be wrong about this, too."

Chapter Thirteen

Kelly was up to her elbows making Swedish meatballs on Sunday morning when Ava told her that she needed supplies for an art project that was due on Monday, so Jack volunteered to take her to the craft store at the mall. It was supposed to be a quick trip to pick up a few things, but since it was almost lunchtime, Ava suggested that they grab a bite to eat. The food court was never his first choice for a meal, but he was still feeling a little bit guilty about the way he'd handled the library incident so he relented. After he'd finished his pad Thai and she'd polished off her tacos, Ava went to the bathroom to wash up.

He glanced at his watch, noting that she'd been gone for twelve minutes. During that time, several other women had gone in and out, but there was still no sign of Ava.

He hadn't moved from their table, and he didn't think she would have been able to leave without him seeing her go past. But he had taken out his phone to check his email, and he'd taken a few minutes to respond to some of those messages. It was possible that she'd snuck past him while his attention was diverted. But why would she?

Because she was still upset with him for what happened at the library. It was the obvious explanation, but he didn't think it was the right one. Ava wasn't the subtle type—if she was upset with him, she would let him know it. She wouldn't hit back at him by sneaking away and making him worry.

Of course another possibility was that her request for art supplies was just an excuse to get to the mall so that she could meet up with someone else. Maybe even the boy from the library. Or maybe someone she'd met online. He felt a trickle of sweat snake down his back. She was smart and pretty savvy, but she was only twelve. And there were a lot of weirdos and sexual predators in the world.

He glanced at his watch again.

Fourteen minutes now.

He couldn't panic—he needed to keep a clear head and figure out a plan of action. His first instinct was to call Kelly, but he didn't dare. If he was panicking, he could only imagine how she would respond to the news that he'd lost their child.

Except that he had no reason to believe that she was lost. It was entirely possible that she had gone into the washroom as she'd said and simply hadn't come out yet.

He pushed open the door, but kept his body outside. "Ava?"

The only response was a soft, almost inaudible "Go away."

The wave of relief that washed over him was so powerful it nearly knocked him off of his feet. While he still had no idea what might have happened to turn a simple hand-washing exercise into some preteen melodrama, at least he knew she hadn't been abducted.

"I'm not going anywhere without you," he said, pleased that his voice sounded calm and rational. "So hurry up and—"

"I can't."

He frowned. "Ava—"

"Can you—"

Her voice broke, and he realized—somewhat belatedly—that she was crying. Damn. He'd been prepared for a trip to the mall, not an emotional breakdown in a public bathroom.

"Can you call my mom?"

Sure, he could call Kelly, and there was a part of him that wanted to. But if he did, it would be like announcing that he was a failure as a father because he couldn't handle whatever had happened to upset his daughter. And Jack didn't like to fail.

There was a cleaning cart outside, complete with sign "Washroom Temporarily Closed." He stuck the sign in front of the door and went in.

"Go away," she said again.

"Ava, please just tell me what's going on."

"You don't want to know," she said miserably.

"I need to know," he said. "I can't help you if I don't know what's wrong."

She sniffled again. "I got…my…period."

Jack sank down onto the sofa in the living room. "Well, that was an experience I never want to repeat again."

Kelly's lips curved, just a little at the corners, as she handed him a beer. "I figured you needed something a little stronger than coffee after the day that you had."

"You figured right." He tipped the bottle to his lips and drank deeply. Despite his determination to handle Ava's crisis on his own, the four words that she'd spoken through the closed bathroom door had him immediately reaching for his cell phone to call in reinforcements. Kelly had been there in less than fifteen minutes, and he had willingly—in fact, *eagerly*—let her take over. "How's she doing?"

"She's okay. I gave her a heating pad to help ease the cramps and put on one of her favorite movies." She sat down on the other end of the sofa, as far away from Jack as possible. "I guess I'm just surprised that you're still here. I half-expected that you would have dropped her at the door and gone running for the hills."

"There aren't many hills in Pinehurst."

She smiled. "You know what I mean."

"And you should know that I don't bail, Kelly. Maybe I wasn't prepared for what happened today, but nothing is going to make me walk away from Ava." *Or you.* But of course he kept that part to himself because he knew she wasn't ready to believe it.

"I think maybe I underestimated you."

"Maybe?"

"Probably," she allowed. "That wasn't a situation any dad would find easy to deal with, and you handled it well."

He shifted closer and reached for her hand, linked their fingers together. She glanced at him warily, but she didn't pull away. "I know I disappointed you. I'm not going to disappoint our daughter."

"I know you won't. You're a good dad, Jackson."

Her simple and sincere statement warmed his heart as no effusive words of praise had ever done.

"It's easy when you've got a good kid to work with," he noted. "So I guess I should thank you for that."

"Does that mean you've forgiven me for keeping Ava's existence a secret for so long?"

"It means I'm more grateful than angry now, because I've realized that although I missed the first twelve years of her life, I have a chance to know her now." He squeezed her hand gently. "But if you're feeling guilty, there is one thing you could do to help assuage your guilt."

"We both made mistakes," she reminded him. "Why am I the only one who's feeling guilty?"

"I'm a lawyer—my moral compass isn't as strict as yours."

"There was a time when I might have believed that," she told him. "I don't anymore."

"Then maybe you won't object to what I'm going to ask."

"You want to change her name," she guessed.

"Not the Ava part," he assured her.

She smiled, but he could tell it was forced.

"You're opposed to the idea?"

"No, I'm not. Everyone knows she's a Garrett, anyway, so it makes sense to make it official."

"You don't sound thrilled."

"I just think it will be strange, for me, when her name's different than mine."

"Yours could be changed, too," he suggested, "if you married me."

Okay, so it wasn't the most romantic proposal—it wasn't even a proposal, really—but she didn't even blink.

"I've been Kelly Cooper for too long to start answering to something different now."

"You could have given the idea some consideration before dismissing it out of hand," he grumbled.

"I got married once for the wrong reasons, Jacks. I'm not going to do it again."

"What if it wasn't for the wrong reasons?"

She still didn't blink, but she did seem to consider his question before responding this time. "Is that a hypothetical question?"

"For the moment." Because as sure as he was about his feelings for Kelly, he was too unsure of hers to put his heart on the line just yet.

"Then I would say that, hypothetically, I'm not opposed to the idea of marriage."

For now, that was good enough for Jack.

Sleepovers at a friend's house were one of the very best rites of childhood, so when Laurel invited Ava to spend Friday night at her house, Kelly didn't even consider refusing the request. She knew they would probably eat junk food, talk about boys, paint their toenails, eat more junk food and stay up too late, and that Ava would be overtired and cranky on Saturday, but Kelly didn't mind.

She knew Laurel and Laurel's parents and she had absolutely no reason at all to be apprehensive about the fact that her daughter was sleeping over at a friend's house. And she wasn't. Nor did she mind being alone in the house. It was the possibility that she might be alone in the house *with* Jackson that had her worried.

But when she got home from dropping Ava off at her friend's house, there was a message on the machine from Jackson, telling her that he wasn't going to be home until late because he was going to help Lukas fix his fence. Apparently his "genius dog" had somehow found a way—or at least a place—to get under it. Listening to his voice on the machine, Kelly told herself that she was relieved and not disappointed. She was glad the brothers were mending fences—figuratively as well as literally.

She would still make her seafood fettuccine Alfredo, but she would make it for one instead of two. And she would even have a glass of wine with her pasta. She'd bought a sauvignon blanc that she knew would complement the cream sauce and she wasn't going to deprive herself just because she was dining alone. After she'd finished eating and cleaned up the kitchen, she poured a second glass and took it up to the bath.

It was a rare event for her to have the house to herself, so she was going to indulge in a soak in the tub. She added bubbles and lit some candles and told herself she had everything she wanted. She didn't need a man to complete the picture.

But with her body feeling loose and warm from the bath and her mind pleasantly fuzzy from the wine, she couldn't deny there were times when she missed having a man around. Times when she missed Jacks. She pulled the plug to drain the tub and wished she could empty her mind of thoughts of her daughter's father so easily.

It didn't take Jack and Luke long to figure out where Einstein was going under the fence. As soon as his master let him into the yard, the puppy made a beeline for the back corner, where the ground dipped just slightly. And Einstein was little enough to be able to squeeze under the boards.

They secured a piece of two-by-four horizontally across the bottom of the other fence boards and, as an added precaution, shoved a big rock against the post.

"Well, that was an easier fix than I expected," Luke said.

"That doesn't mean you get to renege on the offer of pizza and beer," Jack warned.

"I'm not reneging," his brother assured him. "I just figured whatever Kelly's making is probably better than pizza."

Jack shrugged. "I already told her I wouldn't be there for dinner."

So Lukas ordered the pizza and popped open a couple of beers.

"What's going on with you and Kelly?" he asked when the pizza box was empty.

"Nothing," Jack said.

"Then why don't you want to go home?"

There was no point in denying that he didn't. "Because there's nothing going on."

Lukas nodded his understanding. "She's got you all tied up in knots, doesn't she?"

"You don't have to sound so damn pleased about it," he grumbled.

"But I am pleased. When I finally put two and two together and realized that you were the guy who got my best friend pregnant, I was furious—"

"Were you?" Jack casually rubbed a hand over his jaw. "I didn't notice."

His brother just shrugged, unapologetic. "I was furious with you because I was sure that you'd somehow taken advantage of Kelly," he continued. "But the more I've seen you with her, the more I've started to wonder if she wasn't the one who took advantage of you."

"Yeah, I tried to fight her off, but she overpowered me," he said dryly.

Luke chuckled. "Women might look all soft and feminine, but when it comes right down to it, they have the power because they make us weak."

"Aren't you in a philosophical mood tonight?"

"Am I wrong?"

Jack thought about it for a minute, shook his head. "No, you're not wrong."

"So what are you going to do about it?" his brother demanded.

"I'm going to marry her," he said simply.

Luke's jaw dropped open. "Well, hell, Jack, that isn't quite the answer I was expecting."

"I've been thinking about it for a while," he admitted.

"Do you love her?"

"It seems that I do."

"I hope you manage to sound a little more enthusiastic than that when you tell Kelly how you feel."

"It's hard to be enthusiastic about something so terrifying," Jack admitted.

"If it wasn't scary, it wouldn't be real."

"How would you know?"

"Because I've never been scared," Luke admitted.

He considered that while he finished his beer.

When he set down the empty bottle, his brother said, "Go home, Jack."

"That's the thanks I get for helping to fix your fence?"

"We nailed up one board," Luke reminded him. "Go home to your woman and you can thank me later."

Jack decided that was good advice.

Kelly toweled off and dressed in her favorite pajamas. They were soft flannel and covered in pictures of candy hearts, but they were her favorite because they'd been a Mother's Day gift from Ava last year. She had just settled on the couch with a DVD and a third glass of wine when she heard a key in the door.

"I thought you were helping Lukas tonight," she said when Jackson came in.

"I did. We finished." He settled on the other end of the sofa. "Where's Ava?"

She swallowed. "At Laurel's."

He nodded toward the bottle of wine on the table, and the half-filled glass beside it. "She's spending the night?"

She nodded. It was an easy assumption to make, because he knew she didn't drink if she was going to be driving. She also didn't indulge—at least not in more than one glass— around Jackson. She had enough trouble thinking straight when he was around without alcohol fogging her brain.

"Are you going to finish the bottle yourself or can I have a glass?"

"Help yourself," she said, wishing he would go away again. She didn't want to be alone with him, not when her preteen chaperone was away and her blood was already humming in her veins.

"What are you watching?"

"*Casablanca,*" she told him.

He settled deeper into the sofa, but she felt his gaze on

her. "I've never actually seen the end of this movie," he admitted. "In fact, I don't think I've seen anything beyond the first half hour that we watched at that second-run theater the weekend I spent with you in Chicago."

Kelly reached for her glass and sipped her wine.

"You didn't think I even remembered what movie we'd gone to see, did you?" he challenged. "The movie that we walked out of because we wanted so desperately to be together that seeing the end of the movie didn't matter."

"Young lust," she said lightly.

"That's what I thought," he admitted. "What I hoped. That the desire I felt for you would be easily sated. But it wasn't. It didn't seem to matter how many times I had you that weekend, it wasn't enough."

"It was a long time ago."

"More than thirteen years—and in all that time, I never forgot how you felt in my arms. I never stopped wanting you."

She looked up at him, tears shimmering in her eyes. "You're not playing fair."

"All's fair in love and war," he reminded her.

She didn't know if this was love or war. She only knew that she loved him, that she'd never stopped loving him. She didn't really know how he felt about her. He'd told her that she was under his skin and in his heart, but he hadn't actually said that he loved her. But she knew he was physically attracted to her and, right now, with his body angled toward her and his mouth hovering mere inches above hers, that was enough.

She lifted her arms, linked them behind his head and brought his mouth down to hers. She kissed him, deeply, hungrily. Using her lips and her teeth and her tongue, she told him what she wanted, how much she wanted.

After several minutes, Jackson drew away, his breathing ragged. "How much of that wine have you drank?"

"Enough. But not too much." She nibbled on his bottom lip. "I know what I'm doing."

She wasn't sure she wouldn't have regrets in the morning, but right now, she knew she would regret it even more if she didn't give in—not just to the desire pulsing in her veins, but the feelings in her heart.

He lifted her into his arms and carried her the short distance to his bedroom. He set her gently on her feet beside the bed, but it wasn't until he started to unbutton her pajama top that she remembered what she was wearing.

"Obviously I didn't dress for seduction," she said.

"You're sexy no matter what you're wearing." He slipped the top off of her shoulders, then pushed her pants over her hips so they pooled at her feet. "And even sexier in nothing at all."

She wanted him in nothing at all, too, and quickly stripped away his clothes. He eased her down on top of the mattress, then stretched out beside her. She reached for him eagerly, ready for the hot and hungry demand of his mouth on hers, ready for the fast and frantic pass of his hands over her body, ready for the relentless and dizzying drive to the peak.

But Jackson apparently had different ideas, because when he kissed her this time, there was patience to temper the passion, tenderness layered over desire. He brushed her hair gently away from her face and feathered kisses over her cheeks, along her jaw, down her throat. The soft brush of his mouth against her skin made her burn; the tender stroke of strong male hands made her quiver.

"You're trembling," he noted.

"I'm a little nervous," she admitted.

"We have done this once or twice before."

They had, and yet— "Not like this."

He smiled as his fingertips skimmed over her, a tender caress. "No, not like this," he agreed. "I've never before made love with you knowing that I was in love with you." His mouth brushed over hers. "I do love you, Kelly."

She wanted to believe him. She desperately wanted to believe that this was real, that it could last forever. But she was afraid to hope, to want, to believe.

"Jacks—"

"I don't need you to say anything," he told her. "Not yet."

He covered her mouth again, so that words were impossible. Then he deepened the kiss, until her mind was spinning and her body was aching, and he took her hands in his, linked their fingers together.

And when he finally slipped inside of her, they were connected as intimately as any two people could be.

Chapter Fourteen

In the warmth of Jackson's embrace, Kelly had to admit that all her warnings to herself had been for naught. She was in love with him. Undeniably and irrevocably. Just because she hadn't said the words out loud didn't mean it wasn't true.

The first love that she'd experienced as a sixteen-year-old had been little more than a girl's innocent infatuation. She'd been a woman when they'd met again, with a woman's heart and a woman's desires. Her feelings for him had been intense and overwhelming, but without much of a foundation. She'd loved the man she wanted him to be, then hated him when he'd broken her heart, but she'd never really known him.

Since coming back to Pinehurst, she'd realized how misconceived her own emotions had been. She'd accepted that he wasn't a hero any more than he was a villain. He was simply a man. He had strengths and weaknesses, virtues and faults. He was a dedicated attorney, a caring father, a loyal friend, an incredible lover. He could be arrogant and obstinate, but he was undeniably the man she loved.

"Okay." He stroked a hand lazily down her spine. "You can say it now."

She propped her chin up on his chest. "What was it that I'm supposed to say?"

"That you love me."

Oh, yeah, he was arrogant. And sexy. And she was completely head over heels. "I love you, Jackson."

She shifted so that she could press her mouth to his, and the delicious friction of her naked skin against his set off sparks all over her body.

His arms banded around her, holding her tight against him as he deepened the kiss. They'd just finished making love, but sprawled on top of him as she was, she could tell that his body was fired up again, too.

"Energetic." She murmured the word against his lips.

He drew back. "What?"

"I was making a mental list of your virtues and faults," she admitted. "And I realized that I should add 'energetic.'"

"What faults?" he demanded, sounding so indignant she couldn't help but laugh.

"Your super-size ego would be at the top of the list."

With his hands on her hips, Jack shifted her so that her soft feminine center was pressed against the hard length of his erection. "You were saying something about a super-size—"

"Ego!"

He just grinned and continued to rub against her, a slow, sensual caress. He heard the catch in her breath, saw the escalation of desire in her eyes.

"Energetic and insatiable," she said.

"It's your fault," he told her. "No one has ever made me want the way you do."

She smiled as she rose up, gloriously naked and stunningly beautiful. Her long dark hair tumbled over her shoulders, and her eyes—those gorgeous golden eyes—burned with fire when she positioned herself over him. Her gaze stayed locked on his as she angled her hips and took him inside of her.

His fingers tightened on her flesh as he fought for control. She was so hot and wet and tight, and his body was desperate to mate with hers. He had to battle against the instinctive urge to take, to claim, to possess, and focused on caressing, teasing, pleasuring. He let his hands skim over her torso, from her hips to her breasts. His thumbs circled her nipples, moving slowly but inexorably closer to the tight peaks. Her breath quickened, her body tensed. She was close to the edge, teetering on the precipice.

He'd been with a lot of women, but only with Kelly had the reality of making love outdistanced the fantasy. And he knew the reason had as much to do with the connection between their hearts as the joining of their bodies.

She was the one who had left Pinehurst, but it wasn't until she came back that he truly found where he belonged, because it was with her. She loved him, too. It didn't bother him that she hadn't volunteered the words, because he didn't doubt her feelings any longer. He could see her love for him in her eyes. He could taste it on her lips. He could feel it in the warmth of the body that embraced his.

As they moved together now, he knew that it was more than the giving and taking of pleasure—it was sharing and loving. And together, they finally tumbled over the edge.

Kelly squinted at the glowing numbers on the clock and resigned herself to getting out of bed…soon. She'd told Claire that she would pick up Ava around noon, and it was already ten o'clock. She couldn't remember the last time she'd slept so late. On the other hand, she couldn't remember the last time she'd spent most of the night making love. And while she was physically exhausted, she was also incredibly happy.

When 10:14 became 10:15, she eased toward the edge of the mattress—then let out a yelp when Jack's arm snaked around her waist and hauled her back against him.

"Where do you think you're going?" he demanded, his voice still rough with sleep.

"To pick up our daughter."

"But it's not even morning yet," he protested. "It can't be morning—we haven't slept."

"It's not only morning, it's late, and I need a shower."

She wriggled out of his hold, and Jack, with a groan of protest, shifted to sit up.

He looked so cute and grumpy in her bed, she couldn't resist him. She brushed a soft kiss on his lips. "Go back to sleep."

He scrubbed his hands over his face. "If I don't get up, I'll miss out on shower sex."

"I don't have time to go another round with you right now," she told him, but she couldn't deny that the outrageously blunt statement made her tingle.

"If you've got time to shower, you've got time for shower sex. It's basic multitasking."

"Well, I do like to multitask."

He grinned and dragged her into the adjoining bath. "I know."

"We should probably decide what we're going to tell Ava about…this development," Kelly said as she fastened the buttons on her blouse.

Jacks, already dressed, lounged on her bed watching her. "I have no doubt that she will be completely onboard."

"You don't think it will be a little weird for her…her mother and her father…dating."

His lips curved. "Is that what we're doing?"

She wiggled into a pair of jeans. "I'm *not* going to tell her that we're having sex."

"I agree that the 'dating' thing might be weird," he admitted. "Maybe it would be easier for Ava if we just got married."

The brush she'd picked up to drag through her still-damp hair slipped from her fingers, and she slowly drew in a deep breath as she bent to retrieve it. "Is that another hypothetical, Jackson?"

"No." The fingers of one hand circled her wrist, drawing her toward him, as his other hand dipped into the pocket of his jeans. "It's a proposal."

Her heart lodged in her throat when she recognized the Diamond Jubilee logo on the top of the box.

Once, a very long time ago, Kelly had let herself dream about marrying Jackson. Then he had married someone else, and she'd moved on with her life. She'd married and divorced, and she'd never forgotten him. Even when she'd decided to move back to Pinehurst, she hadn't let herself think that she could have any kind of a future with Jackson. She hadn't, until recently, even realized that it was what she wanted.

But now, she knew that there was nothing she wanted more. To marry the man that she loved, the father of her child, to be a family—it was everything.

He flipped open the lid and her heart jolted again.

"It's stunning."

"Ava helped me pick it out," he told her.

"You took Ava shopping for an engagement ring?"

"I wanted a second opinion," he said reasonably. "And I couldn't think of anyone whose opinion would matter more to either of us than our daughter's."

"You were right," she murmured. "And she has impeccable taste."

"You like it?"

She didn't have any words to tell him what the ring meant to her—not because of its shape or size, but because it proved that he loved her enough to make a commitment to her. So she kissed him. Long and slow and deep.

It wasn't until Jack started unfastening her blouse and she wondered why she'd even bothered to put clothes on that she suddenly remembered the reason.

She pulled away from him abruptly. "We have to get Ava."

Jack sighed with obvious reluctance. "Do you really think the Lamontagnes would mind if we were just a little bit late?"

"As much as I'm sure Ava had a fabulous time, I think she's probably anxious to get home."

But as it happened, Laurel's mom called Kelly's cell while they were en route and asked if Ava could stay for a little bit longer. Apparently the girls had stayed up late (as Kelly had expected) and slept late (which she had not anticipated), so their plans to go bowling in the morning had been pushed back—if that was okay.

Of course Kelly said that it was. But since they were already out of the house, Jackson decided to stop by his condo to pick up some legal texts that he wanted to review for an upcoming trial.

The first thing Kelly noticed when she stepped through the door was the shoes. There was no way she could have missed them. The sling-backs with skyscraper heels were like a bloodred stain in the middle of his ivory carpet.

Before her brain could even wrap around the implications, a throaty feminine purr came from down the hall. From his bedroom. "Jackson?"

Jack didn't know how to interpret Kelly's shocked expression. Was it shocked disbelief? Or shocked disappointment? He could only imagine what she was thinking. He knew it hadn't been easy for her to overlook his wild past, to believe that he'd changed. And now that past had reared its ugly head and was threatening to destroy his only chance at happiness.

"Kelly—" He heard the desperate plea in his own voice. "I swear to you, this is not what you're thinking."

The shock that had been so evident only a minute before had been carefully masked so that her face was expressionless now. And her voice, when she spoke, was calm. "I'm thinking there's a woman in your bed."

He shook his head, because he didn't want it to be true. "If there is, she wasn't invited," he promised.

Kelly didn't respond, but she made her way down the hall, following the trail of discarded undergarments. She picked up stockings, a tiny wisp that might have been panties, a matching bra, a dress. He followed in her path, feeling helpless and desperate and—when he saw Norah in his bed—absolutely furious.

He knew it looked bad. Hell, he couldn't imagine any scene that might look worse. And it was immediately apparent to him that this was a scene carefully staged by Norah for maximum effect.

He didn't think her plan had been for anything more complicated than seduction. She couldn't have planned to sabotage his relationship with Kelly because she had no way of knowing that he would bring her to his condo.

When Norah saw Kelly standing in the doorway, the widening of her eyes confirmed her surprise. She'd obviously expected him to be alone. But she recovered quickly, and the slow, satisfied smile that curved her lips proved that she didn't give a damn who got hurt as long as she got what she wanted.

He wasn't gullible enough to believe that she really wanted him. Maybe she'd considered that they would have some fun together and be lovers for a while, and if he'd gone along with her plan, that likely would have been the end of it. But Jack had resisted her advances, and she apparently wasn't going to tolerate any man resisting her.

But Norah's motives and machinations were the least of his concerns right now. All that mattered to him was Kelly. He'd been the happiest man in the world when she agreed to marry him. Now, he felt as if his happiness was slipping through his fingers, like grains of sand in an hourglass.

Dammit, she'd said that she loved him. He would have thought that love would be accompanied by at least a little bit of faith, but he could read nothing in her eyes. He held her gaze, silently begging her to trust him, to believe him, to love him enough. He wanted to plead with her; he was willing to beg. But in that moment he realized that if she didn't trust him enough to know that he loved her too much to even think about another woman when he was with her, then they didn't have any kind of foundation to build a future together.

Kelly didn't say anything to him, but she carried the pile of clothing she'd collected to the bed and dumped it on top of the covers. "Get dressed and get out."

One of Norah's perfectly arched brows lifted. "Who the hell are you?"

"I'm Jackson's lover, the mother of his child, and the woman he's going to marry. And you have three seconds to get your clothes on and get out of here before I toss you into the hall buck naked."

Something in her tone must have convinced Norah that she meant what she said, because she gathered up the pile of clothes and retreated to the bathroom.

"Kelly—"

She shook her head. "I don't want to talk about this until she's gone."

"Okay," he agreed.

He didn't think it took Norah much more than the allotted three seconds to get dressed, but it seemed like forever. Three interminable seconds in which his life hung in the balance.

When she came out of the bathroom, she looked chastened but unrepentant, and she didn't look at him but at Kelly. "I figured the 'Jack-pot' was worth a gamble." She smiled at her own joke, shrugged.

"Was it worth going to jail?" Jack wanted to know. "Because right now, I'm tempted to call the cops to have you booked for breaking and entering."

She tossed her hair over her shoulder. "It's not breaking and entering when you have a key."

"And where in hell did you get a key?"

The fury in his voice must have registered, because she quickly explained. "I have a key to Marcy's apartment, and I knew that she had a key to yours. I was at her place to return a jacket I borrowed when I saw your car pull into the parking lot, and I thought…I guess I thought wrong."

"Where's the key now?" he asked.

She handed it over and walked out the door.

Kelly turned and followed the other woman's path to the living room. She stood at the window, her arms folded across her chest, her expression still blank.

"Talk to me, please," Jack said to her. "Tell me what you're thinking."

"My head is spinning, and the image of that woman naked in your bed isn't likely to fade anytime soon."

Before he could consider a response to that, she switched mental gears and asked, "Who's Marcy and why did she have a key?"

"Marcy is my neighbor across the hall. She's a real estate agent but she works mostly from home. A couple of months ago, her fax machine broke and she asked if she could borrow mine. She was in and out a lot to use the machine, so I gave her a key in case she needed access to it when I wasn't home. She got her machine fixed, but I never thought to get the key back."

"Why would she give the key to Miss Scarlet?"

"She wouldn't have," he answered without hesitation. "Marcy and Norah might be friends, but Marcy would never cross that line."

"But Norah would take it, because she knows how to get what she wants."

He nodded, impressed by the accuracy of her assessment.

"I don't know how I feel about the fact that women always seem to be throwing themselves at you," she admitted to him now.

"I think you should take into consideration the fact that I'm not catching any of them. That I don't want anyone but you."

"I'm trying to."

"You do know that she set this whole scene?"

She nodded, and the tightness around his chest finally eased.

"No doubts?"

"I never would have agreed to marry you if I didn't love you *and* trust you," she told him. "Absolutely and completely."

It was a testament of trust, a leap of faith, and exactly what he needed to hear. He reached for her now, sliding his arms around her waist and drawing her close.

"You did tell Norah that you're the woman I'm going to marry," he recalled. "But you never actually said yes."

And he'd been so distracted by her kiss, he hadn't thought about it at the time. It was only as they were leaving her place that he saw the box on the bed and he realized she hadn't given him a chance to put the ring on her finger. He'd grabbed it and shoved it in his pocket, but he took it out now and opened the lid.

"You never actually asked the question," she countered.

"Kelly Cooper, will you—"

"Yes."

His brows lifted. "Impatient," he said, even as he slid the ring on her finger.

"Excuse me?"

"If we're cataloguing faults, that's one of yours."

"I waited more than thirteen years for this ring," she told him. "I'd say that demonstrates an incredible amount of patience."

"Okay, maybe not impatient."

He lifted her hand and kissed the knuckle of her third finger, just above the ring he'd placed there. Then he kissed her—sealing the promise they'd just made to one another.

When he finally eased his lips from hers, Kelly said, "Go find whatever books you need so we can go and get our daughter."

He sighed. "Bossy."

She laughed.

"I should probably warn you," Jack said, as he gathered the books together. "When Ava and I were shopping for rings, she had some very definite opinions—and some very specific expectations."

"About what?" she asked warily.

"Expanding our family."

Her gaze narrowed. "Did you promise her a puppy?"

"Actually, I think she's got her eye on Puss and Boots now," he said. "But she wants a little brother or sister even more."

Her heart bumped against her ribs.

As an only child herself, she'd envied the Garrett brothers the camaraderie and companionship they shared. And as much as Ava had always dreamed of having a brother or a sister, Kelly had wanted a sibling for her just as much. But she'd given up hope that it would ever happen, and now Jack was dangling the possibility in front of her—and it was even more dazzling than the diamond on her finger.

"I could go along with that plan," she said cautiously. "If you were in agreement."

"I can't think of anything that would make me happier," he said, with such sincerity it brought tears to her eyes. "And I promise you, here and now, if we do have another baby, I will be there every step of the way. From now until forever."

"I'll hold you to that," she warned him.

"I'm counting on it."

"Can I ask you a legal question?"

"Sure."

"Can a lawyer fire a client?"

"One step ahead of you on that," he promised.

Then he took her hand and they walked out of his condo, side by side, toward their future together.

* * * * *

Look out for
Mills & Boon® TEMPTED™ 2-in-1s,
from September

*Fresh, contemporary romances
to tempt all lovers of
great stories*

A sneaky peek at next month...

Cherish™

ROMANCE TO MELT THE HEART EVERY TIME

My wish list for next month's titles...

In stores from 16th August 2013:

☐ A Marriage Made in Italy – Rebecca Winters

& The Cowboy She Couldn't Forget – Patricia Thayer

☐ Miracle in Bellaroo Creek – Barbara Hannay

& Patchwork Family in the Outback – Soraya Lane

In stores from 6th September 2013:

☐ The Maverick & the Manhattanite – Leanne Banks

& A Very Special Delivery – Brenda Harlen

☐ The Courage To Say Yes – Barbara Wallace

& Her McKnight in Shining Armour – Teresa Southwick

Available at WHSmith, Tesco, Asda, Eason, Amazon and Apple

Just can't wait?

Visit us Online

You can buy our books online a month before they hit the shops! **www.millsandboon.co.uk**

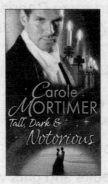

Join the Mills & Boon Book Club

Want to read more **Cherish**™ books?
We're offering you **2 more** absolutely **FREE!**

We'll also treat you to these fabulous extras:

- Exclusive offers and much more!

- FREE home delivery

- FREE books and gifts with our special rewards scheme

Get your free books now!

visit www.millsandboon.co.uk/bookclub
or call Customer Relations on 020 8288 2888

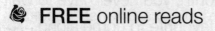